# APHRODITE'S REDEMPTION:

## THE LION ROARS

By

John Hoffert

ISBN   0-7414-2096-1

*Published by:*

**INFINITY**
PUBLISHING.COM

*1094 New DeHaven Street, Suite 100*
*West Conshohocken, PA 19428-2713*
*Info@buybooksontheweb.com*
*www.buybooksontheweb.com*
*Toll-free  (877) BUY BOOK*
*Local Phone (610) 941-9999*
*Fax  (610) 941-9959*

*Printed in the United States of America*

*Printed on Recycled Paper*

*Published  May 2006*

# *Acknowledgements*

Well, here we are again. This is the second installment of the series and there still is plenty more to come! Without further ado, I'll get right to my 'thank you's:

My sister Cyndi was my chief sounding board again and provided invaluable input, as did Tianne Wheat- thank you both for all your help. Thanks to Jennifer Moyer, who also helped make it better. Lauren Franzoni, thanks for your feedback and encouragement. Mark Underwood did another terrific job on the cover art; I appreciate the pains you went through and promise the next one won't be so aggravating.

And once more, I'd like to thank all my friends, family and extended family for your continued support. Now, be warned- this chapter in the series takes a slightly darker turn...

# Prologue

"This would be a great place to die."

John Stratton, his friend from another life, had shocked him with that phrase.

It was June 12<sup>th</sup>, 1989- just weeks after their graduation from law school. Once before John had been to this particular place, which was a high cliff overlooking a river. The history surrounding it intrigued him and probably played a part in why he'd wanted to come. At night, especially when no one else was around, that history weighed in like a heavy, sinister fog that seeped into you. Although you couldn't see it, it was there.

And the longer you were there, the more you felt it.

The very first light of dawn had come; they'd spent most of the night talking about mostly inconsequential things or just sitting. It was apparent that John was not himself. With his profound statement, he further intensified the atmosphere.

John's already troubled disposition had worsened the more he listened to his friend describe the magnetic twenty-year-old dancer he'd been seeing for some time. He made his highly charged remark just after hearing that her name was Kim.

She *was* the same girl John had talked about during one of his rare lucid moments before that night, and she'd been equally glum when she reminisced about her first boyfriend, whose name, of course, was John. Each had been pretty evasive when talking about the other; only on this night did John finally corroborate, in part because of the number of beers he'd put away. It seemed beyond comprehension that they could have fallen so hard for each other in such a short time, and even more unfathomable that after six years apart their feelings for each other still were so strong.

In so many aspects they couldn't have been more different than they were. Kim was strikingly beautiful and John's looks ranged somewhere from average to a little above average at best on the spectrum. Their personalities stood in stark contrast; Kim always was open, warm, kind and giving, whereas John was volatile, often distant and on occasion, a real bastard. Plus, Kim worked to her strengths and assets while John fought against his most of the time, but when he did employ the strengths he had, he was very formidable, if not unstoppable. That was the main reason why he wanted John with him when he carried out the plan John himself had conceived during the last conversation they'd had.

Whatever the case, no doubts remained as to the identity of the obstacle he needed to surmount in order to win Kim completely. He also recognized that it would take time to weed out his competition- *if* he went about it the conventional way.

However, he'd discovered a better way. He'd tapped into a part of her that he was taking full advantage of- one that he believed could make John fade into the background. Prior to what she did- or rather, what she and John did together- on Memorial Day, he'd often used the weapon on her and was happy with the results. Starting the following day when he picked her up from the party, he'd continuously administered progressively larger doses that were breaking down her resistance. When he got her going, which was so easy for him to do, the way she responded was astounding. He'd never come across such a hot-blooded woman and he had no intention of losing her to anyone, especially John.

It also helped that John and Kim were traveling in different circles, and whenever he talked with one of them he didn't give enough of his knowledge away to enable either of them to make the connection.

He pictured her as he'd left her that night to meet John; she was dressed the way he liked her, bound spread-eagle and fastened to his bed by leather thongs. She'd distracted him several times while he tied her. Even when she didn't try, it was very easy for her to distract him- or any man for that matter- and with a smile he'd promised to punish her for delaying his departure. He especially enjoyed her pleas for him not to leave her alone, which were stifled by the very effective gag as she struggled to no avail.

After nearly twelve days of the treatment she was right on the brink.

It wouldn't have taken much more...

As they often did, his thoughts of Kim had made him drift. He'd looked back toward John, who'd moved to the edge of the cliff where he stood, gazing into the gaping, hungry gorge that bottomed out maybe as much as two hundred feet below. The river, somewhat narrow at that point, wound among the rocky bottom.

*I could just push him over.*

*What a fitting end that would be, given our history. There would be no more competition, and that would totally break her...*

*...but then again, I think I'll enjoy this way more. It's more of a challenge, and the victory will be that much sweeter...*

Then, John spoke again. His voice sounded... disembodied.

"Listen to that wind. They say the river's deep enough right below where we are that if you jump and hit it just right, you could survive- provided you could handle the fall. But the wind...it's so unpredictable and at times so strong that even if you made an otherwise perfect jump, a gust could push you far enough off the mark that you'd hit the rocks on either side. Of course, let's not forget that most of the people who jumped so far didn't *want* to survive- not that any of 'em did, anyway. I guess they don't call this place Suicide Ridge for nothing, huh? It looks like a big mouth, just waiting to swallow you."

Again, John was silent for some time after that, deeply in contemplation as he continued to stare into that abyss. There was just enough light at that point to discern some of the more prominent contours of the land around them, and also those of John's face along with the eerie glint in his eyes, but it still was pitch dark in the gorge. He could barely hear the river over the wind, which was gusting pretty strongly that night.

He knew John was hurting because he hadn't heard from Kim since the night they'd spent together at the pool party, and he was sure that had a lot to do with where his monologue was going.

The good part was, John had no knowledge of *why* she hadn't contacted him...

"Listen to the sound it makes...listen to that! Can you hear it? It's like...like a voice- someone down there daring you. 'How much do you *really* believe in yourself? Are you man enough to make the ultimate leap of faith? Forget about everything else- all your supposed accomplishments and all your posturing and macho bullshit mean nothing here.

"It's just you, and...

"...you..."

He took what appeared to be a very purposeful pause.

*I'd love to have been inside your mind then, John...*

His eyes narrowed when he continued. "'*This* is the test. Are you gonna take it, or are you gonna be a coward and walk away? How many more challenges after this one will you walk away from, if that's your choice?

" 'Come on, take your shot. I am your chance for redemption from any failures that have befallen you, and nullification of any that may befall you in the future. I am the sum of every challenge you will ever face. I am life, and I am death.

" 'Conquer me, and you conquer all.' "

John looked back at him, and his further inflection matched an intensity he'd never displayed before that manifested itself clearly through his eyes. "What are we doing? What are we really doing? We're gonna become part of a system neither of us cares for or agrees with: you'll be helping corporate criminals find legal loopholes that allow them to become fatter, and me? I'll be working under a U.S. Attorney who compromises or makes deals whenever he can because he really doesn't believe in what he's doing; he's there to collect a paycheck and make more political connections to further himself once he's finished with this stepping stone.

"Do you realize we're about to do something worse than dying? We're headed right for stagnation. That scares me more than the thought of jumping off this cliff. None of what we did in school will amount to anything because we've both seen what will happen. Those guys we'll be working for- I bet they were just like we are now, and as time goes on, we'll probably turn into them and perpetuate this cycle. And why shouldn't we? What can we accomplish?

"We're not going anywhere, and it's not just us or our supposed mentors- it's everyone. That, more than anything, is the root of the problem. Think about it; the whole fucking society is without direction. It's dead. We're breathing and consuming, but we're dead. We vote for the same wealthy stuffed shirts who aren't the least bit interested in making things better. And you've seen what happens to anyone who tries to do good and make real, tangible changes: the machine chews 'em up. We're just a bunch of parasites feeding off a sick planet and an even sicker society. By doing that, we're feeding on the cancer, and it's making every one of us sick, too. As long as this big crock of shit is perpetuated, we will never accomplish any significant goals again.

"I have no desire to take part in that- any of it. If I had my way, I'd burn the whole rotten system down and start over again. Just as the forest recovers from a fire, no matter how devastating the fire, so would we recover. If only we had the will...

"...if only *I* had the will..."

iv

The longer he went on, the more apparent it became that Kim wasn't the only source of his pain, frustration and anger.

In spite of everything, what John K. Stratton did next totally stunned him. A very weird air came over him- it was like he saw something down there and that was it.

In a split second he was gone.

There was no warning; he just did it.

Was it impulse, or had he contemplated it before? Did he plan it?

*Could* he have planned an act so diametrically opposite from all logic and reason? Would every instinct of survival of such an otherwise highly intelligent man not have prevented him from doing that? Was the ethereal presence on the bluff that pervasive? Was he more intoxicated than he let on? Was he just insane?

Or was that an act of sanity? Of clarity? Was it the ultimate rebellion?

*On the other hand, what if he hadn't jumped? What would he have said or done if I'd had the chance to make my proposition, which in reality was something he came up with during one of his many moments? How would our lives have turned out?*

That wasn't the only momentous occurrence of the crucial night. After giving John up for dead he returned to his place to find that Kim had escaped.

He'd blown it, and badly. After he took such care to have everything in place, she threw a major wrinkle into his plan. As a result, he was forced to move his departure up a few days because he knew there was a very good chance she would go to the police in spite of the fact that she was his girlfriend.

Fortunately, she never did. Even though that might not have caused complications anyway, at the time it could have brought attention he didn't need or want.

He didn't find out John had survived until several days later. That turned out to be fortuitous in one way…

Now, eleven years later, he remembered every bit of it- from their ride up here until the moment John jumped- as clearly as if it just happened. And always on his mind was how everything noteworthy he had done came back to things John had concocted…

…mostly *everything, that is,* he thought with a smile. *I bet you'd give your soul to know the rest, but even if you did it wouldn't be enough to convince me to tell you…*

v

*...so, I wonder how well* you *remember the night on this cliff, John...*

*...or if you remember.*

He was a totally different person now...

...or was he? On the surface it appeared that he'd pulled himself together: Governor, presidential candidate...

...but what if all that was an act for everyone else? What if he just suppressed that part of himself, or chose to ignore it?

As intense as he was and as deep-seated as those emotions were, he probably was horrified when he realized what they'd driven him to do.

Then again, something like that would be very easy to want to deny, or bury.

*I can relate to how you were then, old friend. I feel that stagnation you railed so hard against. You were right about that; it was one hell of an epiphany you had.*

*I think I even understand why you jumped...*

*...what I* don't *understand is how you survived.* A number of others had jumped since the night John did. To his knowledge, none had lived. John was the only one.

He knew everything still could end here. The next step he took could force the confrontation, which would be on his own terms.

Furthermore, the likelihood of the authorities ending the hobby he'd enjoyed for a decade would be much higher- the hobby he'd started with Kim, which would end with her as his ultimate acquisition. She was becoming known now, and once her secret was revealed- the one she apparently had done very well to hide- she would be equally as much a celebrity as John, if not more of one.

*And let's not forget about that other project you were involved in, which probably is the main reason why I haven't been able to find you. In spite of how much it ended up benefiting me, you came damned close to ruining all I worked for. You'll pay for that.*

Once everything became known, even more resources would be allocated to rescue her if he were to succeed in taking her. Maybe they'd end up burning him down, maybe they wouldn't, but something had to give. The routine really was becoming stale.

At this point, he couldn't let himself get caught up in the best case scenario, which he was certain would have happened in the summer of '89, had she not escaped. If that were to come about, the final showdown might not be necessary. He would win in the best possible way, and there would be a second void in John's life- *if* she gave in.

*All the same, it would be nice to see if he could survive a second jump...*

The sky gradually changed from rosy to orange as the sun came up behind him.

"You're right, John: this *would* be a great place to die."


"...so, as expected, the parole board has decided against releasing Rollins, who is the last surviving perpetrator of the heist.

"As we round out our show on this beautiful eighteenth morning of June 2000, we shift focus to the man who became well-known in Maryland as a result of his victory a decade ago in that particular case and well-known nationally for his exploits since then. I'm speaking of John K. Stratton, the twice-elected Governor of Maryland who was on the verge of resigning his post upon entering the presidential race. In fact, he was supposed to have made that official on April 18th For obvious reasons, that didn't happen. It is presumed that he will resign should he decide to re-enter the presidential race.

"It seems you can't mention him anymore without also referring to his companion, Miss Kimberly Francis. Miss Francis is a guidance counselor for a local high school; she's been by his side since that terrible night of April 16th. Both nearly lost their lives by the alleged doings of Governor Stratton's former Chief of Staff, who currently is awaiting trial on multiple charges stemming from that night. Mister Stratton has promised a press conference soon to announce whether he will re-enter the presidential campaign once he has fully recovered from the gunshot wounds he suffered, but as of yet he has given no indication either way.

"As we get deeper into the campaign, it seems his chances will dwindle if he waits too long. He and a rather camera-shy Miss Francis are shown in this clip taken just a few days ago as they took a leisurely walk together alongside the scenic Loch Raven Reservoir, located in Baltimore County. From the looks of him, he seems to be faring pretty well in his recuperation. So, again, will he, or won't he? I suppose we'll find out soon. For the rest of the morning crew, I'm Andrea Fisher. Enjoy your day."


*Camera-shy?! That's a fuckin' laugh!*

Dean Rollins, a ten-year resident of Maryland's maximum-security federal penitentiary, caught a glimpse of her face during the telecast.

That glimpse was all he needed to know she was the one.

*I'm in here because 'a you...*

There still was no doubt in his mind that she'd worked with the cops, even though they cuffed her and her friend and hauled both away in another car after the bust. He was surprised she hadn't gone into witness protection after that. He also was glad she hadn't, as his old plan came back to him.

*Wonder if I'll get another chance ta do that right...*

To cap it off, she was with the one who had beaten his so-called 'unbeatable' defense attorney and put him where he was. Although he had plenty of incentive already for wanting out, she gave him that much more...


It wasn't the same.

He stood at his waterline looking out over the Bay, knowing this was the last time he would see this particular view.

A squadron of seagulls frolicked overhead, and a swan glided by, probably on its way to the pond at the nearby community clubhouse.

The weather was ideal- 85 degrees and sunny, not very humid at all, with a light breeze off the water.

But it wasn't the same.

For six years he called this beautiful and tranquil place home. He fell in love with the house and the locale at first sight and was certain he never would need to move again, unless his job required him to. Even then he'd only be about forty miles away, at most. Once his political career was over, what better place would there have been to retire in?

Over the course of the past two years, his outlook regarding what had been his dream house had changed drastically. Losing Dave Nelson, his campaign manager and closest friend since childhood, shortly after their resounding victory in 1998 had cast a pall. It had been presumed that his death in the study had come from a sort of seizure. That was traumatic enough, but John didn't know what really happened to Dave, which was no accident, as he found out this past April 16th. That was but one of the events of the worst day of his life.

Kim had been abducted and was being held captive here at the house, where John subsequently had been shot and severely wounded. The one responsible for both crimes- John's own chief of staff- also informed him that he'd been responsible for another: Dave's death. Then, after making sure Kim was tied securely, Wally Daniels took her away. Among all the details of that night forever emblazoned in John's memory was her attire.

The daring green dress accentuated her body, and the sexy shoes and nylons served her legs equally well. Her ensemble was much like the one she wore on their first date, Valentine's Day 1983. It had been the perfect choice, given the main event John had in mind for that night, which was to have taken place after their meal. This additional factor made everything Wally had done to them that much more painful, and was the icing on that multi-layered cake of horrors: that was to have been the night of John's proposal to Kim...

...which obviously was on hold now. Everything was.

Not that it mattered before since he never would have considered selling it, but the value of his place had more than doubled over the course of his ownership. Under the present circumstances that had become a factor, although it didn't make him feel any better.

Fortunately, a buyer quickly materialized. After all, this was a spacious, well designed and made house situated on prime real estate. It didn't last three whole days on the market. John hoped this would help everyone move forward, especially Kim. He turned when he realized Tom was standing next to him.

"A lot of memories here, brother. It seems like you owned this house a hell of a lot longer than six years."

John smiled ruefully and looked back at the water. "It sure does."

"When do they settle?"

"I don't have a date yet; they have to do all the inspections first. Shouldn't be long, though. I'd like to have met whoever the buyer is to thank him for cutting down the wait time, but the realtor said the guy insisted on privacy. Not that that's unheard of-the buyer and the seller don't always have a face to face, but it would have been nice. I won't complain, though- this guy's doing me a huge favor, whoever he is. He even paid cash!"

"Damn, must be nice to have half a million in spare change!" Tom thought out loud. "So the arraignment's Friday?"

"Yeah. Can't say I'm surprised Peters took that maggot's case. He's even doing it *pro bono*. Maybe he plans to use this trial to get at me somehow, although I can't imagine what his angle could be. He has to realize the deck's stacked against him- the murder counts, the attempted murders of Kim and me, kidnapping..."

Tom looked at John when he trailed off. "What is it?" He instantly wondered why he'd asked that- he knew what the answer would be.

He turned away for a moment. "It's Kim, she's...I don't know- something's not right. I mean, she's been there for me every step of the way with my rehab; she's helped me recover a lot sooner than I would have otherwise, but she hasn't really talked about what happened to her. All anyone knows is what the New Jersey troopers saw when they kicked the door in and found her tied to the bed and not breathing. She hasn't said anything about what happened between then and when she was taken, and she's been having these terrible nightmares.

"The worst came the night we spent here; I won't forget that one anytime soon. Christ, Tom, I've never seen her so afraid- I've never seen a night terror like that- and she wouldn't tell me about it, just like she won't tell me about any of the others. When I confronted her a couple mornings ago and tried to get her to, she really laid into me. That's probably one reason why she took off so suddenly. I have a feeling..."

Tom clearly saw his implication. "You think Daniels raped her."

He nodded. "He might have. Something happened, anyway; I don't know exactly what he put her through, but I'm pretty certain that whatever it was is mostly to blame for why she hasn't been herself lately. She's been so quiet otherwise..."

"Maybe she just needs a little time away. Although I don't like the way she rushed off, either, maybe the mini-vacation will do her some good. She'll have friends with her, too. God knows I could use a vacation..."

"I hope it helps her." He turned to Tom. "You know, you're starting to look like I did earlier this year. If that's any indicator, I'd say you need one, too. What's going on?"

He released a deep breath. "There's this case- or I should say a number of cases that probably are related- that's been a huge thorn in our side for a long time now. What you said about Kim made me think about it again. Busting up that gang was a big boost for us, but now...this started as a couple of ongoing Missing Persons cases; you know how periodically we get the cases of missing young women that end up never being solved. Many times they're really not pursued like they should be.

"Last week the M.P. reps from several states compared similar open cases dating back to 1990. I sat in on the meeting, and I thought it might be a good idea to get Homicide on the job, too- especially if some or all of the cases ended up as murder cases, which unfortunately is quite possible. I helped put together a conference/meeting of the M.P. and Homicide guys from my department, State, Philadelphia and Pennsylvania, and also from Jersey and Delaware- we held that meeting a couple days ago. The Feds were there, too.

"Between all of us we have ten open cases involving women who probably were abducted. Most are from the Baltimore and Philadelphia areas, and there's one from Princeton University, one from College Park and another from Atlantic City, who seems to be the first. On August 12$^{th}$, 1990, a twenty-year-old cocktail waitress disappeared from a place in A.C. called the Kitty Cat Club while still on her shift.

"It's like we're looking for a ghost, or ten. Collectively we have no suspects or substantial leads; these poor girls suddenly dropped off the face of the earth. No ransom demands- nothing. We want to put together a sting, but we can't find enough of a pattern to profile the perpetrator, or perpetrators, if there's more than one. Hell, we're not even 100% sure these cases are related. All we're doing is spinning our wheels; it's driving me nuts! Everyone at the conference felt the same way; there's just *nothing* to go on. Not a fucking thing...I didn't mean to dump that on you, John- with all you have going on..."

"It's all right- sounds like you needed to."

"I guess I did. With the similarities the girls have, you'd think we'd have found at least a toehold by now..."

"What similarities?"

"All were in their late teens or early twenties when they were listed as missing, but what stands out more than anything is what they have in common physically. They range from 5' 2" to 5' 6" or so in height, they're very pretty, curvy, fit and athletic, and they all have light colored hair and green eyes."

"For ten years this has been going on? Jesus…" He was silent for a moment. "Look, Tom, they need you on the force to help solve this case. They need your experience, expertise and leadership. I really think you should stay where you are."

"What about you? Are you getting back into the race?"

"As for this time, I don't know yet. We'll have to see what happens with Kim. There's no way I could possibly concentrate on running right now. Also, I might not need a campaign manager after all if I do get back in; I'm considering a different approach that makes more sense, given my platform. At any rate, I'll keep you in the loop."

"In that case, I'll stay where I am, at least for now. Maybe I *can* help stop whoever's responsible for all those girls disappearing." Tom noticed the look on John's face that indicated he wanted to say something else. "What?"

"I was thinking…since I'm not gainfully employed for the time being and my life is more or less on hold, do you think there's any way I could help you guys? Maybe a different perspective on whatever you have relevant to the girls' disappearances?"

Tom smiled a little. "That sounds good, brother. At this point, I'll take any help I can get. I don't think we'll have a problem clearing you for access to the files. You always did have that annoying- not to mention weird- way of seeing things differently than virtually everyone else, anyway."

John chuckled, but as he looked back over the water, he thought of the case confronting Tom and his jocularity was gone. "I know this probably sounds bad, but I'm glad Kim isn't in the same age group as those girls…"

# Chapter 1

She stared at the phone, which had startled her.

As part of the healing process she knew she needed, Kim was beginning to reflect more deeply on what had happened to her from the afternoon of April 16th until the following morning. She knew she would be put through the wringer during the impending trial for Daniels, so in order to prepare herself she had to deal with everything she'd been subjected to during those hours.

The more she reflected on being kidnapped, the more she began to draw parallels between that incident and two others that happened back in '89, which was a very turbulent year. The first prevented her from being with John for his twenty-fifth birthday and pre-empted them getting back together. The second happened just before her Thanksgiving break while at Princeton. Thankfully, the latter ended up being a near miss, but even though her would-be abductor that night was not successful, that experience had been every bit as frightening for her.

There were some notable common elements, such as her feelings of paralyzing fear, nausea and shortness of breath when she was initially subdued and bound by intruders who'd invaded her apartments in Towson and Princeton. There also were the feelings of dread and powerlessness while she lay hogtied in Davis' car waiting for John, and as she lay in the same position on her bed in her college apartment waiting for the interloper to come back for her…

*I wonder why* that's *coming back? There seem to be a lot more differences than similarities between Princeton eleven years ago and what Daniels just did to me…*

*…but then again, what he did- and wanted to do- is a lot like what that bastard who said he loved me put me through.*

Just thinking about that ordeal, which happened when she was only twenty, brought back very disturbing memories. That was a chapter of her life she'd never really resolved. She ran away and never looked back- never dealt with it.

Even so, as frightening as that experience of prolonged captivity was…

The phone's ringing gave her a jolt at that point. Only then did she become aware of how aroused her reminiscence of that

1

very trying period made her. Horrified and revolted by her musings and what they did to her, she began to shake, suddenly much more aware that she was alone...

...although she still felt the twinge of excitement...

*Calm down, girl- easy does it. Ted's SWAT team friend is right next door, there's another one on the other side of you, several other policemen in the complex, motion detector lights all over the place- you'll be OK.*

After a few deep breaths, she relaxed.

*Just a little jumpy sometimes- no big deal.*

The machine picked up and a friend of Sue's left a message for her. As Kim gazed at the phone, she flashed back to one particular detail of her night in the motel room with Daniels she previously hadn't paid much attention to- the phone conversation he was in the middle of as she came to and found herself tied to the bed. Although she concentrated hard on trying to free herself, she also tried to listen to what he was saying. She'd only caught a few snippets for the most part, which she'd all but forgotten about.

Now that she was away from him and safe, those bits and pieces began to come back, but as yet they didn't add up to much as she lay down and tried to sleep.

*Maybe I'll remember more as time goes on...*

*...or maybe it had no bearing at all...*

Sleep was difficult to come by that first night of her vacation given everything she'd revisited and what lay ahead of her, which wasn't just the trial and the fact that she still hadn't had her period since early April.

There also seemed to be a very unsettling undercurrent she couldn't identify. On more than one night she lay trembling in John's arms after having him awaken her from a nightmare and on most of those occasions she kept seeing the same face.

Then she lashed at out John, which she still felt badly about even though she apologized. She knew he was only trying to help- it was just a bad moment.

*Honey, I wish I could tell you, but I don't even understand this...*

\* \* \*

2

Even if Jennifer Jacobson weren't so tightly bound, the horror she felt from what was happening to her would have been enough to paralyze her.

Only a couple days shy of twenty, she was one of the youngest girls trying out for the cheerleading squad, having decided to take a shot at the professional level. Her roommate and friend had been kind enough to drop her off, primarily out of concern that Jenny's car was overdue for a timing belt replacement, or something like that. Nothing much was going on in Jenny's life otherwise and she'd done well on her high school squad, so she'd hoped that making this team would give her a charge of self-confidence and help her take her life in a better direction.

She never would have imagined her venture resulting in this.

To make things worse, instead of changing back into her street clothes after the dance trials, she'd chosen to stay in the very revealing custom-tailored outfit, which seemed even skimpier given her predicament. It consisted of a skin-tight, long-sleeved, midriff-baring top made of pink spandex speckled with rhinestones that also showed an abundance of cleavage, along with a matching bikini-style bottom and tan shimmer tights. After he'd finished tying and gagging her, he'd backed away a little to look her over several times. His gaze became more and more intense each time until he finally looked into her eyes and admonished her. With that he'd left her alone to struggle, which she didn't do for long before she realized she had no chance of freeing herself.

She was just as helpless in her effort to fend off the mental picture of what she was sure loomed ahead of her when they reached their destination, wherever that was.

Most shocking of all was how she'd been lured in. She never would have suspected he would do such a thing- him of all people!

Only too late did she realize it wasn't him at all- among other dissimilarities, John wasn't as big as this man was.

The more she thought about the one thing that her abductor probably wanted from her, the more her tears flowed…

"I can make things even worse for you, which I won't hesitate to do. Unless that's what you want, you'd better lie still,

3

and I don't want to hear a peep. Do I make myself clear?" He'd delivered the warning to her in a very cool, even manner.

Trying to shrink away from him, the frightened girl had nodded, her whimpering muffled by the gag. Satisfied he'd gotten his point across, he'd moved to the driver's seat of his van, started it and headed toward the house.

At this point, he was nearly halfway there.

He really wasn't concerned that she might escape- with the way he tied her, she wasn't going anywhere. Her arms were securely bound behind her at her wrists and elbows and her legs were fastened at her ankles and just above her knees. She also was tethered to the small bed by the thongs around her neck and ankles.

He took the young cheerleader as she was taking a break from the latter part of the tryouts. Since it was pretty late in the day he figured she would be tired and drained from her exertions and the stress over whether or not she would make the squad, especially since the tryouts had started at eight that morning. The trials were finished and the girls were waiting for the results. She wasn't in the normal uniform, but what she was wearing did even more for her, not to mention for him. Just as he'd been with the others, he was quite patient with her, waiting for the right opportunity to present itself as he'd trailed her for some time...

*...and this time someone even saw me with her, which will provide a temporary smokescreen and also make things a bit more interesting, since you and I were dead ringers today, ol' buddy...*

She had all the right physical attributes. Although none could equal the beauty of the one he wanted, out of all of the girls he'd taken, Jennifer was very close. He happened across her by a strange twist just two years earlier when making an acquisition of a different kind- in that case, a business, the owner of which was someone he didn't mind eradicating. It was hard to believe Jennifer was the man's daughter; she was his opposite in so many ways...

...and very intriguing in her own right.

She also had the connection to John and Kim that the other girls lacked, which he thought might make the difference. That played a part in why Jennifer was so at ease- in one way- with him at first and also why she was so demure as they walked and chatted.

Better yet, now she was even more terrified than any of them were.

*That just might be enough to persuade you, Kim...*

The chance of success still was relatively small, but he had nothing to lose. Even after all he'd done in his life and could still do, every bit of it amounted to nothing anymore. This was the only thing that gave him a rise, along with what it would lead to.

But he clearly had an Achilles heel- one that he knew could bring him down.

He had to have her again. As close as he came to reclaiming her in mid-April, he'd been closer still a little more than a decade earlier when his overconfidence had allowed her to slip away, which for him virtually nullified the effects of the incredible hot streak he was on at that time. Both those near-misses and his numerous reflections on them only fed his need further. It had been so many years, and to come that close yet again only to have her whisked away at the last moment...

If he was going to do it, it had to be soon or even the small chance he had might be lost. That especially would be true if John was to be elected and the extra security that would bring.

The trouble was, he easily could lose everything on this, probably his biggest gamble. However, the ultimate prize was at stake; there was no way he could settle for those he had now. No substitutes- no matter how many he ended up taking- would do.

What did it matter if Kim didn't bend or break once she was his again?

Just having her would be enough for the time being, and time would then be his ally. He could set the stage...

...but if the unlikely happened and she *did* break, there would be no reason for the final confrontation.

*Well, a little wishful thinking never hurt anyone.*

Quickly focusing again on his situation, he went back to the central problem.

There had to be a better way to get her...

\* \* \*

"I suppose it's time to get out there..."

In a way, Kim was glad Sue and Ted had to miss the first few days at their beach condo, leaving her by herself for that time. The solitude had been welcome.

5

Unfortunately, she hadn't resolved much of anything. After two days of doing little more than pacing, watching TV, napping, or just lying around doing nothing, the same problems still stared her down. For the time being she chose to turn away from them.

Finally, on this third consecutive sunny morning, she'd decided to venture out to the beach. It was a great day to catch some rays, watch the waves roll in, and breathe in the salty air for the first time this year. She normally went to a different beach each year and hadn't been to this one, which was the closest in distance, for quite some time.

Kim donned her favorite bikini and, turning to her side, took a peek in the mirror, focusing on her abdomen. No sign yet.

*Well, it is early. If I am pregnant, I probably won't show for another month or so.*

*Besides, it could just be that all this stress has thrown my cycle out of whack. Again.*

She let out a deep sigh, and after putting on her sandals and cover-up, she grabbed her bag and walked to the beach.

There were plenty of people out on the sand, and plenty more in the water. It was a month into the peak season at Ocean City, and it showed. She picked her way through the families, couples and groups of friends in search of a clear space and finally found one. She was glad- and also surprised- to see it was a fairly large area.

As she set her bag down and pulled out her blanket, she heard a couple not-so-thinly disguised catcalls coming from a group of college-age guys nearby. She chose to ignore them for the time being, pretty sure another girl would come by and provide a distraction.

*No wonder this is such a big space...*

When she unbuttoned and removed her cover-up, after a momentary silence they became even more vocal. Kim blushed as she felt their eyes roaming over her scantily clad body, and also at their comments. It wasn't that they were being outright vulgar and offensive- she just wasn't in the mood and she considered moving somewhere else...

"Oh my God- Miss Francis! Your hair's lighter than I remember, but I thought that was you! It looks like you have yet another bunch of goons drooling over you."

Kim recognized the girl who spoke up and laughed as she returned the greeting. "Kelly! It's great to see you again! I can't believe it's been three years since you graduated; you look terrific! My hair does get lighter in the summer, by the way, and you don't have to call me Miss Francis anymore- please call me Kim." She hugged her former student who, in addition to being one Kim was very fond of, had become one of her success stories.

"Are you by yourself? Why don't you join us?"

Kim looked over at the other girls, and hesitated in her reply.

Kelly noticed her uneasiness. "Is something wrong?"

"Well, I...I was kind of hoping to relax a little. It's not that I don't want to meet your friends- I just..."

"It's OK, Kim- I understand. You want to be alone."

"I don't want to chase you off, though; I am glad to see you."

"Here- let me help you get set up." As she grabbed an end of the blanket she heard yet another comment directed at Kim from one of the guys: "Man, what a *babe*! And wearin' a tiger-striped thong bikini, yet- she oughtta be up on stage!"

Kelly immediately turned to them. "I have heard *enough* out of you!! Not that any of you probably care, but this lady happens to be the best- and coolest- guidance counselor anyone could ever have. I don't know how many students besides me she helped point in the right direction. She deserves a *hell* of a lot better than to have a bunch of juvenile idiots like you all insinuate that she should be a stripper, so knock it off!"

The thoroughly shamed group was silent until the one who'd made most of the comments apologized to Kim, and the rest of them followed his lead. She accepted the apologies and gave them a smile to let them know she wasn't angry. She also mouthed a silent 'thank you' to Kelly as she turned back to her.

Once that was settled and her blanket was spread out, she realized she hadn't prepared herself for the rather intense rays from the sun on this nearly cloudless and increasingly hot day. "Um, would you mind doing my back?"

"Sure." Kelly squeezed some of the factor 8 into her palm as Kim knelt in front of her and swept her long, honey-colored tresses over her shoulder. Kelly smiled to herself as she caught the guys trying not to be too obvious as they enviously watched her apply tanning lotion to the arms, shoulders and back of this sex kitten with her hypnotic eyes and tantalizing curves. Kim really was a stunner; even some of the girls were looking.

Kim knew a number of people were watching, and she was pretty sure they noticed the warm flush on her cheeks as well. "How have you been? How's college treating you?"

"Fine on both counts. I've been on the Dean's List every semester and I'll be doing my internship at this great advertising firm starting in two weeks I have a wonderful boyfriend named Brian, who goes to the same school I do. I can't imagine things could be much better right now, and you deserve a lot of credit for that. Thank you so much for being there for me like you were; I'll never forget that."

One evening in late April 1994, Kelly's mother, a health enthusiast, had gone out for her evening power walk with her neighbor- the two hadn't missed their ritual for anything other than illness in many years. They followed the same path and returned at the forty-minute mark every time.

Kelly expected the same to happen as she sat out on her porch- it was warm that evening and she'd decided to do her homework outside. She was in her freshman year in high school, and at that juncture was holding her own after finally adjusting after the transition from middle school. Her parents always had been supportive and her family was a very close-knit one; it just took Kelly a little longer than most kids to adjust.

As she was putting the finishing touches on her math assignment, she looked at her watch. It was almost that time- in a couple minutes her mother would return and do her cool down.

Right at that moment she heard a loud crash, followed by a woman screaming.

Kelly's blood ran cold when she realized who the screams were coming from.

Knowing something had happened to her mother, she ran to where she'd heard the noise. When she got there, to her horror she saw her instincts were right. A drunken driver, intoxicated well beyond the limit, had passed out as he drove at more than double the posted speed limit of the street that crossed Kelly's. Her mother, walking the same direction the car was careening, never had a chance and was killed instantly when that car ran up the curb and struck her before plowing into a tree.

To make matters worse, not only did the driver survive with minor bruises and cuts, but his license recently had been revoked for driving while intoxicated. That was the fourth time he'd been convicted. He would serve only a year in prison for killing Kelly's mother, whose husband and daughter were devastated. For several days neither of them left the house nor answered the phone. That pattern may have continued for longer if her guidance counselor hadn't intervened.

Kim had worried when they didn't answer her calls or return her messages, so after a lot of internal debate and amid her concern that they might consider it an intrusion, she went to the house to check on them. She was glad- and relieved- when she was invited in.

With the support and comfort Kim gave them that night and many more after that, and with help from time and the rest of their family, both Kelly and her father eventually were able to move forward. They remained close with Kim, who attended a number of their family functions in the years following...

She turned to Kelly and smiled. "You know you don't have to thank me; besides, you were there for me when my birth mother died. I'm so glad to hear you're doing well."

"How about you? Oh- how's Governor Stratton coming along? I hope he's getting better. He's still going to run, isn't he?"

Her smile disappeared as the subject changed and she turned to face forward again. "He wants to, but between you and me, I'm not so sure he should. Please keep this between us, OK?" Kelly voiced her assent. "I worry about him campaigning. There's so much stress and long hours and travelling involved, and he's still in pain- probably more so than he lets on. His therapy's going pretty well, but he's getting impatient with it. Truth be told, sometimes I get a little impatient, too, but I don't want him to push himself too hard, which is *another* worry.

"Anyway, I just needed to get away for awhile, which is why I'm here, although I didn't want to leave him- I want to be with him now. Maybe I do need a break, but..."

It helped that Kim could talk with someone about her concern for John, but there was another reason she was very apprehensive about his campaigning, and also about the impending trial. A lot more attention would be focused on him...

...and on her as well. It was only a matter of time.

*I have to tell him...but how?*

He'd never broached the subject, so she was pretty sure he didn't know. When it came to light, she was convinced it would be

9

a detriment to him as a candidate, even though he himself had nothing to do with it.

Worse, she wondered if it would change the way he felt about her, and also how it would affect the students she'd helped in her tenure, like Kelly...

"You really love him, don't you?" Kelly's question was more rhetorical than anything- the soft tone of Kim's voice when she talked about him gave as much of an answer as her words could. "I remember when-...Kim? Hey, what's wrong?" Her shoulders began to shake, and when she saw why, Kelly embraced her former counselor.

Kim leaned back against her and wept, finally cracking a little under the combined weight of her recent trauma with the abduction, almost losing John...

...and now this. As if things weren't complicated enough...

"It's all right. You'll get through this- both of you will." With a reassuring gesture to her friends, and also to the group of guys who seemed to have a change of attitude, she kept them back so she and Kim could have some privacy.

After a couple minutes, Kim began to settle down. "I'm sorry."

"No need to apologize for that; we all need a good cry from time to time. Are you feeling better?"

She nodded and touched Kelly's hand. "Thanks. You're right; I did need that. I miss him so much and I've only been here for three days. I should go back, I...I don't know. With all that's happened- he's been through so much this year..." She wanted to tell Kelly- or someone- about what played the biggest part in upsetting her so much, but who could she tell? Who would understand without looking judgmentally on her, especially given the position she'd held for the past 8 years? What would the repercussions from it be?

Would what she did just after the end of her first career affect the likely fallout?

Kelly went back to work on applying the lotion. "I guess he has. You've been through a lot, too, though- God, that must have been so frightening to be kidnapped. I don't know what it would have done to me; is that part of why you're so upset?"

"It probably is. It was very frightening, but it could have been a lot worse."

Kelly shook her head. "I hope that's not what happened to Jenny…"

Kim looked back at her. "Hmm?"

"Oh- I guess you haven't heard. Do you remember Jennifer Jacobson?"

"Yes, I remember Jenny- you two were classmates and she was on the cheerleading squad with you. What happened to her?"

"No one's seen or heard from her for a few days now. In the news last night there was a little bulletin about her, and-…I just remembered- today is her birthday."

"Oh, no- that poor girl…" She remembered Jenny well- another victim of emotional abuse and neglect, very similar to what Kim also went through. *And now*… "Do you think she might have run away? Or moved somewhere?"

"She'd certainly have plenty of justification, but Jenny always was shy and hesitant; it took no small amount of persuasion for her to join *our* squad and even afterwards she didn't open up too much. I doubt she'd have picked up and moved- at least not permanently- and she definitely wouldn't have run away. I'm really surprised she went for the spot on the pro team's cheering squad, what with all the exposure."

"You're probably right; she *was* pretty timid…you said she went for a pro squad? Which one?"

"The one for D.C.'s team. I think she made it, too."

"Wow- that must have been quite a challenge for her just to go for the tryout. I remember feeling a little nervous myself until I made the cut there…"

"You cheered for them, too?"

*Oops…*

She realized her little slip. *Well, at least it's Kelly…*

*…then again, I doubt I'll have many secrets left before long.*

Recently she'd begun to doubt the necessity to keep certain things hidden for the reason she had for so long, and not for the distinct possibility that it might hurt her position at the school and John's candidacy as well. This was a different reason altogether. On a few occasions she wondered if she'd been overly paranoid, although considering the source it had seemed to be a good precaution.

*At this point, I think it's been long enough. If that man or anyone else from back in the day really was stalking me, I'm sure he's gotten over me by now. I covered my tracks pretty well.*

"Mm-hmm, back in '90 and '91. I was in my Master's program at the time. I even made it on TV once during a Monday night game my last year; one of the cameramen filmed me. I really enjoyed it. That's another thing Jenny and I have in common besides parents who weren't up to the task; I just hope being abducted doesn't turn out to be yet another similarity between us..."

"Hold on- her father was a little strict, but...you don't think he was abusive like your stepfather was, do you?"

"Well...even though there's nothing in particular I can point to, I always had this feeling there was something going on in that house that wasn't right. I never asked her if she was mistreated, but on a few occasions I told her about the neglect I had to deal with for so long and other things that happened in my childhood. I did that in hopes of getting her to open up to me about any instances of parental abuse she might have suffered. Even though she never did, that feeling of mine never went away. I'm usually right when I have those suspicions, but...then again, I'm not omniscient. Maybe I *was* wrong- who knows?

"Anyway, how long has it been since you've talked with her?"

"She called a couple weeks ago to tell me about her tryout, but I wasn't there. We tried calling each other several times since then, but we never got in touch. It's been a long time since we actually talked, which makes me feel terrible. I went right off to college at the end of the summer we graduated and Jenny stuck around. She had the same boyfriend for a long time; I think the police are questioning him. I don't think he did anything to her. He seemed harmless, but I guess you never know. I hope she's OK."

"So do I." Kim's preoccupations with John and her inner turmoil had put everything else in the background, but she would find out what was going on and what was being done to find Jenny as soon as this short getaway was over, if not sooner.

*In fact, I'm going to call Tom as soon as I get back to my-*

Kim gasped and shuddered as Kelly's fingertips found a sensitive spot at the small of her back.

"Oops- sorry!"

"Oh, don't worry. I'm just a little...um, are you finished?"

"Yeah, you're all set. Let me know if you need anything else, OK?"

She smiled. "Thanks, Kelly. It's great seeing you again!"

After she walked back to rejoin her friends, Kim squeezed some lotion onto her legs and began to rub it in. *I guess I need to keep* some *parts of me from turning red,* she thought, very cognizant of all the glances, stares and outright gawking as her hands glided over her thighs and calves. Apparently, the guys were watching again, along with mostly everyone else around her. In spite of her emotional state she was beginning to enjoy their attention; some things didn't change, no matter what the circumstances.

*A little boost to the ego never hurts,* she thought as she smiled a little. *Any positive is welcome right now...*

In light of their focus on her, Kim's college years began to make their way to the forefront of her mind, in particular the one aspect of that phase that was causing her such anxiety. The shame of it all was that she'd had so much fun doing what she did and she certainly hadn't hurt anyone; on the contrary, nearly everyone seemed to love her. There definitely had been some bad experiences along the way- she'd felt uneasy, even threatened, on a few occasions and there were things that happened to some of her peers that she wished she could forget. However, for Kim- strictly on the personal level- it had been a liberating experience and a surprisingly rewarding one.

*Things sure were simpler then, weren't they?*

As she worked on the tops of her thighs and her hips, she had to laugh when one of her admirers uttered "Dear Lord, just go ahead and take me now". She'd glanced over and saw him gazing openmouthed at her as he made his request- not meaning for her to hear it- and, more than a little embarrassed, he turned away when she caught him. She didn't mind that one and was glad the more blatant catcalls had stopped.

This really wasn't unlike what she felt when she danced.

*On that note, I think I'll wait a bit to do my chest.*

Once finished, she lay on her stomach, found a comfortable position and unfastened her top.

She was glad she'd decided to lay out; the sun seemed to revitalize her. Although her troubles would not go away, this temporary respite was good enough.

As she reflected further on all the attention she was getting, it began to sink in that this was a *lot* like what she felt when she danced at the club. It also was virtually the same as what she felt when she performed on the sidelines, cheering for football and basketball teams on the high school, college and professional levels, although her stint on the college squad didn't last very long and ended on a sour note. On the whole, those had been some happy and carefree days, but in nearly every way, those days were long gone.

In one respect, it just didn't seem fair that what she feared most probably would be the outcome when all was said and done.

Then again, besides being inevitable, maybe it *was* fair...


*You were the best.*

He doubted that anyone who had ever seen her perform would disagree as he again watched one of her sessions he'd captured on film. Fortunately he'd transferred all the much-viewed and eroding tapes he had of her to fresher tapes, and now he had all of them on digital discs, which wouldn't wear out any time soon.

He also had tapes of other performances she'd made during which he was much more than an observer and she didn't have nearly as much freedom of movement...

He allowed himself a pat on the back when he looked at the live feeds from the cameras monitoring his acquisitions. It really was some accomplishment- his score, 11. The police, including the Feds, 0. Jennifer the pro cheerleader rounded out his stable...

...almost.

There was one more he needed to take who would be the crowning piece, and it was appropriate that she would be number 12: the number of completion. She was the reason for all the others- the sum of all the parts.

She was the one moving so gracefully and erotically on his television screen as the digital disc played...

As he got up to check on the girls he had, he wondered if the one he didn't yet have also would be the one who caught on. He paused the disc, freezing her image during a close-up. Those lively, sensuous eyes said so much about her- everything, really, if you looked deeply enough. They burned right through him, as they had countless times before.

There had been many occasions when they were only inches from his, and not on videotape. Even after all the years that had passed since then, her eyes- not to mention the rest of her- still had him under their spell...

...and to think she wanted to be with *him*. Again.

*I know you haven't forgotten about me- about us. I bet he's only scratched the surface with you; he doesn't even know the half of the woman you are.*

*If he did know, he'd never be able to handle you- not like I could.*

*Not like I did.*

But also evident in those green orbs was her intelligence, which he knew not to underestimate. No doubt she would start digging now, if she hadn't already.

*It's probably not a question of if she'll catch on...*

That thought jolted his mental process and again directed it toward possible courses of action that would result in her capture. Nothing less was acceptable, but he had yet to come up with the right plan. So far, he'd only come up with one that had some promise. This one would play into a weakness she had- one he now had the means to exploit, which was embodied in his latest captive. He turned up the sound just in time to hear Jennifer's cries as he saw her unmistakable desperation.

*You look a lot like she did the first time...*

They all had come to that at one point and it usually hadn't taken long. It was amazing how much of a charge he still got from it; he controlled this girl, just like the others, and he was certain that soon she would submit to his every whim. That was the biggest thrill for him, although a very close second was the act of the capture itself, which he had all but mastered.

However, it was good that he had only one more to go- he knew it only was a matter of time before the onset of overconfidence, which played a part in his failure to keep Kim when she was his and his failed attempt to take her half a year later. It probably would be his undoing if it claimed him again. Generally, the only time those who'd fallen victim to that ever realized they had was when it was too late to do anything about it, either in their dying moments, or worse, as they were being led off to jail. Walter Daniels was on his way to discovering both those

15

pitfalls for himself; the latter was happening now, as he was in lockup awaiting trial.

The former would happen as soon as the opportunity presented itself- the sooner the better. *You almost killed her, you stupid, weak piece of shit.*

*For that, you'll answer to me.*

He turned back to the monitor and watched his pro cheerleader struggle.

*You are a beauty...*

He had her on her bed, tied in a spread-eagle. He'd left the ball gag in for the visual effect as well as the audio, and he watched the show she unwittingly was putting on for him, enjoying every second. Since she was locked inside her room, she didn't need to be tied up at all, but he liked her better that way- he liked all of them better that way.

The more he watched her, the more similarities he began to notice between her and Kim. Her very animated expressions ranging back and forth from fear to frustration, her increased agitation when she was left alone...

*...Kim hated that, too...*

*...come to think of it, they look more alike than I thought...*

She would serve him well. Hopefully she would play a key role in his final acquisition.

However, even with Jennifer's help, which he was fairly certain he would get in one way or another, in all probability number twelve would be the most difficult of all of them, and not just in terms of capture.

The question was, how could he play the Jennifer card in a way that his ultimate prize wouldn't be able to trump him? There were a number of ways she could do just that, and if he was going to make this particular plan work, he had to think of- and eliminate- all of them, and fast.

*There has to be-*

Suddenly, he snapped back to something that stuck out before, which was her disposition in the recent news clip- the same one he'd noticed when she was at the press conference with John a couple months earlier.

A possible- better yet, a *probable*- reason for that nervous and somewhat evasive demeanor she exhibited on camera came to him, and the fact that she'd shown it yet again...

16

*...if what I'm thinking is true, you could be even more
vulnerable than I thought...*


"I had a feeling I'd be hearing from you. I saw the report.
Let me guess- no substantial witnesses or leads, right?...I figured
as much. Well, it looks like there's a good chance she's the
eleventh. Thanks for the call, Gil. Keep me posted, and I'll do the
same for you."

Tom hung up the phone and leaned back. This time it was
a cheerleader for Washington, D.C.'s pro football team.

Worse, there was a personal dimension there, which added
to his anger.

At present, their position bordered on untenable. They
couldn't keep tabs on every pretty, well-built young woman who
had light colored hair and green eyes. Even with the widespread
bulletins and warnings the police departments of a good portion of
the Mid-Atlantic area had issued, it was impossible for every girl
who fell under that description to be protected every single
minute.

If there was another connection between all these women,
what could it be?

Since it didn't appear that the perpetrator or perpetrators
would stop voluntarily, there probably was only one way these
abductions would stop- a screwup somewhere along the line,
which didn't seem likely to happen any time soon, if at all. The
responsible individual- or group- was very efficient. So far, Tom
couldn't see any mistakes that had been made during the entire
span.

He went back to what he'd recently been spending a lot of
time on- comparing the notes on all the cases, again looking for
something- anything- that could be the break.

What else could he do?


It had started innocently enough...
*...well, not exactly innocently.*

Kim was eighteen years old and nearly two months into
her freshman year at Princeton, having earned a substantial
scholarship based on her consistently outstanding grades in high
school along with her extracurricular activities and a lofty

composite score on her SATs. Already, she was enjoying the prestigious university and vigorously attacking her studies there.

However, she was missing her friends back home, not to mention their nocturnal outings. They'd had so much fun, and since she only was beginning to blend in at the university- and also since she was very focused on her schoolwork-, her social life was temporarily on hold.

For those reasons, she was looking forward to her Halloween get-together with her group from high school at a famous- or infamous- nightclub back in Baltimore: the old Hammerjack's. She'd picked out a sexy little outfit that, all things considered, seemed to be an excellent choice.

She'd also had to put it on at a friend's place, knowing her adoptive mother would not have approved of it, to say the least.

As soon as they arrived at the club, nearly everyone she passed by or had any contact with showed approval of her costume- or more specifically, what she did for it- in one way or another. Under the watchful eyes of her friends she danced with quite a few guys.

She didn't drink to excess that night, but she definitely had her share, which probably contributed to her actions as midnight drew near.

At that point, the crowd was very loose- it seemed like everyone was having a blast in the forms of dancing, carousing, flirting, boozing or just people watching.

The people watchers drastically grew in number as several of the women there were persuaded to get up onto the bars or tables and dance to the increasingly suggestive music, which helped further charge the atmosphere.

Then, a wide-eyed young girl dressed in a very risqué version of a Little Bo Peep costume, who happened to be an excellent dancer as well, was invited up onto the main bar by one of the bouncers. Many people nearby picked up on that, offering their encouragement. Soon there was a slowly growing cluster of the partying patrons gathering around her.

"*Me*?! You're kidding...aren't you?" Kim's apparent hesitation made all those around her want her up there even more, and they let her know it.

At first she was quite wary, but a few factors began to sway her and she found herself considering that- something she never would have imagined doing before then. She'd never done anything nearly so daring, but the way they cajoled her…

…and begged her…

…and the way the whole situation made her feel…

There really wasn't much of a thought process that led to her decision. Before she fully realized what she was doing, she'd been helped onto the bar and was dancing in her five-inch heels, which her ballet training made fairly easy, much to the delight and approval of the increasingly boisterous crowd. Almost right away it seemed that everyone there was watching her.

It wasn't long before she did something that charged them up even more and simultaneously chipped away further at her natural inhibitions.

The funny thing was, it was the last thing she'd intended to do- an action totally misconstrued by all those watching her. The strings holding her bonnet on had come undone. Without stopping her dancing, she'd simply reached up to tie them together again.

But when she realized what they thought she was doing and what that collective notion did to everyone watching her, the sequence started.

At first, it seemed to happen against her will, but that soon changed.

Even more shocking to her was how natural it felt, and all of a sudden.

Instead of tying the bonnet back on, she made an elaborate show of removing it.

Then she twirled it around a few times, and tossed it into the crowd.

They went absolutely wild and clamored for more.

Kim was a little frightened for a moment when it fully set in what she'd done and what they wanted her to do, but that feeling was chased away by another that felt like a very potent drug that was injected into her and was rapidly coursing through her.

Soon after that the top, apron and skirt of her all-white costume followed the path of her bonnet. She was down to her racy thong and push-up bra, shimmering thigh-high stockings held up by garters, and those 'hooker' pumps with the ankle straps.

She wasn't sure how long she ended up dancing, but she knew she easily had eclipsed the witching hour. Although the

19

crowd couldn't get enough of her, finally she begged off. As the bouncers helped her down, yet another surprise awaited her.

A guy came up to her with a twenty-dollar bill in hand, knelt down and pulled her garter out just enough and slid the bill between it and her thigh. Kim gaped at him, but right after that another one came up and repeated the action.

Then another. And another. She looked around and the same was happening with the other girls who'd danced above the throng, although those girls weren't nearly garnering the attention- and the tips, most with phone numbers attached- that Kim was.

Finally, after they stopped coming, her friend Rob draped her coat over her and she left, flanked by her friends and a couple bouncers, feeling like something of a celebrity. Many patrons asked when she would be back. So did the owner of the club, who also had watched her dance. He pulled her aside and talked with her, asking among other things if she'd be interested in a regular gig there, which obviously wasn't an option.

A week after that he called her to let her know someone a little further north who'd witnessed her display that night was very interested in contacting her about dancing at his club, which was pretty highly touted in those circles.

The owner of that notorious Baltimore mainstay also asked her permission to place over the main bar a blowup of a picture of her someone had taken as she danced. She granted his request, and that poster-sized blowup of her remained on the wall until the club closed in the mid '90s. She went back there one night in the fall of '92 and sure enough, there was her likeness only a few feet away from where she'd held court that night. Just after those doors were closed for the last time the man even gave her the memento in spite of the fact that, according to him, someone had offered him $25,000 for it. She never found out if that was true, but the insinuation alone nearly floored her.

She counted the money when she got to Sue's place and discovered that she'd been given over a thousand dollars, which made for some night of trick-or-treating. In light of that, the loss of most of her costume, which she'd absolutely loved, didn't seem like that big of a deal.

As blown away as she was by the sum of money all those guys- and some girls, even- had slipped into her garters, she was more struck by something that experience had awakened within her.

With the absence of love in her life and her certainty that she wouldn't see John again, she needed something in addition to her studies and her less-than-exciting social life. She believed she'd found a way to help fill in that void.

Although she knew it wouldn't take the place of what she yearned to regain- somehow- with John, or maybe with someone else if it wasn't meant to be with him, at least this could provide a temporary fix.

However, she also couldn't help being a little afraid of whatever this new feeling was and how it had elevated her to a state close to ecstasy.

Even more disturbing at the time was how it had left her wanting more. As she lay on Sue's couch after they got back, she was pretty certain she wouldn't be able to ignore it- that her little performance on the bar was more likely the beginning of a potentially lengthy engagement as opposed to a one night stand.

It took some time- and lots of thought- for her to sort things out and determine what her next move would be...


The news editor from Channel 11 couldn't believe what the caller was telling him.

"You're sure it was her? I'll tell you what- you'd damned well *better* be sure, because if we go with this story and it turns out to be another woman who looks like her, our asses are fried. Now, if it really is her, it'll be one hell of a piece, especially considering what she does and how upstanding she is, not to mention where she could be headed. Can you give me your source, or any substantial proof? I can't go with anything less...Well, until I see some hard evidence, I'm gonna keep this on ice. In the meantime I'll put one of my people on it, too. Thanks for the heads-up, and get back to me as soon as you find something."


"So this is everything?" John had poured over the case files in an empty conference room, making notes as he went. He handed the bundle to Tom and sat down.

"Not quite. A couple days ago a girl disappeared from the D.C. area during cheerleading tryouts for their football team. I just hung up with the lead detective there. From the details they have, it looks like she could be the eleventh..."

He noticed his brother's introspection. "Is there something else?"

Tom looked up. "Remember Jenny- my babysitter?"

"Yeah, Jacobson's only daughter- the really pretty one who had a crush on me-…oh, no- not her…"

He nodded.

John slowly sat down across from him. "Eleven girls since '90. One per year, and one more for completion, if he thinks along those lines…"

"Yeah, 'if'. One of the most hated words in the English language. 'If' we were able to nail him down to a window during the year, that might help, but you saw how he took the College Park girl in November '96, and then the schoolteacher in January '97. Then he didn't do it again until September '98. And the same goes for where he strikes- 'if' we could nail that down. I just can't see enough of a pattern in the way he operates to predict his next-" The second he saw John grimace and clutch at his torso, Tom rushed over to him. "Slow, deep breaths, John. Take it easy. I'm taking you to the-"

"No, it's OK," he cut Tom off as the pain subsided as quickly as it came. He breathing gradually normalized. "It happens sometimes. Doctor Reynolds told me it would, but each time is a little less painful and it doesn't happen as often anymore."

"You're sure you're all right?"

"Yeah, I'll be fine." He smiled to emphasize his point.

After observing him for a moment, Tom gave him a nod and settled back into his chair. "So you think it's one guy, too? If that's the case, it's most likely he keeps the girls he takes for a while and kills them when he tires of them, which I don't want to dwell on too much since now he could have Jenny. Maybe he has another angle- we haven't found any bodies, which could mean he's just good at getting rid of them. On the other hand, maybe he's wealthy and can keep 'em as captives…or maybe he's a white slaver."

"Seems possible- maybe he keeps 'em for a while and sells 'em. For the record, I agree with you; these cases *are* related. It looks like one guy to me, and a smart, calculating, cool-headed son of a bitch at that. If there *is* a pattern to what he's doing- and I have a feeling there is-, he's disguised it pretty well along with his motive."

"He sure has. What could it be that's making him take all these girls? Is it about sex, control, or something else?"

"That's the question, isn't it? I'm sure there's more to it than his preference for young women with that particular look, but at first glance I'm damned if I can see what it is. It could be outright misogyny, or some sort of revenge, whether it's indirect retaliation against an ex-girlfriend who had the same physical traits, or revenge against women in general because he was a high school nerd, like a former acquaintance of mine. Or, it could be he simply enjoys playing cat-and-mouse with the police- lots of possibilities, unfortunately. Worse yet, the trails on most of these cases seem to be pretty cold- especially the older ones."

"Yeah. It seems like it's going to be something subtle that breaks this open- some little thread. I just hope we catch it sooner than later."

"Amen to that. Come on, let's grab a bite." As they got up to leave, John focused again on the pile of case files. "When we get back, there's another file I'd like to have a look at, if you don't mind..."


Kim opened her eyes and looked up as she heard a guy talking with Kelly and the girls next to her; he appeared to be a photographer of some sort.

He glanced over at Kim as he finished up with them and did a double take. He got up and walked toward her, smiling as he approached. "Hello there!"

She smiled back. "Hi." She started to turn over but caught herself just before she gave those around her much more of a show than earlier. She quickly fastened her top, turned onto her side and propped herself up. Looking up at him, she was able to conceal the fact that she wasn't in the mood for company as he squatted beside her. She didn't want to be rude and hoped he wouldn't take long, although she was curious.

"My name's Jeff and I'm part-owner of Kimberly Swimwear & Lingerie. I don't want to take too much of your time, so I'll come right to the point. I'm going around looking for entrants for our Hottest Body on the Beach contest. You've probably heard about it- it's the biggest swimsuit contest here in Ocean City. We're one of the sponsors and every week I help run it. The winner gets a thousand dollars and is invited back to the final competition at the end of the summer. The winner of that gets fifty thousand dollars or a new Corvette- your choice- and also gets to represent Maryland in the Miss Celestial pageant, which has the national round, then the international. If I may say so, you most definitely should enter. I can see you have great taste in bikinis!" *Jesus, I think it's her!*

It was like she'd unconsciously put out a vibe with her musings and reminiscing, and the response was this guy who happened upon her with an offer that could provide a bridge to her past. Ten years ago she'd been approached for the same reason...

...or maybe this could be a fresh start if she came to need one, which definitely was possible. And talk about coincidence- the company was even called Kimberly!

*This could be my last chance. The clock's ticking in more ways than one...*

*...but a bikini contest? Now?! What am I thinking?! It does sound enticing, but...*

"I- well, I'm...very flattered, but...I don't know. This really isn't-"

"You OK here, Miss? This guy botherin' you?" The muscular guy, who a short while ago had asked the Lord to take him, came over and was giving Jeff a very intimidating look.

"No, it's all right, but thank you."

Jeff tried to play another angle- he'd seen hesitation in many a prospective entrant and knew plenty of ways to get them past that. Piling on the compliments usually helped pave the way, especially when they came from more than one source.

Besides, if it really was her, he had another bit of motivation...

He turned to her protector. "Actually, maybe you can help me persuade this beautiful young lady to enter-"

"Hottest Body on the Beach, right? I thought I recognized you." He turned back to Kim. "You should go for it; you sure have my vote! Hopefully we'll see you there later."

He rejoined his buddies and, judging from their reaction, Kim figured he probably told them what was going on. "Well..."

"Looks like you have a rooting section already," he said as he gestured to the guys "and I bet it'll get a lot bigger. You should give it a shot..." He paused, then decided to test her. "Actually, you look familiar- have you competed before? You look just like the girl who became Miss Celestial a few years back..."

24

"Um, no- no, I've never competed before."

*Seems to me she's dodging the question more than answering it...* "Well, anyway, you must work awfully hard to keep that body of yours looking so hot- why not show it off a little? On top of that, with those big green eyes and your smile, you're gonna blow 'em all away!"

Her resistance was weakening by the second. As much as she tried to hide that, she was sure Jeff noticed. If her situation were different, the decision would be a lot simpler; she'd even lied to him about not having competed in a bikini pageant before, let alone not having been Miss Celestial in 1990. "Oh...I don't know. I appreciate your flattery, but this really isn't the best time..."

Even as she resisted, the drug was in her bloodstream again. She hadn't felt the effects of it for ten years, ever since she walked away from what had brought it on that Halloween night in '86 and sustained it for the time in between. Even now she didn't regret her decision to leave that part of her life behind, especially when she was given the opportunity to step into her adoptive mother's position.

But she never forgot how wonderful- and how desirable- she felt when they watched her perform and here was another opportunity if she wanted it...

*It usually doesn't take this much to persuade the really hot ones.* Jeff changed tactics in the face of her continued resistance. "Look, I don't mean to put you on the spot, especially if you're not having such a great day. Why don't I give you my card- this is the address of our boutique at the Gold Coast Mall. Give it some thought- I really do think you'll 'wow' 'em, and I'm not just saying that. Also, being up there on stage in front of all those people might just give you a shot in the arm- who knows? If later on you decide you do want to enter, just call that number and we can set up a fitting for a custom bikini if you'd like to do that. In fact, I have a suit that'll be perfect for you."

"Oh...um...I'll see if I'm up for it later."

"By the way, that's not all I wanted to ask you. I scout for models for our swimwear and photograph them for calendars and our magazine. If you're interested, I'd love to do a shoot with you as my model. I think you're perfect for showing our products- you'll make our bikinis look great. I also do our lingerie layouts; maybe you'd be up for that, too."

"Really?! You want me to-...to model for you?"

25

He noticed her surprise turn to what appeared to be suspicion. "I know what you might be thinking, but I am a legitimate photographer. I can show you my portfolio and credentials, and I can provide plenty of references, including a number of girls from this area. I've worked with many models, and none have ever complained...well, that is unless you don't like my occasional practical jokes. You're more than welcome to bring someone with you, too- maybe your bodyguard over there, or your boyfriend- anyone you like. I want you to feel as comfortable as possible."

Kim looked away when he mentioned 'boyfriend', knowing she couldn't hide what she was feeling.

Seeing her downcast expression, Jeff didn't press her on that front, nor did he give away his reaction. *Boyfriend's elsewhere, too...* "Sorry, I don't mean to pry. Anyway, you have my address and number. I hope you'll consider my offer. Oh- what's your name? I'll need to get you on the list for the contest in case you enter."

She said the first one that came to her mind, which was another link to her past. "Kimberly Fairchild. Thank you, Jeff; I might be interested in modeling for you, but I would like to check your references first. I'm glad you understand."

"Perfectly. In fact, I can give you my resume right now, and I'll save my cheesy cliché about your name and the company's. By the way, what are you majoring in?"

As she took the resume she looked quizzically at him. Then she grinned. "I haven't been a college student for quite some time, but thank you for saying that. In fact, I'm thirty-one."

"Thirty-one?! No way- I don't buy it. You look like you're *twenty*-one, or twenty-two, tops."

"But I *am* thirty-one...seriously!"

"Man...if that's the case, you'll still be turning heads when you're *forty*-one, and beyond!" *Bingo- she's the right age, too...*

Kim giggled and looked away.

"Oh, brother! I see someone else is inflating your ego, Kim, like you haven't had enough of *that* today!" After seeing Kim lighten up, Kelly decided to walk back over.

"Hey, no interruptions from you! Jeff was doing just fine."

With the lighter atmosphere, Jeff greased the wheel some more as he refocused on 'Miss Fairchild'. "FYI, the contest is at

26

six o'clock. You know, now that I've seen you, I don't want any other woman wearing that suit I started to tell you about. It's virgin white with sequins."

"A sequined white bikini?" *Hmm...sounds like what I wore my first night dancing...*

"Some of the girls really get flashy in these contests. Not that you need another edge on the competition; this suit on you would be like the cherry on top of the sundae. You'd need a good pair of heels, too."

"I have a pair that should- I mean, I'll let you...I don't know, maybe I could come up just to try it on..."

"Absolutely, and bring the shoes with you so we can take a look at the result. So you'll try that bikini on for me, then? Ten to one says you'll love it!"

She laughed, holding up her hand. "OK, I'll try it! I'll meet you at 3:30?"

"Great! I'll see you then." He turned to Kelly. "Why don't you and your friends come, too? I'm sure you'll find plenty of suits to your liking."

"That sounds like fun! I'm sure I can talk them into it."

"Now you'll have plenty of company there, Kim," Jeff said to her. "Like I said- I want you to feel totally at ease. Let me know if there's anything else I can do for you, or if you need any special arrangements if you decide to do the calendar and magazine shoots. If you do those, maybe we can talk about setting up a lingerie spread. Once the execs from our affiliates get a load of you, they'll be begging you to show their stuff. Actually, do you mind if I take a couple shots of you now? I really think they'll be excited about you, and you have my word I won't distribute it. You have plenty of witnesses to verify I said that. I'll be glad to sign a waiver sheet, too, if you like; I have one with me."

His resume was pretty extensive, and it was on company stationery. He also had some impressive letters of recommendation.

And, her guard was down. "Um...OK. How should I pose?"

"Just like you are will be great." He quickly set up his camera and had her fine-tune her pose. "Beautiful, Kim. Now give me that smile!" He snapped a couple photos. "Perfect- thanks a bunch!" As he got up to leave, he added, "I have a personal interest in this, too- I have a feeling you could be my biggest

27

discovery, Miss Kimberly Fairchild. See you at 3:30!" He grinned and winked at her, then walked away.

Kelly waited until he was out of earshot. "Fairchild, eh?"

"Well, I…I didn't want to give him my real name."

"I figured as much. Question is, what will you do if-"

"I don't know; I'm not even sure it'll come to that. Let's not worry about it now."


"Even though you said it would be all taken care of, I ain't surprised. It's been ten years and I'm still in this shithole; I'm prob'ly not gettin' out, am I?"

Mark Peters, Esquire, tried to maintain the illusion and do damage control, like he had for the others before their untimely deaths. Rollins never had been much of a problem- especially since he was inside and most likely would stay inside. "I told you I'd do my best, and I did- we both did- and all three board members told me they were going to play. I don't know who got to them, but that wasn't what was supposed to happen."

Rollins nodded, still even-tempered for the time being. "It was the same with you gettin' me a new trial and gettin' that murder conviction thrown out. Guess they just think I'm…what's the word I'm lookin' for…incorrigible?"

*Here it comes…*

"You fuckin' incompetent piece 'a shit'! I've had it with you an' with him, too! Ten years I've been hearin' the same shit outta you. I've had *enough*!!" He pounded his fist on the table to emphasize his last point.

Something felt different about him this time. "Come on, Dean, don't-"

He came up out of the chair. "Shut your hole, you fuckin' overpaid piss boy!! I know I'm right where you both want me. You listen, an' listen good: I'm done with *both* you cocksuckers. I'm gonna do what I shoulda done years ago and tell a certain Governor a story I think he'll be real interested in. You two fucked me for the last time." His eyes bored holes into those of Peters.

He definitely was different. He wasn't just venting as he always had and he'd never even hinted at spilling the beans.

*Oh, Jesus…*

Rollins chuckled as his lawyer looked away, no longer able to meet his stare. "Nervous now, ain't ya? Ya oughtta be…"

After a moment of silence he went on. "Would ya like to go now, Mister Peters, or didja do that already?"

He laughed out loud when Peters' face turned red. It was fun to see the high-and-mighty lawyer squirm, but it was time to think of how to make his next move. "Get outta my sight."

Rollins noted the change in his disposition as he got up to leave- his cage had been rattled and pretty damned hard at that. He wanted to rattle it again. "One more thing, Peters…"

He waited until the bottom feeder looked back at him. When he did, Dean saw beads of sweat on his forehead.

"You better hope you never see me again."


He was about to lie down and take a nap. He'd been up late the night before. Even after all the internal debate, he still was on the fence as to his plan of action.

Then the phone rang.

He almost let the machine get it, but decided to pick it up on the fourth ring. "Yeah?"

"Hey, boss- glad you're there. It's Jeff Newman, and I have some good news. Check your e-mail; I just sent you a couple photos."

"Hang on." He figured he knew what it was- another hot little prospect for modeling. One of his current guests had come from that well. He turned his computer monitor back on and saw the new message.

He opened the file and immediately froze.

"You all right?"

He snapped back at the sound of Jeff's voice, aware that he'd drifted. "Where is she? How long ago did you take these?"

"Awesome! So that *is* her! I thought it-"

"*Where is she?*"

Jeff's blood ran cold from the tone of his voice. He never yelled- for him, that was totally unnecessary to get his message across- and he was true to form in this case. On the whole, he'd treated Jeff better than could have been expected, especially considering the reason Jeff was dealing with him at all. Their relationship was as good as it could be, but Jeff always remembered his place.

He was afraid to think about what could happen if he didn't. The man could scare the devil himself, just like he was

29

scaring the shit out of his photographer/scout. "Uh, I- I'm not sure- I mean, I didn't get where she was staying, I just- just saw her about an hour ago. I'm...sorry, boss, I didn't wanna push-"

"All right. Enough. Settle down and tell me what went on and what you found out about her." After a moment, Jeff was able to do that without stammering. "OK. So you think she'll show?"

*She even used her old alias...*

"Yeah, I think she will. I have everything ready. How do you wanna handle her?"

"For now just keep doing what you're doing. Nothing drastic- I don't want you scaring her off. I'm on my way with a guest, so I'll see you soon. And Jeff?"

"Yeah, boss?"

"Good job."


An hour and a half later he was on his way to Ocean City with his bargaining chip secured in back of the van.

The trip had been delayed as he'd reached a familiar state brought on by Jennifer's beseeching eyes, her very well-proportioned body clad in sexy lingerie, her squirming and whimpering as he carried the tightly bound girl to the van...

...and most of all, his anticipation of having Kim again...

He'd fastened Jennifer to the bed in the van and gone back inside- up to the room where the captive he'd had the longest was.

Lisa was the easiest to control; in fact, he really didn't consider her a captive anymore. She was the one he could always count on to give him what he needed and, as always, she gave it to him willingly, doing all she had to do to prime him and help him along. The live feeds and videotapes of the restrained women made that easy every time, especially the ones of the girls just after he'd taken them. Not only did Lisa know what he liked, as obvious as it was. She loved it, too- maybe even more than he did.

The latest tape, of Jennifer, was the best yet. Given her fearful state, which hadn't abated in the least and came through clearly as she struggled in her bonds, she would be a great source for some time. But, how would she react when the time came?

He already knew how Kim would react. That thought quickly refocused him on the vital matter as he returned to the van.

Once underway, now with Lisa on board, he mused about how he'd taken her, which marked the genesis of his hobby...

30

# Chapter 2

Whenever he thought about it, he always came up with the conclusion that it had to be more than dumb luck. She was the right girl in the right place at the right time.

"Hi, welcome to our club. I'm Lisa and I'll be serving you this evening. May I start you off with a drink?"

He made some small talk with her, more to feel her out than anything. He'd noticed her when he walked into the lounge and observed her briefly and surreptitiously. He saw one of her customers get up and leave, then asked the hostess to seat him in her section, which she did. He seemed to be drawing her in, as she lost track of her other customers. Noting her interest, but not pressing right away, he ordered a glass of red wine and watched intently as the shapely, green-eyed, light brunette went to get it.

Lisa was feeling mixed and equally potent emotions that this very attractive stranger was stirring up within her; if a man could be called beautiful, this man most definitely was that. There was something dark and forbidding- even dangerous- about him, but amazingly, that was one of the things she found so compelling about him. His mannerisms, his total focus on her- and not just on her face and body- and those deep blue eyes…

He was so attentive to her responses to his questions- just very tuned in to her, which was something she was not used to.

Along with all the accessories, her uniform consisted of a strapless, boned satin bodysuit that was too small, cut low at the top and high on the hip, long satin gloves and high-heeled pumps that matched the tiger-striped pattern of her bodysuit, and sheer nylons. It was exactly like the one Kim had worn during her brief stint at the same club.

As Lisa brought him his wine, he saw her reaction as he purposefully leered at her, especially her breasts. She was pretty; her face bore some resemblance to Kim's, although she wasn't a match, of course. She was a little taller and a little more endowed. She didn't have Kim's waspish waist, perfect legs and overall symmetry, but Lisa still had a very nice body. Hers was more along the lines of voluptuous.

She also wasn't as fit as Kim, but that would be easy to remedy…

31

Simultaneously flattered and a little uncomfortable because of his attention- but also even more intrigued-, she lost her concentration as she stopped and dipped slightly to hand him the wine, some of which spilled on her thigh. She fretted for a moment and was about to return to the kitchen to clean it off.

"Come closer." His tone was gentle, but also commanding. She did as he said, and he took his napkin and dipped it in his water. He then reached around and took hold of the back of her thigh. With his other hand he pressed the wet napkin against the front where the spill was to get the wine out of her nylons.

Lisa was shocked. Although many guys had been forward with her, no one had ever been so brazen and bold as he. He was assertive and dominant without being domineering, which turned her on more than any other man ever had. She had to hold on to the back of his chair, certain that her knees were about to buckle at any second.

"Has it been a long evening for you, Lisa? It was crowded when I walked in; you must have done quite a bit of running around."

She only caught the last part of what he said as she continued to watch in amazement while he tended to the spill. "Um...yes, it- it has been a pretty busy shift. I...I also had to cover lunch and help prepare for tonight," she replied in a shaky voice. "I think we've slowed down and-...I have a break coming so I can sit for a while."

She was so taken by him and what he was doing that she never even considered asking him to stop. It didn't matter to her that they were in her place of work, nor did it matter that someone could have seen what was happening between the two of them even though they were at a secluded table, nor did it matter that she had a boyfriend.

He put the wet napkin down and got a dry one to finish his work as he wondered how she would react to his next move. He scarcely could believe what he was about to do, especially considering where they were, but he knew there was no way he could stop himself. He found that a bit unnerving, although his accompanying sense of excitement superceded even what he felt when he and his accomplices shook down the Federal Reserve armored car for all that money. Up until the previous year, he'd always been in control when it came to women.

For the most part, he knew where this malady previously unknown to him was coming from.

Kim's escapes had damaged him badly. Anger had turned into frustration, followed by a lingering desolation. He knew he had to do something to make up for those staggering blows from which he was still reeling. That played a big part in why he was having such irresistible urges with Lisa, whom he hadn't singled out merely because she looked something like Kim.

In a way, she *was* Kim. She had a couple things in common with his real target, so maybe- just maybe- she would be a suitable substitute. With Lisa he believed he was taking the first step toward overcoming his loss.

He made his inevitable and highly risky move...

"You must be tired from all that."

She closed her eyes and sighed deeply, then began to moan as he massaged and caressed her soft, curvy legs, apparently losing herself to his touch as his hands deftly worked. She didn't seem to notice- or care- that the napkin had disappeared. He started with her calves and slowly moved back up to her thighs, feeling the tension slowly dissipating as he went. He was pleasantly surprised and charged up by her reaction; she even leaned against him as she moved her hand from the chair to his shoulder!

Then he reached the inner part of her thigh...

She finally snapped back to reality as she practically collapsed into his arms. He took hold of her and steadied her, and she was slow to pull herself away. She was very excited, but also a little shaken from the fact that she did nothing to stop him. She stared at him, one hand over her heart and the tip of the index finger of her other hand between her teeth.

He was breathing just as heavily as she, but he was the first to regain control. The notion just leapt into his head, and he had to act on it. "You said you're on break soon. Come back over here when you get it; I have a proposition for you. It's something you'll be very interested in."

The bewildered girl nodded, almost against her will. "OK," she replied in a barely audible voice. She backed up slowly, then turned and walked away. She hesitated just before leaving his sight and turned to look at him again for a long moment. As she disappeared around the corner, he half expected to see the manager come back with her along with a couple of the muscular bouncers.

On the other hand, he had an equally strong feeling that she would come back alone. After a couple minutes she did just that. Her disposition was somewhat the same, only her bewildered state was tempered by curiosity. "Um...I'm on my break now. May I sit with you?"

"Let's go outside. I'm sure you could use some fresh air after breathing in all this damned cigarette smoke."

"Well, I- I'd love to, but...I'll get in trouble if-"

She gasped as he took her hands into his and pulled her into his lap. She seemed to melt as he looked deep into her eyes; almost right away she was breathing so heavily that her full breasts seemed ready to burst out of her low-cut outfit.

Then, he took both her hands behind her back and held her wrists together. She didn't resist him at all. With his free hand he again roamed over her hips and thighs. She lay against him, not seeming to mind in the least that he was holding her in place by force, keeping her wrists imprisoned in his hand.

Better yet, she seemed even more turned on than earlier...

At that moment he knew he'd found the right girl. "How old are you, Lisa?"

She was totally adrift, wishing they were alone and imagining what he would do with her if they were..."Hmm? Oh, I'm...I'm twenty." After she answered him, he helped her to her feet and stood up with her.

*Wow- he's so tall...and he's built like a linebacker!*

"Come with me." He took her by the arm and guided her toward the front entrance.

She retrieved and put on her shawl, and she removed the ears and tail to her outfit. The management insisted on the cocktail waitresses remaining within the club while wearing their distinctive uniforms. Although she risked losing her job by allowing this gorgeous stranger to break that rule by taking her outside, she was powerless to stop him. They went through the doors and onto the boardwalk.

When they reached a particular spot, he saw her having trouble negotiating the boards in her heels, so he scooped her up and carried her. She kissed him, then blushed a deep red when he looked at her in surprise.

Instantly she seemed to become weightless, so he kept her cradled in his arms and continued walking as she cuddled against him.

Many people observed the very good-looking couple as they passed, not knowing what was taking place. No one interfered.

Lisa never questioned him or signaled for help, which she easily could have done.

It wasn't long before he got to the street where his car was parked. When they reached it, he set her down, opened the door for her and helped her inside. After he closed her in, she immediately leaned over and unlocked his door, then folded her hands in her lap and watched him as he went around to the driver's side and climbed in. Her eyes stayed on him as he started the car and drove away.

He still hadn't even told her what was happening, and she hadn't asked. He certainly couldn't tell her that, in a way, he was reliving one of his fondest memories with Kim, only he was about to add a little twist to that. He looked over at her to find that she still was observing him. He was amazed that there was not even a hint of fear in her countenance. She was quite calm, and as time went on, he was the one who was becoming anxious. Before long they were out of Atlantic City and heading toward I-95.

Then, he spotted an empty rest stop. Deciding it was time, he pulled into it.

She became nervous when he stopped in the deserted place; her eyes darted around, but nonetheless, she remained still, waiting.

Suddenly, he froze. He was clear in his mind how he wanted the next sequence of events to unfold, but for a moment he couldn't get it started…

…until she moved over and kissed him just like she had as he carried her- very timidly. He was back in control at that point; he took her into his arms and kissed her madly as he turned his hands loose on her body. For all he knew, an hour could have passed before he pulled back from the gasping girl. It seemed like he'd sucked every last bit of air from her lungs with that kiss, but he also took away her fear.

His moment of hesitation was gone as well. "Turn around, Lisa. I'm going to tie you up."

Her eyes widened for a moment in a mixture of fear and excitement. "OK."

That was all she said before she did as he told her. The dynamic of their relationship was solidified. Within minutes Lisa lay, bound hand and foot, in the back seat. She writhed in her restraints, but he could tell she wasn't trying to free herself.

As he prepared her gag, he said, "You know I'm never going to let you go."

He saw a surprising calm take over as she nodded in acceptance of her fate. He gagged her and strapped her to the seat. Shortly they were on their way home.

He had the outlet he badly needed, although it wouldn't be long before he realized she only provided a temporary fix. She wasn't Kim; no one could take her place.

It would be the same with the next girl...

...and the next...

...and the next...

Back at the Kitty Cat Club the manager waited. He'd watched them walk out- with her assets, Lisa was impossible to miss. Upon her return he only intended to reprimand her; he believed in giving second chances when appropriate and Lisa did keep the clientele coming back once they got a load of her.

He had no way of knowing that was the last time he ever would see her.


Kim was becoming more irritated- also more worried- as he continued to pester her. "Look, I don't know what you're talking about; you must have me confused with someone else. I want you to get away from me right now, or-..."

*Or, what?*

*What am I going to do, call the police and tell them he's bothering me because I was a dancer and he probably saw me perform, and suddenly I can't handle that?*

*I wish this damned signal would change...*

"Nah, I'm positive you was her! I never forget a-"

"Leave me *alone*!!" Her blast momentarily silenced him, and thankfully, the signal changed so they could cross the busy Coastal Highway. Even though the guy kept up with his one-way conversation for a bit longer and tossed a few epithets her way in the process, at least he didn't follow them.

*This is getting ugly,* Kim thought as she quickly moved away from him, putting as much distance as she could between herself and the obstinate man who swore he'd seen her dancing at a strip club.

Worse, she and Kelly were walking together, and Kelly witnessed the exchange and her reaction. Her former life finally was catching up with her and she was having more difficulty trying to keep herself in check, having lost her temper with the loudmouth they'd just left behind.

How many more like him were out there? Were some of the glances and stares she'd gotten over the years from former patrons of the club where she'd become something of a star? Guys who recognized her and secretively smiled as she passed?

It was only going to get worse; the press was bound to find out soon.

This all came down to the fact that she'd tried to bury her short career as a dancer because she was certain she would not ⊂ been hired as a counselor, had the board been aware of that. The stabs of guilt she felt early in her career for having harbored her little secret had pushed her harder to make up for her omission by positively influencing as many young lives as she could. As a result, those episodes of guilt had diminished significantly in the face of all the good she'd done and the accompanying respect of her students and peers. It seemed like she'd redeemed herself...

...until recently. Nothing could hide the fact that all she'd accomplished was built on her lack of honesty, and those she held dear would not be the only ones bearing witness to what certainly would arise once the word got around...

*Why couldn't I have done the right thing and told them?*
*Especially John?*

"You can slow down now."

"Oh...sorry." She resumed her normal pace allowing Kelly to catch up.

"Jeez, he sure was persistent, not to mention an asshole. What is it with these-"

"I don't know, Kelly, I just-...could we please not talk about that?"

"OK." *Wow, she's still stewing...*

*...not that she doesn't have every reason to be, though. She certainly has crossed paths with more than her share of mental midgets today.*

She figured it was just a compilation of everything Kim was dealing with that got to her, and quickly became dismissive of the man's insinuation.

*Like she would have done that!*

*Not that she* couldn't *have, of course. She sure turned everyone on the beach into mush...* "So you'll be ready at three? Want me to pick you up?"

"Thanks, that would be great. Three's fine. I, um-...I didn't mean to be-"

"There you go apologizing again. Don't worry! It's all right. You're under a lot of stress and you need to vent."

Kim sighed and then smiled. "I thought *I* was the one who's supposed to give the advice." Kelly giggled as they hugged. "I'll see you in an hour and a half."


"Hey, Boss. Right on time, as always. Good to see you."

He gave Jeff a nod as he walked in and briefly scanned the boutique. There were only a few people there other than Jeff and the sexy little co-ed from Salisbury State University who worked as a salesgirl. Knowing Jeff as he did, he was sure that sales wasn't her only function. Their exchange before Jeff greeted him and ushered him through the door to the stock room lent more than enough supporting evidence...

"That's right- you haven't seen the modifications yet since we bought the space next door. We've got a good setup back here. There's plenty of room for the studio and we added a couple more changing rooms. The models love it," he touted as he showed The Man into the remodeled and expanded studio.

As he walked with Jeff and surveyed the space, he was going over in his mind how he could take her once she was here, and also how he would get her out without arousing suspicion. This was a pretty busy mall and she was bound to put up a fight.

*I guess I'll need the chloroform if it's going to be here...*

*...or, maybe not, if my ace in the hole has the desired effect, which she probably will. Just in case I go the more conventional route, where would the best ambush spot be?*

*Wait a minute...* "You said she's not coming alone?"

"No, she'll have some other girls with her for the bikini fitting. I'll do my best to persuade her to enter the contest or, if she doesn't go for that, to get her back here later for some modeling."

38

He nodded. "Alone, if possible. If not, I'll have to find out where she's-..."

As the idea came to him, he was glad he'd decided to bring Lisa along in addition to Jennifer...

"Regardless of whether or not she does the contest, I want her back here later, or tomorrow. For now, show me the dressing rooms."

"This way, Boss. I already have the big one set up for her with everything you wanted. Miss Fairchild will get the star treatment." Once inside that room, he glanced at his boss, who was totally focused. Jeff knew not to disturb him, so he waited.

The man nodded. "I'm sure she'll love that. There's just one small addition I want you to make..."


"When will he stop with this fucking nonsense?!" Warden Steele barked. "What could he possibly have to say to Governor Stratton that would be of any interest?! You know what it'll be: more of the song and dance he's always had about being set up!"

"It was different this time, Sir, which is why I wanted to tell you right away. He said it had something to do with the Governor's girlfriend."

"His girlfriend?!"

"Yes, Sir. Miss Kimberly Francis is the name he mentioned." The guard could see that the warden was taken by surprise, but that didn't last long.

"Well, I'll tell you this: I'm not gonna let him draw that poor girl into any of his antics or try to put her in some kind of bad light, especially with that trial coming up, which will be hard enough on her. Then again, given the source, I think he'd have a hard time putting *anyone* in a bad light. Do you think he was just screwing around?"

"No, Sir. Not at all. He was dead serious and as cool as I've ever seen him."

Gradually the longtime head of the penal institution leaned back and clasped his hands behind his shaved head, his brow furrowed in thought. "I'm glad you came right to me, Len. This is out of the ordinary- way the hell out of it. It's bad enough that he kept suggesting the Governor knew about the heist before it happened, which Rollins claims is why John was able to put him and the other survivors of the shootout away on what little hard evidence he had. Looking at the big picture, the only thing I can think of that he could possibly want from the Governor is a pardon, but he only can get a pardon from the President since it was a Federal rap. Of course, if John was to win the election...

"As things are, it shouldn't take a genius to figure out that Johnny Stratton's the last guy in the world who would want him anywhere other than where he is right now, but I don't like his girlfriend's name being brought up. I damned sure know Tom, Sr. would have felt the same way. That girl has a hard enough road ahead of her. I don't know what Rollins is up to, but the more I think about it the more it's starting to rub me the wrong way..."

He stood and walked to the window overlooking the courtyard. "Tell him I want to see him tomorrow about this. If he *is* just blowing smoke, that might rattle him into backing off. I know the forty-five days he spent in solitary the last time he tried to pull a fast one taught him a very important lesson about fucking with me."


Just out of the shower, Kim watched the special report and police advisory as she coated her body with after-sun lotion. The police spokesman gave a rundown of the names and faces of the missing girls along with brief descriptions of who they were, what they did and where they were last seen. She slowly shook her head in disbelief.

*All those girls...*

*...I wonder if they're even alive...*

The spokesman wasn't very optimistic about that. Kim recalled conversations she'd had with Ted and Sue when they echoed the rationale that the longer a woman is missing, the less likely it becomes that she is alive.

*Logic sure can be a cold thing.*

Here was a roster of eleven missing women, most of whom had vanished years ago. Among them were two college students, a teacher, a figure skater...

*...a cheerleader from D.C.'s pro football team...*

With Jenny's name added to the list, it became much more personal for Kim. Jenny was such a sweet girl, and Kim had worried about how introverted she was. However, she'd taken the big step forward with cheering, which had infused her with some confidence. During the conversations they'd had, Kim was surprised to find how much they had in common...

...and now this.

Her heart went out to all the girls and their families; she knew firsthand how harrowing an ordeal it was to be abducted...

...and to think, besides the two times it did happen to her, there was another instance when it might have happened to her- back in the tumultuous year of 1989.

*No, there was no 'might have' about it...*

She went back to that night before the Thanksgiving break during her final year at Princeton. Her roommate had left for home a couple hours earlier and Kim, after having finished packing for her own drive back to her adoptive mother's for the holiday, had fallen asleep.

She never heard a thing. She didn't realize what was happening until his hand clamped over her mouth and he pinned her to the bed.

*"Don't move and don't make a sound,"* he hissed as he yanked the covers off her. *"Do exactly what I tell you to do. If you don't, you'll be very sorry. Got that?"*

Firmly in the grip of paralyzing fear in addition to that of her assailant, she nodded and tried to stay as calm as possible, wishing she'd worn more to bed that night than her usual thong.

Her chest tightened as he easily turned her onto her stomach and pulled her arms behind her. She yelped as she felt the strap cut painfully into her wrists.

*"I told you to shut up!! You don't get another warning."*

She couldn't stop herself from trembling, but lay still otherwise as he continued his work. She winced, but stifled her outcry, as another strap bit deeply into the soft skin just above her elbows, locking her forearms together.

As he moved down and began to tie her legs, along with her increasing terror came a sense of familiarity with what was happening...

...how he tied her- so methodically and effectively...

...how and where he touched her while he did...

*Is it...*

*...no, it couldn't be-*

"Josh?"

He seemed to tense up. He'd finished strapping her lower thighs and her ankles, and had placed a ball gag up to her lips

41

when her utterance stopped him cold. She had no way of knowing if that was because she was right about his identity or if he simply had frozen because she surprised him.

Or, maybe she was projecting this incident against what her ex-boyfriend had done to her over the last period of time she'd been with him. The main reason it couldn't have been him was because he had died nearly four months earlier when his Jeep went off the road in a Louisiana bayou...

...so what made her think of him?

Whatever the case, he pushed the gag into her mouth and buckled it in. He left the room, but returned rather quickly. He drew her legs up behind her, folding them until her heels almost touched her rear end, and connected the strap holding her ankles with the one holding her elbows.

*"I'll be back for you soon. Enjoy the last time you'll ever be in your own bed. From now on, you'll be dancing for me. Since you seem to like being tied up and kept in a cage, I'll be glad to accommodate you in those ways, too."* He reinforced her gag with a wide leather strap that covered and sealed her mouth, then he left her.

After some experimental squirming, twisting and tugging, she knew the straps would not yield at all; she could barely move or even shift around. The minutes crept by, and despair and hopelessness intermingled with the horror she felt as she waited for the dark figure to return and take her. She was a little confused as to why he didn't take her right away, but was more than a little glad that he hadn't.

She was just coming into her own- twenty-one years old, only months away from graduating with honors from an Ivy League university and ending her career as a dancer, and emotionally on the mend after the very dark and trying relationship with Josh. Kim was looking forward to returning to the Baltimore area with her dear friends and family having further matured with all she'd experienced, and full of excitement about what the future held for her.

As soon as she was able, she also wanted to reveal to John what she'd done outside college and explain to him why she'd been unable to spend his birthday with him...

...but as she lay on her bed, her world was collapsing and there was nothing she could do about it except watch and listen as her alarm clock ticked on. She tried to focus on who it could be that had accosted her. Obviously, he'd seen her at the Silver Palace at least once- in particular on the night of her twentieth birthday.

She briefly considered as a possibility the professor she had in her sophomore year who saw her perform at the club and tried to blackmail her into having sex with him in exchange for him remaining silent about her extracurricular activity. If word got out that she was a dancer at a strip club, she knew the least it would have resulted in was her having to leave Princeton from all the negative attention she'd have been exposed to.

One thing prevented him from going through with his threat and it wasn't that he was married with three children. It was the fact that he valued being an esteemed professor at an elite university more than anything else- he wanted people to look up to him. Kim was able to pick up on that and turn the tables. They came to a truce, but as a result she was forced to quit Princeton's cheerleading squad. She wasn't happy about that, but her priority was graduating.

The more she revisited her secret war with that spineless, arrogant professor, the less convinced she was that he would exact revenge in this manner. He seemed to enjoy belittling women, but more so via his exaggerated intellect than anything else. Even as angry as she'd made him by outwitting him, she knew he wasn't the one responsible. His attitude and disposition stood in marked contrast to this intruder. Plus, she doubted very much that he was physically strong enough to subdue her so quickly and easily.

That took care of one possibility and she tried as best she could to keep her focus on the process of elimination.

*How long has he been watching me dance? How did he find my apartment? He must have been stalking me for months- maybe even longer...*

That year she'd begun to dance as often as she could- even during her semester, which completed the transition she'd made in her junior year by appearing at the club when she had a light week at school. In her first year she'd kept the two separate. One reason why she decided to perform nearly every weekend as a senior was the incredible amount of money she made each time, which had risen in proportion with her popularity. The other reason was her decision that once school was over, so was dancing.

The more she thought about it, the more she realized how cavalier her attitude toward her own safety had become after Josh

43

had died. She saw him as her only real threat. She'd felt a bit of remorse when she got the news that he was gone, but that didn't last longer than a few seconds. More than anything, she felt relieved and free of him.

Soon afterwards she wasn't as mindful that, among other lapses, she was taking the same route home after her performances at the Palace.

However, as she lay in the cruelly tight and inescapable hog-tie, it was painfully apparent to her that those lapses easily could have increased her vulnerability and factored into the nightmare she was being subjected to.

She couldn't hold off the spectre of what probably lay ahead any longer and just as control over her thoughts was wrested away from her, she thought she heard a noise.

Was it the front door?

She froze and waited, hoping against all odds that it wasn't the door she'd heard-

-maybe whoever did this to her reconsidered, got scared and left. At worst she'd be tied up for a few hours, or maybe a day; someone would be along to check on her-

-or, maybe this was just one of those crazy fraternity guys going overboard with a prank who would come back and free her soon-

-or, maybe her clock's alarm would go off and she would wake up safe and sound, shake off this horrible dream and prepare for her drive home to-...

...*oh, God...oh, God, no...*

She heard the footsteps and panic descended upon her as the chilling reality of what awaited her drew closer with each step.

When the doorknob turned slowly, she made a last-ditch effort to break free as she began to cry...

...and she almost didn't hear Nancy berating her companion for trying to open her roommate's door by mistake and possibly waking her. As it turned out, Nancy had had to turn around and come back because she'd forgotten her little sister's birthday gift. She was just going to leave her car running since Steve was with her, but he had to take a bathroom break, so they both went in.

Thankfully, Kim did hear her and immediately screamed as loudly as she could.

Hearing the muffled cries, which through the door and over Kim's humidifier was little more than a faint mewing, Nancy opened the door and reached for the light.

"Kim? I thought you'd be- *KIM*!!" She rushed over to her helpless and almost nude friend, undid her gags and removed them.

Steve, a mutual acquaintance of both girls, had not yet been inside their apartment. By choosing the wrong door, he'd unwittingly foiled an imminent abduction. He quickly set to work assisting Nancy with removing the confining straps.

A very grateful Kim whimpered, partly from the fresh rush of blood back into her limbs as she was freed, but mostly in relief. "Thank God you guys came back. Thank God..." As soon as she was able, she embraced and clung to Nancy, sobbing and shaking uncontrollably as a torrent of emotion rushed out of her upon her release.

"It's OK, Honey. I'm with you now. Shhh..." Nancy comforted her roommate, who'd become another sister to her during the two years they'd shared the apartment. She was aghast that someone would want to frighten or harm Kim, who was so well regarded by so many...

...unfortunately, plenty others didn't look so kindly upon her. At least one had crossed the line with this assault, which Nancy hoped was the only line that whoever was responsible had crossed.

It took some time for Kim to calm down. When she did, Nancy kissed her forehead. "Are you all right?"

Kim nodded and sniffled as she relaxed her hold on her close friend and co-rescuer.

"Who did this to you? Did he...hurt you?"

"I don't- I don't know who he was. He just-...I mean, I was lying here sleeping and he-" She jumped at the knock on the door and huddled against Nancy again.

"Don't worry, Sweetie- it's the police. Steve called them as soon as we untied you. Here, let's get you dressed so we can talk with them."

Both her friends closely flanked her and held her hands as she told the investigating officers all she remembered. Fortunately they were very sympathetic and went as easy on her as they could; the process didn't seem as long as it actually took.

The local police did their best with the information Kim provided, but she knew they didn't have much to go on. The perpetrator left no physical evidence of any kind- there weren't even any of his prints on the straps and the gags. None of the residents of her apartment complex witnessed any strangers- at least, no one reported anything. Not surprisingly, he never was apprehended.

For several years after that Kim took many measures to hide her whereabouts with help from Sue, her well-placed friend in the police department, and Sue's well-placed friends in the Motor Vehicle Administration and other agencies where records are kept. Those favors did not come solely as a result of friendship, but the relative security they brought her was well worth the risk she took during the sting she helped set up and was involved in not long after that. Even so, although she didn't live in fear, she did have a level of nervousness that only time and the lack of any further incidents gradually lessened.

One thing the police couldn't figure out was how the man had gotten inside. Eventually they reached the conclusion that he must have picked the locks, although they also said those locks were not easy to defeat.

As it always had, the thought of what could have befallen her if the intruder who'd slipped into her apartment late on that fall night had successfully made off with her caused her to shiver...

...and again, even though she knew it was impossible, she couldn't help but wonder if it had been him.

*Why do I keep thinking about Josh?*

*Maybe whoever it was just worked the same way that twisted bastard did when he played his little game with me...*

*...and he was smart enough and thorough enough to get away without leaving the slightest clue...*

When it came to her, a chill slowly made its way from her scalp all the way down.

"What if he didn't stop after he tried to take me? What if-"

In late November 1989 an intruder who never was caught nearly abducted her. According to the bulletin she'd just seen, in August of the following year- apparently on the night of Kim's birthday, yet- a pretty young cocktail waitress with light brown hair and green eyes vanished from the Atlantic City night club where Kim also had worked in that capacity. An unknown man who also was never seen again accompanied her.

46

No arrests were made, no suspects identified.

The year after that, a green-eyed blonde co-ed from Princeton disappeared.

No arrests made, no suspects identified…

"Um, hi. May I speak with Lieutenant Tom Stratton in Homicide, please?"


He looked at the name and number that showed up on the screen of his phone.

*What does* he *want?* he thought, irritated that his total concentration on the third attempt at his ultimate quarry was being disrupted. He jabbed the 'talk' button. "This had better be important, Peters."

"I'm sorry if my timing's bad, but you need to know this. I talked to Rollins this morning and I think we have a problem with him…"

He paid little attention as Peters went on about how much his accomplice knew and how he could land both of them in jail and what were they going to do about it.

Finally, he finished. "All right, I'll give it some thought and let you know what I decide." He'd already made the decision anyway; it was all but done.

"Look, he's serious about this- a lot more so than the last time he-"

"I understood what you said; you don't need to tell me twice."

"But…I, uh, think we should talk about-"

"I just told you *I* will think about this. I don't like repeating myself, especially when I know you're an intelligent man and you understood perfectly what I said the first time. I will get back to you when I've decided what needs to be done, that's *if* I decide you need to know. Now, is there anything else you need clarification on?"

After a few seconds of what he knew was a very nervous silence, his lawyer responded. "No…no, that's all. I'll, uh… I'll wait for your call."

"Good." He was about to hang up, but then a thought came to him.

*Yeah, that could help. It'll push her buttons some more and maybe push her further away from him in the process…*

47

"There's one thing you can do for me in the meantime, Mark. I think you'll enjoy this..."


"My God, Kim...most women don't even have that happen once during their lives, let alone twice. I'm glad your friends came back, too."

"I have no doubt they saved my life that night, just like Sergeant Wilkes and Officer Downes did back in April. I just got to thinking about that again when the bulletin came on. So you're on this case?"

"Yeah, along with the head of missing persons. We're all putting our heads together. Now, this man- did he say anything else?"

"No, that was all. I couldn't pick up on his voice because he hissed. I have no idea who he was Gosh, there were so many possibilities with all the guys who came to see me dance. You saw how crowded the place got when you came up that time...

"Do you think there might be some sort of connection here? Could the same man who almost took me be the one who abducted all those women? Speaking of the others, why haven't we heard about them before now, Tom?"

"Everyone looked at all these cases separately. Each happened in a different jurisdiction with months elapsing before the next abduction. Sometimes it was over a year in between. Nobody picked up on any possibility that they could be related until a few months ago and we just don't have anything to go on as far as good leads go. We can't turn up any pattern at all: when he hits, where he hits, why he's taking them- any aspect of it. To be honest, even if it was the same guy who broke in to your place it still doesn't bring us any closer to knowing who he was- or I should say, is. Even now you can't put a finger on him. No one else can, either. I really wish they'd had something to go on that might have lent support to that. You said you filed a report, right?"

"Yes, I did. I, um...didn't tell them everything...that I was a dancer. It really didn't seem-....I mean, I didn't want Nancy and Steve to know and for the police to think that I-...well, you know what I'm getting at."

"I do understand where you're coming from, but...don't you think it would have helped the police in their investigation?

Maybe they didn't find anyone because they were looking in the wrong direction."

"It seemed like I was the one he wanted. Nothing else crossed my mind but getting another apartment and being extremely careful from then on. I just wanted to get beyond that mess and counted myself as lucky. If I had told them about what I did, I was sure they'd be skeptical at best about what happened. I also was afraid they might think I was playing some kinky game with a boyfriend because they didn't find any sign of forced entry, or something along those lines. I couldn't have handled them- and more so my friends- thinking that of me, especially after what *did* happen with the boyfriend I had until a few months before that incident. I probably should have told them that I was a dancer in spite of my reservations, but I just couldn't- not even later. I wanted the whole thing behind me."

"Do you think it could have been your ex-boyfriend?"

"No, it's impossible for him to have been the one, even though I got this really odd feeling it *was* him. He and a few of his friends were killed in a car accident that summer. I don't know what it was that made me think of him. I guess the fact that my experience with him was still pretty fresh figured in. There were similarities between what he and that intruder did to me, too. In hindsight, it doesn't look like the suspect in all these disappearances is targeting exotic dancers, anyway. One of the girls mentioned was a dancer, but there also was a bikini contest winner, a figure skater, a graduate student from College Park, a couple cheerleaders…"

*This is so weird…*

"I'll get with the guys in Jersey and see if they can send me a copy of it; I'd like to take a look and compare it to what we have on the others." He paused a minute. "Kim, I really appreciate you telling me. It must be hard for you, reliving something like that. Who knows- maybe there will be something we find in your report that helps us."

"I hope so, and this definitely is not my favorite topic of discussion. That's twice I've been so fortunate, and I'd rather not have a third go of it, if you know what I mean. Oh, there's another reason I wanted to talk with you about this. The most recent girl, the one who they say was taken a few days ago- Jennifer Jacobson? She's one of my former students. Is there anything you can tell me about her situation?"

"The bottom line is, as with all the others, we don't *have* much of anything. I'm sorry. Jenny babysat for Donna and me years ago- she was great with our kids. I'm praying we get something, too. We're doing the best we can."

"I don't doubt that at all; if anyone will put an end to all this, it'll be you. I just hope she's..."

"I hear you. I hope all of them are all right." He decided to change the subject in hopes of raising her spirits a little. "So how is it down there? Are you soaking up some rays? The weather sure seems agreeable- guess you picked a good time to go."

"I got a pretty good bit of sun today, and yes- the weather is great! I suppose I did need to get away, but...I miss John."

"He misses you, too." After a brief pause, he decided to ask despite his reservation. "Look, I know it's not my place to bring this up, but...are you going to tell him about your dancing?"

"I know I have to, and yes- I will tell him. I just..."

"It'll be all right, Kim. I think he'll be all right with it now, especially with all you two have been through."

"Is he OK? He hasn't had any more of those pains in his chest, has he?"

"Damn, that's scary- you must be psychic or something. He had one today, but it seemed to go as quickly as it came. He told me the Doc said that would happen. Overall, he's getting better. He had a checkup scheduled for today, anyway. He should be back soon with the results. I just got him into weightlifting; before you say anything, I will go easy on him."

Kim laughed. "You'd better, or you'll have me to deal with!"

"Yes, Ma'am! You also might be interested to know that he'll be working with me, to an extent, on solving these abductions while he recuperates. He wanted something worthwhile to do and suggested that to me, which I thought was a great idea."

"So do I- that's wonderful! I'm glad you two will be working together. Not being able to do much of anything was driving him crazy-" She turned at the knock on her door. "Tom, I need to go now. A friend of mine is here and we're going to do a little shopping. I'll talk with you when I get back home." She decided to put the other thought process she'd started as she talked with Tom on hold for the time being. *First and foremost, I have to clear the air with John, but if there is anything to this little thread I've picked up on...* "When you see John, could you let him know

50

I'll call him a little later? In fact, if he's up for it, I'd like for him to come down here."

"Sounds like a winner, Kim. I'm sure he'll jump at that. I'll tell him to expect your call later, too."

"Oh- um, would you...would you mind not telling John about what we discussed earlier? He might worry more about me and I don't want that. I'd rather tell him myself, so please keep this between us for now, OK?"

"All right, I will. Have some fun down there, huh?"

"Thank you, Tom. I will. Bye-bye."

She hung up and went to the door to make certain it was Kelly. When Kim saw her with a few of her friends, she opened up. "Hi! I'll be ready in a sec. Come on in..."


He kept watching the monitor...

...and waiting.

The time on the screen said 3:06:03.

Sweat beads began to form on his brows and upper lip.

Jennifer was gagged and tied to a chair across the room from where he sat...

...and waited for her...

3:06:59...

3:07:00...

3:07:01...


"Hey, bro. I talked with Kim a while ago."

"How is she?"

"She sounded all right- said she'll call you a little later. She wanted to know if you might be up for joining her in O.C."

"Oh, yeah?" It didn't take him long to decide. "I think that's a great idea; I could use a little respite myself. I'm gonna head home and get a few things together, then I'll be on my way. We'll be back in a few days..." Tom saw a mysterious twinkle in his eye "...or maybe we won't." He turned and headed for the door.

"What's going on in that mind of yours?"

He turned back and winked. "Ne'er ye mind, brother! Got some good news from the doctor today, so let's just say I have some extra incentive to extend my stay."

Tom grinned back. "No further explanation necessary." Apparently, John got the green light from Doctor Reynolds to have sex again...

"Before I go, are there any new developments in the case?"

*You might be ticked at me later, but I gave her my word. Again.* "Not to my knowledge. I'll keep you posted in case anything comes to light. As for now, get the hell out of here- you have a beautiful lady waiting for you who probably has a hell of a tan by now. I bet she'll be as happy about your news as you are."

"We'll soon find out!"


"...and you say she danced there on and off for about four years? Wow...yeah, I'm gonna run this. You just confirmed someone else's story, and don't worry, Mister Peters- you'll remain anonymous. Talk to you later."

He looked at her photo again.

*Wait a minute...*

"I wonder if she's the one Neil mentioned..."


Suddenly his grip on the arms of the chair became vise-like.

He began to tremble as adrenaline shot through him.

He leaned in as close to the monitor as he could.

He couldn't see her face yet, but it was Kim.

There was no doubt.


"Hi, Jeff."

"Kim! I'm glad you made it! Come on back with me- I have your suit ready." He guided her toward the doorway to the studio and turned to the other girls. "Why don't you ladies have a look around? Andrea here will be happy to assist you."

Kim took in the studio as he ushered her in. "Very nice- this is some setup you have here!"

"Thank you- I saw to most of the modifications myself, including-" he opened a door and gestured inside "-your dressing room."

Her face lit up as she looked in. "Gosh, look at this place! I-" She stopped as a sense of familiarity came over her.

*This room is almost scary; it looks so much like-*

What she saw next made her mouth drop open as she went over to it. "Your company makes these, too?"

The white satin short corset on the mannequin looked just like the one she had tucked away among her other costumes. She traced along it, noting that the quality was the same as those she'd ordered some years ago.

*He has a black one, too- also like mine...*

"I'm glad you approve of your suite and yes, one of our affiliates does make corsets. Perhaps we can talk you into modeling one later. In fact, this one looks like it might even be small enough for your waist...but for now," she followed his gesture "your suit is right over here- has your name all over it."

"Oooo..." She cooed as she picked up the bikini.

She had another thought as she examined it. *All I need are the garters. This room, and these outfits- it's like a flashback to my dancing days...*

"I'll leave you alone so you can change- can't wait to see you in my masterpiece. Let me know when you're ready, OK?"

She nodded, and he shut the door behind him.


"...no, Frank, it's just plain stupidity. There are two major thoroughfares through Baltimore, I-95 and I-895, and you have construction closing southbound lanes on *both* of them? On a Friday afternoon, yet, with all the beach travel? Do you have any idea how bad the back-ups are on both those highways?"

John's limo was near the bottom end of I-97 and about to turn onto US 50 for the long stretch that would end at Ocean City as he made his displeasure known to the State Highway Superintendent.

"Well, I have firsthand knowledge of it myself; I just was stuck in one. I saw three cars overheat and stall because of it, and that made the backup even worse, not to mention the fact that those people will face some pretty big repair bills as a result of this needless closure. Routine maintenance is being done on the Fort McHenry tunnel- routine means not pressing, so there's no reason why that couldn't have been put off for a few days until the work on I-895 was done, right?...I'm glad you agree and I hope you

53

won't leave the same- *person*- in charge next time. I'll talk with you soon."

His phone rang again only seconds after he hung up. "Hello?"

"Mister Governor, this is Ralph Miles with the Tribune. I wondered if I could get a comment from you as to how you feel about your girlfriend having been a stripper."

He leaned forward. "Who in the fuck are you and how did you get-"

Click.

"*Hello?!* Don't you hang up on me, you piece of shit!!" He checked the screen on his phone. As he suspected, it was from an unknown number.

"Son of a *bitch*!!"

*Wait a minute…Ralph Miles- where have I heard that name…*

"The press conference earlier this year when Kim was with me. Now I remember…" It was the same piece of trash who'd made the unwarranted and malicious remark about Kim- the same one he'd almost punched out for that reason. John ended up calling the editor of the paper he worked for only to find out Miles already had been fired. The last he'd heard was that Miles was working for a tabloid, which was where he belonged- with the rest of the bottom-feeders.

Still…"Tabloid or not, I'm gonna pound him bloody…"


"Oh, my God…Kim, you are *amazing* in that bikini!"

A few of the patrons got a peek at her as well, and the looks on their faces gave plenty of evidence that they agreed with Kelly's appraisal- although some of those looks weren't very friendly.

Jeff slowly shook his head as he took her in. She *was* amazing; the virgin white of the suit was a perfect compliment to her tan, and the way it showcased that body- it almost was too much, but it certainly would make the beholder want to see more. He stopped at her sexy little white sandals with very high stiletto heels and straps that started at her insteps, then crossed over each other behind her dainty ankles before encircling them. "Wow…and those heels are a perfect addition. Kim, you have *got* to enter this contest! Only thing is, we'll have to make sure everyone there is wearing sunglasses!" She was all woman and as close to perfection as he'd ever seen- her blend of curvaceousness and fitness, the beauty of her face, her golden hair, her genuine warmth and friendliness, her touch of modesty- there wasn't even a hint of pretentiousness or conceit in her...

...he felt a pang of guilt over what would go down later...

Kim giggled and flushed a little at his very thinly veiled compliment and at Kelly's obvious one. "Thanks, you guys. You were right, Jeff; I love this suit!"

"Well, it definitely seems to love you, too! I also was right when I said no other woman could wear it better. So...can I mark you down as an official contestant?"

The feeling was coming back even stronger as she looked at her reflection in the full-length mirror.

She thought of how the crowd gathered around the stage would react to her and she knew the effect that would have on her.

Plus, she was feeling good about something for the first time in weeks, which hastened her decision. "Oh...why not?"

"Awesome! I'll tell the coordinator- be right back."

Kim felt immediate backlash in the form of concern over how this would be received in light of everything else about her past that soon would come to light and hoped she could mitigate it somehow.

"Excuse me for a sec; I need to make a call myself..."


"Hello?!" His blood was still up over the last call and he knew Miles was a big enough asshole to call back and make him say something in anger that he would regret.

"John? Honey, calm down. What's wrong?"

He sighed audibly. "I'm sorry, Kitten...it was just some idiot I had to deal with a while ago. Now that I'm talking with you, I suddenly can't seem to remember what it was that got me so fired up. How are you?"

"I'm fine. I'd be better if you were here, though. I, um..."

He waited a moment. "What is it?"

"I love when you call me Kitten."

"I'm glad you do. You're blushing, aren't you?"

She giggled. "You always catch me on that!"

He laughed with her. "I almost can see you doing it now. Where are you? Have you finished shopping yet? Tom said you told him you met up with a friend."

"Yes, her name is Kelly. This is the first time we've seen each other in a few years. We had fun today and we just finished shopping, now that you mention it. If you're able to make it down here I'd love to introduce her to you; she's a wonderful girl."

"Well, I'd love to meet her, but I hope she'll understand that I'm not available."

She paused momentarily. "What do you mean?"

"I'm sure she is a terrific girl, but...you see, I already have a girlfriend and I'm very happy with her."

This time her pause was for quite a different reason. "I have a feeling she's just as happy with you and that she loves you very much."

"I love her, too. In fact, I'm on my way to see her."

"Really?! You're coming?! How long until you get here? Can you meet me on the beach in front of the Sheraton at six?"

He looked at his watch. "I'll do my best, but I'm not sure. Will you be with your friend just in case I'm late?"

"Yes, she and a few of her girlfriends will be with me. Try to make it if you can."

"I will, Kitten." He smiled as she cooed. "See you soon."

"OK, I'll be here..."


"...oh- John? Are you-"

*Shit!* She couldn't catch him before he hung up.

She'd meant to try to prepare him somehow for what she was going to reveal to him- that being everything about her past, but she got sidetracked.

*Then again, how could I prepare him for that? I need to just tell him. Maybe I shouldn't be doing this contest- especially since John doesn't know...*

*...but that's part of my past- it's part of who I am! I shouldn't feel-*

"Dammit!" She quickly looked around, hoping no one was within earshot of her outburst. No one knocked, so she figured nobody heard.

She stood and walked back over to the full-length mirror. As she looked at her reflection, she began to imagine how John would react if he saw her right now.

There wasn't any mystery as to how he would; she felt the very familiar warmth spreading through her just at the thought of his gaze as he slowly took every bit of her in the way he did. Even on the occasions when he saw her during her not-so-glamorous moments, which she did her best to keep to an absolute minimum, he would give her that smile and make his way toward her. However, he very much appreciated when she prepared herself, as evidenced when he saw her in the tiny red dress.

*I know you'd approve of this…*

*…I just wish there was something you could do about it other than-…*

To John's credit, he was very good at the alternative, but she missed the real thing.

Badly.

"Oh, John- I wish we could make love again…"

She didn't even realize she'd said that out loud.

Once the desire that she herself could only partially fulfill took root in her yet again, she walked somewhat unsteadily back over to her chair and sat down.

After a furtive glance around the room, she unfastened her top.

Her eyes drifted closed and she released a deep sigh as she slipped into her fantasy.

He was more aggressive this time, much like he was the night of the pool party years ago- she could see it in his eyes and feel it in his demeanor.

Then he came after her.

He took hold of her, forced her onto the bed and easily pinned her.

His expression was almost animalistic as his hand ran freely over her. Before she knew it her top had disappeared and he was giving lots of attention to what he revealed.

Practically salivating, he took hold of the bottom and was about to rip it off her-

"Kim? Are you all right in there?"

"Um…yes, I'm fine. Hold on a sec." She put her top back on and scrambled to hide the evidence of what almost happened, but- much to her dismay- didn't.

"Your public awaits, Miss Sex Bomb! We're almost done with our little fashion show, too. Are you all set?"

"Yes, I'm ready, smart-aleck! Come on in." *My God- what was I thinking?!*

*Then again, thinking had very little to do with it...*

"Wow- look at this place! They sure didn't skimp. You must feel like a celebrity- damn, they even have *corsets* in here?! I've never seen these before, other than in magazines."

"Jeff wants me to model them. I don't-"

"From bikinis to corsets...yes, indeed- quite the sex symbol you are! In the very near future a much bigger audience will agree with that assessment!"

She was able to stifle her initial reaction before Kelly saw it and smiled instead. "Maybe. I guess we'll find out soon enough."

"Unh-uh, no 'maybe' about it! Speaking of celebrities, it's too bad that famous boyfriend of yours isn't here to see this. I bet he'd enjoy getting an eyeful of this hot little bikini babe who happens to be the woman he's crazy about! Maybe you *should* do that lingerie spread; I'm sure the Governor wouldn't mind being with you while you did it! Well, I'll let you finish up. See you out front!"

When Kelly closed the door, Kim looked into the mirror. *I hope that's how he feels...*


*This thing sure is ringing a lot today.* "Hello?"

"Mister Governor, it's Jerry Hill."

Jerry was the news director at channel 11 and one of John's friendly acquaintances in the media. *Probably looking for a scoop- I can only think of one thing he'd ask about...*"Hi, Jerry- how are things?"

"Not bad, Sir, thanks. Look, it's not easy for me to tell you this...I think you should tune in to our broadcast. It's on now."

He turned the TV on and set it to 11. "Why? What's up?"

"You won't like it- it's...about your girlfriend's past."

John leaned back. "I think I know what it is..."

58

# Chapter 3

"So you think it's another woman? I'm sorry."

Kim had returned to the front of the boutique where she waited for Kelly and her friends, who were making their purchases, when the woman approached her. Kim was glad to see she didn't have the same malicious look on her face as the majority of the women there did- especially the salesgirl-, which unfortunately was something Kim was used to.

The rather friendly woman struck up a conversation with her. The more they talked, the more at ease Kim began to feel with her. There was something oddly familiar about her and they even bore some resemblance to each other, which Kelly pointed out when she came over to them before going back over to collect her friends.

She was having problems with her boyfriend, which was what they were currently discussing. Kim felt badly for her- it seemed as though she didn't have anyone to talk with otherwise and she needed to unload. For some people it was easier to talk about troubling matters with strangers than with loved ones, anyway. She felt that probably was the case with this woman who picked up on the fact that Kim was a counselor, which probably was another reason why she seemed comfortable talking so candidly.

*I didn't think that was so obvious, but maybe it is...*

*...I just hope I'm still a counselor this fall...*

The more she thought about what the reaction of most people probably would be, the more she began to face the distinct possibility that the career she'd hoped would last as long as that of her adoptive mother might be over...

"Are you all right, Kim?"

"Um, yes- I just...spaced out a little, I guess."

"Are you having man troubles too?" She already knew Kim was having trouble in one aspect of her relationship after having seen and overheard plenty of evidence to that effect.

*If all goes well, I'll personally help make sure that you won't have to worry about that problem anymore...*

*...and that you won't cause any more such problems for me, you little bitch...*

"No,...well, I'm-...no, I'm not. He's probably having more trouble with me than I am with him. I-...how did you know my name?"

She flinched inwardly, especially as Kim now regarded her with a wary curiosity, but she recovered quickly. "Oh- I heard your friend when you came out in that bikini. You really do look terrific in it, by the way." Fortunately she'd overheard them even though she was in the back...

*I must have missed her; I don't recall seeing her before...*

*...then again, that's probably not the first thing I've missed today,* Kim thought as she smiled. "Thank you. I'm sorry, I didn't get your name."

*That was close...* "Diane."

"Really? That's my Mom's name. Now I like you even more!"

She laughed a little. "Thanks. So you're entering the contest? You sure don't seem very nervous about it. I know I'd be a mess. It must take more guts than I have..."

"It's not that big of a deal, really. You'd be surprised."

"Have you done them before?"

"Have I- um, no, but I have been in...well, similar situations."

*Uh-huh,* very *similar situations- both public and private...* It was becoming harder for her to hide the strong feelings of jealousy and bitterness she harbored toward Kim.

Kim, who was looking away, turned when Kelly touched her arm.

"We're going now. You know, from certain angles you two do look like you could be related! Do you know each other?"

"No. Diane and I have never met, but I could swear I've seen her somewhere before. This is a little weird, isn't it?" Kim turned back to her, about to tell her how nice it was meeting her, but she had another thought.

*Maybe she'd like to hang out with us for a little while-might cheer her up a bit...* "Do you have to be somewhere soon?"

"No, not really."

"Would you like to come with us and see me make a fool of myself in front of a lot of people?"

She laughed. "Somehow I doubt that will happen, but yeah, I'd love to come with you. I appreciate you inviting me."

"Do we have room for one more, Kelly?"

60

"That's all right, I can follow you in my car. There's something I'll need to take care of afterwards, anyway..."


"Are you sure you'll be all right by yourself? It might get busy later..."

Jeff shook his head. After Kim and her friends left, the boutique quickly became deserted. "I doubt that. We've probably had our rush for the day. I'll take care of things here- it won't be a problem. Why don't you hang out with your friends for awhile? I heard you mention a party Sheila was having this evening."

"I wonder if you're trying to get rid of me so you can put the moves on that girl who's wearing your white bikini- *Kim*." Andrea frowned when she said Kim's name.

He sighed. "First of all, Kim already is spoken for. After this contest, I'd be willing to bet we'll never see her again..."

He unintentionally trailed off as he again wrestled with what he was playing a part in.

The man promised he would cut the ties once this went down. The boutique, the studio- everything would be his. No strings. He'd looked forward to this day for several years, ever since shortly after his 'partner' took him under his wing and set him up.

Jeff owed him a lot. When they met, his reputation as a photographer was damaged severely and he faced the probability of having to quit the craft he loved for good. When the man made his offer with the stipulation attached, Jeff doubted he would ever have to make good on it. It seemed far-fetched, to say the least, that he would ever even cross paths with the woman in question, who was a short time away from entering a contest she most likely would win.

Really, the whole concept seemed far-fetched...

...that was, until he met her. *I can see how she'd have such an impact...*

Sole proprietorship. The setup he always wanted, and the prospect of expansion as his repaired reputation was growing.

*As sweet as that is...I don't know.*

*This isn't right...*

"Jeff? *Jeff!* See what I mean?! Look at you! You're all ga-ga over her like every-"

"Hey, knock it off! It's not like that. She's a nice girl, and-
"

"Yeah, I'll *bet* she is! You might as well have thrown people out of your way to get to her when she came in and you fell all over yourself waiting on her like she was some kind of a princess or something! Then, your chin hit the floor as soon as the bimbo came-"

"That's enough! She's not a bimbo! What in the hell is wrong with you?! She didn't do anything to you and you're talking all this shit about her! The whole time she was here you looked at her like you wanted to kill her! Why do you feel so threatened?"

"You know what? I *will* leave! Why don't you just bring Little Miss Perfect back here to the studio after she wins the contest so you both can have a good screw to celebrate?! I'm sure you'll do what you can to see that she wins, just like you probably did for me!" She grabbed her things and stalked toward the door.

"Andrea, come on- don't be like that!"

She flipped him off as she stormed out the door.

"Troubles, Jeff?"

He whirled and saw his boss at the door leading to the back.

This would be the night. It was Friday- those other guards who still were here sure as hell didn't want to be and the warden had just left.

Better yet, he was the lead, and his shift ended at eleven. Plenty of time to plan, and he knew the routine of the man whose life he was to end.

It wouldn't be much longer...

He happened across Jeff late in the summer of 1994 in Ocean City as the then-twenty-four-year-old photographer was drowning his sorrows. They struck up a conversation. It wasn't long before Jeff told him about the situation he faced resulting from a grave error he'd made with one of his models back in Baltimore, who at the time was pressing rape charges against him. A lot of damage had already been done just by virtue of her making the accusation. Since he faced a court battle, it was likely that at best he would be finished as a photographer and at worst he would be in for a lengthy jail sentence.

Jeff was in a virtually impossible situation. He lacked the financial resources to fight in court against the girl, who was represented by the office of a State's Attorney whose star was on the ascendant. However, the office was in the midst of turnover since this particular State's Attorney was deeply into a run he'd participated in for months, the finish line of which was at the Governor's Mansion. Therefore, John Stratton would not be the prosecuting attorney- a lucky break for Jeff.

His replacement nearly jumped at the settlement offer brokered via Mark Peters- so did his client. The girl was more than happy to drop her charges for the very generous amount and the case never made it to trial. Out of gratitude, Jeff didn't balk at all when presented with the offer, which benefited him greatly. Gradually, they were able to salvage his career. He was where he wanted to be.

Now it was time for Jeffrey Newman to make good on his end, which essentially he'd already done…

"Does she look *familiar*?! Christ, Pat, she was a *legend*!" The sports reporter from 11 News who'd attended grad school in Philadelphia from '88 until '90 had seen her dance a number of times. He found it hard to take his eyes off the photo his colleague in the news department handed him. "You always knew what nights she was performing, because we'd be packed into the place like sardines. She was awesome- a multitude of other people felt the same way about her. By the time she moved on, they were talking about her all up and down the coast! She also ended up winning the biggest international bikini contest the last year she danced. What a knockout…

"Why are you asking about her? Is she making a comeback or something? Hell, if that's the case, just tell me where-"

"I guess you haven't been following this." Pat remembered Neil's many accounts of boozing and carousing with his college buddies, and their many visits to one club in particular to see a white-hot little stripper who had that whole circuit buzzing.

*Looks like she's the same girl…*

63

"Following what?"

"Well, by all indications, she's headed for the altar."

"Man, whoever she marries will be the luckiest son of a bitch in the-...hold on- she's the girl who's been with...fuck *me*!"

"Sounds like you'd love that, but yeah, she's the lady who's been with Governor Stratton since just before the shooting. Daniels-"

Neil finished the sentence for him. "-kidnapped her after shooting the Governor. Jesus, how could I have missed that? You don't forget a face and body like hers, not to mention everything else she has going on. She used a stage name, of course, but other than her hairstyle, she still looks the same. I guess we all must have gotten so sidetracked with the near-assassination..."

Pat nodded. "Yeah. Not for much longer, though..."


Kim glanced around nervously as she waited for her cue.

She was in a similar state as she'd been on a particularly cold January night in 1987 just before Billy introduced her to the rowdy crowd at The Silver Palace. It took no small amount of reassurance and persuasiveness on his part to talk her into the tiny costume, let alone for him to convince her to take her first walk down the runway. It had seemed so exciting and surreal up until the time she actually was going to do it.

Billy Drake was the quintessential 'gentle giant'- physically, he looked like he should have been chopping wood with Paul Bunyan, but he was very soft-spoken and kind, especially to his dancers. Given the many unscrupulous characters she came across in that industry, she felt very fortunate to have fallen in with Billy. He never came on to her and never was forceful with her. On the contrary, he always was supportive, sympathetic and a wonderful friend for the entire time she danced, and afterwards as well. He understood her plight, which was the same as that of the majority of the girls who performed at his club or any other. He figured prominently in her decision not to walk away that night:

"I'll come back and knock on your door when it's time. If you still want to leave, I'll walk you to your car, make sure you're safely on your way, and that will be that. I won't hold anything against you. I can tell this is a tough choice for you, but I have to say, I think you have what it takes. If you give this a shot- and keep it in the right perspective- I'm willing to bet anything that you'll come to have a following that'll rival the great ones. They'll love you, Kim. You're a lot more than just another beautiful young girl. Something tells me you'll love being up there when you settle down; I saw how you were when you danced on Halloween night. You're a natural. You had that spark and I bet it'll come right back. If I didn't feel that way, I never would've asked about you. You were better than nearly all of the girls I've seen who are veterans!

"I hope you'll at least dance this one night- and you don't have to go topless. You don't have to do anything you're not comfortable with- now or ever- and you've seen the bouncers we have. You're as safe here with us as you can be.

"I'll leave you alone now."

Ten minutes later she went out to where he was. He turned when she tapped him on the shoulder. She smiled at him, and he smiled in reply and gave her a wink before he announced her to the already clamoring patrons.

So it began...

*...and here I am again thirteen years later...*

This also was familiar territory for her- quite familiar, as it was. She'd decided to end that phase of her life back in '90- when she took the Miss Celestial crown in November of that year, that was it.

It felt virtually the same doing these contests as it did when she danced, only her stage was the beach during daylight. Also, any money she won would be handed to her all at once as opposed to being stuffed into her garters one, five, or more dollars at a time, she didn't have to dance and she'd only be on stage for a couple minutes at most.

However, this time she'd be vying with younger girls...

"...and now, for our final contestant. Gentlemen, feast your eyes on Miss Kimberly Fairchild!"


"Uh...no, no trouble. Just a misunderstanding, I guess. She'll cool off."

"She's something else, isn't she?"

"Once you get past the bit of insecurity, she really is a-"

"I'm not talking about Andrea."

Jeff stopped and looked at him. Suddenly, he felt very insecure himself and had a feeling he was on thin ice. The man smiled as Jeff continued his attempt to put together a response that wouldn't make his benefactor angry.

"You don't have to answer that. It was more a rhetorical question than anything. You're a heterosexual male and she's probably the most beautiful woman you've ever laid eyes on. Maybe you can see, in a way, why I've wanted her for all these years. We were together once, a long time ago. Everything stopped when she was with me. All the guys wanted to be me. I felt…ah, you know what I'm talking about. It's a feeling I'm about to experience again, thanks to you. You found her for me, Jeff- you did it."

Jeff still didn't respond. He backed away a little as the man came toward him.

His eyes narrowed and he stopped. "What's bothering you? It…looks like you're afraid of me. Are you afraid, Jeff?"

"I- uh, no, I'm not…"

"It sure seems like you are- you're turning pale," he said as he moved very deliberately the rest of the way over to Jeff, who seemed rooted to the spot. "I can't imagine why you would be afraid of me- you've just done me the biggest favor possible. I couldn't be happier with you…unless you're having second thoughts about all this. That's not the case, is it?"

"No…no, Sir."

"I didn't think it was." He smiled again and clapped Jeff on the shoulder. "You've fulfilled your obligation to me. Our contract is complete. You should be happy; you've worked long and hard for this. Come on, walk me out to the van." He guided Jeff through the doorway into the back. "Thanks for your help with Jennifer, too. She's quite a looker herself, isn't she? She's the hottest young thing I've seen- next to Kim, of course."

He smiled as they made their way deeper into the private section with the studios, away from any windows…

"She sure is." *I have to find out.* "Um…speaking of Kim…"

"Yes?"

"You're…you're not going to…to…"

"What, kill her? Is that what you're asking me? You want to know if I'm going to kill Kim?!"

"Well, I…I just…she's such a nice girl, and…"

"What in the *fuck* kind of question is that?! Of *course* I'm not going to kill her! Do you think I've been searching for her for the past decade just to kill her when I found her?! I've had you recreate the first costume she wore on stage in the form of that white bikini, I've had you fashion the dressing room after the one she had at The Silver Palace, I've had you order custom-made corsets tailored to her measurements along with other lingerie she loves to wear, which you'd *better* have put in the van..."

"Y-yes, Sir- it's...it's all in the van." Throughout the time Jeff had known him, the man had never had anything less than absolute control of himself. Jeff had sensed a crack in the icy exterior a few hours earlier when he got the picture of Kim over the internet.

And now...

"Good man." After a purposeful pause, he went on. "It should be obvious to you what I plan to do with Kimberly Francis. She and Jennifer will keep me company as we ride to their new home, where her final phase will begin. She'll never have any worries again. Naturally, I'll have to make sure her wardrobe for the trip includes some form of restraint, just like Jennifer's."

Again, Jeff saw the coolness descend upon him- the disposition he was used to when it came to his dealings with this man...

...although his instincts told him to turn and run, his legs wouldn't obey.

"So don't worry, Jeff- I can assure you that I won't kill her..." Suddenly he grabbed the photographer and threw him down to the floor.

*I was thinking about letting you go, but this way is better...*

Even though Jeff saw it coming, he was unable to lift a finger to stop him, and he remained petrified as he saw the man draw the pistol with a long tube on the end of it.

A silencer.

They were in the back where there were no windows.

The door to the front was closed.

All he could do was look up from where he lay on the floor as the man pointed the gun at his head.

"...but you, on the other hand..."

\* \* \*

67

Jennifer seemed even more afraid of him than before. She cowered as he climbed into the van with her.

"You've been a good girl so far. I suggest you keep it up. It's time for one more picture; keep your eyes on the camera." She did as he said and he snapped the photo of the tightly bound cheerleader as she lay still before him. As it developed, he checked to make sure she would stay tied up for at least another hour. Once satisfied, he sat with her on the small bed and stroked her. "You're about to get some company; maybe that'll cheer you up a little. She's someone you know, too. Remember Miss Francis, your guidance counselor?"

Her eyes widened even more. "Mmmph!!"

"I can see you do remember. I thought you would. I'm sure you also recall how nice a lady she is. You wouldn't want to be responsible for me having to hurt her, would you?"

She looked at him for a moment, totally stricken, then shook her head and looked away.

He touched her face and made her look at him again. "Because if I come back and see any would-be rescuers or police, I will hurt her. Do you understand?" She nodded in defeat. "So that means you'll lie here nice and quietly while I get her?" When she nodded again, he knew she wouldn't cause any trouble.

"You are a good girl, Jennifer. Good girls are rewarded. I see how frightened you are, but you'll come to find I'm not such a terrible guy as long as you do what I tell you. You've had a hard time finding yourself, haven't you? All those decisions to make…plus, as you told me, your boyfriend hasn't been much of one and your parents have probably stifled you. You must feel so lost and confused. With me, you won't have to worry about anything ever again. Most anything you want, I'll give you," he said as he caressed, then patted her thigh.

"So long as you keep your word, Miss Francis will be fine. I'll treat her just as well, provided she's good, like you've been. I'm sure she'll be relieved to see you, so what do you say we go get her?"


"Are you on your way? She's already on; we don't have much time." Lisa watched as Kim dazzled the audience with her little routine. She playfully teased them, practically making them beg her to take off her cover-up. When she finally did so, from the crowd's reaction there was no doubt Kim would carry the day.

*You really are something else...what a body! You have all these guys eating out of your hand, just like before. I hope you enjoy the last time you'll flaunt yourself like that...*

*...at least, in public...*

"I know; I'm here now. Where are you?"

"Off to the right of the stage a little. She saw where I am. I think we're in luck; her friends moved into the thick of the crowd with a bunch of guys. We might have a chance to take her here after all."

"That might be too risky. We have to wait and see if we get an opportunity. For now, just try to get her into the car with you. I have something I'm going to give you that'll convince her to go with you if you think she needs to be persuaded- that's also if we get the opportunity here. I think...yeah, I see you. I'll be there in a minute."


"You sure you'll be OK, Sir?"

John stared at her as he waited for this spectacle to end and he didn't hear the question.

Herb touched his shoulder. "Sir?"

He turned and looked blankly at his longtime bodyguard for a moment, then the question registered. "Yeah, I'll be all right. Just give me a few minutes."

"OK, we'll be right behind you."

John nodded and turned back to the stage where she stood as the announcer ended the speculation- not that there was much of it. Everyone seemed to know who would win.

*All this time, and all we've been through together...*

*...why couldn't you tell me, Kim?*

*Why?*


"...and your winner- Miss Kimberly Fairchild!"

She walked up to the M.C. amid the boisterous approval of the crowd, smiling and waving to them as she thanked them.

It was another moment for her- the long lost feeling she enjoyed so much. It was one of euphoria, mixed with some good ol' nostalgia.

For that brief moment she was eighteen again and gushing as hundreds of young, energized people- energized in part because of her- were heaping adulation on her.

Then she saw, and instantly recognized, a man who was off to one side of the stage and a little removed from the crowd.

He was not cheering, or clapping, or even smiling.

He just stared at her, bereft of any hint of joy.

Her moment was gone.

He knew…

"John…" Her lips began to tremble. She wanted to go to him, but her legs wouldn't work. All she could do was look back at him as her own joy ebbed away.

On the heels of that came a barb from a heckler. Worse, the voice sounded familiar. When she saw him, she recognized him as the overbearing clod from earlier in the afternoon- the one who swore he'd seen her before. "Take it off- take it *all* off! I *knew* you was her! Take it off! Take it off!" Apparently, he'd convinced several around him of that as well and they joined in.

"*Take it off! Take it off!!*"

The chant grew steadily louder as more voices gave strength to it.

"TAKE IT OFF!! TAKE IT OFF!!!" The whole crowd wasn't yelling, but to Kim it sounded like every voice was ringing in as opposed to the very vocal but small minority it was in actuality.

She covered her ears, but that didn't help.

She couldn't stop it or drown it out- not that she felt she had any right to…


He saw how wounded she was before the chant even started, but she looked away from him and he couldn't catch her eye again…

…the situation was worsening quickly.

In the grip of an extreme sense of urgency, he began to beat a path through the crowd. Herb and the other bodyguard with him fell in with him- one in front, one in back.

Even with the bodyguards, it was very slow going through the unruly mob, but what he and his men saw next made them try harder…

Kelly and her friends also tried to get to Kim, but the crowd stonewalled them completely.

"KIM!!!" Her scream was lost among the chorus that wouldn't stop.

She was a bit relieved when she saw Diane with her, but frowned curiously when she saw the man.

*Who is he? I thought she was alone...*

*...unless it's her boyfriend...*

"It's all right; I'm her friend. I'll take her out of here." She made her way over, ushered by the on-stage bouncers, and touched her arm. "Kim?"

She was a wreck, and seemed to be rooted to the spot.

"Kim? It's me, Diane."

She finally turned around. "Diane?"

"We're going to get you away from here," she said, smiling sympathetically. When Kim nodded, Lisa/Diane turned to the M.C. "OK?"

"OK. There's a quick way out you can take- it goes underneath the stage. It'll take you right to the lot. Oh- here's her bag, too. I'm really sorry about-"

"Don't worry about it; there's no way you could have predicted this. Thanks for your help." She turned to her companion. "Honey? Would you carry her?"

Josh answered, "Sure, I will. Come on, Kim; we'll take care of you." He lifted her up and they followed the M.C.

Kim wasn't even remotely aware of what was happening. She was just grateful that this would soon be over and she wept into the man's shoulder as he carried her away.

He couldn't believe it. It felt like he was on autopilot as he made his way along the golden path, holding in his arms the reason for everything he'd done. Kim's beauty had not diminished in the least. For him, it never would...

*...and to feel her again...*

The one who'd gotten away was nearly his once more. This time she virtually was handed to him, on display in the same

71

costume he'd first seen her in, which was in a venue very similar to the bikini contest she'd just won.

Better yet, she was crying like a little girl.

She was just as he wanted her to be- vulnerable and isolated. His deduction was right on the mark. Then again, for a couple reasons- one of which he saw while she was in her dressing room- she always was vulnerable to an extent, but at this point she had no defense whatsoever. He'd seen the anguish all over her face when she whispered that name- *his* name.

John was here, but apparently, they were on rocky ground. Josh also had heard the story on the radio about Kim, which must have been the cause.

*So you couldn't handle the fact that your angel isn't exactly snow white, eh, John? Your loss will be my gain...*

When it fully sank in how close he was, he stepped up the pace toward the lot.

The crowd had finally settled down and was dispersing. He'd reached the stage, only to find she wasn't there.

"Dammit..."

"Hey, you're not supposed to-...Governor Stratton?!"

John turned to him. "Yeah, I'm looking for Kim- the girl who just won the contest. Where did she go?"

"She left a few minutes ago. A couple of her friends came up and got her. I'm glad they did; she was in bad shape."

Before the man could go on, a young girl accompanied by another of his security team came in between them.

"Mister Governor, I'm Kim's friend, Kelly. This woman we talked to at the boutique and a guy with her left with Kim. I tried to get up here, but I-"

"A woman you talked to? You don't know her? Does Kim?"

"Well,...no, she doesn't. We just met her today...oh, God- I hope..."

John looked at the M.C. again. "How did they get out of here?"

"Sir, what...what's going-"

"I don't have time for questions- *how did they get out of here?!*"

"Uh- this way."

"Kelly, I need you to come with us, too."

She nodded and followed him as the M.C. quickly led the contingent through the back exit.

"I think I'm OK now; you don't have to carry me anymore. Thank you so much- both of you. Would you mind dropping me off where I'm staying, Diane?"

Kim gradually had calmed herself. She knew it was time to face John and whatever consequences would come relating to their relationship. She also had to confront- and be confronted by- the school board. She knew she could lose a lot, maybe everything, but she had to get it all in the open.

As scary a prospect as that was, she knew it had to be done- all of it.

She noticed she still was in the man's arms and neither of them had acknowledged what she said. Frowning, she looked up at him. "Um, I'm all right now. Could you please...put me..."

*What's going on here?*

*And who is he?* He was wearing sunglasses and a hat, but there was something terribly familiar about him...

"Just relax, Kim." Lisa saw the change come over her along with her mounting suspicion. She had to head her off, and quickly.

Kim faced her and that sense of familiarity she felt as they talked while at the boutique returned, only this time it was far more sinister.

*I* have *seen her before, but where?!*

Suddenly she remembered, and the shock that followed effectively paralyzed her: it was the news bulletin.

*Oh, my God...her name's not Diane, it's-*
"Lisa?"

*"...the young woman believed to be the first victim was Lisa Meyers, a cocktail waitress at that club, who took her break accompanied by a still-unidentified man the night of August 12th, 1990. She never returned and has not been seen since. Miss Meyers was twenty years old at the time of her disappearance..."*

Kim was looking into the eyes of the first woman to be abducted...

...and horror descended upon her with the feeling that Lisa was looking into the eyes of the woman who was on the verge of becoming the latest. She opened her mouth to cry out for help, but the pictures Lisa showed her as they continued walking stopped her cold.

Then, he spoke.

"I'm sure you remember Jennifer; this last one shows where she is right now, which is where we're going, too. If you make the slightest motion to anyone, we're close enough to the van that we can throw the door open and kill her. I'll let you watch if that's what you want. As you can see, she's a stationary target. Just be nice and quiet while we reacquaint the two of you."

Kim nearly passed out when she realized who he was, which happened as soon as he talked. Despite what lay ahead, she still couldn't budge.

All the instances recently when she'd thought about him, including the recurring nightmare of him shooting John, obviously happened for a reason. In retrospect, it seemed that her intuition had been warning her.

*But, how could I have known?! This just isn't possible...*

The fact that he was alive brought up even more questions. However, those questions were put on hold when, once inside the van, she saw a familiar face. "Jenny..."

Josh could tell that she recognized his voice as soon as he got the first sentence out. Lisa had slid the van's door open and they'd quickly climbed inside. He glanced down to see that Kim's face was frozen in shock; she even felt a little heavier.

"Get us out of here," he said to Lisa. "Don't be too quick, but don't be too slow, either."

As she shut the door and climbed into the front seat to carry out his instructions, he placed Kim onto the other bed in the back and then gently but firmly pushed her down so she lay on her stomach.

He pulled her hands together behind her back and grabbed one of the straps...

\* \* \*

74

Other than a little shifting around as she tried to get comfortable, Jenny remained still as she waited for them to return.

At this point, she knew it was useless to try to free herself- as before, he'd tied her effectively enough to make that virtually impossible, especially since she wouldn't have had much time, anyway. Plus, there was no way she would risk trying to get away at the expense of any harm to Miss Francis, one of few bright spots during her high school years.

All she could do was wait, and dread what she was sure would happen.

*Maybe he won't get her...please let her be safe, and let her get away from-*

Her last bit of hope disappeared when the door opened and he carried her bikini-clad counselor inside.

*Now he has us both...*


"Did anyone see where they went?"

John's desperation was growing with every second that passed since he saw Kim being carried off by a stranger.

One phrase kept reverberating in his mind: *not again.*

"No, Sir. We've contacted the local police, and we're trying to find someone who may have seen them, but so far..."

"I know. There has to be somebody here who did. We have to keep looking."

*Not again...*


When she saw the state Jenny was in, Kim instinctively tried to calm her.

"Jenny, we'll be all right. Try to- *ah!*" She felt the bite of the strap as he cinched it tightly around her wrists. They really didn't have any chance of escape as it was and now, with her hands fastened behind her, that point was hammered home.

The chilling reality also began to close its grip on her as he just as quickly strapped her elbows together, then moved down to her ankles, crossing them first.

It was happening again...

He finished tying her ankles and turned her onto her back.

Right then she saw it.

His unfathomable hunger was manifest, just like before...

75

* * *

*She's mine...*

For a moment he was unable to move and almost unable to function. His psyche was overloaded as his eyes slowly moved from her unforgettable face to her swelling breasts, which were forced up and out even more so than normal from the way her arms were tied.

Gradually his focus moved lower- down to her tiny waist, and to her shapely hips, and then to those legs...it almost was scary how little she'd changed- her face, her body...

...and the swimsuit was a perfect re-creation. He felt like it was January of 1987 again. Only now, the beautiful young dancer, who embodied everything he wanted, was his. The pursuit was over.

She truly was stunning, in every way.

He needed to feel her...

...he needed her...

...now.


There was nothing she could do.

She squirmed and twisted, trying to escape his hands, but there was no way. He was all over her.

Then he kissed her.


His self-control was faltering; it was becoming increasingly difficult for him to hold back. Doing so now was almost physically painful, and she hadn't even been his captive for five minutes.

Her fragrance assailed him, her unequaled beauty continued to astound him, and the way she struggled...

...before he knew it he was on top of her, kissing her...

...to his amazement, gradually she began to return the kiss!


When she realized what she was doing, she wrenched herself away and stared at him. He was just as shocked as she was.

*What in the hell is* wrong *with me?! As much as I despise him, how could I possibly have reacted that way to him?!*

A feeling of nausea took hold of her, but that was dispelled quickly when her predicament hit her again like a bucket of ice water.

As the shock and revulsion dissipated, instinct took over. "*HELP!!!* Someone please hmmp...*mmmmmph!!!*"

Unfortunately he was equally quick to push the gag into her mouth and in seconds it was buckled in.

Now, her helplessness was complete. She fearfully looked up at Josh as he backed away. "Mmmph..."

"You're still the perfect damsel in distress," he said as his hand roamed over her again. He smiled briefly as she writhed in response, but then he grew serious as he wanted to make everything perfectly clear to her. "I've seen you in that role on a few occasions- the time I had you at my place just after Memorial Day eleven years ago and again about six months after that.

"Let's take a little trip down Memory Lane- back to November 22$^{nd}$, 1989. Remember where you were that night?" He enjoyed her reaction. "I can see you do.

"The month before that I pulled off the heist that made me rich and your now ex-boyfriend famous. With your help, which I guess he didn't know about, he put the rest of them away. Little did you both know that I, the ringleader, had gotten away with all that money. Just like everyone else, you thought I was dead, too, but for the second time in our history you damned near ruined everything for me. You went to the police and helped them set up that sting. It's a good thing Dean threw that little party without my knowledge, or else I probably would have been nailed along with 'em. As you can see, the tables have turned- you've fallen victim to *my* sting.

"I was the one who got into your apartment that night before Thanksgiving in '89. That was easy, by the way; I copied your key one night while you were my guest in June of that year. I'm surprised you didn't have the lock changed- very careless of you. Then again, you *did* think I was dead, didn't you? So, I tied you up and had to wait until there were less people roaming around before I could make off with you; even at that late hour there were too many and I didn't want to take the chance of waiting there with you. As popular as you were, I couldn't risk someone coming in for a visit. I was on my way back for you, but

I saw the police cars out front. You got lucky then. However, as you can see, your luck has run out."

Kim felt nauseous again as he made clear all that was to have happened during that horrible night and clearly recalled her feeling that it *was* Josh who had broken in and bound her. Now that he made the fact known to her, sheer terror held her in its paralyzing grip as what certainly lay ahead of her became abundantly clear. She couldn't stop her mental images of what she knew he would do to her...

"You feel it, don't you? This is your destiny- it always was. You've known since the first time we were together, the treehouse..."

...but she was jolted back to the present when his hand parted her thighs and slowly moved upward. She tried to fight him...

"I can't tell you how badly I've wanted you ever since you left. I want you even more now, which I have no doubt you clearly understand. You've seen what I'm willing to do to have you and I mean to keep you."

...but when he reached the nexus of her legs, she gave up. A whimper escaped her as he cupped her there.

"You're mine, Kim. You won't escape me this time."

*And now, let the games begin...*


Three seconds.

It was going as planned; everything was in place.

His target was right where he was supposed to be.

He even was facing away- he'd never see it coming.

In three seconds his family would be set for life. Chances were, no one would ever know who killed Dean Rollins or why he was killed. Chances were just as good that after a few months, nobody would care, either. He'd just be another felon who got what he deserved in the end...

...however, if that was to happen, it wouldn't be by the hand of Sam Raymond. It was cowardly, sneaky. The guard went to put his knife away...

...but he had another thought and kept it out. An alternative that would work for both of them came to mind.

*Better to go out with a bang than a whimper...*

"Good evening, Dean."

Rollins whirled at the sound of the guard's voice.

*Jesus- I never even heard the fuckin' guy...*

"What are you doin' here, Sam? I thought your late night was-" He froze when he saw the knife in the man's hand and he backed away.

"Sam, what's goin' on?"

# Chapter 4

There was no sign of her.

The local police had put out an APB almost immediately and a news bulletin with Kim's picture was broadcast.

An hour had passed and the police were scouring the area for her, so far with no result, or even a trace. No phone call-nothing.

A few people in the area thought they'd seen them, but they didn't pay attention to where they went, what sort of vehicle they were in- as of yet, there were no solid leads.

She was gone.

Again.

Holding Kim's cover-up, the only vestige of her recovered from where she was seen last, he stared at the wall as he sat in the front room of the condo where she'd been staying. Getting the other key from Sue had been his last stop before he took off from home.

He'd been on such a high as he began the trek from Baltimore, and not only because Kim and he would be able to rekindle their passion. He just wanted to be with her in a relaxed atmosphere- to reassure her that whatever was bothering her would not come between them and that whenever she was ready to talk, he would listen, just as she had for him.

*Yeah...*

"They'll find her, Mister Governor. They will."

He turned to Kelly and tried to smile, but as with Kim when she looked over and saw him after just having won the contest, the smile just wouldn't come. He turned away. "All I had to do was react any way other than how I did. It really got to me that she couldn't tell me she was an exotic dancer, and she saw that. I'm the last person in the world who has the right to be indignant because someone can't tell me about a troubling matter. I could have kept it in for a few minutes and brought it up when we were together and alone. Did I do that? Of course not. She saw how upset I was, and she was so hurt because she knew why..."

When he talked about Kim being a dancer, Kelly flashed back to the idiot at the corner that wouldn't leave Kim alone. *Even though he still was an asshole, I guess he was telling the truth...*

*...which probably explains why she was so flustered about that episode. Maybe it also explains what she did earlier, just after I went over to her and we started talking...*

She took John's hand into hers. "We talked for awhile on the beach and she...I shouldn't tell you this because she confided in me, but...she told me how worried she was about you running for President, with the shooting and all. She said she was afraid you might push yourself too hard. With what you just told me about her past and that jerk we came across earlier emphasizing it, I think I know why she broke down and cried when I asked her about you."

A horrible thought took hold of her. She almost was afraid to ask, but she had to. "This doesn't change how you feel about her, does it? She loves you so much. It would just-...I'm sorry, I can't-"

"It's OK, Kelly; it's OK." John embraced her as she sobbed.

He also was overcome momentarily, but the more he thought about Kim and all they'd been through thus far, the more his resolve began to take hold along with that feeling she- and she alone- could conjure up inside him.

That feeling was becoming an even more potent force than before. Soon he was back in control.

"Shhh...easy, now. You know what? I believe what you said earlier- we will find her. She'll be all right and we *will* find her. Right now, I need your help to do that. You were with her at the boutique when she met up with this other woman, so you might be able to give us clues that could help us track them down. You're our first lead; any little thing you can remember could get us started. Just calm down...that's better. Try to focus on what happened earlier today and take us through it step by step." He nodded at Herb, who pulled out a notebook.

He backed away and looked her in the eyes. "Before we start, I owe you an answer, which is 'no'. None of this changes how I feel about Kim and I'm going to let her know that as soon as I can."


"...to the best of your knowledge, this is what the man you saw with Miss Jacobson looks like?"

"Yes, that's him. I'm sure of it."

Detective Gil Travers of the D.C. Police Missing Persons unit handed the potential witness, a girl who'd been with Jennifer at the cheerleading tryouts, a notepad with the information she'd given as to an estimation of the man's other physical characteristics.

"The same with this description?" She nodded, and indeed seemed very sure. "OK. Thank you very much for coming in, Ma'am. Would you be willing to identify this man in court if he's arrested and charged?"

"If it'll help stop these abductions and save Jennifer, I definitely will."

"All right, we'll see what happens. Thank you again, Ma'am." He saw her out of the office and immediately went to his phone and hit the speed dial button.

As he waited for the man to answer, he stared incredulously at the sketch...


Much to her frustration, Kim realized relief for her would come only when he let her out of her present position.

Before leaving her and Jennifer alone, he'd strapped her thighs together, turned her onto her stomach and finished with her binding as he told Jennifer 'this is one thing that happens to bad girls'.

It seemed ages ago when he put her in the exact same hog-tie he'd subjected her to at her apartment by Princeton, but it probably was no more than half an hour in reality. In her predicament it was hard to soothe Jennifer, but she did the best she could.

All she could do otherwise was try to relax in this form of torment he seemed to enjoy inflicting on her and digest what had happened in such a short time.

The burning question was, what kind of stunt had Josh pulled to make everyone believe he'd died?

On top of that, what had he done for the past eleven years other than kidnapping women and programming at least one of them to assist him in other abductions?

One good sign was that Josh's first victim was still alive-maybe all the others were, too. However, on the downside of that, Lisa contributed quite a bit to Kim's situation.

*She seemed so collected the whole time; it sure didn't look like he forced or threatened her and she easily could have gotten away from him at any point. She even was alone in the boutique...*

*...or, was she?*

*What if he was there the whole time?*

*And how did he know I would be there?*

The picture of what had befallen her seemed frighteningly lucid now, as the answer came rushing in.

Jeff.

He probably worked for Josh, too. He approached her and made his proposition, then let Josh know. She never suspected him, and foreseeing her abduction would have been virtually impossible, aside from the fact that she never should have agreed to take part in the bikini contest in the first place.

*But there were only 4 hours in between when Jeff and I talked on the beach and when I went to the boutique, which means he could be taking us somewhere fairly close...*

*...and he probably had all of this planned in advance...*

*...all this, apparently to get me back. I walked right into it.*

Josh clearly was the driving force behind all of it. One thing she was certain of was what drove him, which was emphasized by what he'd said to her as he groped her.

His words resonated again, and their unmistakable meaning made her tremble. *'I can't tell you how badly I've wanted you ever since you left. I want you even more now, which I have no doubt you clearly understand. You've seen what I'm willing to do to have you, and I mean to keep you.*

*'You're mine, Kim. You won't escape me this time.'*

What really frightened her was that it had been like this before with him. What he was doing to her now made her run away from him a couple weeks after that Memorial Day years ago, only this time she had a feeling she might not have such an option.

It didn't come as much of a surprise to her that fear wasn't the only thing this predicament, which was becoming all too familiar, was stirring up within her. It was disturbingly similar to what happened to a lesser extent with Daniels just months earlier.

But those twelve days, starting on June 1$^{st}$, 1989...

...she squirmed reflexively at the thought, repulsed and frightened- yet in a perverse way, fascinated- by the things he did to her. She'd come to the verge of complete capitulation to him.

*Now he's trying to do it again...*

*...how can I stop him?*
Can *I stop him?*


"Relax. It's not what you think, although it damned near was and you know it." He took a few steps toward Rollins, who regarded him warily and with no small amount of fear, but didn't back away. "We don't have much time- maybe a few minutes, but that's it. First, I'll tell you everything about what I was supposed to do tonight, and after that I'll tell you how you can repay me for not gutting you..."


Night was falling, but they were making progress.

"...no, I'm sure Kim didn't know her. None of us knew who she was. I guess she was just in there shopping."

"Did anything about her strike you as odd- her mannerisms, disposition? Was she browsing around, did she buy anything?" John was walking Kelly through the sequence of that afternoon, totally focused on gleaning what he could from her.

"Um...not that I can think of. It was a little strange that she and Kim looked sort of alike. I didn't see her buy anything. Actually, I don't think she-...no, that's right: she *didn't* have a purse with her!"

"And you didn't see her come in? She wasn't with anyone?"

"No, she was by herself. Now that I think about it, she really didn't seem to be browsing around. It was more like she was just...there. Do you think she was-..."

"Lying in wait? It's possible, but we need to establish a couple more things before we can make that conclusion. She would have had to know Kim was coming, which would lead to the question of *how* she knew, if that was the case. Apparently, she wasn't acting alone. How about the boyfriend? You said you heard her telling Kim about him; you didn't see him there?"

"No, she definitely was by herself. She told Kim she was having trouble with him and-...she asked Kim if she was having troubles, too..."

He drifted for a moment because of what she last said. "So you have a clear image of what she looks like?" She nodded.

"Good- that'll help a lot." He turned to the Ocean City police officer. "How soon can you guys get a sketch artist to us?"

"I'll call HQ right now. It shouldn't be long, Sir."

"OK. In the meantime, I think we need to get to that boutique. Speaking of which, before we go, Kelly, is there anything else you can think of while you were there that stood out in your mind? Anything at all…"

"Hmm…not really, not that I can-…well, there was something that was pretty weird, but probably nothing…"

"What's that?"

"When I went into Miss Fr- I mean, Kim's dressing room, I saw a couple corsets that were on body mannequins in there. I just thought that was strange because I'd never seen one before other than in pictures, and I especially wouldn't expect to see any of them in a swimwear boutique."

"Yeah…you wouldn't, would you?"

"Well, on the other hand, Kim said that guy Jeff told her he dealt with lingerie manufacturers through his company. She said he was interested in having her do some modeling for him; I think he wanted her to model the corsets."

The mere thought of Kim in a corset normally would have sent his imagination- not to mention his libido- into orbit, but John remained focused. After a moment of thought, he shrugged. "Although it probably doesn't have any real bearing here, it's good you remember a detail like that. Sometimes what ends up breaking a case open is something that on the surface seems insignificant. Maybe while we're there, or sometime later, something else will come to you.

"On that note, we need to get going…"


It was done.

One part of it still bothered him a lot in spite of the fact that, everything considered, it was the best course of action. Plus, the man wanted it that way.

The more he thought of how it all went down, the harder it was for him to believe it wasn't a daydream. What especially threw him was how quickly it happened.

Dean drove east on I-70 toward Baltimore. There was only one possibility as to where he might be able to hide out, which potentially was a big risk.

85

However, there was one person he needed to pay a visit to first...


"Oh, that's me." His cell phone rang, and he answered it as they rode toward the boutique. "Yeah?"

"John, I just heard...I'm sorry. Do you know how it happened?"

"Yeah, Tom, we're working on it. I'm with a friend of Kim's who was with her this afternoon. We're heading up to where Kim was fitted for a bikini before the contest she entered."

"She was in a bikini contest? Is that where you saw her last?"

"Yeah."

"How are you holding up?"

"I'm trying to stay busy. I-...she entered that contest and...with what we found out about her and my state of mind..."

"You had a fight."

"I wish we did. I never even made it up there to where she was...this connection isn't so good. I see you're on your cell."

"Yeah. I'm on my way down there, too."

"It seemed like you were buried in paperwork earlier..." A possible reason for his brother's journey came to mind- one he didn't like at all. "Tom, you don't think there's a connection with the other cases, do you?"

"I don't know yet. That's what we're gonna try to find out and it's one thing I need to talk with you about. There's something else, too- a couple things, actually. First of all, Dean Rollins escaped from the penitentiary."

"Shit..."

"Yeah. Apparently he killed a guard, took his uniform and made his way out passing himself off as the guard, which is something I, for one, would love to know how he pulled off so easily, given how effectively that place is run. We're looking for him, but since all his accomplices are dead and we don't know of any friends he had otherwise, we're not sure where he would go to hide out. I have to tell you this, too: Warden Steele said that earlier today Rollins requested a conference...with you."

"With *me*?!"

"Yeah. We don't know what about and I don't like the timing of it. He makes the request the same day he breaks out. I don't know if the one has anything to do with the other, but I'm not about to take any chances, especially given what's already happened to you this year." He didn't tell John that Rollins had mentioned Kim. Given everything else that factored in to her involvement, that was something he would need to tell John when they were face to face.

Totally thrown for a loop, John settled back into the seat as they rode away. "Jesus…how many fucked up things are gonna happen this year? I take it Mister Henry doesn't know what he wanted to talk to me about?"

"No. All he knew was what his guard told him: that Rollins wanted to see you, and he wouldn't say what about. Mister Henry said he most likely would have denied the request."

"Why?"

"Because, as you well know, the guy seemed to have quite a creative streak. I'm sure you remember when he made a similar request before and gave you his song-and-dance, not to mention his allegations that you had something to do with the heist. Mister Henry was going to pick Rollins' brain and get to the bottom of what the meeting was about. This guy does have quite an imagination, but he's no dummy."

"He never struck me as one, either."

"At any rate, Mister Henry turned his hounds loose as soon as they found the guard's body and came up one short in their count of the prisoners. Look, I remember years ago when you confided in me how you wondered if there was someone else involved in that heist, but you didn't have any evidence to that effect. Mister Henry and I are considering the same thing. He wants the three of us and the agent who led the sting to have a sit-down about it."

"I think he's right; we need to meet soon. How long 'til you get here?"

"I'm not even at the Bay Bridge yet- probably two hours or so. In the meantime, State's sending an investigating unit there to link up with the locals. John, you're emotionally involved in this one. I know you want to help, but…"

John saw where he was going. "I'll do my best not to get in their way. I just-…I have to do something, even if it's a little bit. I'll back off once we interview the staff at this boutique.

"Hey- you said there were two things you needed to tell me. What was the other- hold on, something's happening."

87

One of the officers riding along with him piped up. "Mister Governor, we just received a call from an officer at Newman's boutique. You're not gonna like the news..."

He'd taken Jenny inside first. After what seemed to be a second eternity he finally came back for her.

However, he sat across from her for a few additional minutes and watched her before finally moving over to her. He didn't say a word as he only partially released her; he left in place the straps holding her wrists, thighs and ankles.

She was glad to be out of the hog-tie and equally glad he'd untied her elbows. She moved her shoulders around slowly as the blood flowed back into them.

After a moment he scooped her up and carried her inside from the garage.

She lay rigidly in his arms, looking away from him as he made his way into a bedroom and set her down onto a queen-sized bed. The restraints hanging from the posts at the headboard were very conspicuous.

He removed her gag. "You missed it, didn't you?"

Keeping her eyes forward, she moistened her lips and retorted. "Missed what? You keeping me tied up and getting your jollies watching me suffer?"

He chuckled. "Suffer, huh? I saw- and felt- some evidence to the contrary." He smiled as her cheeks darkened and she turned away. "But, that's not what I'm talking about. You missed being the center of attention- more so, the object of desire. You haven't lost the magic, Kim. I've never encountered a woman before you- or since you- who can hold court and stir up a man's lust like you can. What still amazes me is how little you have to try."

She didn't react, at least outwardly, so he took a different route. "I guess you felt a sense of déjà vu when you put your bikini on, didn't you? And when you saw your dressing room? Yes, both were made for you," he further stressed the point when she looked back at him. "I know you remember the corsets, too. In fact, you'll also find a few other things to be familiar when we get you settled into your new life- or should I say, when we pick up where we left off?"

Kim sat very still as he laid it all out for her. It didn't surprise her much that he was proving right the theory she'd put together during the ride; from this point on, she doubted anything would surprise her again.

*I guess I really blew it. I had so many opportunities to tell John and everyone else. It's my own fault...*

"Thinking about John? You still want to be with him. Never were casual about relationships, were you? How many real ones have you been in besides those with him and with me? All those guys you cast your spell over, but you never took advantage of that. You easily could have, which is another aspect of you that really got me. You could have led them all around like a bunch of dogs, but since you were so kind to everyone- even the real dregs-, that made 'em love you all the more. You never had anything to prove to me. I was happy with you as you were."

This was the side of him that not many people saw. However, she saw and felt it many times before and succumbed to it whenever she did. It was so hard for her to tell if he just knew how to push her buttons by saying and doing the right things at the right times, given all he'd learned about her, or if in him she'd found a second man she had such a connection with...

...but his last comment triggered a burst of anger. "Oh, really?! Well, you just had the most wonderful way of showing me how happy you were, which you still use!" She gestured toward her bonds in emphasis of her point, holding out her hands as she did that. "Obviously, trust wasn't something you ever felt for me, or else you wouldn't have kept me chained or tied up for almost twelve days! People treat pets better than you treated me! Forgive me if I didn't- and don't- share your enthusiasm!"

"Nice try, Kim, but you know as well as I do that you were *very* enthusiastic- if I hadn't gagged you when we had sex, I bet you'd have woken up all my neighbors. Even when I got rough with you, you still liked it. I saw right through you." She opened her mouth, but her rebuke never came. Instead she turned away. "You got scared for some reason and decided you had to get away. You wanted to run back to John. And where is he now? You saw how he reacted to you being a dancer, so I know he's never seen the part of you that I found. How do you think he'd react? I bet he'd shrivel up. You're too much woman for him. He's shown his true colors. As for me, nothing you reveal would push me away- and I mean, nothing."

The fact that she was alone with her supposedly dead ex-boyfriend who had just kidnapped her, and that she was tied up, dressed in a skimpy bikini and reminiscing about the relationship the two of them had was as surreal as it was alarming.

However, her fear, which was very real, and pervasive when the full significance of the situation dawned on her, was accompanied by another feeling that was vying for control of her.

As revolted as she was by that...

*I guess I know where this undercurrent I've been feeling ever since I was in that motel room with Daniels came from...*

*...but it still seems so strange that I felt it while that little worm had me. I know why Josh made me feel like this...*

It was nothing less than bizarre that her predicament was resurrecting those long-dormant feelings she had- this in the face of her problems, all of them, with John. It also was ironic how in the dressing room she'd fantasized about John being so aggressive with her- something he'd been only once. On the other hand, Josh generally was very aggressive with her. Obviously, that had not changed at all. The situation was deteriorating by the second.

"It should be apparent to you that John doesn't feel that way. You don't still believe he wants to be with you, do you? You saw the way he looked at you- it was like you had horns on your head. If he really loved you, your past wouldn't matter to him. He doesn't have the staying power you want your man to have, anyway, and I think deep down you know he sees you as a liability now. Knowing John like I do, I'm sure he wants to be President more than he wants to be with you, no matter what he may have told you. He's a chip off the old block- no doubt about it. He just might have what it takes to pull off a victory, too. Hell, he could end up being the greatest leader this country ever had if he goes through with everything...

"Look at it this way. How would you feel if you ended up costing him victory? I'm not saying that to be mean- just realistic. I'm sure you've thought of the same thing. You would hate yourself if that happened. You *know* you would."

He could see the effect his words were having; he'd struck a chord and he would press on. She was confused, upset and isolated; the ground beneath her was turning into quicksand and there was no one else around. No one but him.

"And what about you? What do you have to look forward to? Now that your dancing is common knowledge, you know the school board won't want you to counsel students anymore. Think about all the repercussions; there's no way you can avoid them. What else is there?"

"I don't know. I don't want to talk about this."

He decided to test her. "You don't *have* to deal with any of it; the answer's right in front of you. You remember how great we were together, don't you? I can tell you're thinking about it. I want that again. I haven't been the same since you left. I bet in some ways you've missed me, too. Do you think you could reach the same heights with him as you did with me?"

"John and I *did* reach the same heights! In fact, we went higher together because, unlike you, *he* didn't have to force me!"

It was a heated reply and he knew she meant it, but he could tell she was reeling.

*Plus, she said they 'did' reach the same heights. She spoke of them together like it's past, not present, which is a very good sign...*

She most definitely was on the defensive. Better yet, he had so many ways to keep her there, and to make her retreat even further...

"Were those so-called heights you reached with him real, or were they just part of your little fantasy? Think about it, Kim- all the stories you told me about him. You really believed he was your White Knight. I think you believed that to the point where you just allowed yourself to be sucked into that whole idealistic scenario. So many of you girls buy into that romantic crap and end up missing out on something that *is* real- something that's more suited to you in particular and beyond all that nonsense. I've never come across such a passionate woman as you in my life and I know why: it's because of what you and I have. You know it, too- you always did. You just were afraid to give in to it and feel what true ecstasy is."

He was right on target and he knew it.

*You're still so weak- just like before...*

"One thing puzzles me, though. You say he was never forceful with you? Never? Not even at the pool party? Oh, yeah- I found out about that." For the first time he revealed to her that he knew what happened between her and John at the party, but he still was able to play on the guilt he saw back then.

Now, he pressed his advantage, not wanting her to recover from her surprise of his knowledge of her infidelity, although he still held something back. "I guess that means you didn't tell your friend about how aggressive he was? How he pinned you and held you down, and how much that turned you on?"

"*Stop it*!! Just…leave me alone!"

"Those were your words, and part of the reason why I kept you tied to my bed for those last days we were together. Why did you leave? You say that like it's a bad thing- that I forced you. Then again, *did* I force you? You know how hot it made you when you were under my control. It was just as much you giving in to me as it was me dominating you."

"Please stop…"

She turned away from him, but he took her by the shoulders and pushed her back onto the bed. "Does it feel bad, or wrong, when I do this to you?" He slowly traced along her cheek toward her neck, making sure he lingered where he knew she was so sensitive just below her ear before continuing down her neck. She tried to pull away, whining a little as she resisted. His finger continued down over her shoulder. As he closed in on his target, he clamped his other hand over her mouth as a precaution.

She closed her eyes and struggled in earnest as he touched her so intimately, and she mewed in protest as she felt his finger slide under her bikini top and course ever higher along her breast.

Her hands twisted underneath her and her legs strained as she fought to free herself…

…but Josh and the confining straps weren't all she was fighting against…

…to make matters worse, she was losing on every front…

…and the more she writhed so futilely, the more that intoxicating feeling began to take her over…

As soon as he saw the look- the one he remembered so fondly-, he knew he had a chance, and a good one at that.

*This could change everything…*

He unknowingly stopped his assault and relaxed the hand he was using as an improvised gag on her.

The course of action he really wanted to embark upon suddenly didn't seem like such a hopeless one…

Then, she bit him. She'd caught two of his fingers and clamped down, taking him completely by surprise. He cursed as he practically jumped off her.

However, she couldn't take advantage of the small opportunity she had to scream. Even had he not been so quick to recover and cover her mouth again, she knew Jennifer was

92

somewhere else in the house. Chances were, no one who heard her- if there was anyone close enough- would have been able to react quickly enough to prevent Josh from taking drastic measures against both of them.

At this point, there was nothing she could do. She braced herself for his retaliation…

…but it didn't come.

"If you do anything like that again, you'll remain gagged for the next three days with no breaks, and that hog-tie you were in will be the epitome of comfort compared to what I'll do to you. Do you understand me?"

She lowered her eyes and nodded.

"Don't worry, I'll go easy on you. I can't blame you too much for trying. You've had to digest a lot in a very short time. In fact, we'll play a little game I know you haven't lost your taste for." He pushed the gag back into her mouth and left the room.

In an effort to make herself as comfortable as she could, she turned onto her stomach and lay still as she awaited his return.

Once more, she began to think of John.

*I wish I could turn the clock back and tell you everything…*

*…but, would that have made a difference? I probably still would have hurt your chances and at least damaged your trust in me, if I didn't lose it altogether…*

Right behind that train of thought, which was bad enough, was an even worse notion creeping into her. She tried to ward it off, but she knew she couldn't.

*What if Josh is right?*

What got to her most was how much sense it made. She knew how badly John wanted to be President from the talks they'd had.

*What will people think when they find out about his lying, ex-stripper girlfriend who pulled one over on the school board and on him as well? He'll look like a fool and they'd probably want to run me out of town anyway…*

As badly as she'd felt at the end of the bikini contest, things were getting worse. Her spirits were sinking to depths she hadn't reached since she was thirteen…

\* \* \*

"His name's Jeffrey Newman. The records show he's the proprietor."

"You mean, *was* the proprietor."

With Herb and several local police officers and crime scene personnel, John stood looking down at the body. A single gunshot to the head had put an end to him. "This is scaring me even more. He encounters Kim on the beach, talks her into entering a bikini contest, fits her for a suit...now he's dead, and it sure doesn't look like suicide. No money is missing from the register, there's no sign of a struggle- everything's in place. No one saw or heard anything." He sank into a chair. "When do you think the time of death was?"

Mike Hollis, the lead detective, answered. "Looks to be between four and five this afternoon, at first glance. We'll be more solid on the time pretty soon."

"Have you seen his record? Is there anything on this guy that's out of the ordinary? Any shady dealings, known connections or other black marks? It sure seems like he played a role in Kim's disappearance. Question is, did that figure into his death?"

"He hasn't run afoul of us in a long time, and as far as we know he hasn't stepped on anyone's toes through his business. His record's been clean for six years now- he had an arrest, but no conviction."

"What was the charge?"

"Sexual assault. He made an out-of-court settlement and the charges were dropped."

"Six years...so that happened in '94. Was it here in Ocean City?"

"Actually, it was Baltimore. The girl involved did some modeling for him."

"Oh, yeah? When in '94? Spring? Summer?"

"It happened in early June of that year. You were State's Attorney then, right?"

"Sort of. I officially entered the race for Governor on the tenth. I'd already been campaigning, but just that day I'd become legal to run, and-...wait a second, I remember that case. In fact, I was pretty unhappy that it was settled. From what he told me, it sounded like my stand-in had plenty of evidence to put Newman away. I didn't follow up on it because both sides were happy with the result. Peters was the defense counsel and I'm sure he had no problem pocketing his fee. It must have been a sizeable settlement, too, considering Newman was looking at some hard time. I guess his parents had to dig pretty deeply into their pockets."

One of the local officers got in on the conversation. "I don't know about that, Sir. I knew Jeff, and he came from a pretty modest background. His parents were a long way from well off."

"A modest background, eh? Well, he must have gotten his money somewhere else, then. We're talking about a settlement for a rape charge that probably would have stuck, not to mention the fee for Peters, who never did come cheap, so we're not looking at small change. And then, for him to start his own boutique…when did this place open?"

"'96, at the start of the tourist season."

"That's not even two years after the settlement. What about his reputation? That case made the news, and he got a good bit of negative exposure from it even though it didn't go to trial. We all know how devastating an impact a sexual assault charge- even an unsubstantiated one- can have on the career of a photographer who works with young women, and like I said: that girl who accused him sure as hell wasn't crying 'wolf'.

"So, in two years, a guy from a modest background, who must have had quite a debt to whoever picked up the tab to keep him out of prison, somehow gets the capital to start a swimwear boutique/modeling studio- and a profitable one, apparently…

"I think we need to take a look at his incorporation documents and company records. Under his circumstances, I have a lot of trouble believing Newman would have been able to come up with startup capital on his own. There had to be a friend or acquaintance or someone he formed a partnership with somewhere along the line. I also doubt any financial institution would have backed him. In fact, it wouldn't surprise me a bit if Peters made some kind of a deal with him. With his taste for young, hot girls…" Who could forget Melody Chambers?

*In fact, she's a bikini model, too. I wonder if Peters met her through Newman, maybe as a perk, or…*

"The more I think about it, a conversation with my old buddy Mark just might be a good idea. Maybe his fee was a percentage of Newman's business."

Detective Hollis nodded. "It's a possibility; you might have something there, Sir. Screwing your partner generally is not a good idea. A guy can get himself killed that way. It'll be interesting to see what comes of those records."

"Yeah, that's one avenue that could lead somewhere. Even if it's not *the* answer, it might put us on the right track. It doesn't look to be a crime of passion here; it's too clean. Whoever did this thought it out and didn't want anyone else to see, or at least wanted to buy himself enough time to get away. I wonder if Peters might be connected somehow...

"I can't help but feel pretty damned sure whoever killed Newman has Kim...we need answers, and fast- starting with the identity of that woman Kim was in here with..."

"I'm Lieutenant Stratton." Tom showed his ID.

"Yes, Sir, we've been expecting you. This way." The officer led him to John, who watched intently as a sketch artist worked from the directions of the young woman seated across from him.

John turned when he felt a hand on his shoulder. "Tom. It's good to see you."

Tom smiled. "How's it going? What have you guys found so far?" Knowing how torn up John undoubtedly was over Kim being missing again, he tried to keep focus on the investigation.

Detective Hollis stood by and assisted as John gave a summary of what had happened, what they knew and what they suspected. "So, that's where we are."

"We have the M.C. of the bikini contest at the station; he's with another detective giving a statement and a description. The M.C. was right there with all three of them, so if anyone got a good look at the guy, he did," Mike added.

"Let's keep our fingers crossed and hope he did; that was a chaotic scene. As for the woman Kelly's identifying, she talked with Kim while they were here; she and her boyfriend- or acquaintance- took Kim away. Then we get back to Newman, who earlier today encounters her on the beach, talks her into coming here to be fitted for a bikini and tells her about the contest, then calls the M.C. to include her in the contest after her fitting. Shortly after that he's murdered and Kim is abducted. I don't think any of that is coincidence."

Tom took it all in. "Neither do I. I know what you're about to ask me, John, and it's possible this is related to the other abductions we're investigating. Then again, as far as we know, none of the other cases involved murder.

"While I'm on the subject of the other cases, I found out something about Jenny Jacobson's disappearance, which we're pretty certain *is* related." He glanced around and saw an area where they could talk privately. "Excuse us a sec, Mike."

He guided John toward the cubbyhole, and when he was sure they wouldn't be heard, Tom faced him. "You'd better brace yourself: you're not gonna believe this..."

"Mmmph..."
*Dammit- if only I wasn't gagged...*
...and very thoroughly so. He'd added a wide leather strap that tightly covered her mouth in addition to the ball gag that filled it.

She'd caught a movement at the window; there was just enough space between the curtains for someone to see inside, and sure enough, she saw a young boy looking at her. After glancing around to make sure Josh wasn't there, she tried to divert the attention of the entranced pre-teen from her body.

Not helping matters was the distinct probability that he'd never seen a woman tied up like she was, at least not in person.

What she was- and wasn't- wearing probably figured in as well. The game Josh had referred to was 'dress up'- his version, of course. It hadn't changed at all.

The white corset Kim had seen in the dressing room at Jeff's boutique now squeezed her waist. Josh had taken care to lace it tightly enough to make her only slightly uncomfortable, knowing how pleasurable she found the restrictive garment, which to many women was antiquated and oppressive.

As long as she was his captive, she had no doubt that the corset would be a permanent part of her wardrobe. He also would tighten it progressively until her waist was as small as he could make it without harming her. She clearly recalled his talent in that area. Under normal circumstances, she did love the effect it had on her figure. She also loved the tightness and the feel of its texture, not to mention the feel of her other adornments- that was, most of them.

The rest of her ensemble also was white. Garters from her corset held up the silk stockings that hugged and caressed her legs, and made them shimmer where the light fell across them. They were perched atop fetish pumps with heels as high as she'd ever worn. He strapped them onto her feet and added little padlocks to keep them there. She knew why he had her in those shoes- not only did he love the way they looked on her, but in the unlikely event of her getting free, she wouldn't be able to run very fast or far, if at all. They were another form of restraint.

She also felt the cool, smooth embrace of satin from the opera-length gloves that snugly encased her arms from her fingertips all the way to a few inches below her shoulders. A silken thong completed her clothing.

As much as she would have loved this outfit otherwise, given her predicament the positive effects were lost on her. Instead, she focused on the kid, who was focused on her as well, but not in the way she needed him to be.

Much to her dismay and humiliation, her bare breasts were on display; the corset did not cover them at all. Along with the rest of her showcased assets, they were a major hindrance to her chance for freedom. He'd strapped her wrists together tightly and tied them to an overhead support beam, stretching her out so he could lace her in to the corset without any trouble. He'd left her that way while he went to another part of the house to 'take care of something'.

But the biggest hindrance of all was the gag…

"*Mmmmph*!! Hmmp mm!!" Kim struggled and repeatedly yanked as hard at her bonds as she could to try to pull free of the beam, but the strap and rope held her in place. Her desperation mounted as she tried to convey the very real danger she was in.

"You really are good at this, Honey- looks like you even have our friend here fooled." Josh walked over to the window and opened it. "It's OK, don't sweat it," he quickly reassured the boy, whose face turned almost white as soon as Josh spoke. "I thought I'd closed these curtains. My girlfriend and I are playing-"

That was all Josh got out before the kid bolted. "Dammit," he muttered as he closed the window and the curtains and turned back to Kim, who grew more apprehensive the closer he approached.

"Well, it looks like we'll be leaving a lot sooner, thanks to your attempt to exploit that little opportunity. Just when I thought you were going to be a good girl…I do like it more when you're bad, though. I was going to make you relatively comfortable, but now I get to punish you," he said as he leaned to within inches of her eyes, which widened as her fear became apparent, to emphasize his point. He slowly walked around behind her, took hold of her breasts and squeezed them as he pressed himself against her.

Kim was too afraid to fight him and trembled, trying unsuccessfully to keep her composure as she felt his arousal. There was no mistaking it...

...even so, as before, fear wasn't the only emotion asserting itself...

He roughly groped her for several long minutes until finally pulling away, at which time he produced a leather collar with metal rings fixed into the front and back of it. A short length of chain hung from one of the rings, with a sort of clasp on the end of it- that one ended up at the back of her neck as he fastened the collar onto her. Next, he cut her down from the beam, freed her hands, turned her around and pushed her face-first onto the bed and quickly pinned her underneath him. His delicate handling of her was over- at least, for the moment.

He grabbed her wrists and immediately forced her arms up behind her back. In an instant her hands were together in between her shoulder blades.

"*Mmmph*!!" Kim tried to fight him now, but had no leverage or strength to do so. He took both of her small wrists into one hand and held them fast, and next she felt the bite of the handcuffs as he chained them like they were. It was just after that when she discovered the purpose of the short chain dangling from the ring on the back of her leather collar, which reminded her of something she'd experienced before. He fastened the clasp around the chain linking her handcuffs, holding her arms in that very uncomfortable position.

To make things even worse, he unnecessarily secured her now useless arms against her body with straps that encircled her, one above her breasts and one below. There was no way she could escape the cuffs, anyway- the straps were just overkill.

He turned her onto her back and took great delight in her muffled pleas as she looked up at him. "Aw, come on, that isn't so bad. We both know you can take it- you have before, remember? Plus, we're just getting started. One thing I think we need to do is channel some of that energy out of you so I'll know you won't have much left to try to escape- not that you'd be successful. I want you to be more relaxed, though...hey, I just thought of a great way to relax you," he taunted as he touched her thigh.

Kim looked away. Recollections of the way he toyed with her in the past when he had her in similarly helpless positions made her significantly more uneasy, and seeing the same look on his face as before further worsened her plight.

She dreaded what his next move probably would be...

...but suddenly he changed gears, to an extent.

"I know what you're thinking, but I won't do that just yet. In time, you'll be begging me for it. At the moment, though, I have something else in mind- a substitute, shall we say? I think you'll remember it well. Not that you would admit this, but I know very well how to please you."

She looked back at him as he went over to the dresser and picked up a small box. She frowned at him curiously when he looked back at her and smiled, holding it up so she could see it.

*What's that smirk about? And what does he mean by-*
*Oh, my God...*

Dread sank in immediately when she remembered the box, and worse, what was inside it...

...but along with that dread came something else that was far from welcome at this point...

He looked back at her and smiled as he noticed her focus on what he was doing, but he took more notice of what she was doing. "Look at you squirming around- just what is it that you think is in here, Kim? For all you know, this could just be an empty box..."

Kim didn't need a mirror to know that her face was turning blood red. *Damn you,* she silently cursed him as he kept playing with her in his demeaning way.

"OK, I'll end the drama," he added as he produced the last thing she wanted to see. "Here it is: your magic wand. It sure did conjure up some magic, too, didn't it?"

She wailed and locked her legs together as best she could when he ever so slowly produced the vibrating sex toy he'd used on her before to keep her subdued. She tugged at the cuffs ineffectively as he closed in on her.

"Whoa, look at that face. Such indignation..." He approached slowly, and as he got closer, her anger faded. Taking its place was the mien that showed her feeling of powerlessness, which intermingled with and fed the feeling of arousal she never could hide despite her most ardent efforts.

He sat down next to her. "But we both know that's not all you're feeling, don't we? I already see some telltale signs and I bet if I take a close look...well, what have we here?" He touched the front of her thong with her toy.

She uttered a muffled cry of protest as she tried to retreat from him, blushing furiously at his discovery and deeply angered- but also very excited- by his action. She could tell her thong was more than a little wet and, as she was painfully aware, so could he.

"Just as I thought." He clicked his tongue three times. "A very bad girl you are, Miss Francis- *very* bad. You definitely need to be punished, which I'm going to see to right now..."


"The guy who took Jennifer is a dead ringer for *me*?!"

"One of the other cheerleaders made a positive ID, and yeah- the description she gave matches you. We know it *wasn't* you, of course, but that did raise some eyebrows."

John was incredulous, but also curious. "And that's the only lead so far..."

"In Jenny's case, yes. The girl only saw them walking. She didn't see anything that appeared to be out of the ordinary, so she didn't pay any further attention. She didn't see where they went, the vehicle they might have left in- nothing else. All we got from her was the description of someone who could be your double, who also was the last person Jenny was seen with."

"So we have somebody who looks like me kidnapping beautiful young women who look like-...

"...Kim." He froze for a moment, then looked at Tom, who stared open-mouthed at him. "Christ, Tom, do you think..."

"As crazy as that seems, for what little we've found out over the past ten years you might have touched on something, although I'm not sure what to do with it. All the missing women *do* resemble Kim in a way- and come to think of it, Jenny looks a lot like her-, but...I don't know. At any rate, it couldn't hurt to follow up on it.

"As for now, along the lines of descriptions, let's see how Kelly and the sketch artist are making out..."


*I'm glad I'm still so limber and in good shape...*
*...I only hope this isn't too long a ride.*

As she lay on the cot in the van and waited for the inevitable, she had little doubt he would push her flexibility and endurance to the limit. The position he had her in was worse than any he'd subjected her to in the past.

The plump ball gag and the leather strap still silenced her for the most part, and her arms still were immobilized completely. He'd tied her legs in the usual way, strapping them together just above her knees and using specialized cuffs to bind her ankles, but now those restraints had another purpose besides securing her legs.

They also made sure his other instrument to tame her stayed in place.

He held up the small remote controller box to that instrument as she writhed in the confines of her bonds, her eyes fixed on the box. For the moment, there still was no escape. All she could do was lie there, tethered to the cot by her neck and ankles, and wait for him to hit the switch.

He savored the look of despair- and of anticipation- on her beautiful face. "As soon as I get Jennifer, it'll be time to go to your new and permanent home. While you're enjoying your toy, think about what I'm going to do to you once we get there."

He gestured to the mirror above her. "You can even watch yourself, which I bet will push you along even more. You and this lingerie always did bring out the best in each other. With your little helper thrown into the mix along with the way you're tied...like it did before, feeling how helpless you are will push you *way* over the top. And then, seeing that for yourself and watching as you struggle...I have no doubt your enjoyment of the show will make the result even better. I'm glad you shared with me so much about those hidden desires of yours; you gave me the means to defeat you, which is just what you want."

She whimpered as he put his finger on the switch, but at the same time she couldn't keep her hips still. "I told you- you won't escape me again..."

She flinched as he turned the device on.

"...and no one will rescue you, Kim..."

*Well, at least it's on low...but he's still holding the-*

"Mmmmph!!"

*Bastard! It feels like he turned it all the way up...*

*...oh, my...*

"...no one." He dropped the box next to her, tantalizingly close but out of her reach, and left her.

As soon as he was gone, Kim began a more concentrated struggle against the straps and the cuffs, hoping to find the slightest bit of slack that she could exploit. Simultaneously, she tried her best to break a tether so she could get to the box.

*I think I can get it...just have to get a little closer...*

She twisted every which way she could, trying to get loose. Her fingers fluttered in their very limited range of motion as she tried to get hold of the clasp that fastened her handcuffs to her collar.

She flexed her legs and rubbed them together, also trying to create slack, but considering what the bonds held in, that began to work against her along with her growing feelings of frustration and utter helplessness. Those two emotions conversely were fueling the rapidly escalating fire inside her...

...it wasn't long before it settled in how futile it was for her to struggle.

*It's no use. He's tied me so tightly; I can barely even move...I can't reach that damned box, either...*

The longer the vibrations went on...

...and the longer she watched her own hopeless plight...

Then, it got even worse.

The door slid open and Jenny walked in. Josh made her lie down on the other small bed.

Kim was very distressed to see, through her vibrator and bondage-induced haze, that she and the young girl were dressed almost identically, corsets and all, except Jenny at least was allowed a bra. *She could pass for my sister...*

It distressed her even more how docile Jenny was, which was most apparent when Josh secured her.

*I feel like I'm looking at myself eleven years ago...*

She didn't resist at all and soon her hands were fastened to the rail at the head of her bed. Josh moved down, spread her shapely legs and tied them separately by her ankles to anchor points at the foot of the bed. She opened her mouth to accept the large white ball gag. Once he buckled it in, he smiled at her and patted her hip, then moved to a chair where he could keep an eye on both of them.

Before long they were moving.

As they rode off toward what surely would be another prison, Kim was most alarmed by the way Jenny watched her and how the girl was starting to react to what she saw. Her eyes widened and her breathing quickened when she realized the state her mentor was in.

Gradually, Jenny also began to squirm...

Kim made a last-ditch effort to break free, fighting madly against the unyielding bonds. Her hips gyrated wildly in her doomed effort to expel the insidious invader that she knew would vanquish her.

She battled all the forces working against her for as long as she could, having held them off longer than she thought she'd be able to, but eventually she began to tire. Her cries as she struggled with all she had gave way to a soft mewing as she felt her will and ability to resist slipping away. She was aghast that her audience- especially Josh- also chipped away at her resistance. Incredibly, the knowledge that he was watching his bound and gagged captive as she teetered on the brink pushed her further.

Her frustration from her total lack of freedom of movement, capped off by the tethers that stretched her out, also helped bring about the inevitable. Kim couldn't deny how much she needed it...

...finally, she surrendered.


As the tremors rocked her mentor's gorgeous body, Jennifer watched in awe, utterly fascinated by the intensity of her string of climaxes. Miss Francis had turned her face toward the wall, apparently trying to hide her shame and her ecstasy.

Gradually, she noticed the small box, which was partially obscured. She craned her neck up as much as she could and saw a wire that started from the box, snaked up over her counselor's hip and disappeared between her thighs. She had a good idea of what was at the other end of the wire.

*Will he do the same thing to me?*

As Miss Francis drifted down yet again, weeping a little as she did, Jennifer suddenly realized how aroused she was as well- she couldn't seem to keep herself still.

She turned away, very uncomfortable with her state, and realized the man was watching her!

*Oh my God- he's smiling at me!*

Jenny cried out as he got up, afraid he would come to her and acutely aware of her vulnerability as she tugged at the ropes holding her...

...much to her relief, he went to Miss Francis instead.

However, she was horrified when she realized she also felt disappointment.

*What's happening to me?!*


Josh was entertained very much as he watched his indescribably beautiful and sensuous girlfriend lost in her nirvana, not to mention the fascination of her young protégé, but he also knew Kim badly needed a break from the tight bondage and constant assault from the pulsing toy. As she drifted down from what must have been her fifth, or maybe her sixth, he moved over and sat with her. She'd put up quite a fight, which had made for one hell of a show.

Her eyes were still closed and her breathing was pretty shallow as she squirmed gently in her restraints. She looked up as she sensed him next to her.

"Mmmph..." she moaned weakly, hoping he would untie her. Thankfully, he raised her head, unbuckled the gags and extracted them from her mouth after releasing her from the tether that had been fixed to her collar. As she tried to work her jaw around, he put his arm under her shoulders and raised her into a sitting position. Before she could ask for it, he put the bottle up to her full lips.

A little cry escaped her and she eagerly drank the water she was in dire need of, making small, relieved noises as she gulped it down. "Thank you- may I have more?" He held another bottle up for her; this time she took a little longer to finish, sighing when she polished it off. "Thank you so much. I needed that."

He nodded, waiting.

*He's going to make me ask!*

*Well, I'm really not surprised- not that there's anything I can do about it...*

"Um...could you...oh, Josh, please untie me. I'm so uncomfortable; I can barely feel my arms and shoulders," she begged, looking up at him in supplication.

He looked to be thinking it over, and even though she figured he was purposely doing that to make her beg further, she couldn't help but do it. "Please..." she was on the verge of tears.

"All right, Kim, but if I see you trying to escape or alert someone again..."

"I won't- I promise! *Please* let me out of this!"

*Who could ever deny you anything?* he thought, feeling the slightest twinge of guilt over making a woman of such high caliber- and one he still had very strong feelings for despite her lingering love for his arch-rival- sink to such a state of submission.

On the other hand, it was stimulating beyond words...

First he unbuckled the strap holding her thighs. Next off were the ones pinning her arms against her body, drawing little cries of relief from her, but she whimpered in pain as he unlocked her wrists and drew her arms around in front of her. He left in place the restraints holding her ankles, which were locked on.

As soon as she was able, she went to reach between her legs, but hesitated. "May I...um, may I take..."

The otherwise very confident woman most definitely was wavering. "Go ahead."

She got rid of the still-buzzing monster, sighing deeply after she was free of it. "Thank God. I couldn't have taken much more..."

He noticed she was purposely trying to avoid eye contact with Jennifer.

"With the shape you're in and all that energy you have? We both know you're underestimating yourself; I remember you quite differently."

Kim blushed, but remained silent. She certainly hadn't intended to voice the thought. However, that was quickly forgotten as he retrieved the handcuffs, the sight of which, after just having been released, made her whine. "Oh, no, I thought-"

"Put your hands in front of you."

"In front?" That caught her off guard.

"Unless you'd rather have me cuff them behind-"

"No, please don't!" She quickly did as he told her and he locked her wrists in the manacles once more.

He saw her shifting her shoulders around- no doubt they still were stiff. He sat behind her and immediately noticed her change in disposition. Her breathing quickened, and she began to fidget as she tried to look around at him. She jumped a little as he took hold of her shoulders and seemed near panic.

"Just relax, Kim, it's not what you think. I'm sure you could use a shoulder rub after being tied as long as you were. That's all I'm going to do to you." With that he began to massage her.

In time she did begin to calm down. Fighting him would do her no good, anyway- she could tell he still was very strong by the way he handled her and subdued her, apparently with very little effort. *Even if I wasn't tied up I wouldn't have a chance against him...*

In spite if her ever-present fear, fatigue rapidly began to set in from all she'd been through that day and she found herself unable to stop from leaning back against him as he rubbed her aching muscles.

His heart was already racing from her contact with him, and it kicked into overdrive as she laid her head onto his shoulder. Obviously, she was exhausted and couldn't stop herself, but...

"I'm...I'm going to have to gag you again. Open your mouth."

Kim was totally spent and didn't resist when he put the red ball up to her lips. He pushed it past her teeth and buckled it in.

He resumed the massage, drawing an occasional moan from her as he felt the stiffness leaving her.

After only a few more minutes she was fast asleep. He eased her back down onto the cot, reattached the collar chain to the bed frame and left her to her much needed rest.

Half an hour later they reached their destination. He checked and saw that Kim still was asleep as the garage door closed, and went in to prepare her room as Lisa led a silent and unresisting Jennifer inside.

A couple minutes later he came back out for Kim. He opened the side door of the van, unlocked the chains holding her down, gently gathered the slumbering beauty into his arms and carried her inside.

She stirred, sleepily looking up at him as he laid her onto her bed. After a few seconds her long lashes drifted back together as she dozed off again. She looked so girlish and innocent as she lay there, even though she was dressed- and built- for sin.

*I guess you really are exhausted,* he thought as he fixed her collar chain to the middle of the headboard. He didn't anchor her feet this time, wanting to enable her to sleep as comfortably as possible. With her wrists chained and her padlocked ankle restraints, she certainly wasn't going anywhere.

He was about to place the comforter over her and leave her, but before he did he got rid of the locked straps that prevented

107

her from slipping out of her shoes. He then removed her pumps and placed them on the floor.

She even had the prettiest little feet; he couldn't resist massaging them. After all, they probably needed some attention after being confined in those shoes for so long.

She cooed and wriggled a little as he lightly rubbed them; apparently, he was doing very well. He detected a smile around the gag in addition as he went on.

*Careful- you don't want to get too much into this...*

...however, it seemed like *she* was, albeit subconsciously.

Her hands began to clench and release as they twisted in the cuffs...

... and then she began to moan and squirm, much like she had in the van while she was relentlessly besieged by her toy...

*I seem to have discovered yet another of your many erogenous zones...*

She was heating up again...

*...and what a beautiful display...*

Eventually he became so taken by her and the way she was reacting to his touch that his mind wandered. He was caught off guard when she giggled and pulled away.

He'd inadvertently tickled her and was certain she would awaken...

...but she didn't. Her lashes fluttered briefly, then she turned onto her side, snuggled into the mattress and pillows and dozed off again.

*She's either a deep sleeper or a very good actress...*

Her slow, steady breathing made the former more likely.

He lingered for a bit, wanting badly to massage her legs next, but he knew that would wake her for sure.

*You'll need your rest, Kim.*

Plus, there was plenty of time yet. He'd have more than enough opportunities to rub those legs as often as he wanted...

...and to enjoy every other perk he'd missed for so long.

He then had an unlikely moment. *I must be getting a bit softer*, he thought as he moved to the head of the bed. She really didn't need to be gagged at this point, so he reached over and carefully unlocked and removed the ball, which made a moist little plop as he took it out.

She licked her inviting lips, murmured something, and then was still.

*I'd better get out here...*

Of course, leaving the room was the last thing he wanted to do, but again, there was plenty of time. She was totally demoralized over her situation with John and her perceived betrayal of him, and also by the chance for rescue that she couldn't prevent from slipping away.

She also failed to prevent or hide the re-emergence of her true self- the Kim he knew and wanted to bring back.

*You're right where I want you...*

As she lay restrained and sleeping soundly in her posh, well-furnished cell, which was under his roof and safely away from anyone who could take her away from him, his victory seemed to be complete- a victory that had come about much sooner than he'd planned.

He covered her with the blanket, left her room and closed the door behind him.


It was her.

As soon as the artist finished and Kelly confirmed the sketch, Tom opened his briefcase and pulled out the photos of all the women related to his case who were presumably abducted, all of which were etched in his memory.

One in particular stood out and he handed his photo of her to Kelly, who gasped as soon as she saw it. "Same one?" he asked for confirmation. She nodded in response, and he turned to the artist with the photo. "Do you agree the sketch is this woman with about ten years of age progression?"

"I'd say the probability's 99%. In my opinion, it's the same woman."

Tom looked at it again. "Her name is Lisa Meyers. She's the first girl in this group who disappeared. By all indications, she's just taken part in an abduction herself."


*I see you've been livin' well off my money, ya fuckin' leech.*

He'd double-checked and determined this was the place. He pressed the doorbell and waited.

"Time for you to pay up, Peters..."

# Chapter 5

"Go away...do you hear me?! Go away before I-"

"Before you what, call the cops?" Dean smiled at the door, knowing Peters was looking out through the peephole. "Do ya really think that would be a good idea? If I was so inclined, you'd be dead long before they got here. Even if I *didn't* kill ya, you'd have a hell of a time explainin' why I came to see ya as soon as I busted out. Make no mistake- you'll get what's comin' to ya, prob'ly sooner than later. An' ya know what? It won't surprise me a bit if ya end up askin' me to kill ya.

"As for now, you're gonna tell me why a guard in the pen was supposed to ice me tonight, although I prob'ly know the answer already. Open this fuckin' door."

*I never should have fallen in with these guys...*

Mark had no doubt that his time of reckoning was not long in coming, even if Rollins didn't kill him tonight. The whole situation was beyond his control. Actually, it had been so ever since he accepted Strauss's deal in 1990. Mark had just deluded himself into thinking otherwise.

*I guess this is how it is when you sell your soul and the Devil comes to collect...*

After he called Strauss, for the rest of the afternoon and evening he did nothing but sit in his house trying to think of an avenue of escape. He'd even bought a one-way ticket to the Caymans shortly after that phone call; he had the confirmation number right next to his keys. He had a hundred thousand dollars in cash to tide him over and a few million in an overseas account that the government couldn't touch...

...however, even if he ran he wouldn't be safe. It probably would be easier for Strauss to tie up his loose end if Mark was to leave the country. He had no doubt the man would track him down. It was bad enough that Strauss was out there, but now...

Just outside his door was the man he was sure would end his life- the one who, along with two of the others, had taken the rap and festered in prison for a decade. The one who had more motivation than anyone to kill him.

He jumped as his grandfather clock tolled once; it read nine-thirty.

110

'*It tolls for thee*'. That line from Donne's famous poem came to mind.

Under the circumstances, it was frighteningly appropriate.

He unlocked and opened the door, then stood rooted to the spot, waiting. His single courtroom loss had cost him everything. He stared blankly at the Devil, who'd come to him in the form of Dean Rollins. The ruler of the underworld didn't fix him with a malicious look, he didn't curse Mark and he didn't raise a pistol and fire a bullet into his head.

Instead, he did what got to Mark the most. He kept smiling.

"Damn, Mister Peters, I think ya need some sun. Yer face is as white as Elmer's glue!" he said as his grin broadened. "Ya gonna invite me in, or what?"

"...once again, this man is armed and extremely dangerous. If you see him, contact police as soon as you're able. DO NOT approach him under ANY circumstances."

Josh clicked the TV off. *Guess that's a million I won't have to spend after all...*

*...and I know who he'll visit first, if he's not there already...*

In spite of Rollins being on the loose now as a result of the obviously failed execution, Josh wasn't worried. Apparently, Dean had outwitted the guard or outfought him- or both.

*No doubt what little Sam knew about me died with him...*

On the other hand, there was Peters, who wasn't a concern, either. He didn't know any addresses or anything of real import. Josh always had dealt with him on a need-to-know basis, which Peters seldom did. Better yet, Rollins was a virtual lock to kill him.

That would leave only one loose cannon- one that packed a very powerful punch, but was pointed in the wrong direction, had no resources at his disposal and had no idea where to look for his former partner.

*Plus, ol' Dean will draw some manpower away from the search for Kim and Jennifer, especially if he kills Peters...*

"Mmmmm..." Lying across his lap, Lisa moaned, and he realized he'd been paying a lot of attention to her body as all those

111

pleasant thoughts ran through his mind. Almost immediately, another even more pleasant feeling took hold of him.

Although Lisa really wasn't the cause of that feeling, she would do for now. "Come on, let's go up."

"Mm-hmm." That was the most intelligible answer she could give.

Josh helped the tightly bound and very eager woman to her feet, grabbed her leash and led her upstairs by it. He only gave her the treatment he reserved for the other captives when she asked for it.

Of course, she asked for it quite often...


"You know, maybe Kim's abduction isn't connected. After all, the other missing girls *were* between eighteen and twenty-two when they were taken," John mused as he and Tom reflected on what they knew, which wasn't much of anything.

Tom shrugged. It was plain to see that John was rationalizing to try and ease his fear. It was just as plain to see that he really didn't have much conviction when he gave that assessment. "I don't know. Right now, anything's possible. We have to consider every angle- every possibility. That includes the one you touched on that Kim is the main target, with which you could employ the same logic you just used to make a case for it. She was twenty-two when Lisa Meyers was taken- hell, that even happened the night of Kim's birthday-, which could imply that whoever's responsible had it badly for Kim but couldn't get to her.

"And after a decade plus, he got it right the second time..."

John was so deep in thought he almost missed it, but when what Tom had just said sank in, his head whipped around. "What?! The *second* time?! What are you-"

"In November of '89 Kim was accosted in- and almost was kidnapped from- her apartment at Princeton. A man got into her place somehow and accosted her. He tied her up, gagged her, told her he'd be back for her and left her like that. Apparently, her roommate and another friend came back and freed her before the guy could return. She told me about that when she called earlier today; actually, that was the main reason why she called. She wondered whether the same man who tried to take her is responsible for all the other abductions."

"Jesus...did she have any idea who it could've been?"

"No, she didn't. He told her she'd be dancing for him from that night on. Apparently it was a fan of hers that got carried away, to put it lightly. The police never solved the case, but that didn't happen to her again- until a couple months ago, that is."

"That's another thing she never told me about...she led a totally separate life that I had no knowledge of and she just couldn't tell me. When the school board gets wind of all this..."

Tom saw him drifting. "Don't, John. You're no good to Kim or the investigation when you're like that. I can see how much you're hurting, but you have to shake it off. I need your help here, Brother- we all do."

After a moment John glanced back over at him and nodded.

"Getting back to where we are now, on the other hand, maybe Kim was just in the wrong place at the wrong time. It wouldn't be the first time a photographer or model scout laid a trap for a woman he wanted. Only this one has a wrinkle- somebody put a bullet into said photographer/model scout's head. I'm sure this won't be our last dead end."

The crime scene at the boutique yielded no tangible evidence. So far, no one had a clue as to who killed Jeffrey Newman. All his girlfriend Andrea knew was that someone came to meet with him several hours earlier. She only got a glimpse of the unknown man because she was busy with customers when he arrived. He went in through the rear entrance and stayed in the back for the whole time he was there, so Andrea didn't see him anymore. The only thing Newman said about the mystery visitor was that he was an associate. No one who was in the boutique at the time saw or heard anything out of the ordinary- at least, no one came forward who had.

"On the whole, you have to keep your mind open. Don't focus too early on one angle unless you have a lot of evidence to support it, or one hell of a strong hunch. These cases are a good example: in a vacuum of evidence and also with no foreseeable pattern, it would be easy to jump on the first one that materializes. We need to avoid that."

"I suppose so. It would have been nice if the girlfriend had gotten a good look at the guy."

"Yeah, another 'if'..." Tom picked up the phone as it rang. "Lieutenant Stratton...what's up, Mike?...oh, yeah? Did she

113

get the tag number?…Shit. Well, that's something…ok, let me know what you come up with. Thanks, Mike."

"What does he have?" John didn't even wait until Tom had hung up.

"He just finished an interview with a Miss Rose Perkins, who was in the Sheraton's parking lot around the time of the contest. Miss Perkins said she saw a man carrying a beautiful young woman who was wearing only a white bikini and high heels and was pretty upset, whom she identified as Kim when she was shown a picture. Another woman who resembled her was walking beside them and the three of them got into a white van and drove off. Miss Perkins identified Lisa Meyers as the other woman she saw. She didn't pay as much attention to the guy or the van and she only was able to give a general description of the van; she wasn't close enough to get the tag number even if she would have thought to. What stuck out more to her was how similar Kim and Lisa looked. This woman called in when she saw the bulletin. It's not much- par for the course so far- but it's something, anyway."

"Hopefully someone else will come forward who can give us something a little more solid. I'm even more curious now as to whether Peters *is* connected with this somehow and how much he knows if he is."

"We'll find out soon enough. Seeing you at his door should-…wait a minute: he's Rollins' attorney…oh, SHIT!!!" He grabbed his radio. "Central, this is Lieutenant Stratton. I need the closest available unit sent *immediately* to the home of Mark Peters on Greenspring Valley Drive…I don't care whose jurisdiction it is- *do it*!!"

"Can't do it, can ya?"

Mark didn't even hear what Rollins said as he settled back into the chair, his bones turning into jelly. He lowered the pistol from his temple and just sat still as it all played out before him.

*If only I'd won that case. I'll never understand how I didn't…*

That would have done it. A victory over John K. Stratton on June 19th, 1990 would have netted him his fee and he would have kept up with his practice. He would have been fine on his own with his confidence and killer instinct in the courtroom intact. By now he most likely would have been ready to retire- a wealthy man in his own right. He would have enjoyed the company of more aspiring bikini models like Melody Chambers. Stratton would have ended up as some flunky associate for the firm of Jerkwater and Bushleague instead of possibly the forty-third President of the United States.

Most importantly of all, Mark wouldn't be face-to-face with the Grim Reaper, who'd just called his number...

...but under the circumstances, that didn't seem like such a bad thing anymore...


Dean sighed. "Leavin' the dirty work to me again, eh? Ya don't have any useful information for me as to where the hole that son of a bitch crawled into is, an' now ya don't even have the decency to spare me a bullet? Well, I already killed one guy tonight- what difference will another make?"

He moved in front of the dead man and leveled the Penitentiary-issue pistol at his forehead. "Gotta admit, you'll be a lot easier- 'specially since you're so deserving."

Just one more thing would make it right. "Look up, Mister Peters. At least have the stones to look one 'a your makers in the eye..."

His smiling face and a flash were the last things Mark Peters saw.


"...all right, good. Have them contact me the second they have Mister Peters in custody." Tom turned to John. "Let's just hope that wasn't his first stop..."


As Dean pocketed the pile of money, he looked at the piece of paper with the confirmation number and flight information written on it. It was lying next to the phone and probably would be one of the first things the cops found when they arrived...

...which might not be long from now. Gotta get my ass movin' and get to my next stop, if it's open to me...

He didn't disturb the scrap of incriminating evidence- undoubtedly one of many that would tell the police how dirty Peters was.

As he walked out of the house, he knew it didn't matter if he left prints anywhere else or didn't.

*They'll know I took 'im out.*

*Glad he had this money with 'im, though.*

A hundred grand would tide him over nicely and buy him time, which he'd need a lot of considering the fact that he didn't have the first clue as to where Joshua Strauss could be...

"Stratton." Tom picked up on the first ring. He tried not to let on to John the feeling that he already knew what the officers dispatched to Peters' house were going to report.

Sure enough, they confirmed his suspicion. He hung up.

"Peters is dead, isn't he?" John asked without looking over.

Tom let out a deep breath. "Yeah."

"So for the time being, we have nothing..."

He wanted to say something that would ease the worry that held his brother in a crushing grip. Unfortunately, he knew only one thing could do that- one thing they were even further from achieving, given this latest setback.

"Yeah."

*My God, how long was I out?!*

Kim finally was awake. She'd begun to stir, went to stretch and realized her wrists and ankles still were shackled. It wasn't a dream. Worse, she was tethered to the headboard.

*At least he took the damned gag out, though. Better yet, he took those shoes off me...*

She sat up and tried to get to the laces of the corset, but she couldn't quite reach them.

*I guess I'm stuck in this, too, until he lets me out of it...*

She leaned back against the headboard and looked around the room. Right away she noticed there were no windows, which meant there was only one way in or out. It was very well furnished; judging from the paintings and the quality of the furniture, he'd gone to a lot of expense. A good example of that was the ornate brass bed, which was the most comfortable she'd ever slept on.

At the other end of the spectrum, hanging from the ceiling in the middle of the room was something that was not there for her comfort or enjoyment...

...then, there was the 'toy box', which was on her dresser, in plain view...

She turned as she heard a key in the door. Then, Josh opened it and stepped inside. He just stood and gazed at her for a moment.

She lowered her head and, to her consternation, realized that he was looking at her breasts. She covered them and glared at him before turning away.

However, she grew nervous when he walked toward her. She drew her legs up and curled into a defensive position.

"Oh, knock it off, Kim. I'm surprised at you! You already know how things will be, so drop the act. Breakfast will be ready soon and I'm sure you want out of the cuffs and the collar. I'll let you out of the corset so you can take a bath, which is one of two times that you'll be allowed out of it. The only other time will be when you exercise, so you'd better get used to wearing one again, although I can't imagine that'll be a problem for you. It never was before."

After a pause he added, "Another thing you'd better get used to is me being able to see as much of your body as I want whenever I want, starting right now. Take your hands away, unless you want me to cuff 'em behind you and bathe you myself."

She knew he would make things as hard on her as he possibly could no matter what she did. There was no sense in giving him cause to make her situation even worse, which he wouldn't hesitate in doing.

And the thought of him bathing her...

*What does it matter? I have no idea where I am, it doesn't look like I'm getting out of here and he's probably going to keep me tied up just about all the time, anyway...*

He smiled as she meekly obeyed him, returning her hands to her lap. She wouldn't look at him. He saw her lips trembling as she fought to hold back her tears and keep her composure. This was how he'd envisioned her- how he wanted her...

He couldn't resist. He sat with and faced her, reached over and touched her legs, watching her reaction as he did. Her breathing quickened and her hands clenched into fists, but she

117

remained still otherwise, focused on his hands as they coursed up along her thighs...

...and stopped at the tops of her stockings. He detached the garters before producing a key with which he unlocked the cuffs holding her ankles, and then those holding her wrists. He also removed her collar.

Kim realized he was just testing her. That, however, did nothing to ease her fear, anger and humiliation. What made it so much worse was, as he said, she knew what he would subject her to.

"You have an hour to do whatever you need to do, after which I'll come back and explain the rules to you." He gestured toward the pair of manacles suspended by a chain and set into the ceiling in the middle of the room. "I want your wrists locked into those cuffs before I come in here again. You'll be able to reach 'em when you put your shoes on. Wear the black outfit; I'll finish lacing you in, of course. Don't make me wait, and those cuffs had better be tight enough to hold you." He enjoyed her despairing look at the restraints.

*Let's see how you do with this little test, Kim.* On that thought he got up and left, locking the door behind him.

As soon as he was gone, Kim undid the laces of the corset and took it off, sighing in relief as she did.

*Guess I'd better enjoy the little time I'll have out of it...*

She removed her gloves and stockings, but kept her thong on as she went in to draw her bath. Even though it probably wouldn't make a difference, she didn't want to be totally naked since she had a choice in the matter. While she waited for the tub to fill, she walked over to the door and examined the latch. As she figured, the lock mechanism was on the other side and the door was very sturdy- also what she expected.

*By all indications, I definitely won't be going anywhere soon...*

She walked back into the bathroom and saw her bath was ready, then slipped out of her thong.

*This sure is appropriate,* she thought as she eased herself into hot water.


"I'll be damned..."

*He's got her...*

118

Dean needed a good place to hide from the police and contemplate his next move. Fortunately, he found a place where he still was quite welcome. He watched as the report about the disappearance of Kimberly Francis went on.

Just yesterday morning, while sitting in the rec room at the Pen, he'd seen her for the first time since she'd played her part in sending him there.

She always was Strauss' Achilles heel. He'd never admitted that to Dean, but his disposition and body language whenever they were in the same room gave him away. *Fuckin' guy could barely say his own name whenever he saw her...*

That fact was what led to Dean's ploy for insurance during a little celebration after their job. His suspicion that Strauss was going to screw them all over fueled that ploy, which he never got a chance to go through with. The next thing he knew, he and two of the guys were in jail and the other two were in the morgue. As far as leverage went, it all shifted to the one who wasn't there when the bust went down. Even back then Dean suspected that was no accident, but what choice did he and the other two survivors have other than to play along? If they gave Strauss away, all the money would be gone and their collective effort would have been for naught. Strauss played his hand brilliantly. Dean had no choice at all, and he knew it.

As for Kimberly Francis, who'd always been a highly sought-after commodity all across the male spectrum, she'd been kidnapped for the second time in a few months. There was no question in Dean's mind that Strauss had her this time, which meant that it was a very good possibility that no one ever would see him- or her- again.

Before the heist, the man had so much as told him that once he had the object of his desire again, he would disappear and dig himself in deep somewhere. He'd tried to bring that about twice in '89 and had failed both times- once in keeping her and the second time in getting her back.

*His world revolves around her- it always did...but there's another guy who feels the same way about her.*

That thought led him to a way to possibly get some help in finding Strauss, and also Little Miss Francis.

*I'm bettin' this guy wants his lady back pretty badly and he's one who has a lot of resources at his disposal. Plus, he and Strauss were friends once; that could help...*

119

"What's her name?"

"Vanessa Chamberlain. She says she and Miss Francis performed at the same club and were good friends. She thinks she might have some information you can use, but she asks if she can speak with you alone, Mister Governor."

Tom glanced over at John. "If you want to, and if she agrees to it, you could record what she says. If talking with you one-on-one will make her comfortable, it's what you should do, so go ahead and use my office. Considering the fact that none of our leads are panning out as yet, who knows? Maybe she'll know something that could help us somehow. After you've finished we can review the tape."

John nodded, wondering for a moment about the look that crossed Tom's face when he heard her name. "That sounds good." He turned to Detective Rogers. "OK, Bill- would you show her in?"

"Yes, Sir." He and Tom walked out.

John got up and went to the doorway where he watched as Detective Rogers went over to the stunning and very well dressed woman. She looked to be Amer-asian, in which case she'd gotten the best of the genes both races had to offer. Like Kim, she had uncommon beauty that set her apart and made everyone take notice.

He wondered about the way she regarded Tom as he walked out of the room.

*What was that about?*

John shrugged it off for the time being when she looked over at him. She smiled as the detective pointed him out; he escorted her over and introduced the two of them. John ushered her inside and closed the door. Her light disposition disappeared as soon as they were alone and she embraced him.

"I'm sorry, Mister Governor; you must be beside yourself. I'm so worried about her, too…"

"Thank you, Vanessa. I appreciate you coming," John told her as he comforted her.

She pulled away and apologized again. After a moment she smiled. "So, after all these years I finally get to meet the guy my Kimmy was so crazy about- and still is, apparently.

120

"I feel like I already know you. You were one of our topics of conversation on more than one occasion after she finally told me about what you shared. We performed at a club called The Silver Palace. I sort of took her under my wing in spite of the rough start we got off to and we became really close.

"One night after we danced, shortly before she started her sophomore year at Princeton, Kimmy and I went to my place to have some wine and talk. I was feeling a little down about the boy in my life. She was the best listener and such a wonderful friend; she always knew when things weren't right with you and she would find a way to make you feel better. Most of the girls came to love her and so did the guys who worked there. I miss her so much...

"So, after I'd finished venting, she became really quiet. I asked her what was wrong, but at first she was reluctant to open up. After she started and stopped a couple times, she finally spilled. As I'm sure you know very well, she's really emotional to begin with, which she certainly showed when she told me about you. Poor little thing...she wasn't bitter, though- she never said one bad word about you and she made me promise I never would, either. It was plain to see how much she missed you and...that she loved you."

It was just as plain to see that John loved Kim, too, but Vanessa saw that he was becoming upset, so she changed gears a little. "I'm so glad to see that you feel the same way about her. I was worried about how you might react to her being a dancer."

"The truth of the matter is, I *didn't* react well, which is one reason why she's in this mess."

"Don't blame yourself. You couldn't have known this would happen." When he didn't reply, Vanessa got back on course, hoping to buoy him. "She really was something on stage and I guarantee you she still would be. Believe me, that's a talent you either have or you don't, and Kimmy most definitely has it, along with all her other gifts.

"There were times, I'm sure, when she saw those physical assets as something of a curse. The other girls and I weren't so kind to her initially. We hurt her feelings with a couple of our comments and we thought she'd leave- she was having second thoughts to begin with- but she sure showed us something when she did her routine. We quickly found out that she has much more than just looks...

121

"A good many girls are on stage for the money, and nothing else. They just use their looks, and aren't in to performing at all. Some can't even do the most basic moves without tripping over their own feet, and it's obvious they simply don't care.

"Kimmy was at the other extreme. When she danced, her sexuality just-...it overpowered you. Sometimes it seemed to overpower her, too. I found that it's so potent because, as with everything else about her, she's not forcing it. It made her uncomfortable a number of times, but not enough to interfere with her performances. In fact, that touch of uneasiness just added to her appeal. Kimmy *is* sexuality, which is why I started to call her Aphrodite. So did the other girls, the staff and the patrons.

"She really packed 'em in, and so many of them wanted her- rock stars, actors, professional athletes, business tycoons, oil sheiks- everyone. Some of them came after her hard, too. They sent clothes, flowers, jewelry, plane tickets to exotic places and other gifts all the time- it just never stopped. Oh, there was this baseball player who-"

Having heard enough of that line of conversation, John cut her off. "Look, I really don't need to hear how many guys were after Kim, so let's get off that topic."

"I'm sorry. I just...I'm trying to remember as much as I can. I don't mean to upset you. Anyway, there were plenty of times when constantly being proposed to and pursued really got to her. That was one aspect of dancing that she didn't like. She knew what they wanted her for, yet she always declined so graciously. More importantly, she didn't lead them on. She never was disrespectful or full of herself.

"She never went totally nude- neither on stage, nor for any pictures. She always left just enough to the imagination. We had agents from Hollywood in there wanting to sign her and get her into movies, especially after the little act she did in Vegas, which is one reason why the billboard is there. I have no doubt she could have been a star if she'd wanted that. The more those guys were exposed to her, the more they understood what a wonderful person she is. She just has that way of charging you up. *God,* what an effect she has...

"...and if she wants you, you're hers- no question..."

John took equal notice of her disposition and her tone as she reminisced about Kim and his jaw dropped as it jumped into his mind. "You two were...more than just friends, weren't you?"

122

Her eyes went wide as she looked back at him. "I...I didn't...dammit, this is what made me nervous about meeting you; I *knew* I wouldn't be able to hide that! Please don't-"

"It's all right, I'm not-...look, this is a bit much for me to take. First I find out Kim was an exotic dancer, and now you're telling me you and she-..." He shook his head to clear it and tried to be objective. "Well, for the record, I agree with everything you've said. You can't help wanting Kim any more than she can help being so irresistible- believe me, I understand. It sounds like her appeal even crosses gender lines. If you don't mind me saying so, I can see how she would be drawn to you. You're a very beautiful woman, too."

"Why, thank you- how sweet of you to say that!" She smiled at him, but after a moment her eyes narrowed. "What is it?"

His shock gave way to curiosity; he wanted to know more about Kim's past- wanted to try to understand more about her mindset and why she did what she did. "If you don't mind, would you..."

She smiled again. "Tell you about Kimmy and me? I'd love to. I'm glad you're so open-minded; you're taking this a lot better than many men would. I bet you two make a great couple.

"She and I spent a lot of time together, especially when she wasn't in school. There was nothing we felt uncomfortable about sharing with each other and naturally, one of our favorite topics of conversation was sex. I was a lot more experienced, but that imagination of hers- did she *ever* come up with some great stuff! She was so funny that way; she'd blush when she described what she was thinking on that subject. Even if she was feeling down, like she was at my apartment one night during winter break of her sophomore year, those talks we had would pick her up.

"So, we- oh, that's right: we'd just come back from the Kitty Cat Club that night, and-"

"The Kitty Cat Club? You mean the one in Atlantic City?"

"Yes, that's the one. Why do you ask?"

"I don't know...for some reason that just jumped out at me." That wasn't true, but as yet there was no reason to elaborate. It was nothing more than an inkling. "Sorry about that. Go on."

"Well, we worked there a few times- not dancing, though. A friend of Billy's- he's the guy who owns the Silver Palace- was the manager at the Kitty Club. In order to help boost attendance there, Billy asked me, Kimmy and a few of his other dancers to do some cocktail waitressing and mingling. We were there for a few months. It was such fun and we *loved* the uniforms, which Andy was nice enough to let us keep. By the way, did you ever see the billboard?"

"Which billboard?"

"That means you didn't. You'd have remembered this one, trust me! It was the promotional shoot for the club; Andy came up with the idea and asked Kimmy to do it and she agreed right away. The concept was for her to be wearing her tigress uniform and lying on her side in front of a real tiger- a really *big* tiger, at that. Simple enough idea if the cat is cooperative, which he wasn't at first. He was feeling very ornery, so they were about to cancel the shoot. Then, in walked my friend, as cool as she could be. Kimmy saved the day and made the shot even better than Andy visualized.

"She has the ability to tame the savage beast in all his forms, which she showed us all when she calmed that huge cat. You know the way she coos when she's greeting little children? Well, she lay down on her side, got into her position and cooed to this tiger that just dwarfed her. He settled right down, too. It was unbelievable; he went over and sat right behind her, got into a protective position around her, and the photographer took his shots. The only problem arose when it was time to get the tiger back to his pen; he didn't want to leave Kimmy, so she had to lie there with him until he was lured away with a treat a while later. That billboard probably is one of the most famous ones ever done; you'll see it sometime, I'm sure. It ended up in Vegas after the club closed. I think it's still there on the main strip."

"I wouldn't be surprised...sounds like a great picture!"

"It is! So, getting back to that night, we'd had dinner and she was staying over at my place. It was a little late but we weren't very tired yet. Right in the middle of telling me about this awesome fantasy she had, she got a cramp in her neck. I went over to her, sat behind her and gave her a rub where the kink was. At that point I didn't have any intention other than relieving her cramp, but after a little while when she sighed and leaned back against me...the next thing I knew I was taking her robe off. She didn't resist at all, so I told her to lie down so I could give her a full-body massage and went to get my oils. I came back in and there she was, totally nude, lying on my floor and looking up at me, waiting. I tell you, she could turn the most frigid man or woman into a raving sex maniac with the look from those eyes...

124

"I put some towels down for her and she moved onto them. Oh, God- that *body*...as I'm sure you've figured out, I had it badly for her, but I wasn't sure how she would react to my advances. I know my hands must have been shaking as I squeezed some oil onto her and rubbed it in to her...before I knew it I was touching her breasts. Any doubts I had that they were all natural sure disappeared that night..."

She drifted as she felt Kim's lush curves again along with the blaze she ignited in both of them, which was coming back in a hurry. "I can't tell you how happy and relieved I was when I knew she was turned on, too. The lower I went, the hotter we got...

"Just touching and massaging her was more than enough to get me going, but what pushed me- or more like *threw* me- over the edge was the way she responded. She loves being touched to begin with- I'm sure you know that better than anyone, John-, and from all we'd shared about what we liked and how we liked it I knew how to get *her* going, which I definitely did. I'll never forget her as she was- her hands clenching and releasing like a cat when she's purring, her moans and cries that sound like mewing, and her eyes...when she gave me the look, it was all over. Like you said, I couldn't stop myself...

"John, she was *amazing*! We were amazing together. We just kept going and going; it was all lust and heat at first, but we took our time the longer we went. We knew we could trust each other, so it was total abandon. We acted out so many of our fantasies, and-"

"If you don't mind, Vanessa, I'd appreciate a little less detail, all right? We're talking about the woman I love."

"There is a point here, if you'll bear with me. What I'm about to tell you has a lot of relevance." He sighed and nodded reluctantly, and she went on. "In one of hers- the one she'd shared with me that night- she played the prey to my cat burglar. I was *all* over that one! I surprised her in her 'sleep' and tied her to my bed while she pleaded with me not to hurt her before I gagged her.

"It was obvious how excited she was even while I was tying her, which was a problem, in a way. In addition to being as fit as she is, she's deceptively strong: given how feminine she also is, you'd never suspect that. It was some kind of a task to keep her pinned long enough, even with Kimmy holding herself back, like I know she was. I think the whole experience would have been better for her if she'd been able to resist my efforts at full strength, but if she'd done that, I'd have been no match for her. Even so, she still got plenty out of it, and so did I.

"Just being subdued and rendered helpless as she begged, and then struggling against the sashes I tied her with drove her *wild*, let alone what it did to me. I thought she'd explode when I touched her, and...well, on more than one occasion you could say she *did* explode! It got to where I wondered if she'd ever stop...

"Neither of us had a boyfriend then and we hadn't had any of the good stuff for some time- especially Kimmy. There was this...odd kind of chemistry between us that night- there just was no stopping us. Before we knew it the sun had come up. Finally we just collapsed and slept together until the following evening. I'm not a lesbian and sex with another woman was really nothing more than idle curiosity until that night. Kimmy felt the same way; we talked about it as soon as we woke up. We were a little freaked out, but not with each other. We just got totally swept up in the moment and were so close to begin with, but still, we figured it would be a one-time-only thing, which it was. That didn't hurt our friendship at all, though. There were occasions after that when I wanted an encore, but we never had it.

"I did get to tie her up a few times on stage, though."

He was getting a little impatient and was about to ask her to get to the point when that last comment came out, throwing him for another loop. "You tied her up? While you were on stage?! Wait- you said the *first* time?! What in the hell were you-"

"I know, I know. I never should have-...anyway, she'll probably kill me for telling you that, but those episodes are what I was getting at when I told you there was a point I wanted to make.

"She wore corset ensembles during some of her performances. She had a black one, a white one, a purple one and a pink one, all of which she got from a regular in our club who'd started up a company that made them. There were others like him who gave Kimmy sexy shoes, lingerie and outfits to wear while she danced; she was an exotic dancer and model at the same time. Of all those gifts, the corsets were her favorites.

"Not long after our night of nights she wore the white set and was getting ready to go on. She had all of it; the long gloves, the back-seamed silk stockings, the thong and the pumps with the super-high heels; they were nearly six inches high! I still envy her in how well she could walk in those shoes. She turned that into a form of art, too, just like she did with her dancing...

126

"I'm sorry if I'm rambling a little here, Mister Governor. I'm trying to remember all I can, and this is helping me."

"All right. Go on."

"So, anyway, I helped her into the corset, which was the *last* thing she needed with that teeny waist of hers, but she loved wearing them. She loved feeling sexy and feminine, and nothing made her look the part more than those outfits. Her corsets were short; they were under-the-bust and only covered from her midriff to the top of her hips. She looked like the sexiest bride I'd ever seen on her wedding night.

"I set the stage for what was meant to be a one-time-only gimmick; you know, just a change of pace. Although I had a feeling she was the perfect candidate, I wasn't sure how my idea would go over with Kimmy, so I just sort of sprang it on her."

She fell silent, becoming contemplative for a moment, and her expression darkened. "I'd give anything to take that night back, even though we all made a ton of money from what it led to..."

Kim still had a few minutes left. She'd finished dressing to the extent she was able and sat on the bed, looking up at the manacles she was to lock herself into.

As much anxiety as that brought on, it wasn't what bothered her most.

*Somehow I have to stop him from doing this to Jenny...*

The most prominent thing on her mind was the history between her and Josh- the part of her life she wished she could erase, especially now.

Whenever she thought for even a second that he could put Jenny through the same thing...

*I'm not going to let that happen, even if it means-...*

She had to consider it. At that point, there just wasn't much of anything else she could think of that would save her student from him. There were two other options: escape, which seemed very unlikely, and rescue, which she couldn't even think about.

*I've been so lucky in the past with being rescued twice, but I can't get my hopes up. I don't have much of any control over that, anyway.*

*I can't believe it's coming to this...*

She mused about the night at the club during which the seeds for her present situation most likely were planted...

~ ~ ~

"...you want to do *what*?!" The leather straps in Vanessa's hand suddenly looked much more sinister with what she just said.

Vanessa was sure this would be the coup de grace; given the way Kim was attired, tying her up somehow seemed like the next logical step. "Oh, come on, it'll be fun! You know how you felt when we did this and let's not forget whose fantasy it was in the first place. Besides, I don't just *want* to do it: I'm *going* to do it. You, my dear, have no say in the matter."

She saw a little fear and a lot of uncertainty in Kim's eyes. Had it not been for what else Vanessa saw in her demeanor, the game would have ended there.

As well as she'd come to know Kim, there was no mistaking the intrigue and excitement she saw as she approached her. Her soon-to-be captive turned away and placed her hands behind her. Vanessa fastened her friend's wrists and Kim tested her bonds, unaware of the next surprise that was coming.

"Gosh, Vanessa, did you have to make it so- mmph?!" The ball gag was pushed into her mouth and buckled in place before she could react. "*Mmmmph*!!" Taken by surprise, she could do nothing but grunt indignantly and shake her head a few times in a feeble attempt to dislodge the gag as she twisted her hands behind her.

"Mmm-*mmm*! Look at you- you're gonna make a fortune tonight! Now, let's finish getting you ready..."

~ ~ ~

"...so I led her onto the stage. To make things better I made her sit on a chair and tied her legs to it. It was just this little act we did- a fantasy scenario again. She was like the heroine in some gothic romance novel who was being held captive by a jealous rival: me. We turned it into an ongoing act, and I added a twist at the end by keeping her and ditching the pretend guy we both wanted. Of course, what made the whole act such a huge draw was watching her trying so hard to free herself and the effect that had on her and everyone else as well...it was so *erotic*!

"She told me afterwards how much that turned her on: struggling to no avail while hundreds of people watched her. It didn't surprise me how much those guys ate it up, nor did it really surprise me how much it got to Kimmy. That wasn't the last time we did it, either; we had a few more of our little fetish nights.

"As a club, we did really well before she came on board, but she took us to a new level- especially with her participation in those fetish nights. Although they were my idea, she was what made them so successful."

Her smile disappeared as she went on. "Getting back to her taste for bondage, there was some bad that came from it, which is the crux of all this. I seemed to have helped bring something out of her that in the wrong hands really could be dangerous to her.

"We had another fetish night that fell on her twentieth birthday- on that one we really pushed the envelope. We had various costumes; there were nurses, cops, maids, cheerleaders, and I was dressed as a dominatrix- we had all the bases covered. Of course, Kimmy was the girl everyone was waiting for. She wore the black corset ensemble that night.

"I tied her up and gagged her again, but more thoroughly this time. I got quite elaborate and creative with the way I tied her arms- behind her, of course-, which really tested her flexibility, but she showed me that she could take what I dished out. As athletic as she was, it really didn't surprise me. I had her on a leash, and I made her walk with her thighs bound together. She was particularly feisty on that occasion, too; she resisted me all the way, so when we got to my chair in the middle of the stage, I sat down, pulled her over my lap and spanked her."

She couldn't stop herself from cracking a smile as John's jaw dropped again. "The way you just reacted was exactly how everyone there did. To see this absolutely gorgeous, sizzling-hot young thing being punished...we really 'wow-ed' 'em! And as always, the way she reacted was what really got all of us. She didn't fake anything; I doubt she could, at least in that case. She was *so* indignant, but believe me- that's not all she felt. The way she wiggled that amazing ass of hers-"

She stopped when she saw he was about to cut her off. "I'm sorry, I just-...I get carried away sometimes when I think about her. You're not the only one she had such an effect on, but I'll spare you the details. Anyway, once again we outdid ourselves- every pair of eyes in that place was locked on us- more so on her. For the finishing touch, which also marked the end of our act- the twist I told you about- I helped her up and led her toward this gilded cage we placed right in the middle of the stage.

"When I pulled the cover off it, her disposition totally changed. The defiance was gone and that submissive side of her was bared, but that sparkle in her eyes was still there, so I knew she wanted me to take the next step. After announcing that I hoped she liked her new home and that she would 'be mine forevah!', adding in the cliched villainess laugh for effect, I undid the strap holding her thighs and helped her inside. Then I tied her ankles and locked her in. That cage also protected her just in case anyone wanted to get too close, which as you can imagine, they all did.

"Everyone packed in tight around the cage and watched as she squirmed and played damsel in distress. God, was she ever convincing- for good reason. They almost were fighting to get in close to see her. They slipped bills into her gloves, her stockings, her shoes and of course, her thong- everywhere they could. It got to the point where they just started leaving money in the cage.

"Her body language and expressions spoke volumes; she was burning and everyone saw it, especially in her eyes. By the time I realized how far gone she was, it was too late.

"The guy seemed to materialize in front of her. It was like he was from another world- not only was he the best-looking man I ever saw, he had an air about him, too; I can't explain it. I also knew I didn't like him the second I saw him. He had the opposite effect on Kimmy, though. I saw the look on her face. Almost right away he seemed to take control of her. It was like he put her under a spell; she was begging him to touch her. He pulled a bill out of his pocket and walked around behind her. She tried to turn toward him when he squatted down behind her and reached into the cage.

"You could tell she wanted him like nobody's business. Everyone there saw and felt the chemistry between them; we all were mesmerized. I hate to put it to you like this, but she told me she almost climaxed when he touched her. He just gave her cheek a little caress and then tucked the bill inside her thong: it turned out to be a thousand-dollar bill! He whispered something into her ear and then walked away. I knew I had to get her out of there, so I freed her and took her back to my place. I was so upset with myself for putting her in that position, but she forgave me. That was the last time I tied her, but it definitely wasn't the last time she was tied...

"She didn't talk much during the drive to my place and for the little while we stayed up. I knew he was on her mind, and I didn't want to bring him up but knew I had to. I had no doubt she would call him and I asked her to please be careful. They met the following weekend. Everything happened so fast with them; in a matter of weeks she moved in with him. She told me about some of the things they did and about...the sex- how he dominated her. She really fell for him, but I think it was more infatuation than anything else.

"She was so vulnerable, like a naïve little sister in some ways, even though she was so mature and together in most. I've seen her submissive side personally; when she was with him I could tell he was totally exploiting that part of her. It was like she let him absorb her. She wasn't Kimmy any more; she was just his girlfriend. The whole thing really upset me. He was some hot shot law student- told her he was at the top of his class-" she fell silent when she saw a look of shock on John's face that quickly became one of anger. "I'm sorry, John; I thought you'd want to know."

It just came from nowhere and shot right into his brain- the night on Suicide Ridge with his friend, who was number one in his class at law school at the time...

...more importantly, one topic in particular they discussed, which was the exotic dancer he was seeing... "I do want to know; it's all right. What was his name?"

"Josh," she spat. "I wish I could forget that-"

"About my height, dark hair, blue eyes?"

"Yes, that sounds like him. Did you know him?"

*You son of a bitch.* "I thought I did...how long were they together?"

"About nine months. Even if they'd only been together a day it would have been one too long. It took awhile, but thankfully she started to pick up on some things about him."

"Such as?"

"Well, she's so affectionate, and a number of times when she would want him to cuddle her and kiss her, he would ignore her or push her away. In the latter stage of their fling that really started to get to her. His total and constant control over her started to make her wary, too- by, um, I think it was April or May of '89 when she considered leaving him, but in spite of everything she still had strong feelings for him. It was much harder on her than it should have been, but then..."

131

"So she still was with him in May?"

"Yes, and in early June, too, although during that time it wasn't by choice."

"What do you mean?"

"She told me that you and she were together on Memorial Day, which dispelled any doubts she had about leaving him. She said just seeing you made her heart race again, the same way it always did. The way she described how you two were that night made me think of the story of Sleeping Beauty with a little twist. She told me that in a way, it seemed like she *had* fallen asleep when you separated, but when you made love again it woke her right up. From the sound of it, you two didn't miss a beat.

"More than ever, she wanted to be with you again. She said you'd made plans to be together on June 10th to celebrate your birthday, so she was going to break things off with him during the time in between. She never got the chance."

"What happened? I need to know everything you can tell me about this guy."

"Ok. Even though she forbade me to tell anyone about this- and I know she didn't tell me the whole story-, you need to know, especially with all that's just happened..."


The shock Kim had felt continuously was abating somewhat. Her time to herself and the bath had helped.

However, reality would be back shortly when he walked through the door again. Apparently he'd gone through an awful lot to bring about the result he wanted, which was what she hoped she could prevent.

*The trouble is, how do I resist without setting him off?*

He wanted things to be the way they were before. Even if he hadn't said that to her, she would have known. *Unless that's what he tells all the girls, it looks like I'm the one.*

*If that's the case, maybe I can use it as a weapon against him...*

Although he seemed to hold all the cards, somehow she needed to make him feel like that wasn't the case without pushing him too far. She already knew he'd go to extremes to get what he wanted and she didn't want to risk having him hurt or kill any of the other girls.

*The first thing I need to do is find out how many others besides Jenny he still has and if they're all right, in which case I have to try to persuade him to let them go. If it really is me he wants, maybe he'll go for it.*

*Then I can concentrate on getting myself out of this...*

*...and getting back to John, if he still wants me...*

"You're overdressed, Kim."

She whirled and saw him standing in the doorway.

"Maybe you didn't understand what I wanted, although it should have been clear that I didn't want you to wear the bra."

"Then why did you leave it with the rest of the outfit?"

"That was a test, which you failed. You're also not where you're supposed to be, which makes two strikes." As he walked toward her, the malevolent look in his eyes countered the hint of a smile. "Well, I didn't expect you to make this easy on me."

*Here goes...*"Wait."

He stopped and his smile was gone. "Strike three." He quickly covered the remaining distance between them and took hold of her.

"Please, Josh."

Her soft utterance stopped him again and so did her surprisingly calm demeanor as she looked up at him. This was not what he expected.

"Are the other girls all right? May I see them?"

*I guess I should have expected that, but she'd better understand something, and right now.* "You just don't get the dynamic here, do you? You are my captive. You have no rights, period: that's rule one. That includes making requests of any kind, which will not be granted, anyway. The only privileges you get are those you earn."

"But...this has nothing to do with me. I'm worried about the others. You- you haven't killed them, have you? Is that why you won't-"

"Enough- not another word!"

She suddenly broke his grip, stood and faced him. "Why?! What will you do, Josh?! Tie me up and gag me again?! Torture me some other way because I'm asking you a question you damned well knew I'd ask you?! Why should I do *anything* you tell me to when I don't know whether or not you murdered nine women?! And how do I know Jenny's all right?! I'll tell you this right now: I will fight you every way I can until, first, I have proof

133

positive that those girls are alive and healthy, and second, you let them go: all of them. Until both of those things happen, you get *nothing* from me. You say I'm the one you want? Show me."

He couldn't have hid his reaction if he tried. She surprised him first by her rush of strength that freed her from his grip and again by her outburst. She set him back on his heels, but worse than that, he could see that she knew it, too. However, as soon as the momentary shock wore off, anger over that verbal slap in the face took its place. He grabbed her and pulled her toward the middle of the room.

She knew what was next, but this time she was unable to stop him. She quickly found her wrists imprisoned in the manacles; she was stretched out completely. She also couldn't stop him from pushing the ball gag into her mouth and putting the collar on her.

He didn't say a word to her as he progressively pulled the laces of her corset tight, then gave them a final yank, which made her grunt as her waist was pinched. He tied them off and walked out of the room, but didn't close the door.

Kim stood still and waited for him to return, which didn't take long. She didn't like the looks of what he brought back.

"I see you cringing- no doubt you remember the single sleeve and know there's no way you're getting out of it." He unlocked the manacles, pushed her face-first onto the bed and pinned her, like he did the day before. "I think I'll keep you in it for a while today. In a way I'm glad you're showing your backbone- this will be fun."

She knew he would win this round; it was pointless to fight at the moment. She felt the heavy sheath encasing her arms and he abruptly pulled the laces as tight as they would go, crushing her elbows together behind her. "*Mmmph!!*"

"Objection noted and ignored." He finished securing the leather sleeve onto her. Although he was sure she couldn't slip out of it, he still fastened its integrated strap around her wrists and tied another around her elbows. Finally, he tied her legs just above her knees and attached a leash to the front of her collar. "Come on, we're going to take a little walk."

She swung her bound legs over the side of the bed and struggled into a sitting position, then looked at the strap holding her thighs and back up at him.

"What? We both know you walked pretty well like that when your friend Vanessa led you onto the stage- remember? Those heels are just as high as the ones you wore that night, too- it's the same degree of ease for you." He got a kick out of the humiliation he saw all over her face as he pulled her to her feet, grabbed the leash and led her out of her room. He stopped her when they got outside.

"I was going to show you they're all OK, anyway. I knew you'd ask." He chuckled at the heated look she gave him before turning away as he closed her door. Ready to go, he gestured down the hallway. "That way, Kim. I got a good look at you from the front that night when you were led out in this outfit, so now I want to see the view from the rear. Start walking."

He followed behind her, keeping hold of her leash while he watched and enjoyed.

Kim's thoughts were elsewhere and she did her best to keep them there. *At least they're alive; thank God for that.*

*Just focus on what you have to do; look for a way out of this. He has to make a mistake somewhere along the line, or maybe he has already. Don't let him get to you. Don't-*

Josh whistled at her as she walked with only a bit of difficulty. He was thoroughly enjoying the show and had to let her know it. "You've done a hell of a job keeping yourself in shape and you still walk that walk, don't you? I always did love the way that ass switches back and forth. You always were a teaser, weren't you? Just couldn't help yourself. You might be pleased to know that the routine I have for all my girls is based on what we did and what I saw you do during the time I've known you. In particular, it all stems from what you and Vanessa did in your act."

*I hate you. God, I wish I'd never called you from Vanessa's that night, or any other night for that matter. How could I have been so stupid?!*

She tried to hide her anger and her shame, but could feel her cheeks burning as he poured it on. *Somehow, you will pay for this...*

Certain that things would get worse before they got better, she didn't want to think about whatever else he had in mind for her.

Unfortunately, he didn't wait long to spell it all out.

He gave her leash a little tug and she stopped. "Before we go any further, I'm going to fill you in on the other rule. You are here for my pleasure. Period. There are many ways you can please me, which it's in your best interest to do. You'll do what I tell you, or you'll suffer.

"John never will find you. No one will, so just put any such notion out of your mind. In time you'll accept that as fact, anyway. Food for thought: the law hasn't even come close to me at any point over the past ten years. Only now are they catching on to the things you and the other women have in common- rather, what they have in common with you. They might even figure out you're where this all started and you're where it'll end. Or, they'll just assume all of you are dead, which is logical given the length of time involved and the resources it would take to provide for and sustain all of you.

"Even if they do figure it out, it won't matter. I've buried myself too deep over that time and covered my tracks too well for them to dig me up. With the exceptions of you and Jennifer, all my girls have accepted their positions. I hope it isn't too long before you do the same thing. I'd like to see you save yourself the suffering. Your choice there- one of few things you have a say in.

"As for me letting the rest of my stable go, that will not happen. Ever. If I were to let the others go, what would stop you from trying to escape? I know how you are, especially when it comes to your former students. As long as I have the others- Jennifer in particular- I know you'll stay in line. You're part of that stable now. You are my prize, of course, but don't expect any special treatment…well, not too much special treatment, anyway."
He smiled for a moment at her reaction as he began to stroke her.

*She's reeling again,* he mused as he leaned in close to her ear from his position behind her. "I know you better than you know yourself, and you know I'm right in saying that. You remember how it was and how much you loved your position. I shouldn't have to keep reminding you of that. You made a mistake by running away, but now you're back where you belong: with me. This is who you are. I want you to accept that and face the fact that none of you ever will leave here. I have the means to keep every one of you here for the rest of your lives and you also see that I'll provide well for all of you…

"…especially you, Kim," he said as he continued to fondle her. Her lack of resistance pleased him even more. "Don't get on my bad side. I hope you'll back off from what you told me about fighting me. I want you to realize it won't do you any good. You

136

don't want to cause yourself any discomfort..." He reached up for his favorite pair of targets and squeezed them just enough to make her squirm.

Kim was at a loss. He'd certainly thought it all out and he knew exactly how and where to attack her. This was the worst of all scenarios- the one from which she couldn't see any way out. She tried not to think about it for the time being, knowing that would only make the situation yet more difficult to bear, if that were at all possible.

She felt how excited he was as he pressed himself against her from behind- something he still seemed to enjoy doing-, which agitated her further. She knew he would take every such opportunity he had to demonstrate to her the effect she had on him. She did her best to hide her revulsion and quell her instinct to tear herself away from him as he pawed at her, especially given what he said next.

"...and you don't want to cause Jennifer any, do you?"


"So, what did she tell you?"

"A lot." Tom turned away when he said that. It was the same reaction as before when he first heard Vanessa's name. *I'll ask him about that soon, but for now...* "You said you requested a copy of the police report Kim made the night she almost was taken; have you gotten that yet?"

"No, I'm waiting on it. We should have it soon and I've told the other investigators we have on the case about it. I've given that angle a lot of thought. In theory, it seems very possible that the guy who slipped into Kim's apartment the night before Thanksgiving eleven years ago and damned near made off with her is the same guy who's taken all the other women, and who now has Kim, too. She could be the one he wanted all along. He screwed up that night in '89 and spent the next decade plus making up for that mistake. He's just completed the circle.

"When you look at it that way, it makes sense...I don't know, it's a possibility, anyway- one point of light in this fucking black hole. We've covered every other possibility over the last several months; I can't tell you how many man-hours we've expended on this investigation, not to mention all the other resources we've employed. We're dead in the water otherwise. It can't hurt to go down this avenue and see if something's there.

137

"But if that's the case, who could he be? Kim didn't mention anyone she thought might be shadowing her, even when she was a dancer." Tom was so focused on his train of thought that he didn't realize he'd made another slip with that statement. "Of course, she probably wouldn't know anyway, given the way most stalkers work. How many more like Daniels could there be out there? How many former acquaintances at any point in her life that were enamored with her and gradually became obsessed with her? Christ, we could be talking hundreds- *thousands* of possible suspects..."

"One of which is smart enough and motivated enough to pull it off." In so many ways it seemed impossible, which further convinced John that it had to be the case. He was a brilliant man who had every motive in the world, especially considering all Vanessa had told him and all he gleaned from the source himself. As far as opportunity went, apparently he'd blown two of them...

*...if I'm right, how did you bring the third about?*

*I guess we'll have to start from square one, which is finding out how you convinced all of us you were dead...*

"What are you thinking about?"

"I'm pretty sure I know the answer to your question- that being, who did it."

"How in the hell do you-"

"Just listen. Along with a journey into my past, I need to tell you the rest of what Vanessa told me. After I'm finished, tell me if you disagree with my conclusion."

*I'd also like to find out how long you've known Kim was an exotic dancer and why you never told me you knew.* He'd made mental notes of Tom's slip-ups and added them to those he'd made earlier from his and Vanessa's reactions to each other, and also from Tom's avoidance of her...

*...but right now, our priority is finding Kim and the others.*

"I'm going to tell you about a former friend of mine- one you might remember..."

# Chapter 6

He thoroughly enjoyed her abasement and discomfort.

Before the others got to the dining room, he led her in there. There was a ring-shaped table that took up much of the room. A small section of the table's top was hinged, and he raised it, then led her through the opening to the center of the room, where an iron rung was set into the floor. Connected to that rung were a set of shackles, which he locked around her ankles. That in itself wasn't so bad, but when she realized how he was going to employ the other control measure, she tried to fight him.

Her resistance drew a warning from him: "Keep in mind that any time you resist me, Jennifer will pay for it." She immediately relented and let him finish what he was doing.

He connected the end of a cable that dangled behind her to a small ring at the very end of her single sleeve. The cable ran up to a pulley, which was fixed into the ceiling above her, and then down to a hand-operated winch that was behind her. She knew what was next.

He began to crank the winch, going slowly as he did. As the cable was retracted, it drew her bound arms up behind her and gradually forced her to bend at her waist. He kept turning the handle as she alternately pleaded with him and cursed him in silence. She didn't expect any mercy, and she certainly didn't get any.

By the time he stopped turning the winch and set it, her arms were nearly perpendicular to the floor. Worse, she was leaning forward a little, which meant if she relaxed, her already aching shoulders would bear the burden of her weight. The only way she could alleviate that was by moving her feet as far forward as the chain would allow, which wasn't more than a few inches, and standing as tall as she could. Of course, she couldn't do that for very long either; her legs would begin to tire and she would have to bend her knees a little, which was all she could manage as he'd stretched her nearly to her fullest extent.

He kept her like that while he and Lisa brought the rest of them in, one by one, and she watched the bizarre ritual. Each woman would come in, sit down in one of the big, sturdy chairs and, under Lisa's supervision, lock manacles that were connected to the chair around her wrists and ankles. She would have enough freedom of movement to eat and drink.

Jenny hadn't been brought in yet- no doubt she would be last. Lisa left the room, presumably to get her.

Kim turned her attention the others. The first thing she noticed was that the chairs were far enough apart to prevent any escape collaboration. But then again, looking into the faces of the ten women, escape seemed to be the furthest thing from their minds. As docile as Jenny had been during the van ride, every one of these girls was that much worse. They ate their food in a very relaxed and normal manner. When they regarded Kim, their expressions ranged from slightly sympathetic to relief that none of them was in the new girl's position. There was not the slightest hint from any that indicated a willingness to resist even slightly.

Josh wasn't just showing her that the others were unharmed- on the surface, anyway. He also was showing her what he wanted her end state to be. It was bad enough merely thinking about what he must have put all of them through during their long periods of captivity, but seeing the effects of his treatment made it that much worse...

She endured her predicament as best she could, but as time dragged on she was beginning to tire physically and emotionally. The severe bondage he inflicted on her turned minutes into hours as she continuously tried to pass the time and minimize her agony.

He just smiled at her as he waited. His cruelty was boundless, as she already knew.

Then, the door opened and Lisa brought Jenny in.


"*Josh?* Come on...you're serious about this?"

"Totally."

He shook his head. "I don't buy it. That's too much of a stretch."

"Think about it, Tom; it's the only thing that makes all the pieces fit together. If you look at the whole-"

"I *am* looking at the big picture and I'm telling you it just doesn't jibe."

"Come on, that much coincidence is very unlikely. Look at all the girls we're talking about and how they relate. Kim worked as a cocktail waitress at the Kitty Cat Club; a cocktail waitress who looks something like her disappears from the same club. Kim graduated from Princeton and from The University of Maryland; two students who bear resemblance to her disappear, one from each school. Kim loves figure skating and swimming and was pretty damned good at both; an amateur skater and a competitive swimmer, both of whom look similar to her, disappear. An exotic dancer, a high-school cheerleader, a schoolteacher, a girl who won a bikini contest- all resembling her to varying degrees, all disappear.

"Then Jenny, who from this picture has turned out to look a *lot* like Kim and who's selected to be a cheerleader for the same professional football team Kim cheered for- gone.

"The only one I can't figure is the female cop. I don't know how she fits in..."

Tom caught himself while John was still looking away, contemplating his last statement, which had struck a chord in Tom. *If you knew that Officer Tiffany Holstrom does fit into the theory you've come up with, and worse, the reason why she does...*

*...no, it can't be. The theory- maybe, but Josh Strauss?!*

Nonetheless, he didn't interrupt as John went on.

"Anyway, other than her, the rest of the women fit into the puzzle according to what I know and what Vanessa told me Kim did during the time she knew her. To cap it off, he gets the one who got away from him twice- the one he's wanted all along. You said it yourself; she was in the same age range while she danced, and as it turns out, the same range when he took her the first time and tried to take her again."

He threw up his hands when he saw Tom's lack of a reaction. "For Christ's sake, how much convincing do you need?!"

"John, listen to me. You're too close to this; you're reaching and coming up with this impossible scenario. I can see the possibility of it being an obsessed fan of one of the girls and I agree that Kim is the most likely of them- *if* that's the case. I can even see the possibility of the connection you've laid out, but I don't agree with you on who's behind it. It easily could have been someone other than Josh who tried to take her from her apartment and after he failed, made up for it by taking all the others and then closed the circle with Kim. Then again, there's still a good chance that we're wrong and it could be a white slaver, or worse.

"And now, all of a sudden and out of the blue, you hear a second-hand, eleven-year-old story that a former friend of yours kept Kim in captivity for twelve days. She thinks he has her now, and you're convinced of the same thing. Be objective here: don't you see how easy it would be for you to jump to that conclusion? And do you even know the story she told you is true? What made her come here, anyway- have you thought of that? Could she have a hidden motive for telling you what she did? Did she get any information out of you, or did she try to?"

"What are you talking about?! We exchanged some information, yes. She told me things about Kim's past that are pertinent to our search and I told her a little about us and what I knew about Josh. What in the hell difference does that make?! I didn't give away any details of what we're doing, if that's what you're asking me. Why *are* you asking me that?!"

"Because I don't want you to divulge anything that might compromise our investigation in any way- no matter how insignificant a detail we might be talking! Listen to yourself! You're not in the right frame of mind- in fact, you're *out* of your mind because the love of your life has been taken again. You've latched right on to what Vanessa told you and you've put together your theory that makes sense to you because you want an answer- you *need* an answer."

*Easy, don't push him. He's been through enough already; you don't need to make it worse.* He leaned back into his chair and went on in a more relaxed tone of voice. "I'm not saying this to be harsh. Believe me, that's the last thing I want to do. I know you need something- so do the loved ones of all the other girls. I hope to God we crack this case before long, but I just don't think what you've told me is the answer. It's a cold, hard fact that Joshua Strauss died in Louisiana sometime during the summer of '89. End of story."

"It's not the end of the story."

"Dammit, will you stop-"

"No, *you* need to listen to *me* now. I haven't told you everything; there's…there's more to this than the missing girls."

"What do you mean?"

John took a moment to collect his thoughts before he delved into the darkest chapter of his life- the one that nearly ended it and probably *should* have ended it. "It started with a conversation Josh and I had one night early in '89. We'd just started our last semester at law school and we both were feeling a good bit of angst- at least, I was. We talked about things that would be interesting to do or try that in all likelihood neither of us would ever do. More than any other reason, that conversation came about because we were having doubts about the courses our lives were taking.

"Eventually we got around to how cool it would be to pull off the perfect bank robbery, or something along those lines: a big enough heist to set you up for life. Actually, he brought it up. He laid out this plan he'd concocted to hit the Federal Reserve here in Baltimore."

"He *what*?!"

"You heard me right. He based it on some research he'd done into stories about past robberies. He identified the mistakes the robbers made that had ended up getting them caught, and taking everything into consideration he came up with this plan. Josh always was very methodical and logical about how he approached things. He thinks his moves out very carefully beforehand. One thorough son of a bitch, he is...

"Well, in theory, his plan looked all right at best, but there were problems. The location was good as far as accessibility and escapeability go, but that place is like a fortress. He counted on surprise and a devastating attack, neither of which I thought would get him far in that case. Then, there were the intangibles, like bad weather that could slow you down, a policeman being in the wrong place at the wrong time, extra security being present the day you're going to hit- there were a lot of them. He was so focused on the main points that he didn't even know there was construction taking place on his main avenue of escape that would be going on for quite some time, and I really think he underestimated the contingent of police and guards.

"Then, I told him about something I'd given a lot of thought to. The Reserve makes all the new paper currency every few years, so I'd always wondered what happened to the old stuff. They have to destroy a bunch of notes when they make new ones, right? So there would have to be a process by which old currency is rounded up and sent to wherever they send it, presumably by armored car, to be destroyed. I figured it would be much easier to find out how that's handled, find someone on the inside to give you the right info and take the transport down, because who really gives much thought to old notes? I've never heard of such a carrier being robbed, so the element of surprise would be even easier to achieve. Best of all, since they were so old and used, the bills would be virtually untraceable."

"You've just described the big hit that happened during October of that same year..."

"October 29$^{th}$- Josh's birthday, and coincidentally the 60$^{th}$ anniversary of Black Tuesday, the big stock market crash. He brought the conversation up again while we rode down to Suicide Ridge just after *my* birthday. Kind of weird how that happened. That was the last night I ever saw him."

"That was the case that made you famous around here... Jesus Christ, John!! You mean to tell me those fucking guys used *your* idea and plan to shake down that armored car for over nine million in old notes?! And you even suspected there was someone else involved...have you suspected Josh all this time?"

"No, not until a little while ago after I talked with Vanessa. Just like you and everyone else, I thought Josh died in that bayou, and that the conversation we had died with him. It scared the hell out of me, the fact that I knew exactly how they pulled the job off. That's the only reason why I was able to put 'em away, too; I tricked Baker into corroborating part of it when I caught him in a lie, but that was the only slip any of them made. The rest was on me. I had to convince the jury that my theory about what they did was what happened, and thank God they went for it. I almost wasn't able to persuade the judge that there was enough cause to take the case to trial!

"You remember how Peters was talking about the wrongful death countersuits against your department and the Feds for what happened in that sting? And you damned well better believe if he'd won, not only would he have gone through with those suits- he would have won them as well, and all of you would've looked like shit for years to come! You guys didn't give me jack to go on with your 'sting'; none of them admitted a thing!

"I got lucky through a damned peculiar twist of fate, and as a result, so did all of you. There's no fucking way in the world I should have won that case as it was, and if I hadn't planned the job they pulled off, you can bank on the fact that I *wouldn't* have won it! The money never was found even though all the perps in that heist were put behind bars or killed as a result, which is why I wondered if there was someone else involved...

"...all this time I tried to put him out of my mind, but he never really went away. I just didn't want to think about it because in a way it felt like I'd played a part in that heist. I wanted that chapter closed- period. I don't know...maybe, in some way, I knew it was him all along. It sure makes sense now. There's no one else it could have been- no one else who had more motive."

"What was his motive, then?"

"In spite of how smart and thorough he is, unless he's changed his ways, he has two major flaws: arrogance and rigidity. He always was convinced his way was the right one, and he could be persuasive. He also wouldn't deviate the slightest bit from his way once he set his mind to something, and he always stuck with things that were familiar- things he knew. To his credit, he was right a lot of the time; hell, he was number one in the class. It takes a lot of smarts and dedication to achieve that.

"But that inflexibility- that's how I got him during debates. I would find or create a weakness in his argument and call him on it. I'd take him out of his game and make him doubt himself; he just couldn't react or recover. On that note, I think he had a degree of insecurity, too. The night before any debate, he would spend hours putting together his plan of attack while I was out getting shit-faced and the next day I'd make it look like the opposite happened. I'd just go off the cuff, like I did most of the time during high school. I tore him to pieces every time. I even told him what I was going to argue before one of our debates and he still couldn't get the better of me.

"That drove him nuts. He never said so and never lost his temper, but it looked like he wanted to kill me sometimes. He was number one, yet a fool who drank and caroused his way through all three years of law school and still made *magna cum laude* just danced circles around him while he stewed in his own juices.

"His arrogance won't let him forget that I got the better of him until he gets the better of me. I think that's his motive, Tom: revenge. I've seen his vengeance, too; he never forgets and never forgives. He doesn't rest until he gets payback. Even if it isn't *the* motive, it's fueling him- of that I'm certain. At this point it looks like he's getting it, too, because I have no idea where he could be or how to even start looking for him. He's been out of sight for over ten years.

"Plus, he used my plan to make his mark- just a way to slap me in the face. He even benefited from me putting the rest of his crew in jail because as soon as that happened, all the money became his! He probably *still* laughs about it!

145

"As for Kim, he's exacting revenge on her for escaping him...or for rejecting him."


"Why won't you let me get her down from there?!" Jenny struggled against her captor's grip while the woman named Lisa fastened her ankles separately to each leg of the chair. They kept her hands bound behind her.

She soon realized she would stay tied as she was. Thus far they'd been very thorough each time they'd bound her, and this time was no exception. Her heart went out to her guide and friend, but she could do nothing to help her, which pained her greatly.

"Miss Francis..."

"No talking at the table. That rule was already explained to you and you won't get another warning. Say one more word and you'll find yourself in a position like hers for the rest of the day."

She fell silent and accepted the forkful of food.

Kim looked up only briefly, her eyes glistening, and lowered her head again. She remained still while Jenny was fed.

*She looks so weak...* "I can't watch this any more! *Please* let her down...no, don't-" The rest of what Jenny had to say was cut off when Lisa gagged her.

"Remember, you brought this on yourself. Now, sit quietly and still and just watch."


"Attorney Mark Peters Shot To Death In His Home-Federal Escapee Suspected."

So read the headlines of the morning paper. Dean looked at the picture of him that accompanied the story. *They used the same old shot of me that they used on TV. Good.*

His appearance had changed rather dramatically- he'd eaten pretty well during his time in the Pen and had gotten in to weightlifting. He was a good twenty-five pounds heavier than he was at the time of that picture- maybe even thirty. His face was fuller, reflecting that change. His hair was much shorter, too.

*Probl'y just a matter of time before they catch on and put a sketch on the air that looks more like me now, though. Can't count on 'em using that photo for too long...*

That point emphasized his need to find a way to get to Strauss, and quickly. It was good that he had a place to hide out for a while, but it was only a temporary fix. He needed the money and he needed to find a good place where he could vanish.

He also had another debt to pay that he would make good on somehow.


*This will do it.*

He knew Kim wouldn't be able to endure the position she was in for much longer. Suffering never looked so beautiful.

She had to accept the inevitable- that there was no escape for her. She had to know. She would surrender, like she nearly did before. She would turn her exquisite eyes to him for relief, which he would gladly give her.

From then on, anything she wanted he would give her.

Jennifer would see it happen, too. Despite the fact that she'd surprised him with her first hint of resistance, that wouldn't happen again after she saw her beloved counselor defeated. She also would give in; he'd have them both along with all the others.

It would be game, set and match. All of his girls subdued completely, all at his bidding with his queen at his side once more.

He saw a tear roll slowly down Kim's cheek.

*There's the sign I've been waiting for...*

He looked toward Jennifer and couldn't stop himself from thinking about how much of a pleasure it would be for him when she took the same road as Kim.

It would be just like it was with Kim the first time...

...actually, it would be even better since it was apparent that Jennifer was a virgin, or simply very naïve and inexperienced. He'd suspected as much with all the information he'd gathered about her, and her expressions and actions while in captivity only enhanced those suspicions. Other than a schoolgirl's crush on his nemesis, and a boyfriend who didn't deserve to be called that, based on what Jennifer had revealed to him, there had been no one.

*It would be nice to erase Stratton from you completely- give you a fresh start...*


*I can't take any more...*

Kim's fingers, arms and shoulders were going numb and she was feeling faint.

He'd won. He was right; there simply was no point in fighting anymore. All she could hope for was to make things as easy on Jenny as she could, and angering him by resisting didn't appear to be the answer.

It took what strength she had left to look toward him and give him what he wanted...

...but when she did, she saw him looking at Jenny...

...and there was no mistaking what she saw in his eyes.

At that moment a simple truth burned through her haze and gave her a shot of adrenaline.

*If I give in to him, it's over- for all of us.*

She knew resistance still could prove futile in many ways. She was taking a huge risk that easily could backfire, but she couldn't just hand him victory, no matter what it would cost her in terms of punishment.

*Maybe if I put up enough of a fight, he'll concentrate more on breaking me. He says I'm his most treasured prize? We'll see what it does to him when I become the biggest thorn in his side. It might buy Jenny some time. She even fought them a little when they brought her in. Maybe she'll fight some more so he'll have at least two of us resisting him- maybe one or more of the others, too.*

*Who's to say these girls aren't just putting on a face for him and waiting for a chance to break out of here? With any luck he'll become so angry or shaken that he'll make a mistake at some point and one of us will get a chance to escape.*

*All I know is, if we do nothing, eventually he'll win...*

*...well, here goes...*

"Mmmph..."


"Look, I'm still not sold on this, John, but you've convinced me it's worth looking into. We'll contact the people in Louisiana who were involved in any way with the handling of Josh's case. The first thing we need to establish is the possibility that he could have faked his death somehow. Otherwise, we might not get much in the way of help on this.

"Before I call there, I want to talk about another thing you mentioned. You said you and Josh were riding to Suicide Ridge just after your birthday in '89? I remember picking you up around that area the next morning, but you gave me some cockamamie story about a drunken road trip with some buddies- that they must have left you there. You told me you didn't remember a whole lot because you'd had a lot to drink and you woke up with a major hangover. Even as wild as you were back then, that story seemed pretty weak. You didn't mention anything about Suicide Ridge, either, and now, to hear that it was the last night you saw Josh... what really happened?"

John gave Tom a wry smile. "I never thought anyone would find out about this. Did I ever tell you you're a pretty good detective?"

Tom waited.

"I'm surprised you didn't ask why my clothes were wet."

"Well, judging from what you told me, I figured you'd gone swimming somewhere with your other drunken college buddies..." John answered only with a silent stare. Tom didn't like his expression. "...but that wasn't the case..."

He shook his head. "I wasn't hung over, either- not from drinking, anyway."

Tom felt the blood draining out of his face as it sank in.

*I picked him up not far from Suicide Ridge; actually, he was downstream from where the ridge is...*

*...oh my God...*

"John, you didn't..."


"Is there something you'd like to tell me, Kim?"

She nodded, prompting him to stand and walk over to her.

*A simple look would have done the trick, but to hear her say it will be even better, I have to admit.*

He didn't take notice of the change in her disposition before she lowered her head again. He gently removed the gag from her mouth and gave her a moment to move her jaw around while he remained standing directly in front of her.

"OK, I know you want out of this and you know what I want to hear from you. So, go on and tell me. Tell all of us."

For a moment, she didn't move or respond in any way. He reached out for her chin...

...and jumped back when she spat on his hand.

Then she looked up at him and he saw defiance even stronger than she showed in her room. This time she didn't waver at all. She was far from broken.

Worse, Jennifer and the others were watching.

149

"Yeah, I *do* have something to tell you, Josh. Go fu-unh!" She couldn't quite get it all out before he grabbed a handful of her hair to hold her head still while he jammed the ball back into her mouth. He let her head fall forward and cinched the gag extra tight.

Then he walked around behind her and, as he made sure she was watching him, took hold of the winch handle and began to crank it. A fresh rush of pain surged through her, making her cry out as he cranked until she was fully stretched and couldn't move at all.

"You wanna be stubborn, huh?! Well, you go right ahead; we both know the result will be the same. You don't come down from there until you tell me what I want to hear, and you'd better mean it. We'll all be here watching you. You're gonna get down on your knees and beg me, and if I don't think you're convincing enough, you go right back up," he pointed at Jennifer, "and she goes with you."

Kim looked up toward Jenny and smiled as best she could. When the girl smiled back, Kim gave her a wink.

*Be strong, Jenny. I* will *get you out of this somehow...*

...but she quickly realized that wouldn't happen right away, especially since the adrenaline rush was gone and physically, she was faltering again...


*I have to get her down from there, and soon...*

He cursed silently as he knew that was true. Even with what she'd done, he would not risk doing permanent harm to her. She was beginning to swoon.

*Damn you, Kim...you'll suffer even more for what you just did to me- a LOT more. This is only the beginning...*

And she *still* refused to surrender, which was making him look bad again.

He gestured for Lisa to come to him and she quickly was at his side. He pulled her in close and spoke to her in a voice only she could hear. "We need to get the others out of here now, starting with Jennifer. I have to get her down from there."

"But...they'll know she-"

"Now, Lisa." He gave her a nudge. She looked back at him briefly in question, but went over to Jennifer with him close behind.

150

"Mmmph!" The girl struggled with them as she realized they were about to remove her from the room.

With the last bit of strength she had, Kim looked up at her and shook her head 'no'. Jenny deferred to her and stopped fighting, allowing them to prepare her for the march back to her room. Kim tried to convey as much solidarity, support and hope as she could before she simply could hold her head up no longer.

Her vision blurred as her hold on consciousness was slipping.

"Tom, it happened eleven years ago, not yesterday. I'll tell you more about it at another time. We've got to get moving and get ourselves on the trail of whoever has Kim and the other girls and hope he hasn't killed all of them. You know who I believe is responsible."

"All right- for now." He reached toward the phone, which started ringing just as he touched it. "Homicide, Lieutenant Stratton...hi, Mike- anything new?...All right! Did he get a look at the guy, too?...That is good news- fax that sketch to me as soon as you can, OK? Thanks a bunch, Mike; I appreciate you keeping me in the loop. Hopefully we'll get more leads as a result. Catch you later."

"You got a lead?"

"We just might have. A kid in Dewey Beach was peeking into a window last night and said he saw a gorgeous young woman dressed in sexy white lingerie- she also was tied up and gagged. He said she looked scared, and then a guy came into the room. At that point the kid took off. He called in as soon as he saw Kim's picture on the news today. He said there's no doubt in his mind that she was the one he saw in that room. Along with the Delaware State Police, the guys from Ocean City searched the place. They found a length of rope tied off to a beam in the middle of the room where Kim was- he had her tied to it. They're looking for more evidence now, including finding out who owns that house.

"Other than Kim being all right, the best news we got is that the kid also got a good look at the guy. Detective Hollis is going to fax the sketch to me as soon as it's ready...John?" *Oh, shit...*

151

John's blood was boiling. All he could think about was the image of Kim that he could clearly see- that of her helpless, frightened and at the mercy of a triple felon who was obsessed with her…

…a cunning and resourceful triple felon who he knew very well. John felt just as helpless, reduced to sitting in his brother's office waiting for news that amounted to nothing more than further evidence that they were playing catch-up, and losing.

Josh's very faint trail was getting colder by the minute…

…Kim, Jenny and the others were stashed away…

…and John stewed in *his* own juices…

Tom couldn't get to him before he stood, picked up his chair and threw it across the room, then with a violent sweep, cleared the desk of nearly everything on it…

…and promptly collapsed.


He worried about the looks he saw on the faces of at least two of the others besides Jennifer as he prepared them.

*This could be trouble…*

*…but then again, I'll just need to crack down harder in some cases. I've probably been overly generous with their privileges anyway- time to take some of 'em back from the potential troublemakers.*

Just as Lisa led the last of them out, Kim fainted.

Josh immediately undid the straps from her wrists and elbows and lowered her from that extreme strappado position he had her in. He worried that he'd kept her in it for too long and couldn't believe she hadn't passed out sooner.

He eased her to the floor and removed the single sleeve. She moaned as it came loose, and he went to work on her arms and shoulders, massaging them to get blood flowing back in. After a couple minutes, she reflexively moved her fingers a little, prompting a sigh of relief from Josh. He unlocked the shackles from her ankles, untied her thighs and removed her gag. Once she was free, he lifted her up and carried her back to her room.

As he laid Kim onto her bed, Lisa appeared in the doorway. He looked toward her and said, "Get a plate of food ready for her and bring plenty to drink. She'll need both when she comes to."

152

He turned back to Kim, who still was out, but shifting around periodically. He figured it wouldn't be long before she came around. "Any problems with the others?"

"No, they're all locked away."

She regarded Kim and added, "I thought for sure when we first took her that she'd break pretty quickly. Now, I'm not so sure she'll break at all. She's a lot stronger than we thought- nobody was able to take as much of that strappado position as she just did. I remember how unbearable that gets after just a little while- I didn't last half as long as she did-, but she still defied you, even through all her suffering. Whatever happens, she's gonna be a real problem."

He didn't answer; he just kept staring at her.

*Then again, it seems like she already* is *a problem. I need to say it, because I know he won't.* "Look, I know you haven't considered it with any of the others, but...this one's different. I have a feeling she's gonna pull something that'll end up getting us caught. Joshua? Are you-"

"Haven't considered what?"

It was right on the tip of her tongue, but suddenly she couldn't say it, especially when he finally stopped gazing at Kim and looked around at her.

"Haven't considered what, Lisa?"

Her notion was gone and so was his moment of weakness. He got up and walked toward her as she shrank away. She backed into the wall with him right on top of her, and looked down at her feet.

"You know I never want to hear you suggest that again, right? You understand that?"

She nodded, still looking down.

He touched her chin and raised her face until her eyes met his. "I've been good to you, Lisa- I've treated you well. You've been good to me, too, and you've helped me when I needed you. I need you now, too- more than ever-, but you've known for a long time how much Kim means to me and how much I wanted her back. I'd have thought you would know better than to hint at death for any of them, let alone her. Don't *ever* bring that up again."

Just as quickly as he gave her the stick, he offered the carrot. "She'll break, Lisa- that you can count on. It'll just take longer, that's all. She'll go the way of the others. We've had these problems before, but this'll be the last time. You can help me get her in line. You know how we do it and you know how effective our method is. I also know how eager you were for this moment, just like I was and still am. Look at her- her face, her body…tell me you don't want to possess her and dominate her! The best part is, that's what *she* wants."

He gave her a moment to take Kim in. "You were plenty excited when we took her. I can't imagine your enthusiasm's waned so much just because she's put up more resistance than we expected. The hunt is over; the hard part's finished. We've won. All we need to do is make her aware of that. Think about what we'll do with her…

"So, without further ado, let's get to work, shall we?" He kissed her, and she seemed both placated and relieved.

"OK. I'll be right back with her food, juice and water."

When Lisa left, his uncertainty came back full force.

He couldn't let on to his partner how rattled he was because of what Kim had done. He didn't like that feeling at all. He had to turn up the heat- had to make her fold…

*…but what if it doesn't work?*

"Dammit!" Never during the whole time he'd been taking the girls had he felt anything other than in control until a short while ago when he lost it. Now he was feeling unsure about whether or not he could make his prize capitulate.

*I should have waited until she was here longer…*

As he went back over and sat with Kim, he hoped she wouldn't become such a liability and a disruptive influence that he *would* have to consider what Lisa had implied. There never had been cause for that- they'd all come to accept their roles…

…but none of them showed the resolve he saw in her eyes, and none of them had as much of a hold on him as she did.

Something would have to give.

*No, it won't come to that.*

*She'll come around; I'll make her. She'll-…*

*…wait a minute- of course she's fighting it. I guess I should have expected this…*

He stopped his thought process when she literally did begin to come around.


"More than anything else, it looks like exhaustion to me, Tom, especially with what you told me about him not sleeping well recently and not at all last night. He hasn't fully recovered from his wounds, either. His right lung still is a little weak, which his agitated state did nothing to help. All things considered, I wouldn't worry too much- as long as you can keep him calm. I'm going to keep him here overnight for observation. I doubt it will be necessary to for him to be here any longer. If it is, I'll let you know right away. Once you take him home, I want him on his medication; make sure he takes it until it runs out."

Donna piped up. "He'll take it: that you can count on." She'd left work as soon as Tom called her with the news and had arrived at the hospital in minutes.

Tom smiled briefly at her remark, knowing that was as good as done. There were plenty of reasons why Donna was such an effective and highly respected nurse. "The sedatives *might* help prevent further attacks, but until we find Kim, I'm afraid he'll still be susceptible."

A grim-faced Doctor Reynolds nodded. "I would be, too. Hopefully you'll find her soon."

"Yeah..." Tom looked at John, who was asleep in the bed. "You gave me quite a scare, Brother." He was out of his mind and nearly in a panic while he'd waited for the ambulance to get to the station and only now was he able to relax a little.

"I'll stay here with him, Honey; I know you have lots of work to do," Donna said as she gave Tom a peck on the cheek.

"That I do. I'll be back later; we'll grab something to eat then." Tom hugged her and pulled away to shake hands with Doctor Reynolds. "Thanks again, Doc. With both of you here, I know he's in good hands. Wish me luck."

*I sure could use some about now...*


Kim felt fatigue and some soreness in her shoulders as she came to and her arms still felt leaden, but she was all right. She looked up at Josh, who sat on the bed with her, then immediately turned away.

"Sit up."

She didn't respond and continued to face away from him.

"I said, sit up."

*Pick your battles, Kim,* she thought, as she decided this might not be the best time for one. She raised herself up, wincing as she did when she felt some pain, and didn't try to stop him as he

155

pulled her over toward where he was. He rubbed her shoulders and upper arms for several minutes while she sat rigidly.

"Better?"

She nodded.

He let go of her, satisfied that he'd worked out the kinks in her muscles. "I know why you did what you did."

"Of course you do. I told you why. I want you to let Jenny and the others go and I'm not going to give you what you want until you do."

"Come on- this selfless heroine act might convince the others, but it doesn't fool me."

She looked back at him. "If you really knew me and understood me, you'd know it's not an act. I saw how you looked at Jenny. I will not sit by and let you do to her what you did to me."

"What *I* did to you? I can't imagine time has dulled your memory that much. I do know you, Kim- like I told you, I know you better than you know yourself. You bared your soul to me, remember? I did nothing but pick up on a trait you have, which is the one that makes you lose control. *That's* why you tried to fight the inevitable, because naturally, you have a fear of letting go and being who you truly are. I gave you a glimpse into your true self years ago and you were afraid of what you saw- you're *still* afraid.

"Don't give me that look. You know I'm right. Think of how energetically you're resisting; you'll be every bit as full of fire when you realize you can't win. And you can't, Kim- you can't fight your nature. You love being conquered and restrained. It gets you going like nothing else. You know it, too. I've never seen such intensity as you showed me when your sexual energy is fully unleashed, which is what happens when you're bound and dominated. This fear you're feeling will add even more fuel to your fire, and just like you did before, you'll take me right up there with you.

"I always wondered why you chose the career path you did. You're an exhibitionist, Kim; you love to be noticed. Wearing the high heels, the figure-hugging suits with such short skirts- you just wanted another audience. You loved having the young boys at your school salivating over you; there's no way you can deny that.

"So, why should you worry about society's expectations of you? You are what so many women want to be- not to mention what so many men want- and people are going to tell you that's bad? What woman doesn't want to feel desirable? What man doesn't want to be with a beautiful, sexy and confident woman? They're nothing but hypocrites, and they feel the same way as everyone else. They want an audience, too; they want to make people feel guilty about anything that's risqué or adventurous or flashy, either because they deny themselves what they want and think everyone else should as well, or because they're too insecure to go for what they want.

"There's nothing wrong with what you did. You didn't disclose it on your application because you feel the same way I do about the whole thing and knew that was what would happen eventually: that you'd be flayed publicly by the so-called moral majority. And you damned well can be sure the ones who tell you you're so bad are the ones who cheat on their wives or husbands, the ones who cheat on their tax returns, the ones who frequent places like where you danced, and the ones who advance their own careers by screwing or screwing over anyone they can along the way. They do everything they preach against.

"You have no reason to feel guilty about anything you did. You're an entertainer, and you entertained better than any dancer I ever saw. You know, when we were out together, people just couldn't stop looking at you- seems like that hasn't changed at all. I felt like I was with Marilyn Monroe when she was in her prime.

"You can't help yourself; you *will* give in. You're not a counselor or a teacher, and you're definitely cut out to be a lot more than John Stratton's arm piece. You think you love him, but you don't. Deep down, you know he's not the right one for you, or he never would have let you go in the first place, like the arrogant fool he is. That self-righteousness is hereditary, I guess; he always thought he was better, but I have the upper hand now…"

Kim noted his last spiel and again saw the increased bit of irritation in his demeanor when he mentioned John's name.

*I might be able to use that against him, too…*

"As for you, passion and sexuality- not just what you feel, but what you arouse in people-, and the desire to surrender to the right man; *that's* who and what you are." He picked up the handcuffs he had with him.

She was contemplating what she might say to try and determine just how sensitive about John he was, and also wondering why he'd made that 'hereditary' remark when she heard the clinking sound she knew all too well. She quickly ascertained what was next.

Even though she saw the futility of it, she tried to get away from him, but couldn't move quickly enough. "No!!" She cried out as he pushed her onto her stomach and pulled her arms behind her. She only was able to put up a feeble resistance as he locked her wrists into the cuffs, then turned his hands loose on her again.

He stayed on top of her and leaned close to her ear. "Tell me this doesn't turn you on. You love every bit of it- every step. That's why you're such a great dancer, too; you know what you have and how to use it. You even like being punished for that, don't you?"

"Stop it- get away from me!" But even as she said that…

Much to his delight, he again found that her body was betraying her. "That's it- fight me some more. Make yourself even hotter-" He looked up and saw Lisa in the doorway with the tray of food. "You've gotten a reprieve for now; make sure you thank Lisa. We'll have plenty of opportunity to pick this up again and it won't be long before we do: count on that."

He got up and grabbed a couple straps, which he used to bind Kim's thighs and ankles. As he did that, he gave her a little barb. "It should please you to know that you've just made life less comfortable for your fellow captives. I'll take measures to make sure none of them gets the same urge to fight as you did."

Once he finished with her, he stood and moved toward the door. "Feed her, make sure she has enough to drink and let her use the bathroom if she has to- under your supervision. Otherwise, she stays tied like she is and I want you to gag her and tether her to the bed before you lock her in. That's the minimum she gets until she demonstrates that she's not going to cause any more problems. I'll see you upstairs when you're finished."

Just before walking out he added, "Tie her elbows too, if you want. Your call."


"…No, Sir. Still no tips of any kind about Rollins, either. At this point it looks like he found himself a hole and crawled in. We got the report from Jersey you've been waiting on, though. That fax just came in, too."

"The sketch? Let me see."

158

He perused it briefly and let it drop to his desk.

*I'll be damned...*


"Not a word out of you or else you get nothing. Got it?"

Kim nodded. Acute hunger took the place of her weariness as soon as she got a whiff of the food. She sat still as Lisa placed the tray in front of her.

Lisa sat next to Kim and tucked a napkin inside the loop set into the front of her collar. "You really should make it easy on yourself and just accept that you're here for good. It seems like you'll have it better than any of us, anyway- it's you he's always wanted," she said as she fed her main rival.

As she listened, Kim could detect her envy, which she plainly saw as Lisa began to look her over. *I hope I can make her an ally, but this doesn't look very promising so far...*

The more Lisa took her in, the more jealous she became. That came through loud and clear.

*I have to try to talk with her when she finishes feeding me...*

*...and I hope she finishes soon. She's really starting to look mean. I won't be surprised if she gags me before she gives me all of it, anyway...*

Kim knew she'd need every bit of energy she could get. The breakfast was very tasty, and she gulped down the juice and water.

"These are egg whites, of course. The bacon is lean, too, and the toast is low-cal wheat bread. Joshua doesn't want us taking in too much fat or carbs, not that you and the other new girl have to worry about that- especially you. He'll punish you if you gain or lose more than five pounds, so we all keep in the best shape we can. He's set the ideal weight and measurements for each of us and we have to stay within his standards. We do have a good and healthy diet- he insists on that. Vitamin supplements, filtered water- everything. We all have air purifiers and humidifiers in our rooms, too, as you might have noticed.

"He probably mentioned the exercise period to you. We all work out at least five days a week, an hour to an hour and a half each session. Normally there are two girls at a time, but you'll be the exception to that. You'll work out by yourself. Joshua and I oversee the exercise period; you alternate aerobic workouts and circuit weight training daily. At the end of each session, you'll prepare yourself to be taken back to your room.

"You do that by replacing your collar and gag, binding your thighs and locking your wrists back into the cuffs that you'll be put into just before you're brought to the gym. You'll chain your hands behind your back, of course. There will be no deviating from that. Don't even think about making *any* of your bonds loose enough so you can slip out of them; you'll be checked before you leave the room. You get your daily schedule the night before so you'll know when we'll come for you and you'll find your workout clothes in your dresser.

"Again, there is no talking- well, not that you'll need to worry about that. You're there to work out, so be sure that you do just that. Like with everything else here, you do what you're told. Follow the rules and gradually you'll get used to your new home.

"Of course, you could go the other way. One girl broke a rule one time, but she never did it again and neither did anyone else after they saw what he did to her. That strappado position you were just in while we were in the dining room? It was nothing compared to what she got. Come to think of it, I hope you do break a rule somewhere along the line so you'll find out what her punishment was. The only reason I've explained all this to you is so *I* won't get in trouble for not telling you. Believe me- I'd love to see you find out for yourself how that girl was disciplined."

Kim turned away when Lisa looked back at her while making that last statement. Pure malice flowed from her. *I guess I can't count on her for any help- at least not at this point...*

Lisa grabbed her face and forcefully turned her back again. "Don't you look away from me- that's *very* disrespectful! Joshua hates that and so do I! Remember: I get to help keep you in line. I'm gonna take great pleasure in making things hard on you even if he tries to do the opposite. For starters, as small as he thinks he can make your waist in this corset, I'm gonna make it smaller. He says seventeen inches, but I bet we could take it down to sixteen- maybe even smaller than that."

She enjoyed Kim's distressed reaction. "Even if you don't resist any more, I'll do my best to convince him to keep you tied up and gagged even after he thinks it's time to let you out of that restriction."

Lisa released her face, still getting a rise out of her wide-eyed charge. "Bathroom?" She shook her head in response and

Lisa smiled. "Well, at least you seem to understand me when I say 'no talking'." Kim didn't resist as she was gagged. "Now you don't have that option, anyway, which is just the way I like it." She set the tether and turned Kim onto her stomach, grabbing the last strap as she did.

Kim lay still, waiting for her elbows to be tied together again, but to her surprise, Lisa got off the bed and walked toward the door.

"Remember this little break I gave you- there won't be many more." She closed and locked the door behind her.

*I have to get out of here. Josh is bad enough, but she could prove to be worse...*

Throughout most of her life that was the pattern. Nearly all the guys who ever asked her out were in love with themselves or misogynists in disguise. Besides John, hardly any other decent guy ever even approached her, let alone talked with her.

That, however, was nothing compared to what she got from the other side. Other girls or women who regarded her as competition- and so many did- generally were very nasty and vindictive toward her, sometimes for no reason at all. That started as early as grade school and progressively became worse throughout high school in spite of the fact that she rarely had a single bad word to say about mostly all her classmates.

It became worse still during her college years, especially at the club. The most common affront was someone's boyfriend getting caught while leering at Kim, who would be blamed for it even though it wasn't her fault. She would get verbal stabs ranging from 'you need to wear longer skirts' to 'I wish you would move somewhere else, like the Moon' to 'I'm gonna rip that face of yours off'.

All that history served to bring a strong sense of inevitability to her present situation. Lisa, who apparently had strong feelings for Josh, had Kim- the one Josh wanted- in bondage and silenced, which was the state she had every intention of keeping her in. She also appeared to have as much access to Kim as she wanted.

*How long will it be before she wants- and tries- to do something even more drastic than what she hinted at?*

In spite of her growing sense of alarm and the fact that she was pretty far from comfortable, Kim's fatigue gradually took over.

*I might as well take a nap; there's not much else I can do right now. I'm sure not getting out of these cuffs.*

*Even if I could, what good would it do?*

As she was drifting off, she began to think of John and gradually- for the first time that day- she felt something other than a sense of peril. A very pleasant and welcome fantasy began to take her over as she imagined him bursting through the door...

"I guess I owe you an apology, Brother. Your hunch was right. He is alive and he is our man."

John stared at the sketch. "He hasn't gotten past that arrogance, either; he even showed his face." He tossed the sketch aside. "Problem now is, where do we look for him? Is he somewhere within the triangle from D.C. to Philadelphia to Princeton, or does he just come around here to take the girls? Maybe he has a place further north, west or south."

"We're talking some pretty serious logistics if that's the case, but then again, he did start out with over nine million dollars. God only knows what he did with it. He didn't have to sit on it because all of it was untraceable. The main thing we have to determine to the best of our ability is whether the women are still alive, and if so, does he have them? We know from the Missing Persons Bureaus involved, as well as from the Coroners' offices, that no bodies of any of those women have been found and identified. Based on what you know about him, do you think he has 'em somewhere?"

"You know, I think he does. He liked being in control more than anything. If I had to place my bet one way or the other, I would say yes."

"OK. I want you to think long and hard about everything you know about him- habits, places he liked, things he liked to do- everything you can possibly think of. I have to keep my own search broad and general, but you know this guy a lot better than anyone else, so you're the obvious choice for trying to get a perspective on him. Here's a notepad for you."

As he took the pad, he remembered the other document Tom brought. "What about that report you brought- the one Kim made when the guy broke into her place?"

"Oh, there wasn't much of anything in it that we could use. You can have a look at it just in case. Must've scared the hell

162

out of the poor girl. Had I known that I never would have-" He stopped immediately and looked into John's suspicious eyes.

He'd slipped, and John was right on him.

"You never would have, what?"

Tom knew there was no getting around this. He would have to come clean. He dropped heavily into the chair.

"I've already figured out that you knew Kim was a dancer before all this happened. How long have you known?"

"Since early '89. Some of the guys at the station told me about this girl they'd checked out in Philly. Donna had a girls' night out that happened to fall on the same night they decided to get together and go up there again. I was curious, so I went with 'em. We boozed it up a little when we got there and made our way to the Silver Palace. They had some eye-popping girls who came out and danced, but the guys kept saying 'yeah, they're really hot, too, but you haven't seen *her* yet!'

"Well, the announcer called her name- her stage name, Aphrodite- and there she was. I just stared at her- couldn't move a muscle. There was your first girlfriend, one of the nicest girls I ever came across, in a very skimpy outfit dancing for a crowd of rowdy strip club patrons. She was every bit as sexy and talented as the guys said she was...John, I didn't mean to-"

"Keep going."

Tom glanced at him and looked away again. "There seemed to be something wrong, though; I couldn't figure out what it was. She was out of sorts in a way, even though she was as graceful and sweet as she could be. When her act was over and she was about to go off, she caught a glimpse of me and froze. Then, she walked offstage in a rush. I wanted to leave, but the other guys were bent on staying and I didn't want to give away the fact that I knew her. I especially didn't want to let them know who she was.

"The next thing I knew, one of the bouncers tapped me on the shoulder and said she wanted to see me and asked would I come to her dressing room, which I did. When I saw the look on her face, I felt terrible for her. She couldn't say a word at first, but that look said plenty. It wasn't long before she started to cry. I went over to her and held her until she calmed down.

"We made some small talk for a while and she asked me if I could break away for a bite to eat. Fortunately I'd followed the other guys up in my car, so I begged off, met her out back and we went to her friend's apartment there."

"Vanessa's apartment..."

Tom nodded and hoped John didn't notice what was very hard for him to hide...

"That explains why you avoided her earlier. What happened next?"

He hid his relief and looked back up. "Kim and I just talked a lot while she fixed us some food and drank some wine. We talked about what had happened since the last time we'd seen each other, she asked about Donna and the kids- that sort of thing.

"Then, when she asked about you, that look came over her again. The more I told her about you, the more emotional she got. In spite of that, she still wanted to talk about you, but considering what it was doing to her, I did my best to keep that part of our conversation as brief as possible. She drank more wine after that, and then we ate. She was pretty buzzed; after we talked about you, the conversation dropped off a good bit.

"We were sitting on the couch and she started to cry again. She laid her head onto my shoulder and just cried. Kim begged me not to tell you she was a dancer. She was afraid you'd think badly of her, which was something she couldn't bear. She wanted to be with you again, but she didn't know how you would feel about that prospect. She told me how much she missed you and that she wished she could get out of the relationship she was in.

"Before you ask," he saw a very dangerous look manifesting itself on John's face, "I didn't know it was Josh- she didn't tell me his name or anything else about him. She didn't want to talk about it at all and I didn't push her.

"Eventually she settled down and went in to get herself cleaned up. When she came out of the bathroom she was pretty unsteady and leaned against the doorway. I walked over to her and reached out to try and steady her, and she stumbled and fell into me- she'd had three glasses of wine, maybe four. I picked her up and carried her toward the bedroom; she was pretty much out as I did. I laid her down onto the bed, but I didn't want to just leave her alone given her condition, so I decided I'd wait until Vanessa got back. Since it already was after two, I didn't think she'd be long. But nothing happened between Kim and me- I swear."

However, Tom remembered clearly when he went to cover Kim up, and how he reacted when she stirred a little, untied the sash holding her kimono closed and slipped out of it, then sighed and dozed off again. All she had on was a thong...

164

...and there he was, standing right over her. He shook his head in an effort to clear it of that image of her, which was burned into his memory...

"I think I understand why you didn't tell me she was a dancer; I probably would have handled it even worse then than I did when I last saw her." John looked over at him when he didn't respond, and his expression was unchanged. "What else, Tom?"

"You're not going to like the rest of it. I hated keeping all this from you, but...the missing female police officer does fit into your theory about all the other abductions happening because each girl represents an aspect of Kim's life."

"How?"

"Because Kim worked with us on the sting."

For a long and very uncomfortable moment, John said nothing. He just gaped in astonishment after Tom's admission, and Tom grew more uneasy by the second.

Then, John's face hardened and he turned away. Tom knew that look all too well and given John's condition, a heated argument would not be a good thing at that moment. "I'm sorry, John. I'm not going to try to justify keeping all that from you. I was wrong and I hope you'll forgive me.

"I'm going to leave you alone for now, OK?" Tom didn't expect a response and he didn't get one. "Get some rest, Brother. We'll be back tomorrow."

# Chapter 7

"It hasn't been three weeks yet. Do you really think she's that close?"

"I do; it's time. Besides, you said yourself that she seems to be more compliant than she was at first. I guarantee you what I just told you is a big part of the reason."

"It *seems* like she is, but...I don't know. Don't you think you might be pushing it a little? You held off with all the others and just waited until you were sure."

He tried to hide his irritation with Lisa. She'd never questioned him before and she picked a very bad time to start.

All had gone smoothly- no slip-ups, no escape attempts, nothing out of the ordinary. Jennifer was easy to control, just like he thought she'd be, especially since she'd had no further contact with Kim. They had no trouble with her after that first day and Lisa agreed with his assessment that she quickly was becoming the most docile captive of all.

However, on this morning of the eighteenth day after they'd taken Kim, his main quarry suddenly became the source of their first difference of opinion after he told Lisa about his intention to take the next step toward totally breaking Kim.

Admittedly, it *was* sooner in the process than it had been with the others, but why should it matter to Lisa?

*Why should it matter at all?*

Josh began to wonder if Lisa was going to become a problem. *I hope not, but if she does, I'll deal with her.*

*Before I get ahead of myself, I'll feel her out.* "Look, you don't know Kim like I do. You don't know her nature. For one thing, she can't stand to be alone- to not have contact with anyone. When she comes to terms with the fact that the only people she'll ever have contact with again are you and me, she'll become even more compliant. But more to the point, you know why she's trying so much harder over the past couple days to free herself, right? You see the desperation in her body language and in her eyes; she needs exactly what I'm going to give her. She doesn't just want it-she *needs* it. She *craves* it. She knows it, too, which is why she tried so hard to fight it off, but she can't. If you saw her on the patio this morning...you wash her every day- you know what I'm talking about. Can't you see that in the way she responds when you touch her? Can't you feel it just by being next to her?"

"Well...she *does* seem jumpy and-"

With a derisive chortle he turned away, then back to her. "Jumpy?! Is that what you call it?! She can't stay still, can she?"

"No."

"And she blushes, too, right?"

"Yeah, but I think that's more because she's uncomfortable with me giving her a-"

"Uncomfortable, my ass! Don't you see you've just proven my point? When I had her before, just to see what it would do to her, I made her go without it for three days. It was just as hard for me to keep it from her, but I did that because I wanted to see the effect. I kept her tied in a way that she couldn't help herself out, either, like the way we keep her now. I was giving her a strong aphrodisiac by keeping her like that and there was nothing she could do for release. By the time I gave it to her, she was ready to pull the bed apart. That's the main reason why I agreed with you that we should keep her tied up like we do. That just stokes her even more."

When he saw Lisa's unchanged expression, he lost his temper. "All right, what in the fuck is going on with you?! Do you have some kind of ulterior motive here?! You never had a problem with me having sex with any of the others, but all of a sudden you're balking at me going after Kim? Are you jealous of her...or do you want her for yourself? Is that it?"

Her mouth fell open and for a moment she couldn't respond.

"Answer me!!"

"Fine!! She's all you talk about and all you think about; you've hardly paid any attention to me! It never was like this with any of the others, so yes, I *am* jealous of her! Are you satisfied?!" When she saw his face reddening she backed off and used a different approach she hoped would be effective. "You just don't see what she's doing to you, do you? You're letting her get to you too much and you're becoming impatient. She'll break- they *always* break- but you know it doesn't happen right away. Who knows, with her it could end up taking longer, especially if she sees like I do how anxious you are to make it happen. The worst part is, she's under your skin and she's not even trying to be. If you keep going like this, she will bring you down without lifting a finger- that you can count on.

"You said it yourself, Joshua: the more you try to force something to happen, the more possible it becomes that whatever it is *won't* happen. That's especially true when a woman you try to force submission on doesn't want it."

"But she *does* want it! That's what I'm trying to tell you!"

"Even if that's true, it'll only happen when she accepts that there's nothing she can do to prevent it. We just have to outlast her; time is our ally- not hers. You've told me that before when we've had trouble with some the others. We're in control; *you're* in control. Don't forget that. More importantly, don't let *her* forget it." He backed off from his attack, which primarily was what she wanted.

As soon as he turned away, she shuddered. *That was close...*

*...and I have a feeling this isn't the end of it.*

*He could get worse...*

Her feeling of foreboding had started a couple weeks ago, the second he thought he had even the slightest chance of taking Kimberly Francis. Her wariness rose right alongside his eagerness.

Now, for the first time in ten years, she realized that he wasn't the one who was driving the train.

Kim was.

That was a fact he probably never would admit, even if he did come to realize it, which he probably wouldn't.

*I can definitely see* why *she's in control,* Lisa ruminated as Kim began to take over her thoughts again, too, before she caught herself and came back to the matter at hand.

What if she didn't break after all? What if the one he wanted above all others would not be his? How much worse would he get until he finally erupted?

*I'll see what he does over the next couple days- give him a chance to prove me wrong. Maybe I'm off base with this...*

*...but if I'm not, it might be time to start thinking about a way out of here...*

*...possibly with a very special- and disruptive- guest.*

* * *

Kim sat on the bed and waited for her to come back.

Her routine had become fairly regular during the time she'd spent in captivity. At every opportunity she'd looked for any possible way to escape, but so far she'd come up empty. As she suspected he would be, Josh had been very thorough when he assembled his elaborate and rather posh prison. He was equally as thorough in the way he and Lisa ran it; she had yet to find any flaws she could exploit.

The only positive had come with her period three days after her abduction. A pregnancy now would have proven a complication in more ways than one, especially given how much Josh hated John...

The sequence of events was the same every day. Around the same time each morning, Josh or Lisa would come in and untie her, then wait as she took care of business in the bathroom. Breakfast followed soon after that, then back to her room to await her turn to go outside for a bit. She would be blindfolded and led or carried to a patio where she was allowed to stay for twenty minutes. She was heavily bound, of course- even more so than normal-, kept in her usual attire and under guard. Soon after that would be lunch. Once that was finished, she would be taken back to her room where she would await her exercise period, which always went according to the way Lisa told her it would. Then it was bath, dinner, and bedtime.

Kim still felt the all-too-real fear about what lay ahead for her and Jennifer, but the stale and repetitive routine was evoking other feelings in her that were proving to be very distracting from matters that were much more important.

She was bored and lonely.

And extremely frustrated.

Her thoughts of John eased her in one way, but made things worse in another. She would think back to the times they were together, remembering things he said to her, things they did and what she hoped he would ask her if she could find a way out of the mess she was in. More than anything, she would ponder how she felt with John and long to experience that once more, which would lead to the inevitable. The itch she couldn't scratch would come back again...

...and again...

...and again. Each time it seemed to grow worse. A big contributor was something that fanned the flame even more when

169

it started inside her- her perpetual state of bondage, like she presently was in. They'd just finished preparing her for her workout, and the shackles, strap, collar and gag were all in place and tight enough to serve their collective purpose. This was rather tame in comparison to how they tied her up when preparing her for bed, which took its toll on her in more ways than one.

Inevitably, she would think of John, which under the circumstances would contribute further to her stress level. Josh was doing his best to push her to the breaking point, and denying her any form of release was contributing a lot to that end. The sex toy he left every night for her was yet another way for him to demean her and simultaneously tear at her even more. He purposefully left it in plain sight, but always out of reach. As John's image would come to her she'd struggle for all she was worth to get to the toy, yearning for that sort of release at least, but she'd fail every time, which made her plight even worse. She only could concentrate on finding a way to escape for so long. The more she came back to the fact that so far there simply *was* no escape, the more of a toll it took on her...

...and the more she would perpetuate that horrible circle and think about John. She squirmed as his image came to her yet again along with her desire for him to-

*Dammit, STOP!!* In desperation she thought of anything and everything repulsive enough to reverse her course. Replacing John's image with that of Josh served that purpose pretty well.

She hated what she'd had to do on the patio that morning by playing along with him and trying to convince him that she was turned on by his most unwelcome advances. What choice did she have? If he found out there was no way she would be his ever again, his wrath could push *him* over the edge. The thought of what he probably would do to her became more frightening with each passing day. She was running out of time and as of yet there was no way out...

Kim tore herself away from that emotional black hole. She still wasn't happy about the outfit she had to wear for exercise. It consisted of a white thong and sports bra set made of lycra-spandex that barely was decent, let alone functional, along with a pair of highly reflective tan tights made of the same material. Josh and Lisa salivated over her every time they watched her work out.

One positive that had happened was Lisa lightening up a little on her. Despite how she carried through on her vow of

170

ensuring that Kim's hands always were bound behind her and she always was gagged- not that Josh was in any way against the idea- , she seemed a little less hateful and jealous than she was in the beginning. At least, she wasn't that way outwardly. Kim figured the obedience and submission she'd demonstrated since the first day played a part there.

But she knew that wasn't the only reason- no doubt she'd get another reminder of Lisa's change in attitude when it came time for her bath after she finished working out. She wasn't even allowed to bathe alone; Lisa had washed her ever since the first day.

*Maybe they'll reach the point where at least they don't keep me gagged all the time. Having my hands free for longer increments would help, too, but I'm sure that won't happen soon, unless Lisa lightens up even more on me. I hope I can persuade her...*

She turned as Lisa walked in and stood when she was ordered to. As usual, Lisa double-checked the fetters to make sure they were tight enough. Once she was satisfied, she clipped the leash onto the front ring of Kim's collar, but they didn't leave right away. Kim wondered about the expression on her face.

"As much as I look forward to bathing you," Lisa said as she ran her hands over Kim's waist and hips, and looked her up and down, "there's a good chance I won't be doing that tonight."

Kim waited for her to expand on that, but she didn't. As much as she wished that meant she'd be allowed to bathe by herself again, which would be a most welcome change- and not just for the obvious reasons-, she dismissed that notion almost right away. That was something she hadn't done since the first morning when Josh had allowed her that luxury, and it didn't make any sense that he would make such a concession to her, especially since there was no reason for him to do that. Surely he knew he had the upper hand in every way, and not allowing her even the slightest bit of freedom was part of his campaign to defeat her.

Right on the heels of that came a strong feeling of dread. *What if that means* he's *going to bathe me...*

*...or worse?* Just the thought made her shudder.

The look in Lisa's eyes made that premonition grew stronger.

* * *

When she saw Kim's distress, Lisa felt a stirring of sympathy for her and even an urge to protect her. In spite of all Joshua told her, and what she saw before, Kim seemed so meek.

*Could it be that he's making some of that up, and that I'm wrong about her, too?*

There it was: the shadow of a doubt again.

*She really hasn't resisted us much at all. Maybe I did blow that little flare-up she had on the first day out of proportion...*

"Hey, don't-...look, I- I can't tell you anything right now other than you'll be OK. He won't hurt you."

She'd blurted that out before she even knew what she was doing. With the other women she never had such a thought. Even if she did, she certainly wouldn't have voiced it.

*I need to take a step back here. I can't let her get to me too much because Joshua still could be right. I just wish he would think about me even half as much as he thinks about her...*

She shook it all off for the time being and refocused. "Let's get you to the gym."


Kim was brimming with turmoil as Lisa led her by the leash.

*What just happened? Is she thinking about helping me?*

She thought more about Lisa's new- and more welcome- attitude toward her. As hard as being washed by Lisa had been for Kim to take in the early stage, lately it didn't seem so bad, all things considered. On occasion she even let her guard down and divulged a few things in addition to being relatively civil...

...and gentle- more so each time. Kim found herself doing all she could to be as cooperative as she could with Lisa, who in turn seemed to be rewarding her.

*Maybe it's true; maybe she does want to help me...*

However, when they reached the gym and Kim saw Josh, her dread quickly returned.


Tom watched him as he stared blankly out the window.

John hadn't had any more episodes like the one he'd had in the office, but as he continued to sit there, more distant and

172

expressionless with each passing day, Tom began to think another fit of rage might help him. He was working out, but he wasn't eating right, wasn't sleeping much and wasn't talking much.

Simply put, he was shutting down. Again.

John still hadn't forgiven him for keeping Kim's role in the sting from him, either. Tom knew if the tension between the two of them got much worse, it could become a distraction to his investigation and he might be forced to cut John out.

*I hope it doesn't come to that...*

Other than those they'd gathered over the first two days, no more leads had come up. Even the ones they had had led to nothing. The coroner in Louisiana who'd filed the death certificate on Josh had been shot and killed the following year. The still-open case file the police there had on that murder provided nothing but more questions and speculation. He, John and the other investigators involved had poured over those reports and the one from New Jersey regarding Kim's near-abduction. Each time they came up empty.

Acting on John's suggestion that Josh could be keeping all of them somewhere- a notion a few of the investigators believed possible- they'd even begun to run checks on the owners of houses that might be big enough to securely imprison a dozen women. The problem: there were so many that could be used to serve that purpose in the very large, multi-state area they had to search.

His trail, what little there was of it, was stone cold now. As with all his other victims, neither Kim's body nor Jennifer's was recovered, no ransom demands were made for either of them- nothing. Josh had taken them and disappeared just as quickly.

Without his heart, a man cannot survive. So far, John had gone eighteen days without his and although Tom knew he would never stop searching for her, his health was deteriorating along with his spirits. He also had ordered every single file there was about Josh- from his childhood on-, which were to be delivered soon.

Hope was all that kept him going. Tom prayed he wouldn't lose that as he went back to his notes and files and waited for the phone to ring...

...he also didn't let on that his own hopes were fading.

\* \* \*

173

As Kim worked out on the climber, she grew more leery by the second under his watchful eye. The look on his face seemed even more sinister and lascivious than usual, if that was possible.

Lisa's reassurance rang very hollow now that she saw clearly what was coming.

He'd already escalated the situation with what he did on the patio. He would keep pushing; it was inevitable what the end result would be, and from all indications, that result was imminent.

She shivered involuntarily. Try as she did, she couldn't get that thought out of her head. Stepping up her pace on the machine didn't help, either- even vigorous exercise wasn't nearly enough of a distraction. She saw the whole thing unfolding.

It started with the image of her in the tub...

...gagged, hands fastened behind her...

...not a stitch of clothing on...

...and Josh reaching in-

*No, he will* not*!!*

Just like that it hit her.

It started out as an impulse, but quickly began to mushroom into a plan, albeit an impromptu and very hasty one.

*The only time I'm free is when I'm here. As far as I can tell, this also is the only time I'll have even the slightest chance...*

*...and I'll be* damned *if I'm going to just let that bastard bathe me, or do anything else to me! Even though he has the obvious physical advantage, I have to do something. I'm not too shabby as a kickboxer; I might land a kick in the right place on Josh and be able to make a break for it. I'm not the best runner, but under the circumstances I'll be good enough. I just need to find a way out. God knows this outfit won't hinder me...*

*...or, if Lisa does prove to be an ally, maybe she'll come to my aid and-...wait a minute- when she told me he wouldn't hurt me, is that what she was getting at?*

*Could it be that she's had enough of this situation, too?*

Kim became aware that she'd stopped exercising. When she looked around and saw Josh coming toward her, she jumped off the machine and squared around to face him. Her heart was thumping, and not just from the forty-five minute workout she'd put in...

* * *

174

He didn't know what to make of it when she slowed down, then stopped working out and just stared ahead for a moment. She didn't appear to be hurt or tired, so he went over to her to find out what was going through her mind.

She ended his speculation when she assumed her attack posture. He shook his head, and his smile belied his annoyance with her. *This is getting old. I don't give a damn what Lisa says, I know you're just about ready. You were a hair away on the patio.*

*Time to give you another push.* "Come on, now- you know this is pointless. Give it up and I'll go easy on you, but I warn you- this is *the last time* I'll go easy on you."

She didn't waver, even with his threat. "Why are you being so God-damned hard headed?! Can't you see that it's not me you're fighting?!" he admonished as he started to close in on her. "You're fighting yourself and what you really want."

His anger was apparent to her; she clearly saw and felt it. *Could it be that I'm getting to him, too? Is he starting to wear down?* She sensed that he was struggling to maintain control of himself, which was new. When she'd set him back with her outburst at that first breakfast, she thought his shocked reaction was a one-time occurrence, given his calm state in the period following that incident as well as her first round as his captive.

*Things were different in '89- very different. He never knew I wanted to escape until I was gone. Then again, I wasn't so sure at times that I did want to escape. As for now, I just might have found another way. I need an opening...*

"I had you figured out a long time ago. Everything you did- the dancing, the cheerleading, the bikini contests then and now, all of it- was to make up for what you didn't get as a child. Girls like you need to be loved- or at least to feel loved- and you didn't get that. So you determined to make up for it as best you could through all you did, only it wasn't enough, was it? Nothing you did filled that hole and nothing ever will."

She gave some ground as he moved in, but although he saw how wounded she was by what he said, she remained resolute. "Still playing tough, are you? It doesn't matter. I have all the time and patience in the world. It will be my greatest pleasure when you finally accept the fact that I'm right. You need to be touched, caressed, fondled and stroked- all of which you haven't had for some time. That really has gotten to you, hasn't it? Kitten is a *pretty* good pet name for you, but I have a better one. It's

175

something like Kitten." He smiled at her reaction to that. *Good, now I'm making you angry*...

"So he makes you purr, does he? I remember how you were, too. When you come to realize that I'm the only man who will ever touch you again, you'll be grateful for everything I give you. You can't stand to be neglected. You need affection and lots of attention. I'll give you as much of both as I want to give you and you'll thank me for that. I know everything about what you like and you'll get as much pleasure as I think you need. Better yet, I'll make you beg for it. You will, too, just like you begged me this morning, and also after I held it back from you for three of the days when I had you in '89.

"You begged Stratton back then, too. I saw how you were with him at that party."

He couldn't prevent his smile from fading, nor could he stop himself from continuing. Without thinking, he went right to the heart of it all. He wanted to hurt her- to break her down verbally and make her feel guilty again just like she did before. He also wanted to reinforce to her that she never again would have the opportunity to do to him what she did that night.

"I saw it all. You begged and pleaded with him like the hot little bitch you are- just like a little whore- and that made you even hotter. You're fighting harder and for longer than any of the others, but I expected that. When you do surrender to me, you'll be my most obedient slave. There's no halfway with you- just one of the many assets you have."

Kim stopped listening after his description of when she and John were together in the bedroom of the Memorial Day party's host. "Wait a minute- you *saw* it?! You mean to tell me you *spied* on us?! You told me you heard it from my friend when you saw everything for yourself; the whole time you *knew*?! And you had the gall to use that against me so out of guilt I would let my guard down and ride with you to your place?! You-...oh, my God...

At that moment she saw it. "You had it all planned out, didn't you? It was a test, putting John and me together. You knew I wanted to break up with you and that I felt badly about it in spite of all you did. Then, you sprang your trap on me and kept me from seeing John, knowing how much I wanted to get back together with him and knowing you would sabotage *everything*!! You filthy, deceitful-..."

176

Just as Kim was about to rip into him and vent all her anger, for all the good that would do, she held off, especially when she saw him smiling again.

*That's just what he wants- he wants to take me back to how confused and miserable I was then. I think he really believes that's who and what I still am...*

*...he also wants me to rush him so he can defeat me easily.*

However, picking up on a vibe from his assault on her along with what she gleaned from him previously, she saw her chance to turn the tables and abruptly changed gears. "Well, that explains everything. Even then you knew you paled in comparison to John, didn't you? And let me tell you- you still do. In fact, you compare a lot more to the last worm that kidnapped me, who, by the way, also needed someone else to help him take me.

"You knew that I wanted to be with John again, and that the only way I'd stay with you was if you kept me tied up and locked away, just like now." She laughed at him and with that she already saw her counterattack taking effect. He wasn't smiling anymore. "You know, you really are like Wally Daniels- a *lot* like him. You have no idea how absolutely impotent and repulsive you are, do you?

"John outshines you by far in every way, especially sex, and yes, I *did* like it when he pinned me down. In fact, I *loved* it- all of it! You probably watched when John came after me in the pool, didn't you? I'm sure you must have seen how hot it made me when he caught me!"

"Enough, Kim. I don't want to hear you talking like that and I don't want to hear-"

"Are you kidding?! Talking like what- like a stripper, maybe? Who do you think *you're* talking to?! Besides, I'm just getting started!" She took notice that every time she mentioned John's name, it was like she slapped Josh right across his face, which wasn't the least bit smug now. *What's with that last comment, anyway?*

"I wanted John to catch me because I knew what a guy does to a girl when he captures her in that game- and did he ever live up to that! His hands were *all over* my body- I mean, *everywhere*! Playing with my boobs, grabbing my ass, groping my thighs and reaching between them..." In light of her sexually frustrated state, the memory of what happened that fateful evening sent tremors through her...

177

Judging from the increasing anger he couldn't hide, she could tell that he saw her excitement, which made her press on with her attack. "*God*, how he turned me on! He was *so* strong and he had me completely under his power. I was wet in more ways than one and glad I was wearing the skimpiest bikini I had. I wanted him to rip my top off and squeeze my tits for all he was worth- I didn't care *who* was watching! Now that you've shared with me the fact that you were there, I'm especially glad you saw all that, too, Josh."

She was almost gleeful as she rubbed his face in it, feeding off his near-fury and looking for the exact moment to strike...

...on the other hand, she was starting to enjoy some long-overdue emotional payback...

"I'm warning you: knock it-"

"I was right on the brink of begging John to grab that teeny little thong, yank it off me and fuck me right in front of all your cronies- just like the hot little bitch I am, right Josh?!" He reacted to that like she'd stabbed him in the heart. "And after he took me up to the bedroom, he did just that! We went at it until we barely could breathe! I'm glad John did pin me down; if he hadn't, as hot as I was for him I probably would have torn his back to shreds with my fingernails!

"Of course, having a *real* man- the only one I ever wanted to be with- restrain me like he did sent me into orbit! You thought I was wet when you put that dildo into me? That was *nothing*! John made me flow like a river that night, and every time I came, it was so intense I felt like I would pass out! John and I together are like a nuclear explosion, and you-" she snorted, "you're nothing but a dud."

Kim was starting to enjoy this. A lot.

"Oh, I know what you're thinking," she quickly preempted him. Everything she said about when she and John were together was true. This part would be stretching the truth, but she had him down and she couldn't help going for the kill. "Yes, I did hit it pretty hard when you had me tied up, but you know why I did, Josh?"

He bared his teeth. "No- don't you dare-"

"Of course you know why; you saw John and me in that bedroom. It was because I imagined you were John. Come on, you know it's true! You saw for yourself the effect he has on me.

"You pale in comparison to him in every way. I guess it only stands to reason why John's so much better than you are at debating, too, doesn't it? I never told you this before, but... remember when you mentioned to me that you were preparing for your big debate? The one at the end of your last semester- shortly before graduation?"

She giggled again. She didn't mean to that time, but she couldn't hold it back. "You never told me you went to the University of Maryland and it wasn't long before I realized why. Out of curiosity I decided to go down there when I found out John would be in a debating forum at College Park, which happened to fall on the same night as the one you said you had. Sure enough, when it came time for the one-on-one, there you both were. Did he *ever* make you look silly! I especially loved the set of your face; you *knew* John had made a complete ass out of you and that there was nothing you could do about-"

She saw stars as he slapped her hard across her face, knocking her to the floor. She tasted a bit of blood and the stinging came quickly.

Right away he was on top of her and he had her hands bound behind her before she could recover.

She whimpered as the pain set in and realized she'd overplayed her hand. *Dammit- I had my chance and I blew it. This might have been my only opportunity to do something...*

She looked over at Lisa, who made no move toward them. She was in no position to, anyway, with Josh facing her. Her blank expression made her state of mind impossible to determine.

*I hope she's just waiting for a better opening...*

One positive that came from the confrontation was that she'd beaten him at his own game. Although she didn't know what the repercussions would be, she seized upon that positive in spite of her smarting cheek.

Amid her tears she tried a different tactic, hoping to get her point across before he gagged her again.

"Don't you realize how ridiculous this whole situation is? You've centered it all around a woman who can't stand the sight of you, while one who does care a lot about you is right under your nose- *unh!*" He responded by binding her elbows together and cinching the strap extra tight.

"Of course you can't see the way things are- you never could. You think something will happen just because you want it

179

to, but it doesn't work that way. You will not break me- ever. In spite of what you believe, I'm *not* the same as I was before- even then you misjudged me." Not swayed in the least, he moved down to her legs.

"Hasn't this all become boring? Think about it. You're a prisoner, too, because you have to stay here- day in and day out- and keep tabs on all of us." She gritted her teeth as he bound her thighs and moved down to her ankles. "Why won't you answer me?! Is this really the way you want to spend the rest of your life- just hiding from everything and everyone?! Dammit, talk to me!!"

Still unresponsive, he finished binding her ankles and Kim began to fight as he reached for the dreaded ball gag. She tried to wrench herself away from him, but he held her firm. "Stop this, Josh- *please* let us go!" He grabbed a handful of her hair and pulled her head up. She knew all too well what was next- he put the ball up to her lips. "No- mmmph!!" As always, he made quick work of it.

He rolled her onto her back and she looked up at him. Even though the rest of his face had the mask of calm, she still could see the barely contained rage in his eyes. Seeing him that way and being helplessly bound once more, her fear came rushing back in. It was worse than before and she fought against the straps as the prospect of his retaliation loomed over her along with Josh himself.

"That's more like it. That's what I want to see from you." He leaned in close to her and she turned away, but he took a painful hold of her face and made her look at him. "*You* look *at me!! Don't* ever *turn away from me again!!*"

Kim remembered Lisa telling her how he hated that and she began to tremble.

"You think you know everything about that self-righteous asshole, don't you?!! Huh?!! If you think what I've done to you is bad, you should have seen what I did to-..." He cut himself off.

As gratifying as it would be to tell her everything- to reveal all of the past to her-, something made him hold back.

*Maybe now isn't the time…*

*…but one of these days will be.*

For the moment he refocused on her and what she'd done, and his anger came rushing back in.

"You had your time to talk, which is the last time you'll ever have for that!! I never want to hear another *fucking* word out of your mouth, so forget about any thought of us going easy on you and taking your gag out for anything other than necessity! What's even better is I have more effective gags than this one- *much* more effective, and probably very uncomfortable at that."

He saw from her expression that the curiosity he'd raised in her was gone- her fear and desperation had returned, and he wanted to do whatever he could to make those emotions even stronger.

"You know what? None of what you said to me matters. I have you. You are *never* leaving here. What you want, how you feel- none of that makes a difference to me and in time, it won't make a difference to you. You'll get it through your head that you live to please me: *that's* your only purpose.

"Tonight, you're gonna do exactly that- the way I want you to and as many times as I want you to."

The gag stifled Kim's efforts to plead with him, and worse, her efforts charged him up even more, as they always did.

She could only writhe futilely as his hands quickly were all over her mouthwatering physique. As firm and tight as her body was, it also was so soft to the touch, and so much of it was on display, courtesy of her scanty workout attire. "I'll tell you again- from now on, *I'm* the only man who ever will touch you. I don't care that you don't want me- I want you, which is more than enough. This beautiful body belongs to me. That's right: go on and beg, and struggle. You know how I love it when you do that."

That statement went through her haze of dread. She was surprised at how quickly what he uttered snapped her out of it. She actually became angry with herself for giving him any sort of pleasure and lay still, denying him what he wanted to see. *I'm not going to let you drag me down again while you get your rocks off.*

*Contrary to your delusion, I will get out of here...*

*...I just have to figure out another way. With any luck I'll have some help.*

He stopped toying with her when she stopped responding to him. "The tough girl act again, huh? It doesn't fool me for a minute. We'll see how long it lasts when I have you tied spread-eagle to my bed, just like before...

"...and I keep you there for a week, just like before...

"...while you entertain me, just like before."

She didn't even flinch while she returned his stare. He did see emotion in her eyes, but it was the sort of disgust one has for a cockroach. No longer did she look rattled and his anger began to rise again. "Fine- keep it up, then. Like I said, it doesn't matter." He picked her up. "For now, I'm gonna do the next best thing. *I'll give you your bath, which I'll be doing from this day on.*"

As much as that prospect made her skin crawl, she did her best to keep her cool.

However, she knew this had all the makings of a long night...


Even though he wasn't in prison, Dean began to feel as though he was. It was like he'd escaped from one only to land in another.

He'd just returned from a local deli that Strauss always had been crazy about. He'd taken a huge risk simply by going out at all, let alone to a public place. He was grasping at straws. Even as he sat at his table, looking warily for any stray policeman who wanted to be the one to haul him in or plant him, he knew Strauss wouldn't come. It was a monumentally stupid thing to do, which he also knew.

But he couldn't just do nothing, even though he had nothing to go on. He couldn't keep sitting in her house, waiting. If she kept checking up on his hunches, eventually she would call suspicion to herself and possibly lead the authorities back to her place, which was his only safe haven. He couldn't keep going like he was and putting her at risk as well.

Something had to give, and very soon...


Kim tried her best not to think about it.

The bath was every bit as nauseating as she thought it would be. At first there was no escape from it- neither physically nor mentally- and she couldn't hide her renewed revulsion from him. That only made him keep her in the tub for longer than a normal bath would take, and he paid plenty of attention to certain parts of her body.

Gradually, though, she was able to employ a weapon on him that seemed to be working quite well. No doubt she'd planted the seed earlier when she told him how she pictured John doing the things to her that he was doing. As difficult as it was for her block Josh out during the bath, fortunately she was able to do it because recently John had bathed her- numerous times. He'd even shaved her legs for her, which had pleased her to no end. Coincidentally, that was what Josh was doing at the moment.

She looked up at him, more tranquil because of her daydream. She even managed a deep sigh as she recalled the total pleasure of John doing all those things to her.

She also saw that her weapon was taking the desired effect on Josh. "You're doing it again, aren't you?!" He charged as he lost his temper yet again.

*It's working! He can't even look at me!*

In a fit of fury, he let go. "You wouldn't think he was such a he-man if you saw what he did way back when he was sev-"

He realized what he was saying and cut himself off just in time. *You little bitch...you almost did it to me- again!*

*You will know about that soon, though. Nothing would please me more than to take him down a few notches in your eyes, especially since you think I'm blowing smoke.* She rolled her eyes at him and turned away in reaction to what he almost let out.

*Come to think of it, given what I have planned in just an hour or so, that might be the perfect time...*

A way to keep her in line at that moment also came to him. He leaned in close and added, "we'll see if you feel so smug when I do the same thing to Jennifer later tonight that I'm gonna do to you." He left her and had Lisa come in to finish with her.

As sweet as her second victory in so short a time had felt, it quickly was gone. What she feared most was going to happen, and at the moment there was nothing she could do to stop it. The violent flare-up he had that resulted in him slapping her was just a precursor for something much worse, and not only for her.

Again, Lisa responded to her look of panic. "Just take it easy. I don't think he'll do anything more than tie Jennifer up and frighten her- not tonight, anyway. You know as well as I do that you're still the one he wants, which he'll be showing you in a little while..."

She turned away, missing the look on Lisa's face that showed her feelings about the last thing she said. Kim wasn't the least bit pacified while Lisa finished shaving her legs, then rinsed her off. In spite of her words, he certainly seemed serious and Kim still worried about Jenny. Her sense of worry became more acute because she had no doubt she would be tied up or chained in the most severe way possible, and able to do nothing to help Jenny.

*Of course, I'll be locked up, too, so it probably doesn't make a difference, anyway...*

*...there's only one thing I can do, which in all probability is a temporary appeasement...*

The mere thought made her want to throw up; she tried not to think about it. She would delay the inevitable for as long as she could, which wouldn't be for much longer.

After Lisa dried her, removed her gag and untied her hands, Kim applied the little bit of makeup she usually wore, then slipped into the silk undergarments that were laid out for her and sat in her chair. She contemplated Lisa, who stood beside her.

Kim wondered again whether or not she would help.

She also noticed that the door was open. Josh had gone upstairs several minutes earlier- did he leave that door open as well? Could she knock Lisa out and make a break for it? Even if the door was locked, maybe Lisa had the key...

*...I know I could take her down, then maybe get out of here and run as fast as I could. I just might make it far enough away to get help...*

*...or I could open the doors to the other girls' rooms and we all could rush him...*

*...but if they didn't do anything, which also is quite possible, that might make him kill me- or worse, kill Jenny.*

*Plus, he could be watching now, especially given what I did earlier in the gym room. If he saw me making a break for it...*Kim shuddered at the thought of his retaliation as she sat down. It just was too risky...

*...but there still is the possibility that Lisa could come over to our side...*

Kim glanced up and noticed that she looked quite edgy.

*I have to try...*

"Lisa? I know I'm not supposed to talk, but I-...please help me. Help us get out of here." Kim shrank back from her and held up her hands in supplication, trying to head off a very possible reprisal from a shocked Lisa. "Please..."

After a moment, Lisa spoke up. "What in the hell were you trying to do?! You're lucky he didn't *kill* you in the gym room, and if he sees us-" Lisa took a breath. "I'll give you this much: you do have guts. I never thought...well, after all he told me about you and all I've seen, I never figured you'd blow up at him like you did...

"Look, he's already killed someone. He said he didn't want to, but he had to. No, not one of us," she said immediately as Kim's eyes widened. "It was somebody outside here, but if you make him angry enough, there's no telling what he'll do- and I'm not just talking about what he might do to you. He could take it out on all of us, so for your own sake and ours, just play along tonight. I couldn't stop him earlier, but...maybe later..."

*Who am I kidding? It's you he wants, damn you! As much as I wish he'd do to me what he'll do to you...*

*...I would do or give anything for him to feel that way about me again...*

When she saw Lisa's anger, Kim's hope strengthened.

Lisa held up her hand and preempted Kim from speaking. "No- you don't talk anymore. You're ready now, so go on and put that gag in that he left for you."

*I'd better do what she says. I guess he could be watching, which might explain why she has to be tough now...*

"Come on, Kim, hurry up. It's time to get you dressed."

Kim nodded and smiled at her, then gagged herself with- as Josh promised- the most stifling one yet and put her collar back on. Still, she was encouraged.

*Lisa even called me by name- that's a first!*

Even with the surge of jealousy she'd just had, for a moment Lisa stared at the stunning beauty. Kim sat calmly, looking up at her and waiting, wearing only her elegant but racy black thong and bra, both of which would be cut off her later that night. Lisa handed her the long gloves and silk stockings. She watched as Kim rolled one of the stockings up, stepped into it and carefully drew it up her leg, then repeated the process with the other one. Lisa tried not to give away her grudging appreciation of Kim's gorgeous legs as she did.

After donning her gloves, Kim stepped into her pumps and extended her hands toward Lisa in a silent request for help. Lisa felt a strong current- one she tried to ignore- as she took Kim's hands into hers, helped her up and led her over to the middle of the room. Kim didn't resist as her wrists were locked into the shackles overhead.

*I don't know if you're trying to get to me, or if what Joshua says about you is right and it just comes naturally for you,* Lisa thought as she double-checked to make sure the manacles would hold Kim in place. The whole time, she felt the effect of

Kim's gaze as it was fixed on her. More than once, she couldn't stop herself from glancing into those eyes.

*You sure could be trying to influence me, couldn't you? Using your charms to persuade me to help you- maybe even let you go so you can turn both of us in. Joshua warned me about how smart you are and how distracting you can be...*

Lisa had to make a conscious effort to pull herself away and get Kim's corset. She purposely focused on the garment as she put it on Kim and fastened the closures on the front of it, but she looked up again as she addressed the sensuous captive. "You know I have to make this tighter than before," she said. Kim nodded as her eyes continued to hold Lisa's.

She had to force herself to look away and go around behind Kim to finish her task. Keeping herself from staring at Kim's body was every bit as difficult as avoiding her gaze, which began to make Lisa angry. *If you are trying to use me, you little hussy, by the time I'm done making you regret that, you'll be-*

"Mmmm!!"

Kim's outcry made her realize she'd been tugging pretty hard on the corset laces- more so than she needed to.

"OK, I'm sorry. Take it easy." She was considerably gentler as she finished the lacing. She tied the excess off, having drawn both edges of the garment together, closing it fully. That meant she'd squeezed the captive's waist down to an amazing seventeen inches! It wasn't even twenty-two inches to begin with, and now it was half the dimension of her bustline, not to mention a shade under half that of her hips!

In spite of how envious she was of Kim and how angry she was at the woman for causing so much turbulence, Lisa couldn't help but worry about her a little as she walked around and faced her again.

*This has to be hurting her...* "Are you all right?"

"Mm-hmm."

It was all she could do to stop herself from taking advantage of Kim's helplessness and submissiveness, which Lisa thought about doing more than once as she turned her focus back to those fabulous legs. She slid her hands up them as slowly as she could, one at a time, savoring the feel of them as she took the slack out Kim's stockings. Joshua didn't like to see any creases.

While she performed that very engrossing task, Lisa drifted back to her notion of possibly trying to get away from

Joshua if things got out of hand and she had to take an extreme measure. She mused even more about the notion of taking Kim with her.

A possible way began to form: if she were to tip off the police somehow and they were to come here and find all the women except Kim and herself, it could be deduced that Joshua killed and disposed of both of them.

*That could work. I'd never have thought about taking another woman with me, but you sure are far from an ordinary woman. You could fill the gap very nicely. I'd have to find somewhere to keep you stashed away, though. It would be hard to find another layout like this...*

*...could I do such a thing to Joshua, though?*

*He hasn't been treating me right by any means, but...*


Kim couldn't help but notice all the attention Lisa was giving to her legs. With all the times Lisa had washed her, she knew where Kim's sensitive spots were and she sure was demonstrating her knowledge. She paid a lot of attention to the areas behind Kim's knees before moving up to and concentrating on her inner thighs, but the higher she went, the more she slowed her progress...

*...she's trying to turn me on, from the looks of it...*

*...maybe I should play along...*


Lisa realized she'd drifted. Now back in the present, she noticed that Kim was cooing softly and squirming from her touch.

*Look at her! Joshua was right; she really is aching! She hasn't been able to get herself off for the whole time we've had her here...she even wants* me *to touch her! I guess the girl really* can't *help it...* "Oops- didn't mean to do that," she hurriedly said as she carefully fastened the garters from Kim's corset onto the top of her stocking, then repeated the process on the other side. Once finished, she bent down and added the straps that would prevent Kim from slipping out of her shoes, then stood and faced her again.

When Lisa backed away, she saw disappointment on Kim's face. Then, the captive lowered her head, apparently embarrassed.

187

Lisa couldn't resist; she decided to experiment on Kim with something Joshua had done to her that she'd loved.

She strapped Kim's thighs together, then produced a long silk scarf. She held one end of it in front of the curious woman while she fed the other between her bound thighs and pulled it out behind her.

Kim writhed in her restraints, knowing what was coming as Lisa made a final adjustment, then pulled the scarf up snugly against her and began pulling it back and forth in a slow, steady rhythm.

The eager recipient closed her eyes and moaned. In no time at all, her hips were moving back and forth, and Lisa picked up the tempo a little. It wasn't long at all before the inevitable hit, which was a pleasure to watch, to put it very lightly...


...Lisa reluctantly ended the show right after that. With a quick tug the scarf came out as Kim watched longingly. "No- no more. I need to finish getting you ready for him." Lisa released her wrists from the shackles and helped the somewhat sated and very cooperative Kim over to the bed, motioned for her to sit and sat behind her when she did. Without being told to, Kim placed her hands behind her back. Lisa took hold of her wrists and bent her arms upward until her hands met in between her shoulder blades.

Kim wasn't surprised and sat still as Lisa bound her the same way Josh had just before putting her into the van for the drive that first night.

"That's the way he wants you. There's nothing I can do."

Kim nodded, and Lisa checked the strap that still cinched her legs just above her knees. "Go ahead and cross your ankles; it's more comfortable if I tie them that way." She did so and her ankles were fastened quickly. "The straps aren't too tight, are they?" When she shook her head 'no', Lisa added the small padlocks he'd insisted on to keep the straps on her.

"Let me help you lie down," she said as she eased her back onto the bed, then brought her legs up.

Again she had to force herself not to look for too long as Kim lay before her, securely bound and gagged. Lisa had had so many other very attractive women in this position, but none of them stirred her up like Kim, who shifted a little as she looked up at her, then blushed and looked away.

188

*What* is *it about you?* She wondered as she rolled Kim onto her stomach to finish her task. *Whatever it is, it's too bad we can't bottle it up and sell it...*

She took the length of rope, fed it through the back ring of the collar and pulled it taut as she took hold of Kim's bound ankles and bent her legs backward to hog-tie her.

Suddenly Kim began to struggle. The gag stifled her panicked cries as she shook her head. "What's wrong? What-oh..." She realized why Kim was so distressed: the collar was pressing in on her neck. There was a danger of her being strangled.

"Don't worry, Kim, it's all right now. He told me he wanted you in the hog-tie, too, but I won't do that to you. I'll just leave you as you are, OK?"

Kim's labored breathing from the tightness of her corset added to her distraught state, but Lisa's touch calmed her as she stroked her hair, then her cheek.

"Easy does it...that's it. Just relax now..." *This sure would be nice to get used to...*

It took a few minutes, but gradually her breathing returned to normal. Sighing in relief, Kim softly voiced her thanks.

Lisa quickly blindfolded her before the hypnotic effect of her eyes took control again.

"It's not like you're going anywhere, anyway, the way you're tied. I'm going to try to calm him down; he's still very pissed, so you'll be alone for awhile."

She walked out and closed the door behind her...


*...and she didn't lock it!!*

It was the first time that had happened.

In spite of her severe bondage, Kim sensed an opportunity.

*What about Lisa, though? Should I wait and see if-*

*No. I can't wait and see; there's no time. At best, Lisa is on the fence and I just can't take the chance. Besides, maybe if I can make something happen this way, that might coax her over to our side. But no matter what, I can't assume that she's right about Josh not doing anything more to Jenny than she says he will...*

Then, as she reflected on all that had happened earlier, Kim saw a warning sign that she'd either overlooked or simply didn't recognize before. Lisa was that sign; more specifically, it was the change in her attitude Kim had been mulling over. Although it didn't happen overnight, just the fact that it happened at all made her wary.

Now that she was looking at it more rationally, she came up with more possible explanations for it.

Was Kim's inability to find any way out of her predicament wearing her down so much that unconsciously she was coming to accept her captivity and trying to make the best of it? That could explain why having her keeper bathe her wasn't so hard to take anymore. Or, was her desperate state causing her to jump to baseless conclusions too quickly, such as assuming Lisa might help her? In her deteriorating emotional condition, either could be the case.

*Also, what if it isn't happening at all? What if she still despises me and this is just a ruse that Josh concocted to see if I'd try to enlist some help in escaping? I'm sure he thinks it would be a huge blow to my confidence if I trusted her and she betrayed me.*

*If that's what he's thinking, he's right...*

*...to hell with it. I have to follow my instincts here and hope for the best.* She waited for what she hoped would be a long enough time as a plan even more desperate than her last one formed. Even if he had cameras in the rooms, which she was pretty sure he did, she had to try it.

While she lay on her bed, preparing to take the biggest gamble of her life- even bigger than the move she put on Daniels-, she barely was able to see, at the furthest edges of the blindfold, that the light in her room came on briefly, then went off...

*...that could be my cue. I'll just give it a minute...*


He was checking the wire on the first camera when Lisa walked in. "Is she ready?"

"Mm-hmm. I didn't hog-tie her, though. The collar was pressing against her throat. If she struggled too much or tried to relax her legs, she might have been strangled."

"So why didn't you do that some other way?"

"She's not going anywhere. I blindfolded her, too, just like you wanted. She can't get free, she can't cry out- not that that would do her any good- and she can't even see."

"You're sure about that?"

"Totally. She can't slip out of her heels, either."

190

He turned on the light in her room with his remote switch, checked the monitor hooked up to the camera in Kim's room and saw her lying on her bed. She was tied very well; he agreed with Lisa that she would stay put. He looked at Jennifer's monitor, too.

He had her in the same spread-eagle he would have Kim in soon and he knew there was no way either of them would get out of that. He nodded and went back to what he was doing after turning her light back off.

"You're going to film this?"

"Not only am I going to film it- a very special audience will get to see the whole thing as it happens," he said with a smile.

"How?"

"I'll have a live feed from all three cameras on a secure internet link that I'm going to give to my former friend so he can watch the woman who loves him being pleasured by the one who beat him- the one he'll never catch. It'll remain secure long enough for me to take her as many times as I feel like. The best part is there won't be a single thing he can do about it. He'll never be able to trace the link to me because he won't have enough time. I'll shut it down long before he's able to pinpoint it."

As Lisa took in what he said, something happened that she never thought would.

She began to feel animosity toward him. At the same time she began to feel as though she might have been conned.

She'd followed him blindly for ten years and aided him in his quest to recapture and ultimately break Kim, who possibly didn't do anything other than to make the same mistake of falling for Joshua's charms, just like Lisa herself had.

"You should have heard the way he talked about her. Poor, sweet, innocent little Kim Francis- the one he pushed away. He thought she was the perfect 'girl next door'. You know, it's too bad I didn't tape her tirade a while ago so he'd have more evidence of the trashy little slut she really is. He never even knew she was a stripper. Dumbass. Well, now he's gonna see her being turned into something even better, and he'll get to watch the whole thing live."

Although Lisa's jealousy flared up over him saying that, she was affected in a different way as well. She clearly recalled how much Kim in her subdued state affected her...

...particularly the way she responded to the special silk scarf treatment...

"Well, look at you getting all hot and bothered there."

She snapped out of it and quickly looked away, knowing she was turning red.

He chuckled. "Hey, I can imagine how much she gets to you. She does that to everyone, but you know what?" he said as he walked over to her. "You have that effect on me, too. I, um...I know I've been preoccupied lately and I haven't paid as much attention to you as I should have- not nearly enough. I'm sorry, Lis. I didn't mean to do that. You're the one who's always been there for me. It's because of you that all these girls are still alive and they're gonna stay alive- even Kim. You've been the stabilizing force for me. If not for you and all you've done for me, I'd have gone totally over the edge. Thank you for all the help you've given me and also...thank you for loving me.

"I love you too, Lisa. I promise I'll never neglect you again."

He'd never said that to her- not in any way- and he took her into his arms and kissed her with an intensity he hadn't shown since the first few months they were together.

The same feeling she'd had for him for so long came rushing right back in...


*It has to be now...*

As soon as she felt that stimulus, she put her plan into action.

She wriggled her way over to the edge of her bed, swung her legs over and put her feet on the floor. It was good Lisa didn't make the straps too tight. As a result, Kim was able to uncross her ankles so she would be able to shuffle around. She stood and got her balance, which wasn't going to be easy to keep since she was both strictly bound and totally blind. She'd barely even caught a trace of the light in her room, which hadn't been turned on again.

*I just hope there aren't any obstacles. If I fall, I don't know if I'll be able to get back up...*

Summoning all she'd learned and practiced in ballet, she went as high up on her tiptoes as she could and began to make her way in the direction of the door. She didn't want to risk hopping in nearly six-inch heels, which she barely was able to keep off the ground since her feet were fully arched in them and stretched almost to their limit. They were as high as she could wear- almost *too* high. Even though she easily could fall while following her course of action, the risk would be greater if she tried to hop.

Her pace was careful, deliberate and rhythmic. It also seemed excruciatingly slow given her fear of the retribution he would take if he saw her. Again, the very tight corset hindered her breathing, which already was labored because of her anxiety.

*It's a good thing I don't have far to go...*

Finally she touched and leaned against the wall, taking the briefest rest she could.

Wasting no time, she used the wall to help steady her as she inched along it, feeling for the door.

*Here it is.*

*Since she didn't lock it I only should have to turn the handle, which probably will be easier said than done...*

She moved a little further along the wall until her hip touched the knob. With her hands bound as they were and her arms lashed against her body, she had to slide down the wall enough to position one of her hands to turn the knob, using the strength of her legs to keep her steady and prevent her from falling. As rigorously as she worked them, ordinarily they would be more than up to the task.

*I already worked them hard earlier today, though. I hope this doesn't take too long...*

The problem, as she expected, was turning the doorknob enough. Also, the door opened inwards, so she would have to hold it as it was.

On her first try, because of her gloves and her inability to judge exactly how far away from the knob her hand was, she slipped as she reached for it. She shifted and nearly fell, crying out in alarm before she barely was able to right herself. She had to take a moment to calm down before she could try again.

She didn't fare any better with her subsequent efforts over the next several minutes, either. Her total inability to maneuver her hands was her biggest problem. Only on the last try was she able-barely- to turn the knob enough to open the door, but she couldn't move away quickly enough to let it swing open and it latched itself again.

Frustrated after striving so hard, Kim had to rest again. Her mounting desperation and the constricting corset were taking a toll on her endurance and her nerves; her breathing had become very heavy.

*I'm so close, but I just can't open this damned door...*

*...why does this always happen?*

The tear that fell from her eye couldn't escape, either- it immediately was absorbed into the blindfold as a familiar feeling seeped into her.

It was the same feeling she had after head-butting Daniels and knocking him out, then not being able to free herself when that was all she had to do to make her escape. She was so deflated after her efforts had come to nothing; she still lay there, completely helpless.

What would happen now? The New Jersey troopers, by an incredible stroke of luck, had burst in and saved her that day. She always needed help from someone- the troopers a few months earlier, Nancy and Steve when they found her tied up on her bed in the apartment, the police who rescued her during the sting...

*...and last but not least, if not for the bit of slack in one of the straps Josh used to tie me to the bed the last time he had me, I never would have escaped him then, either.*

Kim wept as all those situations came back to haunt her in this crucial moment and she began to sink to the floor. It would be so easy just to let nature take the same course it always had and become the helpless, imprisoned sex toy she seemed destined to be. No matter how much she tried to get herself on the right path and stay there, inevitably this seemed to be what she came back to. There would be an insurmountable obstacle placed in front of her and she would be defeated every time.

*If only Lisa would have helped me...*

*...maybe Josh is right, and John is just a wonderful fairy tale...*

At this point, he and everything she wanted seemed a lifetime away- somewhere on the other side of the door she simply couldn't open.

She rested on her heels and let herself slide down the wall.

*I'll just lie down and wait for him to take me to his room...*

*...where I'll spend the rest of my life tied to his bed...*

*...while he has his way with me until I hate the mere thought of sex...*

*...and I really will want to die, which is something he won't allow...*

194

*NO!! I can't do this- I can't not try!! It's up to* me. *There is no one else and I probably won't get another opportunity. If I give up, my life is over and I'm his.*

*Worse yet, Jenny will suffer the same fate if I just roll over now. I have to stop being a victim and get out of here somehow! There must be a way to open this fucking door!!*

*Oh, no- the breathing again. Calm yourself down, now; slow, deep breaths. You don't need to faint...*

Although it took some doing, she managed to settle herself relatively quickly.

*Now, get it together and* think!

The first thing she had to do was raise herself back up and at that moment she realized how sore her thighs and buns were from the isometric exercise of holding herself in position for the length of time she had. However, she needed to summon more strength and endurance from them. Concentrating on both lifting and steadying herself, she began to push. Her muscles strained with the effort, but she got to where she needed to be.

*OK, I have to get it right this time because time definitely is my enemy here. I'm lucky he hasn't come for me yet.*

*Plus, my quads really are starting to scream...*

*...all right. Maybe- just maybe- that will work...*

She decided to roll the dice again by holding the knob in place once she had it turned enough, then simultaneously snapping her hand in the right direction to open it and turning her shoulder away from it.

If it worked, she would be out.

It was the best chance she had. She took hold of the knob, turned it carefully and was able to get it all the way over.

*Here goes...*

She flicked her hand and turned away as she did.

It worked! She heard the slight creak as the door opened.

Elated, she quickly straightened her legs out to relieve them and with her shoulder gently pushed the door open the rest of the way.

There was no time to savor this very welcome triumph. As she eased herself out into the hallway, she waited for a second.

*Good- they're not out here. If they were, I'm sure they'd let me know it.*

*Better yet, if he has cameras in our rooms like I think he does, apparently he's not watching mine right now.*

She knew she'd completed only the first couple tasks of many in order to bring her plan to fruition. In spite of all her hindrances, she had to get to Jenny's room, which she knew was three doors down from hers and on the other side of the hallway...

"You always were great in bed. God, what an idiot I've been," he told her as she rested against him in the bed where he soon would have Kim. He looked into Lisa's eyes as he added a point of emphasis. "It's only going to get better for us. All of it."

He certainly had emphasized that statement with his lovemaking, which *was* even better than before. The promise of their relationship getting back to where she wanted it to be placated her almost completely; she'd been at her happiest then. She kissed him and he gave her an affectionate clap on her rear end, which made her giggle and smile at him.

"OK, let's get this done with. Can you help me with the rest of this equipment?"

"Sure."

As they worked on the next camera, he continued to formulate a plan on how he would bring about the change that was absolutely necessary.

"Now, to make a phone call..."

*I'm pretty sure this one's hers...*

Although Kim was amazed that she'd gotten this far, she was focused completely on finishing what she'd started. At that point her calves were getting sore from constantly being flexed in order to keep her high enough to enable her to shuffle as far as she had. For the same reason, her feet were getting sore as well. It had been a very long time since she'd done anything like this in her ballet classes.

First she had to open the sliding bolt, which, after locating it, she found she barely was able to reach. *I guess in that respect it's a good thing I'm wearing these heels...*

She manipulated the bolt open, then lowered herself a bit so she could flip the latch of the deadbolt and then turn the lock mechanism on the knob itself. This time she was able to lean against the frame for support as she turned the knob. It was much easier opening this door since it opened away from her...

*I hope* this is her room. *I'm sure she'll have the courage to leave, especially if I have to tell her his plans for us tonight...*

"Mmmph!!"

"Mm-mmm!" Kim immediately shook her head to quiet her; she was sure it was Jenny and was very encouraged by her spirited response. She heard another welcome sound of creaking- this time from the bedframe- as the young girl struggled.

*I don't hear chains clinking, which also is a good sign. Hopefully she's not in handcuffs or any kind of shackles, or my plan ends here,* she thought as she moved toward her.

Finally Kim felt the bed. She called softly to Jenny, who responded in kind- now Kim knew where her head was. She turned and sat down, then lay next to her. Given the position of her arm and leg, Kim knew he had her in a spread-eagle. She wriggled her way up until she felt Jenny's hand touching her head. It was only seconds before Jenny tugged at the buckle of her blindfold and pulled it off.

There wasn't much light in the room for her to adjust to- only a little plug-in nightlight. She felt Jenny's fingers on the buckle of the repulsive gag. *Good job- you almost have it...*

Once the buckle was undone, Kim turned toward her. Jenny extracted the conjoined plug and strap monstrosity from her mouth.

"Oh, thank God..." Kim breathed as she winced in pain. Her jaw had been held wide open for some time by that large plug.

Jenny whimpered and tugged at her restraints as she couldn't contain her joy at seeing her counselor again, but then she gasped as she saw the red mark on Kim's face.

"Shhh- it's all right, Jenny. Let's get you out of here." She turned over so she could grasp the thong holding Jenny's right wrist in her teeth. She worked it loose, then quickly pulled it open.

Jenny unraveled it and went to work on freeing her other wrist, which she did without much trouble. Then she removed her gag. "What did he do to you, Miss Fr-"

"It's nothing, plus it was well worth what I did to him. Keep it down to a whisper. No, don't try to untie me," Kim stopped her as she reached over. "You can't do it, anyway. These padlocks are holding the straps in place and I'm in handcuffs. Finish freeing yourself while I tell you what we're going to do.

"You have to move fast, Honey- we don't have much time..."

"Well, that should do it, Lis. Sit on the bed, OK? I'll give it a quick test…"

"No! I'm not leaving you here! How can you expect-"

"Shhh- keep it down! Jenny, please don't argue with me; you *have* to do this. Believe me, I don't want to stay here either, but you can't get me out of these cuffs and straps, or these heels- I'd only slow you down. My legs and feet are so sore, anyway. I doubt I could walk very far, let alone run. Most importantly of all, their focus on me will give you more time.

"Hurry, now. You'll have to carry me back to my room. Grab your dance outfit and let's go."

"Looks like we're all set," Josh said as he confirmed the camera links to the computer. The site was secure as well. *We're only talking an hour max, anyway- plenty of time to get offline before he gets the bloodhounds to where they can track me down.*

"Time to get the star of our show."

He was so confident that he didn't bother to double-check his monitors and look in on his captives before walking out.

Jenny had shut her door and set all three locks before putting Kim over her shoulders again and carrying her back inside her room. She laid her onto her bed, then pulled the door most of the way closed, leaving enough of a crack for the light of the hallway to aid her in what she had to do. Given what Miss Francis had told her about cameras being in the rooms, she wasn't about to turn the light on.

She went back over to her liberator who, much to Jenny's chagrin, still was so tightly bound and would have to stay behind. A look of pain crossed over her face and she shifted around; her discomfort was obvious.

Jenny rubbed her shoulders and she relaxed a little. "Thank God they left your door open."

"Yes, we sure were lucky with that." The nauseous feeling started to come back- it was time for the final phase to begin. All

Kim would be able to do was wait, and then provide the most detestable diversion possible in hope that it would be good enough not only to give Jenny the opportunity to get out, but also time to get as far away as possible. She tried not to think about it.

"OK, Jenny, you have to blindfold me and gag me again before they get here. Don't be afraid when you hear them. They won't find you. Get changed and be ready. Keep all your stuff in the bathtub with you and keep the curtain closed, just in case. Don't leave *anything* out. Wait about five minutes after they leave, then get out of here. Run as fast as you can and as far as you can. Try to reach a main road as soon as possible."

*And pray they don't lock the upstairs door...*

"They haven't locked my door after taking me out of here and I doubt they will now, but if they do, just stay hidden. If they don't see you in your room, they still might run out of here in a panic and go looking for you. When people panic, they make mistakes. Just be cool, Honey, you'll-...you'll do fine." Her voice cracked in the middle of her last sentence.

Jenny hugged her and felt her trembling. The tables were turning for the two of them. *She was so brave to do what she did to give me my chance to escape, but now...*

*...God knows I'd be scared, too- she's the one who has the harder job ahead of her.* "Don't you worry, Miss Francis; I'll get you out of here. I'll get to the police and bring them. I know you're afraid, but think about what you just did for me and how much courage that took. You've already proven that you're much stronger than he'll ever be. He can't win; he'll never get the better of you. Just hang in there, all right?"

When she pulled back, Kim nodded. This time she was able to hold back her tears. "Thanks, Jenny."

"I hate to do this, but...are you ready?"

She nodded again, and Jenny was about to lay her back down and reach for the gag. "Wait- just one last thing." She leaned in and kissed Jenny passionately. "In case I don't-...well, just in case, will you give that to John for me and tell him...tell him I love him?"

She felt every bit of love Kim wanted to convey in that deep, sensuous kiss. It took Jenny a moment to recover. "Wow," the reeling girl said. She shook her head to clear it and smiled. "I'm sure he knows how you feel. Besides, I think *you* should tell him."

Kim smiled back. "OK, now I'm ready."

Jenny replaced Kim's gag and blindfold, lay her gently onto the bed and collected her things. It was very hard not to pick her up again and make a break for the door, but she knew her mentor was right. This was the best chance they and all the other captive women there had- everything rested on her ability to escape.

*They're all depending on me...*

So many times before, she'd crumbled when she was faced with situations that demanded a lot from her, but with this one- easily the most demanding one she'd ever been in- she inexplicably felt confident of success.

She knew a lot of that came from the woman she was about to leave to their captors- one of the very few who believed in her.

"I won't let you down, Miss Francis," she said as she kissed her cheek. Kim's urgent cry prompted Jenny to get up. "OK, I'm going. I'll see you soon..."

She closed the door to the hallway and made her way into the bathroom.


"What did you say, John?"

Tom looked intently at him, waiting. He'd been so quiet for so long that day that Tom nearly jumped when he spoke.

John turned toward him. "Corsets."

"What about 'em?"

"They're custom made. Since they're not exactly in demand, I can't imagine there are too many manufacturers of them. Maybe if we get a couple investigators to work on finding out who does make 'em and getting lists of their clientele..."

Tom shrugged. "Couldn't hurt, I guess." He took care of that quickly, and looked back at John, who continued to stare ahead. "Is there something else?"

"Well, I've been looking through all this other stuff on Josh that came in today- all the records from his childhood and everything. I see some things in there that don't make sense, given what he told me when we used to hang out..."

"Oh, yeah? What did you see that-" The phone rang again, throwing both of them off track. Tom answered it. "Lieutenant

200

Stratton…OK, have it sent up. We'll be waiting." He hung up. "A message is being sent up here- eyes only for you."

John's eyes narrowed. "Wonder what that could be…"

"Why isn't this locked?"

Josh stared at the door to Kim's room before turning to Lisa.

"Well, I…didn't think it mattered, you- you saw the way I tied her up and blindfolded her- she couldn't walk or see." Lisa backed away a little. "I'm sorry, Joshua, I didn't-"

Her voice always got higher when she was afraid, just like it was now. He held up his hand. "Let's go in." He opened the door, turned on the light and there was Kim. She'd been lying on her stomach, but when she heard them come in, her head turned toward them and she began to struggle and tried to move away from them.

*It doesn't look like anything's out of the ordinary, anyway,* Josh thought as he walked over and sat on her bed. She jerked as he clamped his hand onto her hip to hold her in place. He slapped it as she tried to pull away. "*Stay still*!! I don't want *any* more of this from you today, do you understand me?!"

She nodded, and obeyed him for the most part, other than a little squirming as yet again he ran his hands over her. However, she knew very well how much he enjoyed that. *That's it- focus on me…*

"Much better, Kim. This is how you need to be. You don't want your breathing to become too heavy since your corset's even tighter now. Once I show you what you've been missing over the past eleven years, you'll fall in line.

"Plus," he looked at Lisa and winked, "you'll have an added bonus. Another beautiful ex-Kitty, who happens to be here with us, will be joining in on the fun. I'll let you in on a little secret- she wants you just as badly as I do." Lisa blushed and looked away as he smiled at her. "I'd say you did an excellent job of tying her up, Lisa- very good work! I see you added the locks, too," he kept groping Kim as he inspected her bondage, and then he ran his hand up along the back of her corset where it was laced together.

"The ends of the corset are touching, too. Perfect!" Kim whimpered as he squeezed her breast, then got up.

"Time to go to your room?" Lisa asked.

"In a minute. I need to use the bathroom."

*Oh, no!!*

Kim froze as she heard him go in there. Please *don't tell me he was watching us the whole time...*

"Did you pull the shower curtain, Lisa?"

"Um, I might have, but I'm not sure. Why?"

"Just wondering..."

Kim was about to lose her tenuous grip as she fought to reign in her emotions. All of her senses were channeled into that of her hearing.

She waited for the sound she prayed she wouldn't hear.

*No...oh,* God, *don't let him find-*

She gasped as she heard him pull the curtain.

Jenny managed- barely- to control her trembling.

*I'm glad I decided to hide in here...*

She'd opted for the small linen closet over the bathtub because she didn't want to take the chance of him having to use the toilet and doing what he just did- looking into the tub, which was too close in proximity for her comfort. She'd already hidden her corset, heels and everything else he'd made her wear behind the towels.

She froze as he turned and looked toward the closet.

This was it: the crucial moment had come...

...and it passed. After his exchange with Lisa, he flushed the toilet and left the bathroom, prompting Jenny to heave a deep sigh of relief.

*Now get the hell out of here- both of you- so I can get the hell out of here...*

"Well, maybe it's better if you keep it pulled. Less worry about mildew that way," Josh said as he went over to Kim and clapped her on the hip again- not so hard this time. "I told you, Kim- you really need to control your breathing better. Come on now, you already know what's going to happen. It's not like we haven't done this before."

202

Relief washed over her; Jenny was safe- for the moment. *Now, let's hope she can find a way out of here...*

"Anyway, ready or not, here we go." He scooped her up and carried her out with Lisa following right behind.

She shut the light off and closed the door behind her, then looked at him. "Do you want me to lock it?"

"Why? It's not necessary now. Just don't leave any door unlocked again when there's a girl inside, no matter how well you've tied her. We don't want to take any chances."

"I understand."

They made their way to Josh's room, both eagerly anticipating what was next.


"Mister Governor? I have that message for you." The runner handed it to him.

John thanked her as she left, then opened and read it. He froze a moment later. Tom watched as all the color drained from his face, and the slip of paper fell to the floor.

"What does it say?" He didn't answer, so Tom reached down and picked up the note:

*Nine PM. Yourworstnightmareandherslive.com. Watch and enjoy.*

*Sincerely,*

*You know who.*

"Oh, my God..."

"He's gonna kill her, Tom- and he wants me to watch..."

# Chapter 8

"All right, we're ready. Help me fasten her down."

Josh had removed all the straps that bound Kim, then removed her handcuffs and allowed a few minutes for her to work the kinks out of her shoulders- with Lisa's assistance. Her gag and blindfold were left in place; the latter was more important at the moment.

*I'm sure she wouldn't make this so easy for us if she saw everything that's about to happen,* he thought as he made her lie down. He took hold of Kim's right wrist and Lisa got her left one. They spread her arms and pulled them toward the solid posts at the headboard, where the leather cuffs were. Kim didn't fight at all as her wrists were secured in the cuffs. After testing the restraints to make sure she wouldn't be able to free herself, they spread her legs and cuffed her ankles separately to the footposts.

Once that was done, he took a moment to enjoy the view.

"OK, Kim, time to get rid of that blindfold. I wouldn't think of depriving you of the pleasure of watching as we relive our history," he said as he pulled it off.

She emitted a soft cry, squinted and turned away, writhing in the restraints as she adjusted to the light. When she was able, she looked back up. He watched her for her reaction as she took in her surroundings and smiled at her dismay as she saw the cameras.

However, he was disappointed that she didn't react more heatedly, as he was sure she would.

"Just like old times, right?" His attempt to rub some salt in had little effect as well. He was the one who became a little angry when she gave him the look of utter contempt that was becoming a common reaction from her. He got up and walked it off.

*Let's see how you react to this- I bet you won't be so fucking cool for much longer.* "I'm sure you're not surprised to see that I'll be filming us, but that's not all the cameras are for. This isn't just for me. What do you say we get our audience in on the entertainment?

"However, before the main event, there's something I want to share with you and our exclusive video guest. It's

204

something you and he will find very enlightening," he said as he typed in the command on his keyboard.

Now, they were live. His moment was at hand.

*Dammit! They turned out the hall lights, too!*

Jennifer had opened the door very slowly and made that discovery as she peeked into the hallway that was so dark it seemed to consume even the faint luminescence of the nightlight in Kim's bathroom.

To be on the safe side, she'd waited closer to ten minutes, although doing so had put her further on edge. When she couldn't stand the tension any more, she knew it was time to try to get out.

She'd opted to wear her dance outfit- the same one she'd worn the day he abducted her. In her cross-trainers, she'd be able to run much faster than in the footwear she'd become used to over the past two and a half weeks.

*OK, here goes, although I didn't count on pitch-blackness...*

When she stepped out, she knew to turn left and make her way past where they worked out every day- she and Kim agreed that the exit had to be somewhere in that section.

Not wasting a second, she moved off in that direction.

There was a very hollow feeling in her stomach. At any moment he could step out in front of her, or sneak up behind her and grab her before she knew he was even there.

However, the fear she felt at the prospect of any such thing happening only served to motivate her more to find the way out of this well-developed underground prison complex. All the floors, walls and ceilings were tiled, paneled or carpeted- nothing was left unfinished.

She felt her way along the wall and eventually reached the first junction. The gym room was to the left.

Each time she'd been led to the gym in the thoroughly humiliating manner- on a leash, of all things- she would look a bit further down that hall to where she figured the exit was, aching for freedom. She'd been carried up a single and rather long set of stairs on many occasions- while restrained, of course- and allowed a little time on the enclosed patio.

She knew the stairway had to be somewhere close, so she continued along the wall, wishing she could move faster...

* * *

"...maybe he's not going to kill her- maybe it means something else."

"*What* else? Kim dying, especially by his hands, *is* my worst nightmare!"

"I know, John, I know- the way you see it, obviously that's your worst nightmare, but maybe he's trying to rattle you some other way. It seems to me he's somebody who would want to draw things out, especially with what you've told me about him added in. We can only hope that's the case; we might get more time that way.

"Think about this, too- his communiqué to you is the first time he's made contact with any of his victims' loved ones. We have to look at that as a positive. Plus...I hate like hell to use this, but if you're right and Kim was the reason he's done all he has, why would he kill her so quickly?"

"I don't know...I don't know what he's thinking. I just know that I can't face life without her. If she-...if she doesn't come back, I won't rest until he's dead. I don't just want him caught, Tom- I want him *dead*"

"John, you've got to stop this! Don't you know you're letting him win? Can't you see what he's doing to you?" Another approach- probably a better one- came to him. "How do you think Kim would feel if she saw what was happening to you? If she saw how much you're deteriorating? You know how upset she'd be. I can see the toll this has taken already- you've lost ten pounds minimum since the day she was taken. You probably have ulcers, too, which is all you need given the fact that you're still recovering from the wounds to your vitals, not to mention all the surgery you had to go through.

"You can't keep going like this- you've *got* to take care of yourself! If you don't, you're going to waste away until you're too weak to recover. Can you imagine what it would do to Kim to survive this ordeal only to come home and find that you didn't?!"

John's disposition changed immediately.

*Christ, she'd be devastated...*

Tom took notice of the change in him and eased up, then he had to take the opportunity he saw. "I know you're still angry about me keeping what I knew about Kim's past from you and you have every right to be. We've had our share of problems over the years and what I held back is the latest example. I'm not trying to minimize it, but for God's sake, John, you're the only brother I have left. I want you to be around for a while. We have to pull together- for Kim's sake, if nothing else. What do you say?"

John lowered his head for a moment, then turned to Tom. "You're right on both counts. We do have to work together, and I'm not doing Kim or you or anyone- including myself- any good going the way I am. All this speculating is just making me stress even more.

"For now, we'll see what kind of shit he's trying to pull."

As John stared at the screen and waited, Tom glanced over at him several times. Although still intense, he wasn't as touchy; he appeared to have taken a step back. *Thank God for that...*

"Oh, I meant to tell you- the investigators we have working to track down every corsetier there is have made a good bit of progress. They've all been cooperative and our people already have gathered a lot of lists of clients from '89 through-..."

He trailed off when Kim's image replaced the blank screen. Seeing the predicament she was in, he walked over and laid his hands onto John's shoulders.

John couldn't stifle the pain in his gut when he saw her, knowing there was nothing he could do to help her.

Then, Josh stepped in front of the camera and the pain got worse.


"Good evening, John. Welcome to our program."

When he said that, Kim lost her cool. *No...oh God, don't let John see this...*

She had no more chance of escaping the cameras than she had of escaping the cuffs that held her down. Every way she tried to turn her head, one of the three cameras had an angle on her. She cried out and yanked ineffectively at the restraints, then cursed Josh through the gag. Tears of anger and shame soon followed.

He turned back to her. "Well, it looks like our budding starlet already is demanding our attention," he said as he walked over and sat on the bed facing her. "Or, maybe that's not the right way to put it. Her looks and presence alone demand attention- wouldn't you agree, John?" He touched her thigh and began to caress it. "And since she's all tied up, I think that only serves to enhance her even more. I especially like the fact that she can't talk right now."

Kim bucked wildly as she fought to escape his hand, even though she knew that would only serve to excite him. She couldn't just lie there and pretend not to be affected- that was impossible.

"You've never seen her like this, have you? You must be thinking, 'damn- what have I been missing?' Look at her, John- look at how she struggles! Turns you on, doesn't it? Well, I'll share this little tidbit with you: it sure turns *her* on! It always has."

Sure enough, he became more intrusive with his hands, with John watching. She was certain he was watching, too, and she tried not to picture the reaction he surely was having to her being so thoroughly humiliated. As much as she wished she could convince herself of it, she knew Josh wasn't putting on an act with this setup.

And that only was the beginning.


Jennifer tried to swallow the cantaloupe in her throat.

She'd reached the door at the top of the stairs after a painstaking and nerve-wracking trek through the catacombs of this lavish hell and had her hand on the knob of its gate.

She had to turn it, which made her more nervous than anything.

What if it was locked? What would she do?

She couldn't go back and re-fasten herself to the bed in hope that they wouldn't know she was free- that simply was not an option for any reason.

*It has to be open...*

*...all right. I have to try it...*

*...just a half-turn should do it...*

"Come on- just turn the damned thing already!" she hissed to herself.

She took a deep breath, turned and pulled.

Nothing.

*No...no, it* can't *be...*

She turned and pulled again.

It still didn't budge. Her heart sank as she leaned forward--and fell onto the floor as the door swung outward.

For what could have been an eternity, the stunned girl couldn't move a muscle.

She lay still in the normal and humble-looking sitting room, waiting…

…but no one came. There was no commotion anywhere.

*They must not have heard me. The door didn't creak, and thank God the carpet on this floor is thick…*

Sighing heavily in relief, she gathered her wits and was even able to snicker at herself for almost failing the 'push/pull' test as she looked around.

There was a door about twenty feet away from her that looked to be the front door. No sooner did she see it than she found herself in front of it.

After checking behind her to make sure the coast was still clear, she unlocked the deadbolt, opened the door slowly this time and stepped out, then closed it gently behind her.

Not three seconds later, Jennifer was running as fast as she could down the long driveway.


"Before we get down to business, Kim, I want to let you in on a little something- you and John. This'll lend even more credence to the inevitability of you being with me." He turned to the camera. "To bring you up to speed, John, I've been trying to convince Kim here that her life with you is nothing more than a fantasy- an aberration. It's only a matter of time until she realizes that and you do as well.

"As far as I'm concerned, you turned your back on her when you found out that she'd been a stripper. Let's be honest: you definitely would have looked down on her if you'd known that before. I did you both a favor by keeping you apart. You'd have turned the cold shoulder to her when she was most vulnerable and it would have crushed her. Besides, she especially was vulnerable then because her true self had emerged and she was afraid of what you might think of her. She always worried about you and your feelings.

"And look what you did when you saw the real Kim. You proved me right.

"Now, back to what I was about to tell you both." He looked back at Kim and his hands picked up where they left off. He chuckled at her efforts to escape his attention and how she first scowled at him, then gradually whimpered in defeat and turned away when she accepted the fact that she couldn't evade him.

*Wish I could see your face, John...but I can picture your reaction easily enough.*

When she became more compliant, he went on. "I'm sure you recall being in the same predicament a few months ago, Kim- full of fear and despair, at the mercy of somebody who wanted you for himself and wanted to keep you locked away. I guess that's a familiar feeling for you, isn't it? Sort of like a feeling of destiny. Eventually you'll stop fighting when you realize you can't beat it. You can't escape your destiny, just like you can't free yourself from these cuffs." He smiled before adding the lead-in for the punch line.

"Starting to get used to this position, aren't you? Being tied spread-eagle like you are? Isn't that how Daniels had you?"

Kim's head whipped around and her eyes were wide, which made his smile grow wider. "He had you naked, too, and how about the motel where he kept you? Did it look familiar? It should have, unless they remodeled it..."

He watched as the realization hit her, and hard. He expected her to struggle violently in the grip of rage, or close to it, but she only wailed weakly- she seemed paralyzed and he saw horror in her eyes. She barely reacted as he squeezed her breast.

"You're finally starting to understand it all, aren't you, Kim? Are you coming to accept the fact that your place is with me? The inevitable already has happened, for the most part. It's been a gradual process and you were very elusive, but I caught you. Even though for our eighteen days together you've resisted this fact, you *are* where you belong. I'm going to keep reminding you of that until you do accept it.

"Daniels was my puppet. I was the one who convinced him to take you. He was hesitant, but I talked him into it. I promised him a million dollars when he turned you over to me. He did a pretty good job, only he didn't succeed in killing John. Then, the dumb bastard almost killed you, which he will pay for...

"I also told him where to take you, which is why you ended up where you did. I didn't get a chance to see the inside; maybe they did remodel it. I didn't get that chance because, for the second time, there were police cars outside the place where I was to pick you up. Oh, well- doesn't matter now, does it? Third time's the charm, right?

"Think back to the last night in '88, when you worked at the Kitty Cat Club. Remember when we were on our way back from there? You were sitting right next to me, wearing that hot little outfit...I couldn't wait until we got to my place- there was no way. I kept the heat up enough so you wouldn't put your coat on. We didn't even make it fifteen miles outside Atlantic City before I had to have you, so we went to that motel. Of course you remember...

"Sorry, John, I didn't mean to leave you out. She really was something; you should've seen her in that Tigress uniform. When Daniels asked me where we should meet, that motel came right to mind. Kim and I had quite a time there. In fact, I'm getting worked up just thinking about it while I have the lady herself right here in front of me, all tied up like she was that night...

"On that note, Kim, you have my undivided attention now. It's about time we I show John what real sexual chemistry is..."

Kim's shock wore off. She fought with all her strength against the bonds that wouldn't budge. She paused briefly, looking up at him in helpless fury as he produced a small knife and pulled one of the narrow sides of her thong up off her hip. He was about to cut it and the other side and pull away her bit of protection from him.

"Look how damp your panties are- again. Just can't help yourself, can you?" As her cheeks turned blood red, a tormented, stifled scream erupted from her and she struggled even harder, which was turning him on more by the second. He could smell her scent.

*Christ, I can practically taste you...*

"Oh, SHIT!! Where is she?!!"

He froze, his blade against Kim's thong, staring at Lisa.

"Who?! *Who?!* Lisa, what-"

"Jennifer- she's gone!!"

He dropped the knife and rushed over to the monitor.

Sure enough, Jennifer's bed was empty.

"*FUCK*!!!" He flew out of the room and down the stairs and was in Jennifer's room very quickly, seeing firsthand that the monitor was not malfunctioning.

She *was* gone.

He ran back upstairs- as he reached the top of them he heard the car starting. He locked the door and bolted it, then went to the garage and met Lisa at the door.

"Come on. I have cuffs, straps and a gag in there. I thought the car might be better."

"Good. I'll drive. She can't have that much of a head start. We have to get her back or else the game could be over. Let's go."

*How could she have gotten loose?! I checked those thongs again before I left- no way was she getting out of them...*


Tears were streaming down John's face as he stared at her. It was all Tom could do to keep himself from smashing the monitor to bits. *John has to be on the brink again- can't let him see me like this...*

The computer experts continued to work on a trace of the weblink- fortunately they were on the job quickly, but so far they had no luck. Again, for John and for him, it was a waiting game, which was taking a terrible toll on both of them.

Tom turned and was about to walk away, unable to watch what Josh was about to do to Kim, but then looked back as the situation changed drastically. He watched the quick exchange between Josh and Lisa Meyers, then saw them both rush out almost in a panic.

"Did you hear that, John?! It looks like Jenny got away!"

John nodded, now on the edge of his chair, still intently focused on Kim. "Let's hope she can get to someone's house, or flag down someone friendly- especially a police officer."

"Speaking of which, I'm gonna make sure every station between D.C. and Jersey has every available officer out there looking for her. If we find her, we find all the other women."

He made the call and right away the wheels were turning.

"She looks healthy."

Tom was glad to hear John's change in perspective. "You're right...she does."

"Did you see her fight him? In spite of how frightened she must be, she has the will to resist. Look at her- she's still trying to break free." He leaned forward and touched the screen where her face was. "Hang in there, Kitten. We'll find you..."

"John, I need to get out there. I'm one more guy who could be on the street looking for Jenny. Do you want to come?"

After a moment of contemplation he shook his head. "I know this might sound weird, but in a way I feel like I'm with Kim right now. I know it's only her image, but I'm closer to her here than I would be out there. I just don't want her to be by herself, especially if things get-..."

"I think I know what you mean. All right, I'm going. I'll let you know as soon as I hear anything, or if I find her."

John's response was not much more than a mumble of acknowledgement.

He continued to gaze at the monitor, mesmerized as Kim renewed her struggling and simultaneously heartsick because he couldn't help her...

When Kim heard the car pull away, she allowed herself a smile as a tear rolled down her cheek. Jenny had done it!

*Now, if only she can avoid being recaptured and come across the right person who will help her, and us...*

But she also couldn't help but feel fear about that. What if Jenny was successful and she came back with the police? Josh most certainly would come back before they were able to find the place and he would be enraged if it came down to his fortress being stormed.

There were ten defenseless women upon whom he could unleash his wrath...

On top of that, she suddenly realized how close she also was to freedom. She twisted and tugged, wriggled and writhed for all she was worth, but she couldn't do that for very long before she was out of breath. The tightness of the corset thwarted her efforts once more.

*Not that I had much of a chance, anyway...*

As she lay back and slowed her breathing, she looked up at the camera.

*I almost forgot- John is watching...*

That notion had two effects on her- first, it eased her fear and made her feel like John literally was watching over her.

The other feeling it began to evoke was most unwelcome...

She cried out in frustration as she looked longingly into the lens and began to squirm involuntarily as that presently unwanted feeling was waxing ever stronger. What fed it more was the looming possibility that this could be the last time he'd ever see her. That notion brought on another set of emotions as well.

*No...I can't cry. This already must be hell for you, Baby...*

In spite of the acute pain and desire she felt she was able to stifle her tears, but she had to do something- and quickly- to keep all those forces working against her from dragging her down.

*What am I going to-*

*-what in the hell is that?* She shifted around as she felt something cold.

*Oh my God- the knife!!*

Josh had dropped it. She looked down and there it was, lying on the pillow against her hip.

Not only did the feeling of the cold steel on her skin alert her to the presence of the knife, it also brought her out of her funk. Immediately, she set about formulating a plan of action.

*The cuffs are stiff leather. Even though I can't cut through the chain connecting them, maybe I can saw through the one locked around the bedpost...*

*...but how can I get the knife into my hand the way I'm tied?*

A possible way came to her- the only way, at that. It would take time and concentration, and with any luck, it wouldn't require more of a range of movement than she was capable of.

*Well, it's not like I have anything else to do.*

*I just hope I can get it before they come back...*


"Help! Please, stop!"

Jennifer waved wildly at the driver, who slowed down.

This was the moment she feared most out of all the trials this night had brought.

There were two people in the car, which scared her- she couldn't distinguish any of their features. Were they young? Older? Male or female?

How would they react to a young girl in the middle of nowhere, dressed as she was?

Whatever the case, she couldn't afford to wait- they would be coming for her. She had to take the chance, especially since she'd been running hard for a good fifteen minutes and this was the first car she'd seen. It was coming from the opposite direction, too, which hopefully meant it wasn't the two of them in the car that was stopped a few feet away from her.

Even as winded as she was, when the driver got out of the car and began to walk toward her, she backed away and was ready to run again, as long and as far as she had to.

"It's all right, Miss- don't be afraid."

With that she stopped and momentarily was unable to move.

"What are you doing all the way out here by yourself? What happened to you?"

As he approached, Jennifer saw that he was a man who looked to be middle-aged. When he reached her and stood in front of her, she saw that he had very kind eyes. Suddenly she felt as though she was a child as she looked into them.

She would have fallen had he not caught her and all she could do was cry as he lifted her up and carried her to the car. Her exhaustion from running and the surge of relief after three weeks of captivity were just too much for her.

"You'll be all right- you're with us now. We'll get you to safety." He turned to the woman who'd gotten out of the passenger side. "Would you open the back door, Allie? I'll get her inside so we can get out of here." Once he did that, the woman- probably his wife- sat with Jenny and drew her close.

Thankfully, they were underway quickly.

Jenny lay against her, still unable to say a word, as the woman comforted her. They drove on for a couple minutes when they came upon a car that was moving slowly along the shoulder.

"Looks like this guy might have lost something-"

Jenny reacted like ice-cold water had been thrown on her. "Keep going- don't stop! That's him...that's *them*!! Please, you have to-"

"Don't worry, I'm not stopping." He noticed the girl ducked down as they passed the car. *Poor thing's scared out of her wits...* "It's all right now. We've passed them."

At that moment, she finally felt safe. Simultaneously, the crucial mission she had to accomplish came back to the fore.

"Um, Sir, could we please go to the police station? There are others, including Miss Francis. We were kidnapped, but she helped me get away. I have to get to the police and-...where are we?"

"We're near Kaolin, Pennsylvania, not far from Delaware. There's a state police barracks nearby; we'll go right to it."

"Thank you. Thank you both so much."

215

"You're quite welcome. What's your name?"

"Jennifer Jacobson. I can't tell you how glad I am to meet you- you may have heard about me on the news." From the looks on their faces, she could tell they had indeed.

* * *

John never looked away from the screen. He watched as Kim fought against the cuffs, but soon she lay still, panting for breath, no doubt because of the corset. He couldn't believe how constricted her waist was; he was amazed she could breathe at all.

He then listened to her grunts and cries as she renewed her bid for freedom. He watched as her arms and legs strained, her hips gyrated, her breasts jiggled...

...but most of all, the look in her eyes drew him in. She was intent on her fight, but there was something else there, too.

It was a look he was familiar with- one he loved to see normally but hated to see now, which became even more prominent as she lay still, spent once more after her exertions and panting for breath.

Then she looked up at the camera and right into him. It was like she flipped a switch...

...*my God*...

Was it only because of the potentially inescapable danger she was in that it was flowing? It was abundantly clear by the urgent way she writhed and mewed to him that she was very much aroused...

...and so was he, despite his efforts to deny it. He wanted badly to pull himself away from the screen as seeing her in this state was tearing him up, yet he was glued to the spot...

...suddenly, her disposition abruptly changed and she was focused again- on something else.

"What are you doing?"

Then, he saw the knife, too, and with it a ray of hope.

"That's good...that's good, Kitten- try to get it..."

*If only she has enough time...*


"Joshua, we've been out here for so long. She could be anywhere now. What are we going to do?"

"Be quiet for a minute. I'm thinking..."

216

He'd given up any real hope of recapturing Jennifer. His only chance would have been to catch her in the act of escaping, but his focus on Kim had given Jennifer possibly as much as a half-hour head start. The girl was in great shape and had plenty of motivation. There was no sign of what direction she took when she ran- there was no trace of her at all...

*...I could have done a lot with you,* he thought as he reflected on the young girl, who was the most impressionable he'd come across- even more so than Kim had been when she was the same age.

*You might have given me as much pleasure as Kim did...*

*...but I can't dwell on that. She's gone. I can't spend another minute looking for her, and I can't take the chance that she's lost in the woods somewhere, or that she fell and broke her leg, or she was hit by a car, or any other scenario that would prevent her from leading the cops to my place...*

*...it's time to implement plan B and concentrate on who I do have and can keep.*

"All right, let's go back. We don't have much time- I'll explain what we're going to do on the way..."


It had taken every bit of concentration, patience, coordination, endurance and flexibility she had, but through her exceptionally taxing effort, Kim was able to maneuver the foldout pocketknife from her hip up to her left shoulder.

*I think the hardest part is over- now I just have to work it the rest of the way up to my hand...*

*...this is easier. Just a little further-*

She heard a door open, then heard Josh talking to Lisa.

The knife was just past her elbow.

Kim frantically worked to get it the rest of the way to her hand as she heard one of them coming up the stairs.

*Oh, God- please give me another minute...*

The sound of the footsteps got closer...

*...come on...*

...whoever it was approached down the hallway.

The knife was so close, but she still couldn't reach it. She stifled a despairing sob as Josh walked in.

"I'm so glad you're still here, Kim. Breathing heavily again, eh? Looks like you've been doing more of that fruitless struggling- no doubt our audience enjoyed seeing that."

He looked into the lens of the main camera. "Show's over, John. As you may have guessed, I've experienced a most unexpected setback, but it's all right. Kim still will be with me. Even if this place is found, you won't have any clues as to where my next destination is. I'll be going to a place neither you nor anyone would ever think to look, but if you should happen to think of it, you'd better hope it's you- and you alone. If I see any police or anyone else besides you or with you, I promise you this: Kim will die. I'll send you that video for sure. Of course, if you come, I'll kill you, too. Food for thought.

"As for this place, you might want to pass on to the police that they should exercise extreme caution in trying to get inside. If they're not careful, it could be fatal- not only for those who would breach the door and those within a hundred feet, but also for the nine young women who are trapped inside and have no means of escape."

"*Mmmmph*!!!"

He backed away and smiled as he watched Kim tug at the cuffs again with a horrified expression on her face. "I see the lovely Miss Francis realizes that I'm not joking. I hope you and they will realize the same thing. Bye for now, John." He wanted John to see Kim in her state of alarm just before he shut down the link and the cameras. *I hope you're still watching.*

*This will make a good parting image of her for you...*

After killing the feed, he turned to Kim before he left the room. "I'll be right back."

Kim watched him go, fearing for the other women. However, knowing there was nothing she could do for them, anyway, she quickly came back to the other pressing matter.

*He didn't notice it!*

She'd been successful in shielding the knife from his view- fortunately he hadn't come any closer to her or else he probably would have seen it. She worked it the rest of the way up and finally was able to grab it. The first thing she thought to do was to get the blade back inside the handle. She pressed the tip against the bedpost, depressed the release and it was done.

*There's still a good chance he might realize I have it.*
*Then again he might not, since the handle is black, like my gloves.*
*It's a chance I have to take, anyway. I have nothing to lose...*

*I can't do anything with it now, since he's back, but*
*hopefully I'll get another opportunity when I'm alone- IF I can*
*keep it hidden from him. As long as he doesn't use handcuffs on*
*me I finally might be able to free myself...*

As she lay still and waited for him to come back for her,
she couldn't help but feel a fresh rush of fear. The threat he'd
made to kill her hung over her. That was something he'd never
even insinuated, but it wasn't much of a stretch for her to assume
that he could be getting desperate, which would make him more
dangerous to her than he already was.

*I just hope the others will be safe and that Jenny's OK...*


"You're a very brave young woman, Miss Jacobson.
Don't you worry: once you've led us to where we need to go,
we'll take over and we'll get him."

Detective Russo turned to the Donaldsons- the couple
who'd brought Jennifer to the station. "Thank you folks very much
for your help. At minimum, it looks like you've saved one life
tonight."

"So you're sure you don't need us anymore? You can get
back all right to the spot where we picked Jennifer up?"

"Yes, Sir, and thanks again. I know the area well; I'm
familiar with the road you're talking about. We'll get there, no
problem. If you'll excuse us, we need to get moving right away."
He turned to the beautiful girl. "Are you ready, Jennifer?"

She nodded and smiled, although her heart was pounding
again.


"Mm-mm! *Mmmmph!!*"

Kim cringed and tried to twist away as he took out the
bottle of chloroform. *If he uses that on me I'll drop the knife...*

"Maybe that isn't such a good idea; she could throw up,
you know. It happened before with the high school girl, and if Kim
does that while she's gagged..."

Josh though for a moment, then put the bottle back in his
pocket. "Good point. All right, Kim- Lisa's going to undo your

219

hands from the posts, then re-fasten 'em behind your back. If you fight her at all," he produced a large-caliber handgun, "you'll die right here. Understand?"

She nodded and Lisa undid the cuffs, then raised her up to a sitting position. Kim didn't resist, but her heart sank as her captor used one pair of the restraints to fasten her elbows, which would make it next to impossible for her to free her arms.

It sank even further when she heard the dreaded clinking of the metal handcuffs; Lisa quickly had her wrists imprisoned in them. Once that was done, she moved down, unlocked Kim's legs from the footposts and brought them together, then used one of the pairs of leather cuffs to bind her ankles.

*Well, at least she stopped him from chloroforming me.* Unfortunately, that small positive only stayed with her for a moment.

"That'll hold you for now. Do you have everything in the van, Lisa?" he asked as he scooped Kim up.

"Yeah, we're all set."

"All right. I think we'll have enough time to get away from here." He looked into Kim's eyes, again savoring the fear he saw in them. "At least, you'd better hope we do."


"Shit. I'm not surprised to hear that. I will say this; it's a good thing you stayed back and kept watching, or else we wouldn't have known. Obviously, we can't take the chance that he's bluffing...hold on, John- it's my other line."

John had just finished passing on Josh's warning that the place where he kept all his captives was booby-trapped.

*I hope they're not already-*

Tom came back on the phone. "They found Jenny! She was about twenty miles southwest of Philadelphia- Scott Russo just let me know. He's their head guy on the case, and I passed on your warning. He's notifying their bomb squad right now; I'm headed up there to hook up with 'em."

"That's great news, Tom. I hope they get the others soon. Is Jenny all right?"

"She's fine- a little drained, of course, but she's fine otherwise. She told Scott she needs to see you as soon as possible- she didn't say what about. We're close now, John; we're gonna get Kim back...John? Are you still-"

"Yeah, I'm still here. They won't find Kim- not where the other women are. Josh has taken her with him by now. He gave me a little parting shot before he killed the live feed. He's on the road and he'll probably be well out of the area by the time the guys up there find the house."

"*Dammit!* Just when I thought-...did he give any hints as to where he was headed? And were the computer guys able to trace the link?"

"No on both counts: they couldn't break through the security measures he had in place and Josh's hint was nothing more than a cryptic one. He said he's taking Kim to a place where no one would think to look. That could be anywhere."

He kept the rest of what Josh said to himself.

"Well, once we've found his place there should be some kind of trail we can uncover- at least a clue...I hope."


"This is where the Donaldsons said they picked you up, Jenny. Which direction did you run from?"

She took a moment to look around. "That way," she said, pointing east. "I remember the bend in the road. I didn't see them until they were almost up on me. It's definitely that way, probably a couple miles up or so."

"All right. Good." With the task force behind him, Detective Russo covered the distance pretty quickly. "We'll go slower now. There aren't many houses along this stretch, so it shouldn't take us long to find it..."

He was right about that.

When she saw the end of the driveway, all Jenny could do was point to it. Her mouth refused to work.


"You thirsty, Kim?"

"Mm-hmm," she nodded quickly to emphasize her answer and hopefully get a break from him and the gag.

She still had the knife in her grasp.

"Thought you might be." He reached into the cooler and grabbed a bottle of water.

So far, she'd spent the entire ride in his lap, still corseted, cuffed three ways and gagged, and also subjected to his intrusive hands and slimy lips. Each time he touched her disgusted her more than the last, but also as before, there was nothing she could do to stop him. She'd kept her eyes closed and simply tried to block him out, which unfortunately wasn't working so well anymore.

*At least he hasn't gone further than groping me yet, although what he's done- and is still doing- is sickening enough...*

*...and as long as he has me in these cuffs I have no chance of getting free...*

He rubbed more salt in. "Just think, now you don't have so much competition and I have who I want. I could get used to the simplicity after so many years of being weighed down. You were right about that; I'd say this way is much better..."

He was supposed to be severely shaken, if not frantic. Jenny had escaped and his house- the prison- in all probability was about to be overrun by the police. However, he didn't seem the least bit worried, which began to worry her as he finally unbuckled the gag and pulled it out of her mouth.

She winced as she moved her jaw around- this was by far the most uncomfortable, oppressive gag she'd been subjected to.

"Ready?"

She nodded again and accepted the water.

He watched as she gulped it down, then licked her luscious lips after finishing. Her innocuous action made him grab her hair to hold her still while he kissed her every bit as greedily as she drank the water. He couldn't stop himself if he wanted to.

It had been such a roller coaster day for Kim. First there was the realization that the inevitable was about to happen. Josh was going to cross the line in some way, which spawned her tirade in the gym room and also the harrowing journey from her room to Jennifer's. Next came her relief when she was able to free her former student, the agonizing wait for Josh and Lisa to come and get her, and her fervent hope Jenny wouldn't be discovered as she hid. After that was the horrible feeling that set in as she was sure Josh would rape her while John watched, the high she felt when Jenny escaped, her yearning for John, her success in getting the knife into her hand and the stress of knowing Josh might find it...

...and now this- the man she loathed more than any other, sticking his tongue down her throat. She couldn't pull away from him and there was no way she could make him stop...

*...oh, yes, there is.*

She bit down hard on his tongue and held it. Instinct had taken over completely, fueled by her anguish, frustration and all the hatred she'd come to feel for him.

Even though she knew it was very possible she'd committed her last act, she also knew she'd done the right thing. She released his tongue and could taste his blood. He screamed in pain and cocked his hand back to slap her. Instead, he grabbed her up and threw her onto the bed, then pulled his gun and pointed it right at her face.

Kim lay still, trying to accept her fate, if this was what it was coming to. She looked up at him and waited...

...but there still was a faint glimmer of hope.

*Lisa, if you're going to come around, now is the time...*

"You're not gonna beg me? You're not gonna plead with me to let you say goodbye to John?"

That triggered her anger yet again. "Why should I?! You know you're just baiting me- you wouldn't do that, anyway, just because you take the greatest pleasure in watching me suffer! Fuck you, Josh, you spineless piece of shit!! I'm surprised you can even mention John's name without cringing! You know you don't have the balls to face him- not in *any* arena! I bet it's the same with virtually everyone else, too!

"You made your mark- if you can call it that- by screwing over your partners and leaving them for dead or in prison to rot! They probably did all the work in the robbery, didn't they?! I don't buy for one *minute* that you didn't know about the sting I helped set up; you just wanted them to take the fall for you! You hid behind your little disguises and burrowed yourself into the ground; in fact, how can I be sure that Josh Strauss is your real name? Whatever the case, you've been flushed out and I know you're a lot more afraid than you're letting on- I can see it!

"Another thing: knowing me as you say you do, do you really think I could just allow you to rape me and not do anything about it?! Are you so delusional as to think you can make me forget about John just because you want me to and that I could accept being your slave?! If that or dying is my choice, I want you to pull the trigger because I can't- I *won't*- live like that! You may have destroyed the lives of ten innocent women, but thank God you won't get that chance with Jenny and I'll be *damned* if you're going to destroy mine!"

Josh started to shake. What he worked so hard to achieve was slipping away...

He turned when he heard Lisa behind him and just noticed that she'd stopped the van.

"Joshua? Are you listening?" When he shook his head she went on. "I was saying, why don't you go ahead and kill her?"

She smiled a little as she went on. "We're on a side road that looks pretty deserted- there are woods all around. You can take her outside and shoot her, and we'll be gone. We have more than enough money to just go somewhere and live out the rest of our lives, plus there are all the other bank accounts. All your records are here with us, too; no one can trace you. It can all be over. We'll be rid of this manipulating little slut once and for all."

Kim looked up at her, and her fear began to surge. Even though she wasn't really surprised that Lisa was back on Josh's side- and firmly so, apparently-, Kim fully realized that her situation was becoming more perilous by the second. When Lisa continued with her train of thought, that sense of foreboding worsened. Kim saw the resurgent hatred in her eyes and tried to quell her own antipathy. If she wasn't careful...

Lisa moved to the back of the van and stood over Kim, who glowered at her. "Think of all she's put you through...and worse, she tried to come between us. You should have seen her when I washed her, and also during other times when we were alone- especially earlier this evening. You were right about her all along. I think she was trying to use her looks and her body to get on my good side."

Kim's mouth fell open. "You lousy, lying-"

Lisa cut her off by slapping her as hard as she could. "*You shut your God-damned mouth, bitch*!! In fact, *I'll* shut you up right now!" She grabbed the gag and forced it back into Kim's mouth. She made sure she pulled the buckle tighter than it was before, making her cry out in pain. "There. Now you can try to talk all you want."

She turned back to Josh. "Think about it, Joshua: all your past baggage will be gone once you kill her. In fact, I'll be glad to kill her myself. Once she's out of the picture, you and I won't have anyone between us ever again." She pulled a revolver out of a gym bag and leveled it at Kim. "I can take the cuffs off her ankles and make her walk far enough into the woods so no one passing by will see anything. By the time they find her dead body,

224

we'll be long gone. Think about how much better that will be; she sure won't charm anybody anymore."

Kim's eyes already were tearing from the slap and now she was afraid as well as helpless, which was making them tear up even more. She did her best to fight them back.

It felt hollow where her stomach was supposed to be and she couldn't stop herself from shaking as she looked down the barrel of the second pistol that had been pointed at her in a very short span. The woman holding it had a stronger motive to want her dead than Josh did and she was one who Kim was certain wouldn't hesitate to do it.

Her hatred of Kim seemed to run even deeper than before, when she made her tremble after that fateful first breakfast. Josh no longer was the enemy she feared most. Her survival instinct superceded the moment of defiance she'd had with Josh. She thought of the experiences she yearned to have, especially the family she so badly wanted with John- more so now than ever...

She turned away from the gun and desperately looked up at Josh. He was deep in thought. She prayed he would have a change of heart, if for nothing else, to buy her time.

*I don't want to die- not like this...*

"Scared now, aren't you? You should be; you really did it this time. Just give me the word, Joshua, and it's done."


*Things would be easier that way...*
*...but then, I'd prove her right.*

Even though logic told him to just let Lisa kill her and be done with her, Kim's rebuke had cut deeply. Her words still reverberated in his head. That outburst, combined with the one she'd unleashed on him in the gym room, resurrected the spectre of the one who for years now had made it a habit of getting the better of him- the one with whom Kim's bond truly seemed unbreakable.

*You've sure paid me back in a lot of ways, haven't you, you bastard? It wasn't supposed to be like this...*

For so long, he'd believed that just physically having Kim with him would be enough- that what she felt for John didn't matter-, but now he realized how wrong he was about that. He was only fooling himself. It *did* matter. As long as John was alive, it always would matter, and in more ways than his bearing on Kim.

He was winning. Again.

The confrontation was unavoidable. He had to get rid of John; he had to beat him, once and for all…

*…and I know the perfect venue. You'll come, old buddy; you'll come for her.*

*We'll have that confrontation after all.*

"Joshua?" Lisa looked back at him- her last statement still hung in the air and he was staring straight ahead.

Finally he turned to her and shook his head. He saw her disappointment but held up his hand as she opened her mouth, no doubt to protest his decision. "Not yet, Lis- there's one last thing I have to do before all is settled. She tried to tempt you, eh? I'm not surprised, but I'm impressed with your ability to resist her charms.

"I have something in mind that you might find even better than killing her- at least, right now, anyway. If I can make it work, that is. If I can't, I'll take you up on your suggestion. You're right when you say that would be the easiest solution…"

He enjoyed the terror he saw in Kim's eyes before she looked away from him. He'd already made his decision and was only toying with her, but he didn't let on to her that he was.

Kim's disposition now was a sudden change- and most definitely one for the better. She was cowering and trying to shrink away from Lisa. *She even looked to me for help while Lisa had the gun on her…who knows, maybe if I play that card right…*

*…maybe there is still hope to ultimately break her. No one can take this kind of predicament forever, with the constant threat of death or worse hanging overhead…*

*…plus, if the best thing in her life is taken away from her, and it's done right this time…*

"Stay back here. Keep her company and keep her in line, using any means you feel the need to, or the desire to." He paused for a moment while that directive took root in both women- Lisa had a sadistically gleeful look on her face and Kim was visibly trembling as her fear deepened yet more.

"Make sure you don't leave any marks on her, though. I'll drive; we're not too far from where we need to be, so it won't be much longer. With any luck, we'll beat the storm that's coming.

"I need to think about this…"

226

# Chapter 9

"Here you are, Mister Governor. This is the last of the lists of customers from the corsetiers. It'll take us awhile to get through the ones we have and we figured you might want to check these out since you know who to look for...something to help keep you occupied." The officer handed the small stack of papers to him.

"Thanks, Janie. I'll let you know if I find anything." She smiled and left him alone.

Immediately- and carefully- he began to scan through them. There were ten lists in all, and they were rather lengthy.

*Looks like corsets aren't quite so unpopular as I thought...*

*...of course, we're talking a ten-year period, which might help in a way.* "That's a long time to go without making a mistake. You're good, but you can't be that good. You must have screwed up somewhere..."

*This is a well-timed storm. Everyone's probably indoors...*

The rain had started in earnest ten minutes earlier, so even though it was early summer, no one would be out roaming. Chances were no APB had been put out on the van as of yet, anyway, but he still was cautious- even more so since Jennifer's escape.

He turned onto the access road leading into the community and went past the lighthouse and the pond. *It'll be nice if I can enjoy this place for awhile, but I have a feeling that won't happen. It makes a good way station for now, though...*

He turned into the driveway and hit the garage door opener, drove inside and let the door close behind them.

"OK, Lis, let's get Kim's quarters ready for her. Blindfold her first, though, and take the cuffs off her upper arms while I check the inside. By now she needs a little break."

It was taking forever.

However, under the circumstances, Tom knew the painstakingly cautious procedure of the bomb squad was

227

necessary. Along with Jennifer, who told him how Kim helped her make her escape, he waited. The girl still was quite shaken- justifiably so- and hadn't left his side since he'd gotten there. She also cried on his shoulder more than once.

His admiration and fondness for Kim, which already were very strong, became stronger still. It didn't surprise him to hear that she'd been instrumental in the successful breakout given the way she'd put herself on the line years ago during that sting, but it hurt him, as it surely did John, that Kim would not be among the captives they were about to rescue.

"I'm curious, Jenny; what is it you need to tell John?" He became more curious when she looked away and began to fidget.

"Um…well, it's kind of personal. Miss Francis wanted me to give him a message from her. Will we be going back soon?"

"Yeah, we'll head back as soon as I know things are under control here. It shouldn't be too much-" He looked around when he heard someone yell 'All clear!'.

"Stick around here with the officers for a bit, OK? In fact, you can wait in my car if you like. I can't imagine you want to go back in there."

Jenny shook her head at first, but suddenly changed her mind. "Actually, do you mind if I go in with you? I think there's something of mine in there."

"Just tell me what it is and I'll-"

"No, it's- it's all right. I'll only be in there a moment. Besides, you and all the other officers will be inside, too."

Tom nodded and led the way.


"I think I have something here, Janie. Would you mind coming up for a second?…Ok, thanks."

John hung up and looked over the list again.

To his astonishment, not to mention his self-directed anger, it was on the first one he'd picked up that he saw it. Just as he'd asked, the investigators got records from the corsetiers dating back to 1989. *If I'd have thought to do this when Kelly mentioned the corsets, we could have nailed him almost right away…*

Hindsight truly was 20/20.

The New York-based manufacturer listed one purchase under Josh's name made per year from '90 until '93. Each purchase occurred very close to the date one of his victims had disappeared in that particular year. The mailing address was even listed- Pennsylvania, most likely where Tom and the rest of the team were right now. Then, in September of '94, a corporate order was made under the name of Kimberly Swimwear & Lingerie- Jeffrey Newman's company- not long after Megan Reilly, the competitive swimmer who in all probability was among Josh's captives, had vanished. Newman's company had placed the subsequent orders in the years leading up to the present one.

What really grabbed him was the order Newman had placed for two corsets- one black, one white- on April 16$^{th}$, the day he was shot and Kim was kidnapped. Given what Josh had revealed during his webcast a couple hours earlier, John knew why those orders were placed when they were.

*Chances are, they were the two corsets Kelly saw in the dressing room the day Kim was taken yet again. He had them ordered when he thought Daniels was going to turn Kim over to him.*

"What do you have, Sir?"

John looked at the young investigator. "Pull up a chair. We have the first hint of a paper trail…"


"So, did she behave?"

"Oh, yeah," Lisa smirked as she looked down at a very docile Kim. "She's a model prisoner now."

"Glad to hear it. I see you blindfolded her, too. Perfect. I want this surprise to have the same effect as the last one, if not better." He gathered Kim up into his arms, where she lay almost perfectly still. "Let's get her upstairs. I have everything ready."

On the way up, Lisa asked, "How long will we be here?"

"Not very long, unfortunately; a couple days at most. It really is a nice place, isn't it? The last owner even left the furnishings; apparently he and his girlfriend had some bad memories here."

He walked into the bedroom and set Kim down onto the bed, then he straightened up and smiled. "Here's another one you'll enjoy, Kim." He undid her blindfold.

When he pulled it away and her eyes adjusted, a chill started at her scalp and slowly moved all the way down.

She couldn't breathe and little whining sounds began to come out of her.

"What's with her?"

Josh turned to Lisa. "Until a month or so ago, this house belonged to Kim's boyfriend, the illustrious Governor of Maryland. Also, it was in this very house on this past April 16th that Miss Francis here was held captive by a would-be associate of mine while he and his accomplice lay in wait for the Governor, who killed the accomplice before being shot three times by my associate. I bought this place when John put it up for sale." He looked back at Kim, enjoying the sheer terror he clearly saw in her unfocused eyes. He couldn't see very much green in them because her pupils were fully dilated. "Fitting, isn't it? You might spend the last night of your life in the place where your loving man almost spent the last night of his.

"As for Lisa and me, we'll be leaving the country. We have to take off in a bit to meet up with someone who will make that happen for us, so you'll be by yourself for awhile. I'm not sure exactly what I'll do with you yet. I haven't ruled out killing you, especially since it had to be through your doing that Jennifer escaped and all the other girls by now have been rescued. Your door was the only one that wasn't locked at the time. I don't know how you could have pulled it off, but I gotta hand it to you: that was quite a feat.

"I'm sure you know Lisa's campaigning pretty hard for your death. If I end up taking her advice, which I will say is very good advice, you'll pay the ultimate price for those rants of yours and the other disruptions you've caused and all will be done.

"But, see, that's the problem, too. If I kill you, it's only one quick punishment for all and that's it. I really want to make you regret what you did. If I can bring that about I'll do it, which is why there's a chance you'll be making the trip with us. On the way here I came up with something that I think will help get us back to the way things should be and settle an old score in the process."

He pulled out his phone and moved in front of her. She'd managed to calm herself a little, but she still looked very disconcerted and afraid, as evidenced by her breathing and the much lighter than normal shade of her face. He gestured to Lisa, who sat next to her.

"So you don't believe I have the balls to confront John? What do you say we put your assumption to the test? Just think, you could have that last moment with him after all. Would you take that gag out of her mouth for a minute, Babe?" When Lisa did that, he went on. "What's his cell phone number?"

That jolted Kim back to the present. Her mouth fell open and her eyes locked onto his, then narrowed as she sealed her mouth like a vault and glared defiantly at him.

Josh smiled. "That's all right. I didn't expect you to give it up; I only wanted to see that contrary look on your face. I'll just get your cell phone out of your purse. I already know John's number's programmed into it."

"*NO!!*" Kim struggled with renewed vigor and tried to stand, but Lisa pulled her back down and held her down.

"Cover her mouth- no, use your hand for now." Lisa dropped the gag and took a firm hold of her. She clamped her hand tightly over Kim's mouth, then Josh grabbed the purse and took out her phone.

"MMMMMPH!!!" Kim fought her until she raised the gun to her temple and cocked it. She lay still against Lisa and watched in despair as Josh pressed a few buttons, found what he was looking for and raised her phone to his ear.

She began to weep when she heard John answer.


"...so if we can get credit card numbers- or better yet, cancelled checks- maybe we can nail down his bank account. One of 'em, anyway. We cut off his money supply..."

"...we shut him down," Janie added, finishing his thought. "I'll get right on it, Sir- looks like I handed you the right pile!" She smiled as she went off toward her office and her computer.

John leaned back in Tom's chair and looked at the monitor on which he'd seen Kim not so long ago. Almost right away, he saw her again, dressed and bound as she was. That image would be a hard one to get rid of.

He prayed it wouldn't be the last way he would see her...

The ring of his cell phone disrupted his thoughts. He reached into his pocket and pulled it out, figuring it was Tom calling to give him an update.

When he looked at the screen, his heart stopped.

KIM-CELL.

All he could do for a moment was stare at the phone- he couldn't move or think...

*...the knife!! Could she have gotten away?!*

231

That desperate inkling finally jarred him out of his haze and he frantically jabbed the 'talk' button. "Kim?! Is it-"

"Hi there, John. She's here, but she can't talk at the moment. I'm gonna get right to the point here just in case you have any thoughts of triangulating me, although I can't imagine you were expecting this call.

"You and I are going to meet. Tomorrow night. I'll call you with the time and place. I know it might be tough for you to ditch your security detail, but for Kim's sake, you'd better find a way. If I sniff any police of any kind- even if I see one in the area by happenstance-, she dies."

"How do I know you won't kill her anyway?"

"You don't, but you and I both know you'll come. You have to see her- there's no way you could live with yourself if you didn't make the effort, so let's just knock off the-"

"Is that her? What are you doing to her?!" During Josh's last statement he was sure he heard Kim's muffled cries. When he didn't respond, John became frantic. "Let her talk with me...do you hear me?! Put her on, you son of a-"

"Tsk, tsk- such language! You know, I like this situation a lot more. All those times you got the better of me and now it's the other way around, isn't it? I could simply ignore your request, but I'll throw you a small bone. Here she is..."


Josh covered the mouthpiece, turned to Lisa and nodded. When she took her hand away, Josh looked Kim straight in the eyes. "No mention of where we are unless you want John to come here and find your corpse. Of course, if you have no problem doing that to him, I have no problem doing it to you. Your choice." He took his hand away from the mouthpiece and held the phone up for her.

As much as it pained her to know that yet again she would be used as bait for John, she also knew that Josh was right- there was no way John wouldn't meet him and he probably would blame himself somehow if he didn't and Josh or Lisa killed her.

There was no way around it.

Her love for John and her anguish from the apparent hopelessness of the situation overwhelmed her. She cried harder as Josh raised the phone to her cheek.

"Shhh, don't do that, Kitten, try to take it easy."

Just hearing his soothing voice further intensified both emotions that held her in their grip just as effectively as the restraints fettered her arms and legs. "I love you so much…"

"I love you, too, Honey. I'm so sorry about-"

"No, please don't apologize, John. I should have told you, but-…" Suddenly she thought about what would happen very soon.

*They'll be gone for a while, and they'll be leaving me here. It might work, if I can only find a way to tell him where I-*

She found one that quickly, and under the circumstances it was very easy for her to convey her panic through her tone of voice. "Baby, I'm so afraid; I'm having that horrible nightmare again…" She tugged at her cuffs and struggled against Lisa's grip. "*Please* get me out of hmmr- *mmmmph*!!"

Josh took the phone away and Lisa easily subdued her again- her hand quickly covered Kim's mouth. Kim could only listen and watch as Josh finished the phone call.

*I hope you got that, John…*


"Finally, I doubt it's necessary for me to remind you of this, but if you tell anyone about this call or what you have to do tomorrow evening, which I will know if you do, Kim will cease to be. You have your instructions. I'll call you."

He killed the connection and dropped the phone. "You really are afraid when you're in this place, aren't you, Kim? A lot of demons here, huh? I've hardly ever seen you in such a state…"

*…which could be very useful in one way, but it also could push you to try even harder to escape. Good thing I've taken every precaution to make sure you'll be tied up tight and then some. Wait 'til you see my last little present for you,* he thought with a smile.

"Guess we need to get you situated so we can take care of our business. Like I said, we'll have to leave you alone for a while. So, needless to say, we'll have to make sure you're extra comfortable. Do me a favor, Lis- freshen her up, but make it quick. After you gag her again and bring her back here, grab the special little gadget we brought for her." *I doubt very much you'll be wriggling out of that one,* he mused as his smile made its way to the outside.

Lisa grinned evilly at Kim. "That will be my pleasure."

233

* * *

Dean stared blankly at the television screen. Yet another night of sitcoms.

His mind seemed to be turning into mush and it wouldn't be long before the rest of him followed, if he kept up with his present course. Going to a gym was totally out of the question, as was jogging or any outdoor activity, for that matter.

He still didn't have clue one as to where Strauss could be. Things were looking very bleak, especially since his options were almost non-existent. *Somethin's gotta give here...*

An interruption by the local news anchor brought him to attention and he listened in.

"We have breaking news to report regarding the ongoing investigation involving the string of abductions of a dozen young women from Maryland, Pennsylvania and New Jersey. Apparently one of the two latest victims, Miss Jennifer Jacobson, managed to escape from where all twelve of the women- all still alive, as we've just learned- had been kept. Ann Warner is live at that house with the latest developments and the full story as we know it thus far. Ann?"

"Thank you, Jim. I have Detective Scott Russo here with me. Detective Russo is the head of the Pennsylvania task force assigned to the case. His team has worked alongside similar task forces from the two other states involved and the FBI. Thank you for giving us a moment; could you bring us up to speed with all that's happened?"

"Certainly. With the help of one of the other captives, Miss Kimberly Francis, Miss Jacobson was able to make a daring escape. She was exceptionally brave under those circumstances. Then, Pete and Alice Donaldson, a couple who happened to be driving along a side road off Route 41, came across Miss Jacobson, picked her up and brought her to the station. Since that road is so lightly traveled, we really lucked out there- the Donaldsons were a Godsend.

"After Miss Jacobson told me what happened and what the situation at the house was, my task force along with a bomb squad converged on this location as quickly as we could. There was fear of a booby trap, which was the reason why the bomb squad was with us, but fortunately that turned out to be a bluff.

234

"Once inside, we found nine more of the captives, who'd been kept in what amounted to an underground prison probably for the entire duration of their captivity. I'm happy to report that all are in excellent condition physically and their families are being notified as we speak.

"Unfortunately, Miss Francis was not among the captives we found here. We believe that the perpetrator, Joshua Strauss, along with Lisa Meyers, the first abductee who is now believed to be Mister Strauss's accomplice, returned to the house before we could get here and took Miss Francis to another as yet unknown location. Every state and federal law enforcement agency is on the trail; we will spare no effort in tracking them down.

"Excuse me, Ann, I have to get back now."

"Of course, Detective Russo. Thank you very much for your time." She turned back to the camera. "Jim, we have pictures of the suspects, Joshua Strauss and Lisa Meyers, and also of Miss Kimberly Francis- the last of the captives- that Detective Russo requested we put on the air. It is unknown at-"

Dean clicked off the set and leaned back.

*Looks like you fucked up, pal- big time...*

*...but now you're on the run with all the bloodhounds on your ass. If they catch you, I'm out all that money. Worst of all, I still have no fuckin' idea where you could be headed...*

*...or, do I?* One detail of what he'd learned over the past weeks and the circumstances surrounding it came back to him.

However, some doubt sprang up almost immediately. *It wouldn't make sense for him to do that. He's got all the cards- most importantly, his and Stratton's Queen of Hearts. There's no reason why he should take such a risk...*

*...unless...*

He thought of a reason that made sense, in a way, especially considering how much he hated Stratton...

*It's worth a shot. Time's running out and other than that I got nothing to go on...*

*At least she changed my gag,* Kim thought as Lisa took hold of her arm and led her back into the bedroom. *I never thought I'd consider a ball gag comfortable...*

Once more, she was trying to seize upon every little positive she could in order to avoid focusing on where she was, but those positives were very few in number and very small in significance.

The thunderstorm was growing worse and starting to nullify any good thought completely. It was another reminder of the night of April 16th. In light of that, she was growing ever more alarmed about being left alone, especially here. She was sliding down into a chasm of fear and it seemed that she had only one hope left...

*...please come for me, John. I can't take much more...*

Lisa handed her over to Josh. "I'll be right back." With that she left, and Kim was alone with him.

"Have a seat." He gestured to the bed and Kim did as he said. It was a very long and uncomfortable moment between then and the time Lisa returned, in part because he didn't say another word. No gloating, no sexual innuendos- nothing.

Other than the sound of the fusillade of raindrops hitting the house and thunderclaps that were increasing in regularity and getting closer, there was silence...

...except for the alarm clock ticking. An icy hand reached in and took hold of her stomach the instant she picked up on that. It sounded just like the one she'd had in the bedroom of her apartment near Princeton- the same one that marked the passing seconds and minutes as she lay on her bed waiting for Josh to return for her.

Just then, she saw Lisa in the doorway, holding a metal bar that she also recognized pretty quickly. Kim mewled as her morale fell even more and she looked away.

"You remember your posture bar, Kim? Ah, I see you do. That'll prevent you from doing what you just did. It'll keep you nice and erect, just like you need to be." Lisa walked over and handed it to him, then stood by to assist him as he began to lock Kim into it.

He started with the high, stiff black collar that functioned as a neck corset, which was locked on to the top of the bar. He fastened it around her neck and tightened it enough to 'hold her head high', providing the upward tilt to her chin that gave her an appearance of pride and superiority. Given her state of dress and bondage, the latter of which he only was getting started with, he found that very amusing. *You have to love the irony...*

Next came the shackles for her upper arms. As usual he clamped them on just above her elbows, which were held closely together as a result. He fastened the belt tightly around her waist. Finally, he locked the heavy handcuffs onto her wrists. All those components were integrated into the posture bar. When he finished securing her to it he removed the other handcuffs he had on her.

That done, he helped her to her feet. "Come on- it's time to bed you down for the night. I have a special place all set up for you."

She glumly walked into the hallway with her captors on both sides of her. *I hoped he'd tie me to the bed, but no such luck. I'm in handcuffs again, which still makes this knife useless.*

*All that effort I put out to get it, and for what? It probably wouldn't matter if I got rid of the damned thing now, especially since I could make them angry if they catch me with it. Now, I have this cursed bar to put up with for God knows how long...*

*...what will they do to me next?*


Again, John had to wait.

It had been over eighteen days already and now it looked as if he'd have to wait yet another. Seeing that Kim was all right and then hearing her voice made him feel better in one way, but also twisted the dagger in his side. There still was nothing he could do other than be at his enemy's beck and call, waiting to jump when he said to- right into a deathtrap.

There was no question as to whether or not he would go; Josh was right about that.

As he sat there contemplating the endless possibilities as to what could go down in twenty-four hours or less, he kept replaying what Kim had said. Each word from her was a precious drop of water, but there just weren't enough of them, nor could there be.

Nothing short of being with her again would do for him.

The next thing he knew, someone was shaking him.

"John?"

"Yeah, I'm...oh- hey, Tom. Sorry about that, I was just- Jenny!" He got up and embraced her. "It's great to see you and to know you're all right." He backed away and smiled at her. "My God- look at you! I haven't seen you since you were fourteen...*wow!*"

She'd always been very pretty in the face, but the slightly chubby girl had blossomed into a very well-put-together young woman, which he clearly saw as she stood before him in that outfit.

The more he looked at her...

*...no- don't dwell on that. It won't help...*

When he shook that off, he noticed something about her that had not changed at all- her shyness. She seemed to blush from head to toe as he took her in.

Jenny's hands fidgeted as she continued to look down. Eventually she glanced over at Tom and then back to John before she looked down again.

Taking the hint, Tom excused himself. "I have to go downstairs and check with my team- see if they have anything new to report. I'll be back."

"OK, Tom, catch you in a bit." After he left, John turned back to Jenny. "Come sit down. Are you hungry? Or thirsty?"

"No, thank you. I'm fine. The guys at the station gave me lots to eat and drink."

He nodded. "By the way, I heard you made the cheerleading squad. Congratulations! Will you still be joining them?"

"Mm-hmm. I think I'll be all right by the time we get into the season. Plus, I worked hard for that spot on the team and I enjoy it. I'm looking forward to cheering again."

"Did Kim tell you she also cheered for them? They won the Super Bowl the last year she was on the squad. I just found that out."

"No, she didn't...we didn't have much of a chance to talk."

"I suppose not." John turned away. "You know, it's almost scary how much alike you and she look..." He changed gears and tried to steer himself away from the dread he felt over what could happen to Kim, which yet again loomed right in front of him. "Anyway, I'm glad to hear you'll be joining the squad after all. It's good you're not going to let what he put you through ruin your life."

She saw his spirits sinking and tried to buoy them. "Well, it...things would have been much worse for me if-...if Miss Francis hadn't done what she did." That statement brought Jenny to her other purpose, which would be rather complicated for her given how she'd felt about John when she babysat for his brother's children.

The longer she sat with him, the more she felt the resurgence of those feelings, along with her desire to make him feel better any way she could. Although the window was open and it was a cool night with the wind kicking up- and also in spite of the little bit of clothing as she was wearing-, the room began to feel very warm. "I, um...there's something I need to give you from-...I mean, Miss Francis wanted me to tell you that she-..."

John regarded her curiously as she looked away again.

Then, suddenly, she embraced him and gave him a very deep kiss that in short order turned him into a lump of gelatin.

She retreated as she finished, breathing raggedly and unable to face him. "She, um...she wanted me to- to tell you that she loves you and to give you...well, *that*. I- I wasn't sure how you..."

It took a moment before John's shock wore off. It really did feel like Kim kissed him. Jenny's stammering brought him back; wanting to calm her, he touched her hand. She fell silent, although she still trembled and her eyes darted back and forth. "Thank you, Jenny."

She finally was able to settle down and collect herself. When she looked back up at him, she was filled with sympathy for him as his expression remained a downcast one. It didn't take much insight to know where his thoughts were.

"Tell me about Kim; tell me everything that happened. I need to know."

She did that, holding nothing back. She told him about the moment their abductor brought her into the van and the next morning when she defied him at breakfast. After that, the next time she saw Kim was when she came into the room a few hours earlier and freed her, so unfortunately there wasn't much for her to tell him.

"I wanted to take her with me when I made my break, but she wouldn't let me. The way she was tied, I couldn't free her, anyway. He put locks on the straps he bound her with and we didn't have knives or anything. She also was in handcuffs. She had to tiptoe all the way from her room to mine in those super-high heels- she even did that while she was blindfolded! She was so tired and sore when she got to me because she'd already worked out earlier.

"He was so horrible to her the whole time; he even slapped her! I could tell he had because her cheek was a little red.

I don't know how she was able to keep herself together, but she did. I admire her even more now than before; she knew she was the one he was focused on and she used that against him.

"She always was so kind to me and so helpful when she was my counselor, but now…she risked her life for me- for all of us- and there was nothing I wanted more than to return the favor and get her away from him, but we were too late. I'm sorry, John- I'm so scared for her. What if he-…what if he killed her?"

She stopped when he took her into his arms and couldn't keep herself from crying in spite of her efforts.

"Don't say that; just calm down…I-…"

*I have to tell her. The poor girl's feeling such guilt because she got away and Kim didn't.*

He pulled back from her and raised her chin, making her face him. "Kim's all right. I…talked with her about an hour ago."

Jenny took hold of his hands. "Really?! Did she get-" The set of his face answered that for her. Obviously, Kim didn't get away. "I mean…was it- was it a ransom call? What did she say?"

"We didn't get to talk for long, but we got to tell each other what matters most."

"Did you? That must have made both of you feel better."

"It did, but…God, how I hated hearing and feeling the fear in her voice. As strong a woman as she is and always was, to hear her breaking down like that and not being able to help her or calm her…that's what hurts more than anything.

"I've never picked up on her being so afraid, except for a few months ago at my old house when she-"

He froze like he'd looked right into the eyes of Medusa.

*It changed…*

*…the tone of her voice. I knew she was afraid, but suddenly her voice got higher…*

*…and she had that night terror while she was there, mainly because she was there, given all that went down…*

*…was she trying to tell me-*

The same kind of gut reaction he had when Vanessa told him about Kim's boyfriend in college being the number one student in law school seized him again…

*…Jesus- he has her at my house!!*

As soon as that came to him, he knew it had to be true. Josh said he was taking Kim to the last place anyone would think to look, which the house that had been John's most definitely was.

240

It made perfect sense…

"…hey, what's wrong?" His intensity was beginning to intrigue Jenny as she watched him. He seemed to have forgotten she was with him.

All of a sudden he'd zeroed in on something like a fighter's radar locks onto an enemy jet. In that instant Jenny's fear was gone and her curiosity was piqued. She recalled what he talked about just before whatever it was grabbed hold of his cognizance…

*…could it be…?*

He jumped when she touched his arm. He glanced at her, then quickly stood up. "I have to get out of here. Tom will drop you off at your house. I'll talk with-"

"Wait a minute…what are you going to do?"

"You'll be all right here. Tom said he'd be right back. I don't have time to talk- I have to go." He moved toward the door.

Jenny got in front of him. "You know where she is, don't you?" Even though he didn't say a word, he couldn't hide his answer. "You *do*!! Where immmph-"

"*Shhh!*"

*Dammit…*

As he stood in his brother's office with Jenny pinned against him and his hand clamped over her mouth, John quickly ascertained that the situation was on the brink of becoming even more complex than it already was.

*What in the hell am I going to do now?*


Kim's legs began to feel heavy. She realized they were guiding her toward the last room in the house she wanted to be in.

It was the place where she was certain she saw John die.

Josh just wouldn't stop tormenting her. Every little detail he could think of, every thing or place or event that was in any way traumatic for her, he would use against her.

She took a deep breath and closed her eyes as they reached the doorway…

…and when they took her into the study, a tiny cry was her reaction when she saw what was right in the middle of the room, waiting for her. That barely audible wail seemed to signal the last shards of energy and hope leaving her.

A feeling of complete desolation took control of her.

"You know, you could show a little more appreciation for the accommodations I'm making for you, Kim. All the trouble I went through to put this together- I did it myself, you know. Looks just like the last one you were in, eh? I know we're talking about twelve years ago, but I'm sure something like this stands out in your memory, doesn't it?"

He was about to needle her some more but stopped short when he saw her expression, which he was able to sum up with that one magical word: capitulation.

The deeper he looked into her eyes, the more he knew it was true. She was totally lost, like a little girl separated from her parent at a grocery store. He didn't see that in her at any other time. He was certain that she was on the verge eleven years ago, at the same juncture where they were now- with him having to take a short trip.

Until this moment, she'd resisted him.

*Not any more, though...*

She just stood there, staring at the gilded cage that waited to swallow her. It was the perfect symbol of her defeat- the fitting end of his campaign to subdue her.

He had won.

He looked over at Lisa, who smiled at him. She'd seen that look on the faces of all the other captives; she knew it just as well as he did.

"All right, time's a-wastin', so let's get you inside." They led her to the door of the cage and helped her down into it and onto the pillow he'd put down for her. "Scoot over and sit against the back there, just like you did for your friend that night...good girl. Now, cross your ankles- in those heels, you'll have to sit Indian-style." When she did that he clamped the shackles, which were bolted to the bottom of the cage and on the end of a short chain, onto her ankles.

Her expression remained almost blank as he shut the door and locked her inside. There was no chance of her escaping and no one would hear her above the storm and the ball gag if she cried out for help.

*Best of all, no one knows where she is,* he thought as he stood to leave.

"Mmmmph!!"

He looked down at her.

*Please don't leave me here alone!*

242

He barely could tell that was what she was trying to say. Her muffled entreaty- and more so the way she made it- dispelled any inkling he had that she might have any remaining will to resist. He clearly recalled how she was the night she escaped, when she also begged him not to leave her by herself. She was right on the verge then, just like she was now…

…and the more he looked at her, the more convinced he was becoming that he had her. Her eyes and her body language were virtually the same as they were the night of June 12th, 1989.

The mere thought of her coming to that state had distracted him while he tied her that cool, breezy spring night over a decade ago; his anticipation was such a distraction that he obviously ended up making a mistake when he tied her hands. He doubted it was her intention to so preoccupy him then.

As he looked into her eyes, which were filled with panic, he had no doubt whatsoever that was not her intention now. Better yet, he was certain that a repeat of the result of that long-ago night would not happen on this night. This time his focus was absolute, and he knew her slide into total submission was at hand.

Her fear seemed even more pervasive than it was in the van on the way to their present location. He was certain that in that fear he now had the best weapon of all to use against her. "Another reminder of the past- kinda similar to the last night of your last stay with me, isn't it? Only this time you're more securely bound, plus you're locked inside the cage. There's no escape for you, Kim. You are where you belong. Like I've told you time and again: John won't come to your rescue, nor will anyone else. Maybe you're finally beginning to accept that as fact.

"We'll see you in a few hours; we'll have time to play when we get back. You'd be too much of a diversion now, so you'll just have to be a little patient." He leaned in close to her to make his next point clear. "Maybe the next time the impulse to defy me in *any* way crosses your mind, you'll think about this experience you're about to have and reconsider.

"I'll leave you alone with your memories…then again, maybe I shouldn't put it like that. You have plenty of spectres from the past to keep you company, so you really *won't* be here alone, will you?"

He went to get up, then stopped himself. "Oh, I almost forgot something."

From his pocket he produced the small clamps attached to the ends of a short chain. As he reached in to the cage and pulled down the cups of her bra, he couldn't prevent his smile from breaking out- even though she knew where he was going to put the clamps and he knew that she absolutely detested them, she made no attempt to back away. All she did was watch, her despair apparent, and wince as he fixed them onto her where they would cause the most discomfort.

*With that, the prosecution rests. No further proof will be necessary.*

"Well, have fun, 'Kitten'. See ya soon!"


"Mmmm!!"

It finally registered in John's mind that he still had his hand over Jenny's mouth; she reminded him of that orally, and with a frown, as he looked at her. He quickly removed it. "Sorry."

"I'm coming with you. Whatever it is that you're doing, I'm going to help and I won't take 'no' for an answer."

"Jenny, you were abducted and held for three weeks. I won't let you put yourself at risk again. Don't you want to see your parents?"

"Well…I guess, but Miss Francis is more like family to me than they are, especially now. You're not going to keep me from-"

"You know Kim would not approve in the least of you putting yourself in danger again, especially after all she went through to spring you. Think about it: what if something was to go wrong and he ended up capturing you again?"

She thought for a minute. "All right, maybe I'm not the best person to be directly involved in her rescue, but I'm sure there are things I can do to help you."

"Please don't argue with-"

"You're wasting time, and if you try to go without me I'll tell your brother…hold on- why are we even discussing this, anyway? And why are we keeping our voices down? You'll have police with you along with your bodyguards, right? I can stay with them- in fact, isn't that where you'll be? You're not a police officer, either."

He didn't say anything and looked about ready to erupt.

*No…he wouldn't do that…*

*...on the other hand, as much as he loves her...* "Oh my God- you're going to act alone?! Have you thought this through?"

"How in the hell-" he stopped and lowered his voice. "No, I'm gonna have to make this up as I go along. I didn't even know I would take this course until I saw the reason for it a few minutes ago. Yes, I'm pretty sure I know where he has her and I've got to get there now. I have to go alone, too- I have no choice."

"No way. I am *definitely* going with you." A thought came to her that she figured could help to the end. "If you're not taking your bodyguards, don't you have to get away from them? Do you think they'd just let you go and do whatever it is that you're going to do without them? Isn't it their duty to protect you? To keep you *out* of harm's way?"

He looked away. "Yeah."

"So, you'll need to shake them somehow, right? In fact, I remember you doing that earlier this year when-" She stopped abruptly when he held up his hand.

"Don't remind me of that. Jenny, I need you to get to the point- seconds could be crucial here."

"Do you have a way to slip out of here without them knowing?"

"No, I'm trying to think of one. With that attempt on my life, they've been sticking very close to me. The only reason someone's not in this room with me now is because we're in the police station where my brother works and everyone here knows me. The building's secure, too."

"Maybe some kind of diversion would help..." Her brow furrowed as she thought.

An idea came to John as he looked at Jenny, a very beautiful, attention-grabbing young woman, who happened to be clad in a flashy and revealing spandex dance outfit. "You must have gotten plenty of glances and double-takes as you came in."

She giggled and shifted around a bit, then coyly replied, "Yes, I suppose I did. I think everyone in the station must have..." She trailed off when she saw a strange little grin on his face, but in a matter of a few seconds, a big smile of recognition lit her face up as she moved close to him and touched his chest. "That just might work! What a great idea! So you will take me with you?"

John couldn't help but chuckle. Her exuberance was very good to see, considering how timid she'd always been. "You could be a big help, so yes, you're coming, too."

"I do want to help you and Miss Francis; I promise I won't get in your way. What do you want me to do?"

"Well, our first concern is getting out of here, which you'll play an important role in..."


Kim jerked yet again as another deafening clap of thunder came almost immediately after a flash of lightning that looked as though it could have been from a nuclear explosion. There was no way she could hide from the storm. Knowing how much squalls like this one frightened her, he'd positioned the cage so it faced the window and the addition of her posture collar forced her to look directly at it. It was even worse for her than it had been when she was six years old and confined to her room the night another bad storm hit.

Her mother wasn't home that night and her stepfather, without saying a word to her, had marched her up the steps and made her go into her room. He shut and locked the door behind her. Kim hadn't even done anything wrong. It wasn't her fault that he didn't see the cup of water she'd set down on the table- the same one he ended up knocking over and spilling onto the paper he was reading. However, that didn't stop him from blaming her.

The severe thunderstorm struck about half an hour after she'd been locked in. When the first big clap came, she began to cry and ran for the door. For what seemed to be an eternity, she repeatedly twisted the handle and pounded on the door, all the while pleading with her stepfather to come for her. He never did.

When it sank in that neither he nor anyone else would let her out, she sought refuge in the best place she could find- her closet. She shut herself in there and huddled with her favorite teddy bear in the farthest corner where she prayed for the storm to go away.

In a way, she stayed in that closet for the next eight years and even afterwards went back into it from time to time.

Kim sobbed as that memory she'd kept at bay for so long came back with a vengeance. What made it worse was her inability to take refuge in her closet this time. She was forced to languish in the cage, totally restrained, silenced and imprisoned both physically and emotionally, as the storm raged on and her demons continued their assault on her.

This time, it felt like they were winning...

* * *

"I thought for sure he'd recognize me. That was some class-A improvisation you pulled in there." *You almost were too effective...*

They stood half a block away from the station, on President Street in between Baltimore and Fayette Streets. They'd stopped for a moment to let the aftershock wear off from another kiss that was even more intense than the one she'd given him for Kim. As it did, John saw clear evidence of guilt on the girl's face.

"Jenny, it's all right. You had to do that or else we never would have gotten away from there. Kim would understand, too."

"I hope she would. I hope she'd understand about...well, all of this. I mean, are we doing the right thing? You haven't explained why-"

"No, I haven't- not yet. Come on, we have to get moving."

"Where can we go? Do you have a car here?"

"No, and I know you don't, either. We'll need to hail a cab."

They hurriedly walked down President Street toward Lombard and avoided The Block, a notorious part of the city on Baltimore Street which, ironically, was located right next to the Central District Headquarters of the City Police- the very station they'd just left. With the way Jenny was dressed, The Block was the last place she needed to be.

"Are you sure you don't want your brother in on this? You know he'd want to help and that he'll be very upset once he finds we've gone."

"I know. We have another more immediate problem: I only have twenty bucks or so on me, which won't get us a cab ride to where we need to go. Is your car at your- dammit, that's right, he took you while you were in the D.C. area at your cheerleading tryouts. I guess your car's there, too."

That was something she didn't have cause to think about until now. "Yeah, it probably still...no, wait- it's at my house! My roommate dropped me off and I was going to get a ride back with her after I was done. May I use your phone to-" She didn't even finish asking him before he handed it to her. "Ok, I'll give her a call to make sure she's there. My keys are in my purse, which I never was able to find..." She dialed the number and waited.

247

No answer. "Damn, I got our voicemail. Maybe she's in the shower or something…Gina? It's me, Jenny. If you're there, I need you to call me back on this cell number- it's very important. It'll be so great to see you again. I'm free, I'm all right and I'll catch you soon." She left the number at the end of the message, then handed the phone back to John when she was finished.

"I just thought of something else. They'll be looking for both of us, which means they'll probably go to your place before long. We really need to- *hey!*" He whistled as loudly as he could, and fortunately the cab pulled toward them. "All right, he's stopping! Come on, let's get in and hope your roommate's home."

"Even if she isn't, we hid a spare house key inside a phony rock in case we got locked out. If we end up having to use that I just hope I can remember where my spare car key is."

"Well, there's some food for thought for you during the ride to your place. Once we have your car, which hopefully will start, I'll tell you everything so you'll know what the situation is and understand why I can't tell anyone else, including Tom.

"With any luck, I'll come up with some kind of a solution on the way…"


Kim desperately tried to fight off the panic she knew was on the verge of claiming her.

Right on the heels of her recollection of that terrible experience she'd had as a child came the one that was so prevalent given her position and her location- that of what happened the last time she was in this room. It was the same event that triggered the night terror she had as she and John lay in bed in the next room over.

In that horrible vision, she saw Josh- not Walter Daniels- standing over John holding the gun. With all that had happened over the past weeks, she'd come to realize why it was Josh she saw when she reached the room and the lightning flashed.

That vision seemed almost certain to become reality.

Never in her life- not in any single experience she'd ever had- had she felt so afraid and helpless. Every impulse she felt was negative, every thought she had was just another powerful wave crashing down on her- they rushed in relentlessly, one after the other, and their combined force further eroded her beleaguered and severely weakened defenses. There didn't seem to be anything she could latch onto- Jenny and the others were probably safe, but as much as that had helped her earlier, it did nothing for her now. Her chance to escape had come and gone; she remained in bondage and things were about to get even worse. There were no more diversions to keep Josh away from her tonight when he returned.

Worse still were his intentions toward John…

"*John*!! Where in the hell are you?! I was just picking up the phone to call you; your bodyguards are in an uproar and I was just about to put out an APB! Are you out of your fucking mind sneaking out of here like that?! And where's Jenny?"

"She's with me. In a way, I guess I am out of my mind- I have been since Kim was taken. I didn't tell you, but…I talked with her."

"You talked with Kim?! Is she-"

"She's scared, Tom. We weren't able to talk for long. Josh wants me to come by myself. He told me if he sees anybody other than me, he'll kill her. I know what the risks are by doing this, but I have to go. I can't take the chance that he's bluffing."

"John…listen to me. Step back a minute and think about what you're doing. You told me how much Josh hates and resents you. Don't you think he'll kill you, too?"

"Do you remember the talk we had when you dropped me off at Kim's this April?"

It took a moment for Tom to reply. "I remember every word and I know what you're trying to tell me, but…what will you do, John? What *can* you do? Can't you see he's setting you up? I want you to tell me exactly what he told you. Maybe between us we can find another course of action."

When John told him, Tom wished he hadn't asked. From what John spelled out, he couldn't see another way, either.

*Even though that fuck so much as told John he'd kill him, he didn't hesitate. He went right away…*

"She *is* everything to me; I realize that now more than ever. As soon as Josh told me all he did, I knew what I had to do. I can't be without her, Tom; I can't go back to the way things were before we got back together, now that Kim's helped me see how happy I can be. I know what it means to really live, and now…

"I can't even stand the thought of her in his hands, and of him doing all he's doing to her, only some of which Jenny told me

249

about. What happens to Kim happens to me. You'd feel the same way if Donna was in this predicament and you'd do the same thing if this was the choice you had. Then again, it's really not a choice at all, is it? I know there's a very good chance we won't come out of this, but I won't let her go through it alone- I just can't. If you could have heard her on the phone...how frightened she was..." John's throat tightened and he had to stop for a moment.

Knowing he had to get the rest of it out, he gritted his teeth and held his emotions back. "You were right to keep all you knew from me, Tom- even her role in the sting, because that would have led to me finding out the rest. I think you knew that, too, which is probably one reason why you did. There's a good chance back then that I would have just thrown away all we had; I wouldn't have handled it right because I was nowhere near together and focused. Only recently did it finally dawn on me how much we mean to each other and I finally can appreciate the woman she is. You helped in that process, Big Brother- in more ways than one. I'm...I'm sorry for all the times we fought and I'm sorry I was such a shithead over the past three weeks."

Tom knew why he said the last part and he sank into his chair. The same feeling he had when he saw John lying in a pool of blood in his study and also when he had to make the decision that ended Doug's life came back full force- the most horrible feeling he'd ever had, and hoped he never would experience again.

Even though in all probability it was an exercise in futility, he scrambled to think of anything at all that might prevent John from putting himself into another situation that most likely would prove to be a fatal one. "*Please* don't do this, John- think of all you could do as President. Think of the impact you could make on the present and future of this nation if you can bring about all the changes you laid out to me. You told Kim what your plan is, too, right? Don't you think she'd want you to-"

"I know what you're trying to do. I love you, Tom, and I know you're in a bad spot, too, to put it lightly. I'm sorry."

"There *has* to be a way I can help!"

"I wish there was, but there isn't and there's no time. I have to do this and I have to do it now. Most of all, I hate what this could end up doing to our family and I know in a way I'm being selfish by going there, but...I have to. If I didn't try to get her out of there, or at least...I don't know- just be there for her, if nothing else-, I never would be able to live with myself."

As much as Tom wanted to keep working at it to try to dissuade him, he sensed the finality in John's voice, which he'd heard many times before. There simply was no talking him out of what he'd set his mind to do; that always had been the way with him, and Tom knew it. "I do understand, and…you're right. If that was happening to Donna, I'd probably do the same thing."

"There's no 'probably'. You *would* do it."

"Wait a minute- you said Jenny's with you, right? You're not going to-"

"No, she won't be directly involved and she understands that. I needed her help in getting away from the station and she's driving me to where I need to go."

"So…you're already going to meet him? You said he'd call you tomorrow evening with instructions as to where to be, didn't you?"

"Yeah, but I'm-…Tom, don't do that. Don't try to trip me up. I know you-"

"Ok, take it easy; I'm sorry. I had to try, though."

John sighed. "I'd have been disappointed if you hadn't." He smiled when he heard Tom chuckle. "It's not over yet. You know if I can get us out of this mess, I'll do it. I've beaten him in debates and who knows- maybe I'll find an opening this time, too…

"Hey, I have to go now. It won't be long before we're there; I need to focus. Wish me luck, huh?"

"Good luck, Brother."

# Chapter 10

Suddenly, Kim visualized the face of her stepfather, which brought everything to a standstill. The thunder and lightning and all the unwanted visitors they helped conjure up from her memories and her present situation were halted in their tracks.

Just that quickly, she started to look at the whole situation from a different perspective- one she'd never considered. Instead of fixating on the result of what Steven Francis had played a large part in causing that night, she homed in on the cause itself.

Because of his selfishness and indifference, she'd spent much of that long-ago night cowering inside her refuge, waiting for the storm to pass. She remained in there until she was nearly fourteen.

For many years- specifically in several key situations- she'd felt the fallout of that pivotal event in her life. In part because of that event, she'd made some bad decisions that led to much of the heartache and stress she'd felt.

In the present, she'd spent the last couple months fearing what most likely would happen if her past as an exotic dancer came to light. More than anything, she dreaded the effect it would have on the students she'd mentored and on John's candidacy for the presidency, not to mention the probability that the career she loved was all but over.

After her ordeal while in Josh's hands for those twelve days in the late spring of '89, which was even worse than what he was putting her through now, she'd hidden again, afraid to reveal to John what had happened and afraid he would want nothing to do with her. She'd been so certain that was the case when he saw her on the beach just before Josh abducted her again…

…but it isn't- that's not how John feels at all! Baby, I was so wrong to run away and to keep all this from you. I thought the worst- that the opposite was true. I was just afraid to lay it all out to you…

…never again. I'm going to find a way out of this mess and make things right. I am sick of being afraid and hiding! I'm not a horrible person because of my dancing! I deserve a hell of a lot better than to be treated like this…

Relieved and thankful that she finally felt something other than fear, she began some experimental squirming and tugging against the manacles. That action energized her; fighting back physically felt good, too, even though- as usual- there didn't seem to be any way she could overcome the restraints.

It wasn't long before her anger made its way to the surface and caused her to fight harder still. She was infuriated with Walter Daniels for what he'd done to her, but even more so with Josh for causing her to put her life on hold for all those years and for putting her in this situation once more. Although she also was very irate with herself for allowing him to exercise such control over her life, no one could deny that he was mostly to blame.

*You came close to breaking me, you sick, conniving control freak, but you didn't!*

The more she thought about him- the one who, for so many years, had been the primary antagonist in her quest for happiness- and how she'd let him get the better of her, the angrier she became. Her more spirited struggling reflected that, but the bonds wouldn't give in the least.

Her frustration steadily mounted- she grunted from her efforts as she pulled and twisted, stretched and strained against the unyielding shackles, just like she had earlier while tied to his bed...

...once more, the tightness of her corset forced her to stop fighting. As she yet again tried to control and slow her breathing, she tried to think of something to calm herself down- to divert her thoughts somehow. Gradually she found a way, given where she was. She found a sort of temporary mental escape, which was good since there was no way she could do so physically.

*I wish we were together in there right now, John,* she thought as she turned her eyes longingly toward their bedroom...

...and began to drift away as a much more pleasant preoccupation took over...


John ran up the driveway of his former house after leaving Jenny in her car. He'd told her in no uncertain terms not to follow him- and she promised him she wouldn't- before he got out and bolted through the driving storm to where Kim was.

*I hope Jenny follows through on her promise...*

He also hoped the house wasn't as empty as it looked, but as he made a quick circuit around it, he confirmed what he was afraid of: there wasn't a single light on.

"Dammit!!"

As he stood there in front of his door, he temporarily became oblivious to the rain as he tried to think of where they could be.

*I thought for sure they'd still be here. It's been just a few hours since he was flushed out of his other place...*

*...but I have no idea where else they could have gone. I bet I didn't miss 'em by much, either, for all the good that does...*

The pattern still was the same as it had been throughout. There was nothing for him to go on, which gradually sank in after he kept coming up with nothing in spite of his efforts...

...but as he stared at the door, he began to think in a different direction.

*Maybe he left something behind...*

*...and I'm here, anyway. Couldn't hurt to have a look inside...*

*...question is, how do I get inside?*

It wasn't long before he thought back to how they'd gotten into Jenny's place. They were forced to use the key hidden inside the fake rock in the little garden out front. John had done something similar with this place. Given his occasional tendency to lose, misplace or forget things such as keys, he'd covered one up with plastic wrap and hidden it inside a flower pot that sat on a window ledge on the side of the house...

...which was something he'd forgotten about long before he sold the place. In a matter of seconds he was at the ledge, looking at the undisturbed flower pot. After a quick dig, he produced the key, still in its wrapping.

*Now it's time to see if he changed the locks...*

Given what Josh had kept himself preoccupied with over the years, it was possible he hadn't. John opened the outer door-the locks appeared to be the same, but that still didn't mean he couldn't have had them re-keyed.

He slid the key into its hole, closed his eyes...

...then turned it.

\* \* \*

*'John! Baby, you've come!'*

*She couldn't voice that because of the gag, but it didn't matter. He was with her- sort of. He bore more resemblance to a rabid wolf than a highly skilled political prodigy as he practically flew around to the front of the cage and ripped the door off, unlocked her ankles and took hold of them.*

*In one motion he pulled her out of the cage, grabbed her up and took her over to the wall, where he set her down onto her feet and promptly tore off her thong.*

*She was very unsteady and her knees were sure to buckle as she willed him to hurry. All she could do was pant, eyes wide with excitement and desire, as she watched him drop his trousers as quickly as if someone pulling a prank had yanked them off him.*

*He grabbed her up again and put her back against the wall. Kim locked her legs around his waist and off they went...*

*...while Josh stared in disbelief.*

*And rage...*

*'I hope this hurts you, you bastard!', Kim thought, smiling at Josh's anger while John took her almost savagely, right in front of him...*

*...wait, what's that noise?*

Kim jumped when she realized she wasn't imagining the beeping. After that jolt she sat perfectly still.

Someone was inside the house.

*Oh, no! Josh is back...*

*...and when he sees the state I'm in from that daydream...*

She renewed her fight. Every last bit of strength she had left went into it and despite her severely restricted mobility, she was making some noise, especially as her legs worked against the shackles that were bolted to the floor of the cage and holding her ankles...

...but when she heard the voice calling out, she froze again, certain she was hearing him because she so badly wanted to, especially after the vision she'd just had...


Once inside, John immediately turned to the alarm system control box and instinctively punched in his old code. It didn't work, which when he thought about it, didn't surprise him at all.

*That was stupid, and it's strike one. I have two more chances to get the code right before it goes off...*

255

…worse yet, he only had thirty seconds, six of which were gone…

…*come on*, think…

…*all right, that's worth a shot.* He punched in 102962, Josh's birthday.

The result: 17…16…15…

"*Shit!*" he hissed. *Only one shot left…*

…12…11…10…

…*other dates- graduation dates, the trial date, when he met Kim, which I don't know…*

…there were so many possibilities as to what it could be and none of them took the forefront…

…7…6…5…

…*Kim's birthday!* It was what stood out most, and it seemed logical. As soon as he thought of it he punched it in: 81268.

He hit 'enter' and the green light came on. He sighed heavily and leaned against the wall…

…but stood bolt upright when he heard what sounded like metal clinking.

"Is someone up there?"


It *was* John!

Immediately Kim made as much noise as she could and prayed it would be enough.


Even before he heard the muffled cries, he knew it was Kim and raced up the stairs. "I'm here, Kitten; where are you?"

"Imm hmmr!"

He rushed into the study and stopped in his tracks, not believing what he saw. His blood began to boil again.

*He's keeping her in a* cage*?!*

Worse were the manacles that just about locked her arms together from her elbows down…

Kim's distressed cry brought him back to the present. He moved toward her, hoping there would be a way he could free her…

…and stopped in his tracks when he heard the voice.

* * *

"Hey there, Johnny boy! You're still a pretty smart one, I see- figured out where I'd hole up, eh? Don't you just love the irony? Guess I should've brought Kim along on my drive after all...oh, well, it doesn't matter. I'm sure you're all pleased with yourself and everything, but unfortunately for you two, it's not quite over yet. This time, you will be there when I get back, Kim."

John looked around and found the speaker from which Josh's voice was coming, then he noticed a camera over the doorway and another one above the window looking right down on Kim. *Son of a bitch...* "I don't see how it isn't over, *old buddy*. I'm about to pick up the phone and call my brother to let him know Kim is with me and she's safe and sound. Once that's done, the next step will be tracking you down, which shouldn't be difficult given the fact that you'll have at least four state law enforcement agencies coming after you, not to mention the FBI. Actually, if you'll excuse me I'll make that call now. Watch me, if you like."

"Not so fast. Come on, John, don't you think I'd have taken precautionary measures to prevent what you think you've achieved there? Give me *some* credit, huh?"

"What are you talking about?" He didn't like the self-assured undercurrent when Josh chuckled in response before he continued.

"I can tell you now that picking up the phone won't do you any good, anyway. I never had the service activated there, but if I see you reaching for your cell phone or trying to leave that room, either move will be the last that you or Kim will ever make."

John looked at Kim and saw in her confused but concerned expression that she didn't know what he was talking about, either...

...then, he remembered Josh's threat of the booby trap he'd supposedly emplaced for the police to trip as they stormed the house where he'd kept all the girls. "Sorry, Josh, you already used that bluff. I don't think I'll fall for-"

"Look under Kim's cage. You'll see more than enough explosives there to take out the whole house, let alone both of you. Kim, I'm sure you remember hearing a 'beep' as I was leaving the room? I can see by your reaction that you do. That was the sound

257

of the detonator going live. All I need to do is press a button and it's all over, so if I were you, John, I'd do some serious thinking about how you're going to spend the time while you wait for me to come back. Don't worry, though, I won't keep you in suspense for long. We're already across the Bridge on Route 50, so we shouldn't be any more than twenty minutes."

*Dammit! That's not much time at all...what in the hell am I going to do?*

In spite of his knowledge that the situation was about to get worse, John was glad he hadn't addressed Jenny by way of his improvised communicator. It most definitely could have meant the end if Josh even suspected that someone else was listening in, no matter who it was. Also, Jenny still would be safe.

*At least that's something I did right...*

"In addition to the two things I already warned you not to do, I also don't want your hands anywhere near the bomb. Both of you will wait right where you are- not that the lady has much of a choice in the matter- and make sure you don't move away from the camera, John. Remember, I have my eyes on you; I haven't missed anything.

"I guess I interrupted any, um, celebration of your reunion, shall we say? I'm sorry about that...well, no, I'm not. Looks like you'll just have to stew even longer, Kim, since I'm sure John will keep his hands to himself. Too bad he won't witness a display- or should I say, *many* displays- like those you gave Jennifer and me during the van ride we all took.

"We'll see you in a bit. Be good, now!"


Kim's cheeks burned from Josh's last barb. She wasn't the least bit surprised that he would humiliate her in front of John- again.

Worse than that was the returning surge of dread since he'd be back so soon.

She wriggled and tugged at the unyielding cuffs again when the visions of what would happen next rushed into her. When John embraced her from behind, she fought harder as she was reminded once more that she couldn't do the same to him. *If you'd tied me up with rope or straps or anything else, at least John could have freed me, but you had to put me in chains, didn't you?!! DAMN you!!*

* * *

John was still for a moment, at a loss as to what to do. There was no way to free Kim- that much was obvious as he examined her manacles. He certainly wouldn't do anything to risk getting them both killed, either.

*I couldn't possibly have prepared for this...*

The clanking of the chains from Kim's efforts caught his attention. He moved to the front of her cage and knelt down before her, and talked in a very low voice. "Easy, Honey, try to calm down. I know it looks bad right now, but we have to focus and look for the right opportunity. It'll come, but we have to recognize it when it does. Just relax now- save your strength..."

He reached in and touched her cheek, tenderly caressing her. In no time at all, her eyes were brimming and a tear spilled over as she abandoned her efforts for the time being. She still squirmed a little in her bonds, trying in vain to move closer to him. Her fear of what lay ahead for them was plain to see in her eyes.

Hoping to ease her more, he smiled and said, "Even though this isn't exactly the reunion I had in mind, it's great to see you again, Kitten."


So many emotions were running through Kim at the same time. For a moment, her joy over seeing him, strengthened by his comforting words, offset her uneasiness. She smiled at him as best she could around the large ball gag...

...but not for long. Although she tried her best to keep those other emotions at bay, she couldn't help but wonder- again- if these might be their last moments together. She cried out softly as she tugged at her restraints again, yearning to be in his arms...

...but imprisoned only a couple feet away from him. Frustration began to resurface; try as she did, she couldn't hold it back. That made her renew her vain effort to free herself yet again.

Amid her struggling she saw, in spite of his effort to shield it from her, that he also was contemplating the possibility that they might not live to see tomorrow...

...then she saw something else materializing in his eyes, brought on in part- no doubt- from that possibility...

...she felt it taking root in her, too...

* * *

*This could be it...*

John had to face the possibility, as much as he hated to. It might happen in his house, of all places.

...nonetheless, something else was taking hold of him.

The longer he looked at her, and caressed her, the stronger its hold became...

...more appropriately, the stronger *her* hold on him became, in spite of the fact that, physically, she was completely helpless.

The steel shackles and other implements bound her fabulous body every which way. Her sexy bra restrained her firm, full breasts and nasty-looking clamps pinched her nipples. The satin corset imprisoned and further compressed her waist. A pair of fetish pumps confined her feet. Last but not least were those legs, sheathed in silk and straining in futility against their fetters...

...and so soft and smooth to the touch. Every part of her was complimented by adornments or restraints, or both.

John had never seen such total, inescapable bondage...

...she was utterly irresistible...


...feeling like she was on the brink of madness, Kim whimpered as the state she was in was becoming physically painful. It became even worse with what he did next.

When he realized what he was doing, John took his hands away. "I'm sorry, Kim, I-"

"Mm-mm! *Mmmmph!!*" *Please don't stop, Honey...* "Hmmp..." She blushed as she begged him so shamelessly, desperate to entice him with her erotic writhing. That further act of submission kicked her engine into warp speed.

With the look in her eyes there was no mistaking what she was expressing to him through them. This time it was even more manifest; the hunger he saw was primal. Her intensity was almost scary as her muffled pleas and her body language further emphasized to him what she needed him to do. She yearned terribly for release from another kind of bondage altogether.

She tried further to press that home to John, but again, the cursed gag hampered her effort. She bucked madly, crying out as she fought with all she had as he moved around behind her.

260

For a moment John was so taken by her that he could do nothing but watch her as he temporarily put the dire situation they were in on the backburner. In spite of his efforts to contain it, there simply was no denying how much she turned him on as she was, which was even more so than normal. The novelty of seeing Kim in the fetish lingerie and all chained up along with the dire circumstances they faced were proving to be an unstoppable combination.

Also, her very energetic struggling factored in...

...and her submissiveness...

...to his amazement, she was becoming even more enflamed although her struggling was abating. Not only could he see the evidence of that- he felt it, too. Her baby-soft skin felt like it was burning everywhere he touched her, especially as he kneaded her breasts...

...then ran his hands down along her pinched waist to her hips...

...and her thighs. Her cries were much softer now...

He realized that he was fondling her again, which apparently was contributing to her state.

The signals she was sending were obvious. She beseeched with her magnificent, restrained body as she writhed uncontrollably in distress that was so sensuous- so erotic. Tears fell from her mesmerizing eyes as she simply couldn't restrain her boundless passion and undeniable craving for release.

Her need was even stronger than it seemed to be when she was tied to the bed in the last prison she was in. Her piteous cries for him to help her, her total inability to respond to him in any way other than to squirm in her bonds and mew to him through the stifling gag got to him in a primordial way.

He thought back to the night he pinned Kim to the bed and how much more that charged him up the night; their session that night after six years apart was off the charts in terms of wild. As he had that night, he felt a very powerful urge to dominate her...

*...for the time being, there's no way out of this predicament anyway, so why not?*

"Since we don't have much time to ourselves, anyway, and God knows what will happen next, what do you say we make the most of this? There are far worse ways to pass the time..."

261

He noticed the slight dampness of her stockings as he stroked her thighs again, clear evidence of how much energy she'd expended in her fight for freedom.

She leaned back against him as much as the cage would allow and sighed deeply when he kissed the back of her head. She was capable of touching him only with her bound arms, which made her grunt petulantly.

*My God, she's white hot...* "Here, at least let me take these off you."

Kim flinched and whimpered a little even though he removed the clamps as gently as he could. His anger toward his former friend was rising drastically, especially as he saw her pain.

But at the same time...

"I'm sorry, Kitten. I love you."


She cooed softly in response as she tried to look back at him, which wasn't necessary since her feelings for him flowed from her. Again he cupped and gently kneaded her breasts.

Kim allowed the feeling of her utter helplessness to take over- the cuffs seemed to embrace her now, as she knew she wouldn't be denied. In a way, this was so much like what she was feeling one fateful day in the middle of the summer of 1981, with a couple very big twists thrown into the mix. The effect was even more intense, and there was much more yet to come.

She gently squirmed, almost blissful in her confinement as she drifted away in this fantasy scenario, only this time it was much more than a scenario. She really was the captive damsel and her hero had come for her. Although she was far from certain that this one would end as well as her dream had, for the time being it was good enough...

His hands roamed all over her, touching every part of her they could. Her fire blazed ever hotter and her hips began to gyrate as she moved toward the release she craved. In no time at all a small climax hit her, but instead of coming down, she was propelled right through it and raced even higher in spite of the camera that relayed everything to Josh.

As she glanced at that camera, a last voluntary thought came to her. It stemmed from another part of her little fantasy- the diversion she'd needed just before John arrived. In that part of it was a way to take a stab at her longtime tormentor.

262

*How better to rankle him than to show him what he'll never conjure up in me?*

Immediately she felt better about the situation- for the moment. *I know we're still very much in danger, but maybe throwing it in his face will help somehow- if for nothing else than to knock him off balance again. God knows it'll be easy enough for me to pull off, especially considering who I'm with and how long it's been. And, if this is our last night together, I'm going to make the most of it every way I can...*

She allowed the impetus John was fanning in her once more to imbed itself even deeper inside her. She encouraged him as best she could while he bestowed his full attention upon her, urging him to keep it up by way of her impassioned responses to his loving manipulations of her restrained body.

It was blissful torment, but she knew it would end up as simply bliss as she surrendered to the feeling that held her in its grip even more effectively than her shackles. This was a battle she was only too happy to lose- one that really wasn't a battle at all, as she had no will or ability to resist. At least, not in this case.

His next words added more momentum to the irresistible force that was on its way to claiming yet another victory over her.


"It'll be all right, Honey. We're together and that's how it always will be- that's how it's *meant* to be. I'm not going anywhere this time. I swear to God I'll never leave you again and I'm not going to let him hurt you." The protectiveness he felt toward her swelled right along with the desire she so effortlessly stirred up in him, and he kept squeezing her tender globes, which rose and fell rhythmically with her rapid and shallow breathing.

He almost ignored the metallic thud as something fell…


…Kim cried out as the surging force fed on the feeling his comforting words stirred up. In spite of their predicament, she believed nothing and no one would harm her. She needed to feel protected, which he seemed to know intuitively; it was just another example of how deeply connected they were.

She jerked as John's fingers again brushed across her nipples, now hypersensitive having been clamped for so long. That action in itself almost did it, which she tried to let him know, but again the gag defeated her effort, adding still more frustration. She was so close...and then he shifted his focus lower.

Her extremely charged state was rubbing off on John as he fondled her. That was all he could do, which frustrated him more than it did her.

Kim's cries were almost animalistic as John's touches and kisses pushed her even faster and higher, the lower his hand moved on her body. Her total inability to touch him channeled every kiss she wanted to give him, every caress, every nibble, into all her nerve endings. She hated, but also loved, that she was chained and gagged so securely. All she could do was feel.

That sense was heightened to the extreme, especially where he touched her...

...and teased in that excruciatingly gentle way of his...

Totally out of control, she hurtled toward the inevitable: a climax that was becoming cataclysmic in proportion. Everything was hitting her- the lingerie, the bondage, the danger, being in the hands of the man she so deeply loved and feeling how turned on he was, too...

...and her measure of revenge that she hoped Josh was feeling the sting from. That combination was more than enough...


*Jesus, Kim, how many can you take?*

She'd already hit the peak four times and she showed no sign of slowing down. John got the clear impression she was trying to draw every last bit of pleasure from each one, which was no surprise, given their circumstances and what they faced.

Nonetheless, he could tell she was left wanting more...

...and so was he...


From her vantage point, Jenny watched and listened.

John had insisted on her waiting in this spot, which was just off a side street that fed into the one his house was on. She was far enough away to avoid detection, but not so far that she couldn't see what she needed to see. He'd also come up with the very good idea of calling her cell phone with his and leaving the connection open with the hope that the man who'd kidnapped her would screw up by falling asleep or divulging the location of where they were going next or some other way. He didn't want to risk calling the police in at first because there was no telling whether they would be detected as they approached. He didn't have to remind her what the consequences of that could be- and probably would be.

Jenny was glad to be helping him and knew she had a very important role to play. She was safe as long as she stayed put.

Staying awake, on the other hand, was proving to be a tall order. The main thing working against her was the lateness of the hour, especially given all she'd been through the past evening. Her clock read 2:24 and her supply of adrenaline was running low. If not for the very unexpected sounds she heard- and the activity they undoubtedly indicated-, in all likelihood she would have fallen asleep not long after John went into the house.

Upon hearing the kidnapper's voice, which happened only minutes after John had gotten inside, she feared he'd been there the whole time. Fortunately, it turned out to be his voice over a speaker. When he mentioned the bomb directly underneath Miss Francis, Jenny's blood froze. It really was a good thing they hadn't called the police, and also that John hadn't said anything to alert Joshua that Jenny was listening in...

It wasn't long after the man who'd held her captive stopped talking that Miss Francis and her lover were at it. They didn't seem the least bit hindered by Joshua's intrusion.

Even though Miss Francis was caged, gagged and thoroughly restrained as evidenced by the clinking of the chains when she struggled, Jenny knew what was happening. The same muffled, impassioned cries had erupted from her helplessly bound former counselor so many times during that long van ride to their prison.

What amazed her most was how much stamina the woman had- the one who'd stirred up such desire and outright lust in so many- and Jenny certainly hadn't forgotten how charged up she was just from watching and picturing herself in the same situation.

A twinge of excitement sent ripples through Jenny as she thought about that again, remembering clearly how she'd pictured herself tied so tightly like Kim was and writhing in ecstasy, penetrated by the sex toy, while Joshua watched her...

...but this time it wasn't a toy drawing them from her...

...and from what Jenny was hearing, John was doing an even better job of it. Jenny let his words wash over her, which surely contributed plenty to Kim's powerful burst of passion...

*... 'We're together and that's how it always will be- that's how it's meant to be. I'm not going anywhere this time. I swear to God I'll never leave you again and I'm not going to let him hurt you.'...*

*You really are lucky to have him, Miss Francis- and you* sure *do have him...*

*...even with the danger, I'd love to trade places with you...*

She drifted as that thought began to take root while she clearly recalled the deep, lingering feelings for him that the kisses she'd given him earlier had brought back...

...but she also thought about what had happened only a few nights earlier, which to her surprise only served to turn her on even more. She was trying to deny the mixed feelings she was having about the whole experience now that it was over, but it wasn't working.

Joshua became so gentle with her, even though he'd been so heavy-handed with Kim...

Those ruminations almost made her miss the van pulling into John's driveway. She sat bolt upright and shook her head, then focused on the vehicle as it stopped in front of the garage door, which was already opening.

*That's him.*

Even though she couldn't make out any identifying features of the van, there was no doubt. Jenny still heard the sensuous cries coming from Miss Francis even after the garage door closed.

*I wish I could warn them, but since he could still be monitoring them I can't risk him hearing me...*

All she could do was listen and wait...

...although a small part of her wanted to go inside...


"I'm coming upstairs, John. If you're not standing by Kim with your hands where I can see 'em, I'm going to kill her first, then you. Are we clear?"

After John assented, Josh went up to the room while Lisa watched the small monitor to make sure John didn't try anything. He peeked inside and saw John where he was supposed to be, then called downstairs for Lisa to join them. He glanced over at Kim, who was wiped out and would be easy to control. Undoubtedly,

266

she was running on vapors by virtue of her ongoing ordeal, the exertions she must have made in order to free Jennifer and the fact that she'd barely slept and the night wasn't far from over.

Most of all, the show she'd just put on by way of John's coaxing most assuredly took what little was left of her energy. That display also gave Josh even more incentive to make his former acquaintance suffer instead of the quick end he'd considered for him during the ride back.

*I was thinking about killing you now, but the other way will be far more satisfying.*

As for John himself, according to the reports he still hadn't fully recovered from the gunshot wounds and all the surgery he'd undergone because of them. In fact, recently he'd had a relapse of sorts, so controlling him wouldn't be too difficult, either.

"I hope you enjoyed yourselves, because I guarantee you won't like what's next."

"Give me the keys, Josh."

"Why should I?"

John looked at him, his anger working its way up to the surface. "You know why. You've probably had her like this for hours, haven't you?!"

"Probably. I don't think I like your tone- maybe I'll-"

*"Give me the fucking keys- NOW!!"*

Josh actually took a step back. Generally, people didn't shout orders when looking down the barrel of a ten-millimeter automatic, but then again, John had been in a similar situation three months earlier and had ended up killing a veteran- not to mention psychotic- state trooper with his bare hands.

Josh decided not to push him; he tossed John the key ring.

"The big one's for the cage and the shackles holding her ankles. The gold one will unlock the cuffs on her arms. The key to the padlock on her gag is on there, too- it's the little one, which also will open the locks over the straps holding her shoes on. Nice touch, don't you think? Although, as much as Kim enjoys wearing high heels, you wouldn't have thought she'd need any extra persuasion to keep 'em on. Oh, well…"

John paid little attention to Josh's chattering as he opened the cage and eased Kim out after freeing her ankles. She felt like a rag doll as he carried her over to the chair and gently set her onto

267

it. He brushed a few damp strands of hair away from her forehead and she smiled at him as he leaned down and kissed her.

"Give her a rub after you free her, if you want. She needs to be washed, too; I want her nice and clean before we take our little trip. In fact, you can give her a quick rubdown while you're in the shower- emphasis on 'quick'. Lisa will get some water for her to drink."

First he undid the high collar and the belt from around Kim's neck and waist. When he unlocked the steel restraints, Kim mewed and winced as her arms finally were allowed to return to a natural position. It felt like a thousand needles were pricking her at once from her fingertips to her shoulders, which burned for a moment. As soon as he opened the three padlocks, enabling him to remove her gag and her to remove her shoes, John started massaging her aching muscles.

After only a couple minutes, Josh spoke up. "Get her ready for the shower." When John looked at him he added, "Right now."

Knowing she might not be able to do much of anything for herself, John undid Kim's gag, which took a bit of persuasion to extract from her mouth. He hated the look of pain that again crossed her face when he finally got the large ball out. He rubbed her jaw while she worked it around slowly, then stood and helped her up.

"Undress her here."

"What?"

Josh cocked the hammer back. "Don't make me repeat myself. I know you understood me perfectly, so do it- after you put your cell phone on the table, that is."


*Oh, no!*

As soon as she heard him say that, Jenny hit the 'end' button and killed the connection, just like John had told her to. He'd been certain the kidnapper would make him hand over the phone at some point and sure enough...

*What happens now? He never said where they're going, or when, so I still can't call the police yet...*

*...or can I?*

But, again, she remembered her promise to John. In spite of all he told her about the man who'd held her and eleven other women captive and had eluded police for over a decade, she promised him she wouldn't call unless he was able to wrangle a location out of his enemy.

Unfortunately he wasn't successful, and worse, she had no idea what was going on.

In a matter of only a few minutes, anxiety had her pulling at her sweatshirt and biting her lower lip.

*What if I don't call the police and they end up dead? A promise is a promise, but...*

"All right, John, I'm not giving you much more time. I'm going crazy as it is..."


"Nice and slowly, John."

John did as he said, very deliberately putting his hand into his suitcoat pocket. Once he made the exchange and got the phone out, he placed it onto the table and backed away.

"Very good. Time to get the lady undressed."

Kim stepped out of her pumps as John moved behind her to undo her corset.

"Turn around the other way. I want both of you facing me."

This was too much for John; he put his hand on Kim's shoulder to stop her. "No, Kitten, stay as you are." The anger took over as he looked back at Josh. "Haven't you humiliated her enough?! I'm not gonna stand by-" He stopped when Kim touched his cheek.

She rose up and kissed him. "It's all right, John."

"But-"

She touched his lips with her finger and shook her head. "You know it could be a lot worse. Like you said, we're together and that's all that matters. To Josh's credit, he *has* been kind enough to give you the chance to wash me, which I do need. More than that, I need out of this corset. Please help me with it, Baby." Once she saw that she'd succeeded in calming him, she turned away and let him go to work.

The whole time John was freeing Kim's waist, she kept her eyes trained on Josh's.

As much as he wanted to, Josh couldn't turn away from her. How could she have such a hold on him in spite of everything? Her heart obviously belonged to John; nothing would

269

change that. He could see no plotting or scheming going on within her and it didn't seem likely that she would beg him to spare their lives- she probably knew better.

Still, she was totally calm and devoid of fear, even though there could be no question that she clearly understood what ultimately would happen...

...or did she? Was she simply at peace, or *did* she have something up her sleeve?

*No, that's not possible. I'm in control here. I have the gun, Lisa's on my side, I'm sure John didn't call the police and we'll be out of here shortly. So, what could she be-*

*Dammit, she's doing it* again!

"It won't work, Kim. Your little 'psych-out' game won't work on me."

"What do you mean? I'm not doing anything."

She continued to look deeply into him- deeper than anyone could. How could a woman seem so meek, yet be so disruptive, unnerving and outright powerful? "Like hell you're not!! Stop looking at me like that!! Just...stop looking at me, period! We're not gonna play these fucking games! Get those gloves and stockings off- now!! And you get the rest of your clothes off, too, Mister Governor...let's go- move your ass!" He turned to Lisa. "They get ten minutes; we'll both keep tabs on 'em. Is everything ready?"

She nodded.

"Good." He turned back to the naked couple. "All right, get in there. You heard me: ten minutes."

"...still nothing, Eddie?...Dammit, where could they have gone?!...No, don't do that. I mean it, do NOT have them pulled over and do NOT have them tailed- neither Miss Jacobson's car nor the van if any unit happens to come across either one. Anyone locating either of them will give the location and direction of travel, then pass them off to the next available unit. If any of our people are anywhere near Strauss, or if he sees one of us anywhere near John, I have no doubt he'll follow through on his threat and kill Kim...I don't know. I wish I *did* know what to do, but with no location, no idea where they could be going and no idea if John's with them yet we have no choice but to wait...I've been a hell of a lot better. Keep on 'em, Eddie."

Tom hung up and looked out the window of the unmarked patrol car.

"Where to next?" Detective Rogers looked over at his boss, colleague and friend with no small amount of concern. Although the man needed it, sleep was nowhere in his near future, nor would it be if the situation remained the same.

He just kept staring out the window. Rogers knew better than to disturb him.


*I wish we had more time in there...*

Despite the brevity of the shower, Kim felt refreshed and reinvigorated, especially after the massage John gave her. Better yet, he'd given her the release she'd been denied for so long, which removed a distraction that probably had been a big obstacle for her. One thought kept replaying: *this is* not *the end.*

While she would comply with her captors on the surface, she also was determined to seek, recognize and exploit any opportunity to get John and herself out of the mess they were in, or create one if she had to. She knew John had the same focus- he'd said so when he first knelt in front of the cage- and she prayed they would get such an opportunity sooner than later.

She prayed more fervently when she saw the black single glove she hated so much as they walked into the bedroom after toweling each other off. Her confidence was shaken a bit; the difficulty level had just shot up.

Worse, it also dawned on her that she'd lost something.

*What will I do, once he has my arms tied in that thing? What* can *I do?*

"I see you've spied the sheath, Kim. I'm sure you know where it's going to end up." Josh enjoyed that look of despair that always came across her face when she was presented with that prospect. "So, John, you like to see your girlfriend tied up good and tight? Well, it doesn't get much better than this," he touted as he held the implement up. "It's totally escape-proof. Of course, I've got something for you, too- have to keep you both out of the way. Time's a-wastin', so get dressed- and hurry up."

Kim's mouth fell open when she saw what was laid out for her to wear. Along with a pair of sheer, tan-shaded nylons that shimmered to the point of looking wet was an exact duplicate of the Tigress uniform she'd worn at the club in Atlantic City.

271

"Like it?" Josh quipped to her. "I hope so, because it's that or nothing. Put it on."

When she got the nylons all the way up, she gasped as she felt an unexpected draft. She glared at Josh, then stepped into the suit and worked it up. As tight and unyielding as it was, it required some wiggling and tugging to get it past her hips and into place.

Lisa moved behind her. "Breathe in and hold still," she ordered as she took hold of the reinforced zipper of the rigid satin bodysuit that purposely was too small for its occupant. With some difficulty, she pulled the zipper all the way up.

The effect the suit had on Kim's body was much like that of a corset- her waist was pinched in and her breasts were pushed together, up and out, almost spilling over its low-cut top. The very risqué outfit also was cut quite high on her hips. It was a perfect replica of the one she had in her closet. A bow tie and collar completed her ensemble along with the obligatory and very high-heeled pumps she stepped in to, the color pattern of which matched her suit.

This pair even had the same ankle straps, which she used to buy time.

Kim bent down and fastened them as deliberately as she could get away with, using Josh's blatant leering to buy time while she tried to figure out how she would escape from the single glove. She also knew he wouldn't object as she slowly ran her hands up her legs to smooth out her nylons. It was so easy for her to command his attention.

Unfortunately, she had her weakness as well.

Her need, and the loss of focus it led to, already had cost her a way out- the knife- while John was scratching her itch. How many other chances had she missed besides that one?

*Can't dwell on that now. I just have to be sure not to miss the next one...*

"We won't bother with the ears, gloves or tail," Josh said as he grinned at her and turned to John, who had just finished dressing. "Sure is something else, isn't she? I always did think that aside from the corset, this outfit brought out all the best she has to offer. Tell you what, ol' buddy- I'll give you the honors of putting the lady's arms into the sheath. You get it started and-"

John grimaced and sank to his knees while clutching at his midsection.

272

"*John!!*" Kim rushed over to him and knelt down with him. "Try to relax, Honey- slow, deep breaths. Where does it hurt?"

Josh kept his distance and motioned for Lisa to do the same while Kim tended to him. *He could be trying to pull a fast one on me- trying to improvise, just like before. If he is, he'll need to come up with something better than that...*

*...if he's not, getting rid of him might be even easier than I thought. Hell, if his condition becomes bad enough, which is possible since he had that attack a couple weeks ago just after I took Kim, he might die, anyway. Maybe he's not bluffing...*

Whatever the case, after a moment John straightened up and got to his feet with Kim's help, assuring her that he was all right.

"I hope you're up for a little ride, John. I promise I'll make it as brief as possible, given your, um, condition." Josh couldn't see the effect his verbal jab had on John, but he could feel it. With a chuckle he turned to Lisa. "Grab the sheath, Lis. I want her tied first."

"Sounds good to me." In short order, Lisa was behind Kim and encasing her arms in the soft leather single glove and lacing it up. Kim flinched a little when Lisa tightened it as much as she could, locking the captive's elbows together. "I'd think you'd be used to this by now," she sneered as she tied off and double-knotted the remaining laces at the top, which was a few inches above Kim's joined elbows, and tucked the excess inside it. She finished the task by fastening the securing straps that ran from the top of the sheath, fed through her underarms and over her shoulders, then crossed over each other and formed an 'X' between her shoulder blades. At that point the free ends fed through and were secured into the short ends with the buckles, which came out of the other side where the laces were tied off.

Lisa double-checked to ensure there was no way she could slip out. As icing on the cake, she also picked up both ends of the integrated strap just above Kim's hands, took them around her wrists and buckled them together, smiling as Kim winced again. She made sure the strap was tight enough to be uncomfortable as well as secure.

"All done," she said to Josh. He tossed her a wide, thick leather strap, which she used to gag Kim.

During that time, Josh had cuffed John's hands behind him and gagged him as well. "What do you think, John? The sheath really enhances her assets, too, doesn't it? It especially does that for one pair of 'em!" It didn't look like it would take much more than a sneeze to make Kim's breasts pop out of their confinement, which now seemed even less adequate.

"I'd say we're ready; let's get out of here. I hope, for the sake of both of you, that this is an uneventful walk to the van."

He made John lead the way with Lisa right behind him and holding a gun on him. Josh put his arm around Kim to make sure she didn't fall as they walked down the steps. They got to the van and inside it without incident. Lisa kept her gun trained on Kim while Josh locked a shackle around John's ankle and clamped the other end around the lower rail of the cot he was on. There was about a foot and a half of lead on the chain that connected the shackles, which would keep him where he was.

Next, staying true to form, Josh bound Kim's legs just above her knees and at her ankles with a couple straps. Once finished, he sat on the other cot with her. Lisa handed him the hairbrush she'd brought at his request and took her place in the driver's seat.

As Josh began to brush Kim's still-damp hair, Lisa started the van and they were on their way.


"That does it. I'm calling-"

Just as Jennifer was about to dial Tom Stratton's number, the garage door opened and out came the van. She watched it turn left; there could be no doubt they were heading toward the highway...

*...maybe that's not what they'll do, though. If I were to call the police now and stay where I am, it could turn out that he would take some back route to somewhere the police might never think to look Who knows where he could be going? After all, they probably never would have found him last night if I hadn't gotten away...*

It didn't take much of any thought or debate. Jennifer started her car and pulled out after them, but she didn't turn on her lights- that would wait until they got out onto the main road. It was a chance she felt she had to take.


274

*I'll follow them at least until I get some idea where they're going.*

*Then, I'll call Mister Tom…*


John was out of ideas.

Using the cell phone to allow Jennifer to listen in was the best thing he could come up with. He'd hoped Josh would divulge his next move, or at least give some kind of clue- *something*- that Jennifer would be able to relay to Tom so he could come after Josh with as much force as he could bring down and end this.

Josh, however, did not cooperate.

Then, there was the knife, which John doubted would be a factor even though his ruse of faking the pain in his chest was successful and, as a result, Kim had it again. He'd watched as Lisa put the single glove on her and fastened it so tightly around Kim's arms that the leather looked to be perfectly smooth; there wasn't a single wrinkle in the material. It didn't appear that she had the slightest chance of getting out of it as things were.

Worse yet, the longer she remained secured in it, the number her arms would become. She'd already spent the better part of the night bound in a similar way. She had to be more fatigued and sore than she'd let on.

*If only I'd had more time to think about this…*

*…I should have told you, Tom. I know you'd have come up with a better plan- something that would have turned out a lot better than this one did.*

John felt every bit as foolish as he did powerless. He'd acted impulsively and now Josh had them both…

He looked over at Kim, who had no choice but to sit ramrod-straight since her arms practically were fused together behind her. She was still while Josh brushed her hair and her eyes constantly remained on John's. He saw and felt her concern for him, but he was a little surprised that he didn't see fear or uncertainty in her. She seemed so composed in the face of what lay ahead that he began to feel ashamed of his negative disposition and looked away for a moment.

"*Mmmmph!!*"

He looked back up and saw what caused Kim's outcry. Josh was molesting her, squeezing her breast with one hand and groping between her thighs with the other. She struggled with him and tried to pull away while John yanked at the handcuffs and hurled muffled curses at Josh.


Kim's state of calm had gotten to be too much for Josh.

He'd already had more than enough of her tranquil countenance earlier. That more than anything had led to him letting loose on her if for nothing else, to at least shake her up and give John a jolt in the process. "Go ahead and cuss me out; that's all you can do, too, isn't it, John? The man who aspires to be the most powerful in the world and you can't do any more than that in order to help your lady. Absolutely *pathetic*!

"As for you, my dear Kimberly, you should know better than to fight. I've tried to get it across to you that you're nothing but a sex object. Look what Mister Wonderful over there did to you when he 'came to your rescue'. For a minute I thought he'd be a hero and charge me, throw something at me, or do something else to take me out, but what did he do? Nothing!" He finally let go of Kim and didn't stop her as she stood and hopped over to John.

She sat down, turned and lay across him, and worked her way between him and the wall of the van. She cuddled against him, buried her face into his shoulder and wept as he positioned himself to shield her from Josh.

"Ah...I shouldn't be too hard on you, John. All of this was inevitable, I suppose. Gotta hand it to ya- it took a lot of guts for you to come even though you knew I'd kill you, which I will do. Charging me back at your house only would've sped up the process. There's no way around it. Your other choice was to let Lisa and me get away with Kim, never to know what we would have done with her. I knew you wouldn't accept that, especially after what happened to your Old Man. Kim also knew you wouldn't accept that.

"You might be thinking that you should have told your brother about our little talk. Be glad you didn't. Make no mistake; had I smelled any police, I would have killed her and I would've made sure everybody saw it, especially you. There wouldn't have been a final shootout, a standoff, negotiations, or anything like that. Again, you wouldn't have been able to live with yourself had that happened. As for myself, I'm prepared to die and have been for some time, so it wouldn't have mattered to me.

"You made the best choice- the only good one you could have made. Take whatever comfort you can from that." Josh stood and moved close to the driver's compartment, then took a seat just behind Lisa. "I'm gonna keep you company for the rest of the drive, Lis. You must be pretty tired by now, but you're doing great. We should be there in another hour-and-a-half, tops."

He turned back to John and Kim and added, "I can keep watch over you two from here as well, just in case. This is the last time you'll ever spend together, so enjoy it."

*They're headed for the capital beltway. I wonder if he has a hiding place in D.C...*

Fortunately for Jenny, there was some traffic on US 50, even at this late hour. She was able to blend in with the other cars as she followed the van. They'd already crossed the Bay Bridge and after passing Annapolis, the van continued west on US 50 toward I-495 and Washington D.C. All was going smoothly in her pursuit thus far...

...until she passed the town of Bowie. The engine suddenly and drastically lost power. "*SHIT*!! Oh, God- don't let this happen now..." She pumped the gas pedal, but that didn't help.

She had to pull off to the side of the highway, where the engine seized up completely. It wasn't long before she realized why.

The timing belt- her roommate's boyfriend had warned her about it shortly before that fateful day she went to her cheerleading tryouts. Given all that had happened between him telling her that and now, she'd all but forgotten about that previously minor detail, which no longer was minor.

When she picked up her phone to call Tom Stratton, the situation worsened.

Her phone had no signal.

# Chapter 11

Fortunately, it wasn't long before Kim's efforts to curb her anger and humiliation were successful. She knew she had to keep her focus on finding the way out, which she believed she already had.

*I won't let him win- it's not over...*

*...besides, I managed to rattle him yet again.* That thought made her feel better right away.

She nuzzled John's neck and cooed to him. When he looked at her, she smiled as best she could in order to let him know she was all right. She also hoped to alleviate the grave concern he had, which she felt while she lay against him.

Unfortunately, she wasn't very successful in that.

*Hang in there, Honey. I'll do my best for us.*

The problem was, she had to wait to get to work until Josh wasn't looking, which seemed as though it might not happen until they got to where they were going. She couldn't risk drawing his attention to her efforts- any suspicion at all on his part could mean the end of her plan, which also would be the result if her arms went numb. She did her best to keep the latter from happening by rotating her shoulders as much as she could and clenching and releasing her fists.

*I just hope we're not on the road for too much longer. I can't keep the circulation going indefinitely...*

"I-66 is coming up, Joshua. I go west, right?"

"Yeah, we've already passed the turnoff for eastbound, anyway, and we definitely don't want to be in D.C. We're making good time, which certainly will help in the short term, not to mention in the overall plan to get us to a safer and more friendly place. We'll be on 66 west for a while. Once we get out toward the sticks more, the speed limit'll go up to 65. When it does, set the cruise control on 73- no higher. We don't want to risk being pulled over for speeding."

"OK."

Josh looked back at John, who wasn't looking terribly confident. "Finally accepting the inevitable, ol' buddy?"

He briefly looked at Josh, then away.

*No, he's not looking the least bit confident...* "Well, you'll be happy to know that our next stop along Nostalgia Boulevard, which will be your last stop, is a place we both know very well." He smiled at John when he looked back.

"You know where we're going."

As soon as he said that, Josh saw his look of recognition. "Yep, that's the place- Suicide Ridge. Just thinking about it brings back all those memories. It was one hell of a night, wasn't it? Not just in terms of what I witnessed you doing- the lady lying next to you also played a part. You remember where you were the night of June 12<sup>th</sup>, 1989, right, Kim?" She didn't even look at him. "You're no fun, you know that? Neither of you has a sense of humor.

"To fill you in, John, you were just a trifle upset that night and I knew why before you even said anything in that same roundabout way you always used whenever you talked about your lady there. You two had made plans to spend some quality time together on your twenty-fifth birthday, but she stood you up and you never knew why. Well, I suppose after eleven years I can end the mystery for you- no sense in having any secrets, given what's gonna happen very soon. Kim was tied to my bed. I left her that way when I came to pick you up so we could take our ride to the ridge. I-...wait a minute, you know this?" He could see the rage burning in John's eyes, but there was no expression of surprise. "I'd like to find out how you got that info, but it really doesn't matter- not now.

"I even had her dressed the same way she was when you found her in the cage a couple hours ago. Had her all set for yet another sex-filled night, like most of the eleven days prior were when she was my guest during that timeframe. She really is something in bed, especially when she has no choice in the matter. She always did love being tied up and you saw how much she gets off that way during sex. I didn't know how you'd react to seeing the real Kim when it came to that, but I gotta admit- you showed up to play tonight! You found out for yourself how much a dose of good bondage gets to her.

"Needless to say, I was more than a little pissed when I got back to my place that night and found that she'd escaped. It was an unexpected complication, given what I had planned for later that year, plus the fact that I had to make arrangements for my death. That in itself wasn't difficult to do, but I'd already planned it out and the clock was ticking at that point, so unfortunately I couldn't go back and look for her. Besides, there was too much of a risk of her calling the police, which fortunately, she never did. Of course, I had no way of knowing that, so I couldn't chance it. I had to execute my plan, with which you helped a lot.

"The execution was pretty damned good, too, buddy; you really should have been there. In fact, that was the primary reason why I went down to the ridge with you. I was gonna ask you to join us. I figured since you came up with the idea, the least I could do was make the offer for you to join us in pulling off the heist."

He noticed that Kim had finally begun to pay attention, but she rolled her eyes and looked away at that point. "What, you don't believe me, Kim? You don't believe your man there could have come up with something like that? Well, maybe you don't know him quite as well as you thought you did. You should've heard him plan out the hit we ended up making on that armored car; we did it the way he laid it out. Hell, it might have gone smoother still if he'd been there with us, but I never got the chance to ask him, considering what he did.

"Christ, John, I knew you were a little down, but never in a million years would I have guessed you were feeling suicidal, which, given the name of the place where we were, was quite fitting." He could see that he had Kim's full attention now. She looked up at John, who turned away.

"That's right. You're looking at a man who should have died eleven years ago."

"Mister Tom? It's me, Jenny. I-"

Tom reacted like someone had used a cattle prod on him. "*Jenny*!! Where are you?! Is John with you? What's going on?"

"Please don't be angry with me. John made me promise not to call you because he said they would-"

"I'm not, Sweetheart- I'm not angry at all. I can't tell you how glad I am to hear from you and that you're all right. Just take it easy and tell me what's going on."

"They had Miss Francis at John's house on the eastern shore. He went inside to try to get her out of there, but he couldn't because they had her chained up- they even put her in a cage! They planted a bomb under her, too, so she and John had to wait until they got back. I was listening in until that point, but he told John to hand the phone over and I had to hang up. A while later I saw their van pulling out of the garage and I followed them until my car died on me about half an hour ago just past Bowie on Route 50 west. I don't think they knew I was behind them and they kept going west toward 495."

One phrase stuck out and caused a ball of ice to form in his gut. "Half an hour ago?"

"As soon as my car broke down I tried to call you, but I couldn't get a signal. I had to get out and walk around until I finally did. I was afraid to try and flag someone down since...well, you know why. I'm sorry, Mister Tom..."

"It's all right. There's nothing else you could have done. Did you get close enough to see the tag number?"

"I did get that. It's a Pennsylvania tag: KFJS 121."

"That's *great*!! So you're still on 50?"

"Yes, my car's on the shoulder on the right side."

"All right. I'm going to contact the state police and have them send an officer out to pick you up- one should be to you shortly. How far from your car are you?"

"Not too far. I could be back there in a few minutes."

"OK, I want you to start walking back to it. I'll stay on the line with you until the officer they send gets to you. You did very well, Honey; I know you must have been scared. We'll take it from here. I'm going to put a call through on my other radio- don't hang up."

"What now, Tom?" Rogers inquired.

Tom picked up the two-way and turned it to the 'group' function, which would connect him with everyone in the task force. "This is Lieutenant Stratton from Baltimore Homicide: everyone listen up. I have a positive sighting of the subject vehicle- the late-model white full-sized van, Pennsylvania tag Kilo-Foxtrot-Juliet-Sierra One-Two-One, probably the same one used in the recent abductions. Their last known location and direction is US 50 West just past Bowie approximately 30 minutes ago, so heads up, everyone in the D.C. area and vicinity. I'm inbound from Baltimore and will be in the area shortly to lend a hand, over."

Rogers didn't need to hear it twice. He hit the siren, stomped on the accelerator and headed toward I-95.

"Copy that, Tom. This is Todd Stone. I'm in command of the Virginia contingent tonight; my call sign is Victor Six. What's your ETA from there, over?"

"I should hit 495 in twenty minutes or less, Victor Six-hope you don't mind my invasion of your turf, over."

"Not at all. In fact, I might need an assist from you with command and control if you're available for that; I'm running on vapors. My Lieutenants and I have been going hard lately; this case on top of everything else we have on the table has caused a bit of an overload on all of us. I made 'em go down for a few hours, so I'm it. Mike One is a call sign that's not being used-we'll make that yours. Make sure you switch to our frequency when you get here, copy?"

"Roger that, Six, I'll help any way I can. Mike One, out."

Tom switched to an alternate Maryland State Police frequency and gave Jenny's situation and location. He also had a crime scene unit and a bomb squad dispatched to John's former house to diffuse the explosives and hopefully find something that would give them an idea of where Strauss could be headed. Once he got confirmation that a unit was on it's way to Jenny, he switched back to the frequency the whole multi-state task force was on.

"Christ, now Captain Stone could go down for the count? What's next?"

"Well, maybe that's the last bad thing that'll happen tonight, Bill. Hopefully a unit down there'll spot the van. If ever we needed a break, it's now."

He picked his cellular back up and tried to glean any more information Jenny had while he made sure she was safe.



"As far as I know, John's the only person ever to jump off Suicide Ridge and live to tell about it, although I can't imagine he *did* tell anybody about it. Apparently, he never told you, anyway." He paused a moment to let the weight of that sink into Kim.

"I couldn't believe it, either. He told me about all the wrong he saw in the world and how he wished he could change it, and also how much he loved you, which- if you want my opinion-ultimately was his reason. Next thing I knew, he was gone. Just like that.

"He never did what a lot of would-be jumpers do; you know how they get to their spot and tell everybody who cares to listen how they're gonna jump. Mostly it's just people who need somebody to talk to. Then, they spill their guts to the negotiator or counselor or cop who's sent to talk 'em down, which many times they're successful doing because the people really *don't* want to die. They get to the edge and lose their nerve, then they turn back.

"To say the least, John didn't lose his. It was like he had a moment of clarity and just acted on it. No warning- nothing. It was the damnedest thing I ever saw; I know I'll never forget it. It was too dark for me to see him. The pre-dawn light was all we had and we really didn't have much of that, either. The blackness just swallowed him up. I mean, he couldn't see *anything*! He told me how it was possible somebody could jump and survive, but he couldn't see where the rocks were or where the water was deep enough- he had no point of reference to work with and *could not see a fucking thing*!! Yet, he jumped.

"After he did it, I don't know how long I just stood there, staring down at where he'd gone. I mean, he was *dead* What other possibility was there? I never had more respect for you than I had at that moment, John: you either had balls of steel, you were drunk, or you were just nuts. Or, maybe it was all of the above. You had to be afraid, but you did exactly what you said. You didn't screw around with indecision. You did that with the same focus and decisiveness you had when you demanded the keys from me to release Kim.

"At any rate, when I found out you'd survived that fall I was even more blown away. I thought, 'what, is this guy Superman? Did he sprout wings on the way down, or something like that?' There just was no logical explanation. I do want you to tell me what happened before I kill you. You know, I might even let you jump again, if that's how you choose to end your life. We'll talk about it when we get there."

He smiled as he looked at Kim again. "Given the expression on your face it almost would be worth it to take your gag off and hear your thoughts about the new light I've shined on your man. You have to love the irony, don't you? He thought it was such a big deal when he found out about you being an exotic dancer while he had an even bigger skeleton buried in his closet; he tried to commit *suicide*, for Christ's sake! It's just too damned funny!"

283

His smile disappeared. "Whichever end I choose for him, he'll be dead when the sun first peeks up over the horizon."


"That half-hour lag really hurt us, Tom. They could be anywhere. Shit, he could be headed northbound on 95. Who's to say we didn't just pass him? He could be hiding in D.C., or maybe heading south toward Richmond- God only knows."

The siren warned off anyone in their path. A number of cars had slowed and pulled into the right lanes of the interstate. Rogers had the car over 120 miles per hour. Given the circumstances and the sparse traffic at 3:45 AM, the excessive speed was warranted.

"Mike One, this is Victor Six. What's your location?"

"I'm a couple miles from 495, over."

"Roger. I can barely keep my eyes open, so I'm taking myself out of the game. I'm giving you temporary tactical control. You'll have thirty units at your disposal. Stand by, I'll make the announcement to the group." After a moment, he came back up. "All Victor units, this is Six. Lieutenant Tom Stratton from Baltimore Homicide, call sign Mike One, is in command now. He will be until oh-seven hundred when the new shift comes on. Victor Six, out."

"All right, Tom, it's your show. Carl Warner is Victor Five; he's your second in command and he'll bring you up to speed. I hate like hell to have to bow out like this."

"I know, Sir. Losing you won't help at all, but you don't have a choice in the matter. Get some sleep; I'll take care of this."

"Nobody has more motivation to find 'em than you do. Take charge, Marine- get 'em out of that mess."

"Aye aye, Sir. Mike One, out."


"Is this the road, Joshua?"

He got up and looked out the windshield. "Yep- that's the one. Take a right and follow it on up. There's another turn-off you'll have to take soon, though. It's easy to miss, so I'll stay here with you until it comes up."

\* \* \*

For the time being Kim put what she'd just learned aside. With Josh temporarily occupied, it was time for her to take advantage of the small opening he'd given her.

Step one was getting the blade out without cutting her fingers off. *I sure am glad I held on to this knife after all, and more so that you got it back to me, Baby. That was one smooth move you made,* she thought as she carefully opened it. At the height of her frustration, she'd nearly ditched it.

Now, it would be essential to any hope she had of bringing about a better ending to this drama for John and her...

"This is close enough. Stop here. You can keep it running if you like; you'll probably need the heat on." Josh moved back to John and Kim. "All right, you crazy kids. It's about that time. Say your goodbyes, but make 'em quick. Oops, forgot- you *can't* say goodbye, can you? Oh, well, that'll just save time, then."

Their foreheads touched and they looked into each other's souls one more time.

Kim was very distressed by the resignation she saw in him. There was an air of finality, just like what she sensed a few months earlier when she saw him lying on the floor of his study in the pool of blood and reaching out for her in vain while Daniels took her away. She wished she could convey that they still had a chance, but she was determined not to give away to Josh or Lisa the slightest hint of what she was doing, so she dared not.

All the same, she couldn't prevent her sheer dread over what John faced from forcing its way out as Josh reached down and unlocked the shackle from around his ankle in preparation to take him away.

"Hey, Lis, come back here and take hold of Kim. Keep her in here while I take care of things with the Governor; she's yours to do with as you like." He waited until she was in position. "Oh, there is one thing I need you to do. Switch license tags- I don't want to take any chances that somebody got the number. The Virginia one should make us blend in well enough. Go ahead and use that one." He pulled John to his feet.

285

"*Mmmmph*!!!" Kim fought against Lisa's grip when Josh opened the rear door and pushed John out. Lisa held her down as she cried and tried to no avail to wrench herself away.

The door closed behind them.


"This is Victor One-Seven, I have a vehicle matching the description of the suspect vehicle heading south on I-95 below the Springfield interchange; present location is two miles north of the Occoquan River. The vehicle's tag appears to be an out-of-state, but I do not- I say again, do not have confirmation of the tag number. Standing by for orders, over."

"That's about the right distance given their last known location, direction of travel and the speed limit." Tom said as he picked up the two-way. "Victor One-Seven, this is Mike One. Are you marked or unmarked?"

"We're marked, Mike One. Over."

"Mike One, this is Victor Three-Four. I'm approximately five miles below the Occoquan heading south on 95 and I'm unmarked. Exit 102 is coming up now- I'm pulling off and looping around. One-Seven, let me know when you hit the mile 103 marker and I can ease back onto 95 and pick up the subject vehicle, over."

"Roger, Three-Four- sounds like a plan. Let me know the second you have that tag number and we'll make the call on our next move from that point. One-Seven can act as your backup just in case. Mike One out." Tom gestured toward the cell phone Detective Rogers had just put down. "Was that our State guys?"

He nodded. "The unit they dispatched just picked up Miss Jacobson. She's fine."

"Good."

*Give us some more good news, Victor Three-Four,* Tom thought as Rogers got them underway again.

"We're heading toward those Victor units, Tom?"

They'd reached the I-495, the Capital Beltway, in a little more than half the time it normally took- even with the stop they made. "Yeah, just follow 495-..."

Tom was just about to tell Rogers to head south on 495, but he trailed off. Although that was the quickest way, his gut told him it wasn't the *right* way...

"South, right?"

He shook his head. "Take 495 west, Bill. Don't ask me why."


"Hasn't changed much, has it?"

After making John sit on the ground, Josh undid his gag and put it in his pocket. "It's not too bad out here, either- not much of a bite in that wind. I'd say we picked a good night."

He just stared over the edge, not saying a word.

"You know, John, if you're not gonna say anything, maybe I'll just shoot you now. I can't imagine you not having anything to say, though. Don't you wanna challenge me to a debate or something? Talk about old times for your last, oh, forty-five minutes or so?"

"What would the point of that be?"

Josh chuckled a bit. "Wow. You're really throwing me for a loop here. As good as you always were at talking your way out of things and you don't even want to try?"

"No."

"Aw, come on, ol'-"

"Look, if you're gonna shoot me, just do it and get it overwith. I'm not in the mood for your bullshit or your gloating and I have no desire to put up with another one of your delusional rants."

Josh responded by putting the barrel of his pistol next to John's temple.

John closed his eyes.


"Nice boobs, Kim."

Unfortunately, Lisa had decided to stay with Kim in back of the van and wait until later to switch the license plate. Worse, she occupied herself with Kim's body as if she owned it. As her malefactor idly toyed with her breasts, Kim didn't bother trying to pull away since there was nowhere for her to pull away to.

"They're almost as big as mine. Of course, with the help from the lift the suit gives 'em and from the way you're tied, it looks like they *are* as big as mine...well, no- they still don't look as big. They're close to mine, but not quite."

All Kim could do was lie there and listen to the irrelevant, immature drivel while she battled to keep her frayed nerves at bay.

Every minute- every second- was critical, and it didn't look like Lisa would leave her alone at all.

If that happened...

...or worse, if Lisa decided to take advantage of her total inability to resist any advances she could make, just like Josh had suggested...

*Just settle down- the worst thing that can happen here is for you to panic. If you do that, she* won't *leave you alone. You've seen how those two love to use your fear against you.*

*Don't let them. Don't take this bait she's putting out; you know that's what it is. At the same time, don't ignore her, because you know the effect that has.*

*Just let her have her bit of fun, maybe even throw in a little meekness for her and look for your next opportunity...*

"You know, I've been thinking..."

*That must have been hard on you; I'm surprised you have enough functioning brain cells to pull that off. You'd better take a nap so you can recover.*

"...that was quite a show you two put on back at the house. I really enjoyed it, and I wouldn't be surprised if you and your boyfriend had a quickie while you were in the shower. Joshua's right: you *are* one hot little bitch. It's like you can't control yourself when it comes to sex. Maybe we should keep you around after all- take you with us. As you can see, he'll want me to play with you, too.

"We could have *lots* of fun together, but one thing I will teach you is discipline. When we get to where we're going, you'll start out eating and drinking just like a pet Kitty Cat- from bowls on the floor. Of course, you'll be tied up like you are now. You'll get used to that, too, or you'll get nothing- no food or water. See, I'm not so sure that Joshua's right and you've learned your lesson after those stunts you pulled. You've gotten a little better, but you still aren't where I want you to be. I'll teach you some real humility; when *I* think you're ready, you'll be allowed to eat at the table again."

That rant gave Kim even more motivation to free herself, as if she needed any more. *Just when I thought there was no way I could hate anyone as much as I hate Josh...she'll do it, too- all of it...*

*...I wish she'd just shut up and get away from me so I could-*

"Hey, you know what? You could be our maid! That'll give you a function. Besides, that type of work is something you're very good at. I could give you a personal reference."

*Huh?*

"I was training for the job the last night you worked at the Kitty Cat Club. All everyone could talk about was you and your other stripper friends who worked there, including that Vanessa bitch. I hated both of you. Of course, you're the one they talked about the most. All the customers loved you. They always talked about how *beautiful* and *sexy* and *sweet* and *vivacious* you were, and that you were their favorite waitress and how much they wished you would have stayed there. Having you on the billboard promoting the place didn't help, either; they would not stop talking about you, but what pissed me off most was when they told me that I looked a little like you. They never told me how good *I* looked without adding that in.

"Well, things have changed, haven't they? I'll give you the chance to pick up where you left off. You even have your old uniform on- that should help get you back into the swing of it. It'll be a little different, though, because you'll only have two people to wait on. Your, um, 'tips' will be a little different, too."

She laughed as Kim mewed a little and tried to twist out of her grip. "Oh, knock it off. You can see it does you no good to fight, so why bother? You enjoy this, anyway. You sure didn't mind when I ran that scarf back and forth between your legs, did you? Believe me, there's plenty more where that came from, too. Joshua said it well- you're nothing but a sex object.

"And now, you're *our* sex object." Lisa moved her hand down along Kim's body. "You sure are built for that role, too. Even without the corset you've got the hourglass figure going on big time, and I have to admit: I've never seen a sexier pair of legs than yours," she said as she stroked them. "You do like this, don't you? Not that you can answer me...but then again, you are, aren't you? I can see you like it. It won't be so bad for you; you'll get used to the way things will be."

Kim let out a sigh and squirmed a little, feigning resignation to her fate as Lisa ran her hands along her legs, but behind that façade her mind was racing.

*I'm really starting to lose time now. I have to do something about her, and fast...*

289

"Well, I think I'm gonna take a nap after all. I am kind of tired. It's time to tether you like the pet you are." She got up, grabbed a length of rope and moved to the foot of the bed.

"We'll start with these legs of yours."

Kim finally saw a way. "Mmmph..."

"What? Oh, you want to turn over. Guess you'd be more comfortable that way, and you will be tied like this for a while longer...OK, go ahead."

As Kim turned onto her stomach with some difficulty, bound as she was, Lisa didn't hesitate to take advantage.

"*MMMM!!!*" Kim yelped as her captor delivered a painful slap to the vulnerable target she'd just been presented with. It was very difficult for Kim to hold back her fury over this latest assault, but she knew she had to stay focused. Her anger possibly had cost her a chance for escape that day in the gym, and she couldn't let the same thing happen now. She also couldn't give Lisa reason to keep toying with her, which a heated reaction to the slap surely would. Kim took a deep breath and slowly released it.

"Besides the sexiest legs, you have the most spankable ass I've ever seen, and as usual it was just *begging* for the treatment! Just couldn't help myself. I'm sure glad you didn't flex it, or my hand would be hurting!" she laughed as she went back to her task.

Kim looked back over her shoulder, and waited.

Please *let this work*...

She couldn't stop thinking about Lisa's revelation of what lay ahead for her if she failed, or if her chance didn't come...

...but thankfully, it did. Lisa never saw it coming. As soon as she leaned forward, Kim aimed a kick at her jaw and struck it full force with her right heel. Since her legs were bound together, Kim was able to use their combined strength, which was plenty. Lisa fell heavily across her, then slid off onto the floor.

She was out cold.


"Mike One, this is Victor Three-Four."

Even if Tom had not been able to glean from the tone of the officer's voice that the van he was behind was not the one they were looking for, his instincts probably would have told him the same thing. "Go ahead, Three-Four."

Not surprisingly, he confirmed Tom's suspicion with his next transmission.

290

"The license tag does not- I say again, does not- match that of the suspect vehicle, over."

"Roger, Three-Four. At least we know. Keep your eyes open. Mike One, out."

Tom glanced at the sign they were passing under as he put the two-way down.

The I-66 interchange was coming up soon…

…and the same instinct that told him to head west on 495 came back.

This time, however, he was starting to understand why. "Victor Five, this is Mike One. In a couple minutes I'll be heading west on 66, so I want you to hang around the D.C. area just in case we have a sighting there, over."

"Roger, Mike One. Do you want any additional units out that way, over?"

"Negative, Five. I don't want to go too heavy in one area. The allocation of units is fine the way it is. Until we pick up the trail, we have to keep covering as much ground as possible. Keep your fingers crossed. Mike One, out."



He laughed and took the gun away. "I'm sorry you lost your sense of humor, John. However, mine is alive and well. Shooting you would be too easy- too quick," he walked over to the ledge and looked down, "but if you really want me to do that, all I'll need for you to do is get up and rush me. Hell, I might not hear you if you're quiet enough. The river down there and the van's engine might mask any sound you'd make." He used his peripheral vision to its full advantage as he observed his adversary. "Still not biting, eh? Well, you can't blame me for trying to liven things up a little, can you?"

John didn't respond to him at all, but he scooted to the edge and swung his legs over.

Both looked into the abyss. Dawn still was a ways off; as yet there was no light at all.

"None of this was supposed to happen, you know."

"Well, that's one of few things you've said that I agree with."

"I don't think you follow what I'm getting at."

"What *are* you getting at?"

291

"You made your decision and you chose to end your life. There's no way you should be here right now- no way I should be talking to you. You died. You jumped off this ledge and *died* It was over. The only obstacle in the way of Kim being mine was out of the picture. All that was left was the way I was gonna break the news to her, or *if* I was.

"She was on the ledge that night, too. She was so close. She can deny it all she wants, but she *loved* the sex. Just one more step forward- like the one you took off here that night- and she was mine. You were gone and she was mine. There's no way you survive the fall and there's no way she slips out of those straps I used to tie her to my bed. *That* is what was supposed to have happened. That was her destiny; to belong to *me*- her body, her mind, her soul, her essence- all *mine*! The third and final part was the heist we pulled off. I had it all planned out and it was a good plan. I knew it would work as soon as I put it together.

"When I left this place after you jumped I saw clearly in my head how things were going to turn out. The heist was gonna work and even with splitting the money six ways we'd all be very well off. We'd get away with it and we'd all be free in the best possible way. If each of us played his hand smartly, none of us would have had to work another day in our lives. No one would have caught us- the only one outside our little ring who knew of the plan was you.

"As for me, just by virtue of my share I'd have been able to provide very well for Kim- give her the things she liked, spend lots of time with her while her new life grew on her. She was so young, and she was innocent in the right ways, not to mention curious. At that point, even though you set me back with your interference at the pool party, she'd have broken. All the pieces were in place and all I needed to do was execute. That's where my focus was as I drove back that night from here. I was happy, John- for the first time in my life- and she was the reason why.

"She was *not* supposed to be gone when I got back. She even begged me not to leave her alone, which is how I knew she was so close to giving herself to me. Obviously, I *shouldn't* have left her alone, and if I had the night to relive, I wouldn't have- we wouldn't have met here.

"You know something? Even as beautiful as she is normally, she's not her *most* beautiful- not her most sexual. When she's restrained and helpless is when the rest of her essence comes out. That last little part of herself she hides from everyone else is revealed. You've never seen and never *will* see a more dazzling display of sexuality when she's that way. I don't have to tell you, John- you saw it, too. Think of the times before when you had sex with her- how she responded- and compare that to what you saw a little while ago. You know exactly what I'm talking about, so don't even try to deny that you agree with me."

That did it.

Even if it meant that Josh would kill him sooner, he wasn't about to listen to any more of this and remain silent.

He unsheathed the weapon he'd always beaten Josh with, and would again.


*So, how do you like my legs now?*

Knowing how low on time she was, Kim didn't dwell on her success. Unfortunately, since she didn't know how long Lisa would be out, she temporarily had to divert her main effort from cutting her way out of the sheath to getting out of the straps binding her knees and ankles. Just in case Lisa came to while her arms still were bound, which given all that had gone wrong was a chance Kim couldn't take, she once more would be able to use the strength of her legs to squeeze Lisa's neck enough to make her pass out again.

Given the way her arms were tied, Kim knew she'd be unable to cut the strap that fastened her thighs since she couldn't reach it with the knife. So, along with her grunting, there was a constant swishing sound as she feverishly worked her gleaming, flexing legs back and forth in her attempt to rid herself of it. As much as she normally would love how her nylons looked and felt, at the moment she was much more appreciative of how they were aiding her effort to slip out of that first strap. The smooth- and in a way, slippery- texture of the pantyhose allowed her to work it lower, which would have been much more difficult had her legs been bare. It wasn't long before the strap was below her knees.

Again, the nylons helped as her tapered knees gave way to her well-developed calves. After some more concentrated writhing and twisting, the strap finally slipped over and below them.

*I always did appreciate good hosiery,* she quipped, relieved as she kicked the strap away. Next, she widened the hole she'd made in the single glove enough that she was able to put one of her hands through it and she drew her feet up to get rid of the other strap. She couldn't quite reach the buckle, which Josh had fastened over the fronts of her ankles, so she went to work on cutting the strap itself.

Fortunately, the knife was a sharp one. In a matter of seconds the strap parted and her legs were free. That victory gave her another boost of confidence as she went back to work on the sheath.

*Stall him as long as you can, John. I need more time, especially since this will be the hard part...*

She tried to maneuver the knife into a position that would enable her to cut the lacing.

After dropping it a few times, she came to realize that even if she could put it against the target, which she couldn't, there was no way she would be able to exert nearly enough pressure on it to cut through.

*DAMMIT!!*

Her anger and desperation boiled over- a small whine escaped her as she had to take a break. There was another reason why her repeated attempts to cut the lacing of the sheath, which started just above her wrists, were totally unsuccessful. For more than one reason, the strap that bound her wrists so tightly was the primary culprit. There was a good chance it was covering the lacing at that point. Plus, having her hands bound palm-to-palm drastically inhibited her range of motion with them.

The situation was becoming critical. It wouldn't be long before her fingers went numb from the duration and severity of her bondage. Moving her shoulders around and clenching and releasing her hands no longer was enough. She wasn't getting the blood flow she needed.

Time was running out in more ways than one. Sunrise wasn't far off; everything rested on her ability to escape. Lisa's gun was in the open gym bag across from her. She would need to be able to use that gun if she were to have any chance of saving John, which she was determined to do.

*I can't fail- I can't. Otherwise, John will be murdered and this time I will be made into a sex slave and kept in a state of bondage for the rest of my life...*

*...there is a way out of this sheath. I just have to find it...*

She looked around the van for something- anything- that might help her.

There weren't any sharp edges, at least none that she could see. There weren't any hooks or anything like that she could use to try and get out of the securing straps- they were cinched too tightly over her shoulders, anyway.

*Have to keep looking- I know there's something...*

*...maybe in the gym bag?* She moved over to the other cot and sat next to the bag, reached over to it and grabbed enough of it to pull it all the way open.

She shook her head as she perused its other contents besides the handgun. *It looks like they have enough handcuffs, rope, straps, gags and duct tape in here to restrain half the female population, which I'm sure he wouldn't-*

She froze for a moment, then looked back at the duct tape...

...and then at the exposed upright section of the cot's frame, which extended about half a foot up from where it joined the horizontal rail. There was a plastic or hard rubber cap- that meant the tubing was hollow...

...and it looked like that hole might be wide enough...

*...if I can secure the knife so it won't move when I rub the sheath against it...*

As soon as that notion materialized, she went into action.


Rogers glanced over at the Lieutenant. "Care to let me in on the secret, Tom?"

"It's something my brother told me about. I just might know where they're going."

"I know what you said to Victor Five, but maybe we should call for backup. If your hunch is strong enough..."

Tom shook his head. "Not yet. There's just as a good a chance that I'm wrong about this and I don't want to draw a lot of units away from the search in case I *am* wrong. I don't want a mistaken assumption to cause us to lose them altogether. I'm close to this one, Bill, and you know what that can do to your judgment if you let it.

"Plus, if I'm right and he sees a lot of heat, it's very likely he'd kill John and Kim. For now, we'll handle this on our own."

"How?"

"I'll let you know."

295

"Contrary to what you're trying to make yourself believe, it never was just sex, Josh- not when Kim and I reconciled a few months ago, not Memorial Day of '89 and not on the night of my Prom, when we made love for the first time. That's exactly what it was and what it is between Kim and me: love.

"Deep down inside, where you *can't* twist things to suit you, I think you know that's true. Not everybody looks at things the way you do- thank God-, which is something you never cared to realize. You know what else? Kim doesn't have to be tied up in order for me to see her true essence. I saw it and felt it the first time I looked into her eyes. She never hid it from me or tried to hide it from me, like she probably did from you. You want to talk about destiny? How things were meant to be? At that moment I knew I wanted to spend the rest of my life with her.

"For you to say you can't see her essence unless she's tied up...that only goes to show that you *can't* see who and what she is- period. You don't know and probably don't care how terrific and influential she is as a guidance counselor, which she loves doing more than anything else. You can shake your head all you want, but it's true. All you're seeing in her is what *you* want to see, which is not necessarily what's there. You're forcing something on her instead of giving her the choice, which comes naturally for you, doesn't it? You can't or won't see how truly fucked up you are. You think you can just impose your will and that everybody will yield to it. Welcome to the real world, where it doesn't work that way."

"Is that what you think? Well, guess what, John? It *is* working that way! In about twenty minutes when I either put a bullet into your skull or throw you off this fucking cliff, you'll *see* that it works that way!" He sneered as he went on. "Anyway, you're one to talk to *me* about imposing my will! All that bullshit you fed me that night about wanting to change the world...I remember everything you said. Even back then you knew it was futile to try. You knew you wouldn't make a bit of difference and you couldn't accept that. The sad part is, you could have done something better if *you* hadn't been so full of yourself. You could have been part of the group that *beat* the world. But what did you do? You damn near brought all of us down- you and Kim both. If things had worked out the way they were supposed to, all would have been well. If not for you, we *never* would have been caught and none of us would have been in stir or dead."

"You just proved my point. Things didn't go your way, Josh, and obviously you weren't able to adjust- not that you ever could. And why are you talking like that bothered you? You never gave a damn about those other guys- you used 'em for what you could get out of 'em and tossed 'em aside, which became one of your trademarks. As for your latest venture, you got away with it for a long time. We'd never have caught on if you'd left Kim, Jennifer and all the others alone and quit while you were ahead with Lisa. Needless to say, that wasn't enough. You never did know when to quit or when you were beaten. You don't always win. Even killing me won't be any kind of a victory for you."

"You're saying that because you're on the receiving end. On the contrary, killing you will be my ultimate victory. Look at all that happened leading up until now- other than Kim pulling her stunt and freeing Jennifer, everything has gone right. Thanks to investments I made through- and with- Peters, I'm wealthy beyond even my own expectations. I also have both my chief antagonists.

"I played you like a fiddle over the last several hours. You knew what I'd do to you, yet you still came when I told you to. Now, I'm going to kill you at the place and time of my choosing."

Josh glanced over the edge again. "I talked to a guy who was a parachutist in the military. He told me the first jump isn't the scariest; it's the second one that gets you. You know why? It's because you know what you did, and what you're in for. You've actually done it; it's not just talk or imagination any more. Plus, you still aren't comfortable with jumping yet, which adds to the fear and increases the possibility of screwing up.

"Yep, I think that's how I'm gonna end your life. It just seems more fitting that way." He smiled as he turned back to John. "You're wrong. I *have* won; I have all the cards. Those couple minor setbacks were just that. Ultimately, *I'll* be the one who's still standing and *I'll* be the one who ends up with Kim."


*Good thing Lisa didn't tether me by my neck first, which I couldn't have prevented her from doing. I also wouldn't have been able to do this if she had…*

Kim positioned the tip of the knife over the middle of the cap covering the rail, pushed it through to the hilt and withdrew it.

297

*Ah, the cap's plastic, not rubber. That should help...*

She was careful when she inverted the knife in her hands. She knew the blade was very sharp given the ease with which she'd cut through the leather of the sheath. Once she'd done that, she worked the base into the slit she'd made in the cap and pushed it through until she felt resistance enough to hold it.

There wasn't enough time to run the duct tape around it in order to make sure it would stay put. Besides, she easily could cut herself if she tried that, given the awkward way she would have to do it. She'd have to take the chance with it lodged as it was. Since the cap was hard plastic, it might hold the knife steady for long enough, provided she didn't push against it too much at the wrong angle.

The laces would have to go first.

She sat on the cot and turned her back to the knife. As best she could, she'd fixed it in a way that allowed her to sit as she worked on freeing her arms.

*Looks like I did that well enough- the edge is pointing right about where it needs to.*

She positioned herself to where the tip of the knife touched the sheath where her elbows were- and hopefully where the lacing was. She leaned back a little and then inched herself upward, moving her arms along the edge, then slowly back downward in a sawing motion. At first, she didn't feel any difference, so she put a bit more pressure on it, hoping she wouldn't push the knife down into the tube. She repeated the motion again, and again...

*YES!!* Suddenly she felt some give in the sheath! She moved a little further along and cut the lacing at more points, then moved off the blade as she'd probably sawed through enough of it. She twisted and pulled as much as she could against the weakened restraint.

Gradually, the single sleeve came undone. For the second time in a few hours, she felt the pain as blood freely rushed back into her shoulders and arms, which for the most part had been deprived of it for some time. While she got used to normal circulation- a process she had to speed up as much as she could- she bowed her elbows outward and raised her hands a bit so she could slip out of the securing straps, which proved to be relatively easy. Using her chin, she pushed those straps off her shoulders, which put her on the verge of getting out of the glove completely.

Only the strap that bound her wrists so tightly still remained.

*It could be a little tricky getting that blade in position to cut it, but-*

An almost inaudible moan came from Lisa.

*Oh, no- she could be coming to! I have to get out of this right now...*

*...but I can't panic, especially since this is one sharp knife, which I have to use since I can't slip out...*

Lisa flinched and Kim saw the whites of her eyes briefly.

*Easy, now. Very carefully...*

The tip of the blade touched the palm of her right hand. She adjusted a bit and then felt the tip between the heels of her hands. Those sensations meant that the circulation of blood in her arms was beginning to normalize. Had that not happened, she could have cut herself badly without knowing she'd done it.

As it was, the pain was easing and all her feeling was coming back quickly.

*Good- just a few inches upward...*

*...and now to get the tip through...there!* She moved her hands a bit lower, then stopped when she could tell the edge of the blade had made contact with the strap. Without hesitation, she pushed down, putting pressure on the blade, and began moving her hands back and forth slowly to allow the knife to do its job.

Lisa groaned and began to stir.

*Come on...this strap can't be-*

Suddenly it gave.

*I'm free!!*

For the first time, she didn't have to rely on someone else, or some lucky twist. She'd overcome her bonds her own way and she felt a rush of confidence that she hadn't experienced for quite some time.

But again, Kim didn't waste a second by savoring her victory, as she still had work to do. She immediately moved across and grabbed the most torturous-looking gag she could see, which coincidentally was the same one she'd been forced to use on herself yesterday evening and endure for hours on end after her tongue-lashing of Josh. Lisa had to be silenced as much as possible, and as Kim pushed the gag into her mouth, she knew it would serve that purpose very well. She noted the bruise on Lisa's jaw, which made her smile.

Fortunately, Lisa was very slow in regaining consciousness, which aided Kim greatly in her task. However, with as much anger as she had toward her suddenly former tormentor, Kim was sure that even had she been fully conscious at this point, this was a fight Lisa would not have won.

*I must have clocked you pretty good,* Kim thought as she locked Lisa's wrists behind her with one of the million pairs of handcuffs that seemed to be in the bag. She cuffed her ankles with another pair, and then with a third she completed a handcuff hogtie on Lisa that she had no chance of escaping. For good measure and some more personal satisfaction, she locked another pair onto her enemy's arms just above her elbows. Kim made sure the cuffs were locked tightly enough to hold her, then reached into the bag and took out the gun after she removed her own gag. After checking to make sure the pistol was loaded and ready to fire, she zipped the bag closed.

"Mmmph?"

Kim looked down at Lisa, who just now was being made aware that she was securely shackled and gagged and lying on the floor of the van. When her eyes focused, they immediately widened and she pulled at the cuffs very briefly when the · realization of what had happened hit her. Just as quickly, she seemed to realize there was nothing she could do.

Dismissing an urge to rub Lisa's face in it, which she deserved most definitely, Kim gently opened the rear door, slipped outside and quietly closed the door again.


*"MMMMMMPH!!!"*

Only too late did Lisa think to scream while Kim had the door open- she'd still been in shock from the sudden and drastic change in the situation. As a result, she'd blown the only small chance she had to warn Joshua.

Also, she quickly realized how much her jaw hurt, which the gag was making even worse.

All she could do now was try to find a position that would make her the least uncomfortable, lie still and wait.

# Chapter 12

"This is an ugly one, Tom. As lousy a thing as this is to say, it couldn't have been placed or timed any worse."

Tom and Detective Rogers waited for the ambulance, tow truck and police units to arrive after they tended to the victims as best they could. The driver of a box truck had fallen asleep behind the wheel, crossed the center line of the narrow two-lane highway and hit another truck head-on. The only way Tom knew of that led to Suicide Ridge was blocked.

"No doubt." Tom picked up the two-way. "I'll have to get some more units out here. I have a hunch Strauss has 'em on that ridge; I don't know where else they could be. Nobody's reported a possible sighting since the one near the Occoquan.

"All units, this is Mike One. Is anyone who's unmarked in the vicinity of Suicide Ridge, the bluff over the Shenandoah?"

"Mike One, this is Victor Two-Niner, I'm unmarked and approximately half an hour from that location, over."

"This is Victor One-Six, I'm marked but I can be there in half an hour, too, if you need backup, over."

"This is Victor Three-Three, my deal's the same as One-Six, but it'll be closer to an hour before I'm there, over."

*Well, one out of three ain't bad, I suppose, and the backup wouldn't hurt...* "Roger. Two-Niner, how familiar are you with that area, over?"

"I know it pretty well, Mike One- been up there plenty of times, over."

"Roger. I need you to double-time it up there and let me know when you arrive so we can coordinate our search. One-Six and Three-Three, that's a roger on the backup. Check in with me when you're in the vicinity. One-Six, find a good rally point that'll put you as close to the ridge as possible- preferably one that'll give you a quick response time when I call you. By the way, if you're coming off I-66, there's a nasty accident a couple miles below the exit on Route 340. Take another way if you can; the road is blocked. In fact, if any of you know of another way for me to get there, I'd sure appreciate you telling me."

"Roger, Mike One. Let me know when you're ready to copy."

"Well, that didn't take long at all," Rogers said as the patrol car responding to the accident report pulled up.

"That's a good thing. Now we can get out of here." Tom keyed the two-way again. "I'm ready, Two-Niner. Let's have those directions…"


"What's the matter, John? Kitten got your tongue?" He laughed out loud, very happy with himself. "Can't argue with that logic, can you? How fitting that I get the better of you in a debate just before I kill you."

"Is that what you think? That you got the better of me? You're even more delusional than I thought," he said as he chuckled, "and this much is for sure: you're still one sorry debater. You're supposed to get *better* with age!"

"All right, let's see what kind of smoke and mirrors you conjure up this time. I can hardly wait."

"Oh, I don't need any of that. As usual, you've beaten yourself. Even though it's a lost cause, I'll do my best to enlighten you as to why.

"I've come to realize a few things during my journey and one of the most important among them is that the end result doesn't mean a damned thing if you had to resort to cheating or lying to get it. It's just another way to prove that a house built on a bad foundation will fall eventually. After all the perks lose their value, which they will, you'll be left with the knowledge that you didn't have what it took to win the right way. You had to resort to deception, lies, screwing over someone else or something along those lines to get to where you are. And there's nothing you can do to gloss that over- nowhere you can hide from reality, because whatever stunt you pulled will catch up with you.

"You can say all you want about how it'll all roll off you, but that's a load of crap. One of two things will happen. Someday a conscience, which is something most people have that you either lack or have managed to suppress all your life, will force its way through your megalomania and torture you for the rest of your days. Or, if that doesn't happen, somebody will come along when you have your guard down and give you a dose of what you doled out. It might take months- maybe even years-, but one of those things will happen. When it does, you'll realize that what appears to be your biggest victory will turn out to be your biggest defeat."

"Is that the best you can do? That 'reap what you sow' bullshit?! That's something your old man would have said."

John's head snapped around. "What did you say?"

After a slight hesitation Josh looked back at him. "Well... you told me a couple times that's one thing he pounded into you." Then he laughed. "God-damn, you're easy. All I have to do is mention something about Kim or anyone in your family- especially your father- and it sets you off."

"That's because I love all of 'em, which is something I bet you've never felt for anyone other than yourself- *if* you even love yourself. It would be easy for me to believe if you didn't. Love is hard to deal with sometimes, but it's the best thing in the world. I know both of those things to be true. Part of the reason I wanted to come here that night eleven years ago was because I was feeling the bad part of it, which you knew.

"You played a big role in my decision to jump, Josh, because you needled me about her in your own way. You knew she was the same girl I always did and always will love. You knew how much I was hurting and you used that against me. I figured, 'how much worse could it be if I jump?' You could've stopped me. In fact, with what you knew you could've helped bring us back together, which is what a true friend would have done. But what did *you* do? You kept her as a captive at your house. You betrayed us both."

"You can't possibly be trying to make me feel-"

"I'm not finished yet. To finish and respond to your statement, no- I already know it's futile to try to make you feel guilty about anything. Frankly I couldn't care less how you feel, anyway. You don't know what it means to be a friend. Apparently, you never did. Just like love, friendship takes work. It entails giving and sometimes sacrifices, neither of which you would know the first thing about.

"You've always taken the easy way out, Josh. You'll only fight on your own terms; you can't handle adversity and you only can see things your way. If you think there's even the slightest possibility you'll lose or be proven wrong, you just shrink away."

He turned and looked over the edge. "Here's a perfect example. You wanted so badly to come here so- in your mind- you could complete the circle, which is funny since here is where I had the ultimate triumph. You said so yourself on the way over here- hell, you even sounded a little envious."

303

"Envious? How do you figure?"

"Because this is where I did something you never would have the guts to do. There's no way for you to alter the rules or the scenario in your favor. It's just a matter of courage."

"Courage?! Are you kidding me?! You were drunk, and stone crazy, at that!"

"Ah, now you're backpedaling, just like before during our debates. I caught you again- during the ride here you said that I had to have courage and decisiveness to jump. And, I wasn't drunk, Josh- I wasn't even close to it. On the contrary, I knew exactly what I was doing and was in complete control. I still remember every thought that passed through my mind that night.

"I hated where I was in life and hated even more where I thought I was headed. I felt like I had no say in what would happen and that nothing I ever did would amount to anything. That really got to me that night along with my state of mind over Kim. Let me tell you something: at that moment I felt like I had nothing to lose, so I decided to go for it. The worst thing that could have happened was death, which I was ready for if that was what it would have come to, so I stepped up and took a swing.

"Did I *want* to die? Of course not, but I knew I *could* die. In retrospect, I'm sure I didn't think it out very thoroughly, even though all of a sudden I was crystal clear in my mind that I wanted to make the leap and that I was going to. I don't know, maybe a sort of insanity did come over me. As soon as I jumped, I realized how much I wanted to live. Christ, I couldn't believe how many thoughts and memories went through me on the way down.

"I've thought about what might have happened if I'd hesitated- delayed it somehow. Your amazement over my decisiveness at that moment made me think about it again. If I'd waited just one second, would the winds have shifted enough to make me hit the rocks? Was that like a window opening- one that only was open for that precise moment? From the sound of it, things sure would have turned out differently if I didn't act on that impulse. That was one of the defining moments in my life- no doubt about it...

"At any rate, I landed right in the channel. Not only did I luck out in where I hit: the same applied regarding the water level. Thankfully it rained a lot that year, and the river was running high. So, my feet- and then my ass- hit the bottom, but not too hard. Damn, was that water cold! It woke me up in more ways than one.

"Once my head popped up and I realized I'd made it, that fog I'd been in was gone. I took the ultimate challenge and I won. At that moment I accepted two things as fact: first, no matter how difficult or impossible the obstacle I faced, instead of running away from it I'd take my best shot at defeating it. Second, I never would do such a stupid thing as jumping off this ridge again. I was granted one hell of a Mulligan that night, so I vowed to do all I could to justify that gift to whoever or whatever gave it to me.

"In spite of the probable lunacy of what I did, I proved to myself that I could overcome any fear, including that of death. I had what it took to pick up the gauntlet the Reaper threw down and slap him in the face with it, even though I knew the result easily could have gone the other way. Instead of the end of my life, in a big way that moment marked the beginning of it.

"I never looked back, either; I never got so down about anything again...well, that's not true. Recently I went through a bad spell, but I got past it. I got smart and finally reached out to Kim. She helped me out of that funk. Sometimes you need a nudge, no matter how strong or together you might be. You know what the ultimate irony of my jump was? In a way, *you* helped me. After the wake-up call that leap gave me, I still made a few mistakes along the way but I was on the right path. I was moving forward and now, here I am.

"By all indications, you just stopped and hid in the woods. You were afraid to go on and take your shot in the legal world, or in any legitimate pursuit. Because of that you got angry and blamed everyone and everything else because *you* weren't up to the challenge. You just started to waylay other people who were on their own journeys and robbed them outright of the lives they could have had. Or, you manipulated them with promises of riches, used them until they no longer were any good to you and then cast them into the pit of fire. Not only have you failed in your own life, you've cheated others out of theirs- probably more times than anyone even knows about. How does that make you feel? Then again, that's a stupid question, isn't it?

"One thing I find totally comical is that after all your railing about how much better and smarter you are than Daniels, you're just like him. You're a cockroach. You can't bear the light of scrutiny and truth, so you go scurrying away for cover. Well, there is no cover now, is there?"

* * *

*I'll have to get closer...*

Once she'd closed the rear door of the van, Kim had made her way to the front of it to find that she had a pretty clear field of fire. After resting her arms on the hood, she'd lined Josh up for a shot. The only problem was, they were a bit too far away.

She had to be sure she'd hit him solidly, because she knew she might not get a second shot if she were to miss with the first.

Keeping the gun and her eyes trained on him, she moved forward slowly and very carefully. Fortunately, Josh was holding the gun at his side.

*That's good, Honey. Keep him occupied for just a little longer...*


"You son of a bitch..."

"What's the matter, Josh? That's not exactly the reaction the winner of a debate has...unless you've changed your mind about that, maybe? That wouldn't fall in line with your theory, though, would it? That you're always victorious and never wrong?

"In fact, when did you *ever* better me in a debate? Hmm- let's think about that...the answer? You never did! Add in the fact that after my jump from here I was able to pull myself together and make something of my life- I, who you always thought inferior. You can't handle that, can you? You had your grades and your position of number one in the class, which you reminded me about when you needed to repair your ego.

"On second thought, how am I to know that you even did *that* the right way? How am I to know you didn't cheat or bribe professors or something like that in order to be number one? Let's face it: you sure aren't above doing something like that, are you?"

Josh looked away without responding.

"Why should that period have been different than any other for you? You were a spoiled rich kid who never had to work for anything in your life. You never appreciated anything as a result and figured you could do whatever you want. You're just like the vast majority of those other rich kid assholes, who turn out to be self-absorbed and worthless."

"That goes to show how little you know about me."

306

"Oh, yeah? How so? I can't imagine that means you're not going to take the typical way out and blame something or someone else for how screwed up you are- or Eric and Hilda, maybe."

"Who?"

John was taken aback by the blank look on Josh's face; not the slightest sign of recognition dawned. *What in the hell...?*

"Your parents."

"My parents? What are you talking about?"

He seemed to be out of sorts, reeling...

*...has he lost track of who he is?*

*Or was I right about those inconsistencies in his bio?*

"My parents don't have shit to do with how I turned out. He didn't even acknowledge me, anyway- not for a long-...I mean, they didn't-...It doesn't matter. Money's all they were good for."

John waited to see if he would go any further down that road, but the shroud fell over him, so John resumed his attack. "Which wasn't enough, obviously, in spite of the fact that your parents were millionaires. You put it to such good use, too, with the prison complex for the women you took. You never could attract women the right way, could you? I guess you've proven the point that looks really aren't everything, huh? Hell, you even had to disguise yourself as me to lure Jenny into your van! That must have been a hard pill to swallow, eh? Having to take on the face of the one you envy the most to get a girl? Have you done that with any of the others?"

"I needed a good way to keep my identity hidden, so yeah, I did. Don't you just-"

"-love the irony, right? If that's the real reason you did it, but I wonder if you're being honest. You didn't say that with much conviction, which tells me there could be something else... why, Josh, ol' buddy, were you envious of me to the point of wanting to *be* me? You used my plan to rob that armored car, you tried to take my girlfriend...that's it, isn't it?"

"You always were an arrogant son of a-"

"Oh, now I've heard everything! *You're* calling *me* arrogant?! Can't come up with a way to counter my argument- as usual- and now you're resorting to name-calling?" When he turned away, John couldn't hold back his laughter. Knowing he was facing death, he wanted to get every last jab in- sink every psychological dagger he possibly could into the one who would take his life. "Pathetic- absolutely pathetic!! I'll rephrase my question; how *often* did you disguise yourself as me? Did you do that every time?"

"Fuck you," he muttered in a barely audible voice.

John's smile faded as a possible explanation for that came to him. Seeing the damage he'd inflicted, he decided it was time to begin his final argument. "In all seriousness, why you did what you did means nothing to me, although I think I see what you're trying to do now. You think by killing me you'll solve all your problems, don't you? Do you really believe *I'm* the dragon you need to slay? Have you pinned every bad thing that's ever happened to you on me? Well, guess what? Even if you kill me, you won't have wiped our past history away and you won't have killed the dragon- not by a long shot. Like I told you, eventually he'll get you."

John took a step toward him. "You never could- and never will- face up to *any* real challenge, let alone the ultimate one. You thought you were so ingenious by pulling your disappearing act, robbing the Reserve, covering your tracks, kidnapping all those innocent young women because you wanted Kim and then finally taking her because that was the only way you'd ever have her. You're a coward- a soulless coward.

"One last thing: all that bullshit you laid on me about the second jump being the worst? How would *you* know anything about that? *Any* of it? I've stared death in the face three times and on each of those occasions, death blinked- I didn't. I was confronted by a psychotic state trooper who held a gun on me, was shot three times in the back by your minion and I jumped off this very ledge. Guess what? I'm still here and I always will be.

"As for you, you don't have the guts to challenge anything or anyone on equal terms, let alone death. You danced your way around it and tried to pull a fast one on it, just like with everything else, including law school."

John took a moment to let him digest all that. "That's about all I wanted to say. You might find this hard to believe, but I wish I could bring myself to feel some kind of sympathy for you. I think it's a Goddamned shame when the only thing someone's capable of feeling is hate, envy and a need for vengeance against the world, in part because he's certain that he doesn't have what it takes to make it in the world. Worse, he's not even willing to try. He's just given up.

"But now that all is said and done between you and me, considering all the damage you've done- some of which is irreparable-, I can't feel anything but contempt for you."
With that, he turned and faced out over the ledge.
"Do what you have to do."

*I think this should do it.*
Since Josh had turned his back to her, Kim was able to get to a comfortable range.
However, before she could make her presence known, he said something that made her freeze.

"Funny you should put it that way. I caused more damage than you realize..." With that statement Josh turned toward him.
"You know something, John? You've never been so close to your father as you are right now."
"That's the second time you've mentioned him, you-"
"Don't worry, you'll join him. Oh, you're gonna. I just wanted to let you know before I sent you to be with him that in more ways than one, you're as close to your father in his last moment as you possibly could be. You followed his course and in a way you're right where he was when he was killed. He was on the verge of going very far- possibly all the way-, just like you were, but you both suffered untimely deaths. As it was with him, no one's gonna know what happened to you."
He was about to reveal to John the full extent of the damage he'd caused in the life he was about to end It only would take one phrase- the phrase he was certain John would remember. He smiled broadly, savoring his imminent victory as he raised the gun...

...and had it shot out of his hand. In shock, he turned around to see Kim holding a pistol on him. There was enough light now for him to see her eyes, which scared him for the first time ever. In those beautiful emerald orbs he saw clarity of purpose...
...and death.
"Hi, Josh. I guess I never mentioned this, but when I trained with the police for my part in the sting, a very patient

309

detective taught me how to shoot. I'd say he taught me very well, wouldn't you agree?" Her moment of levity was gone as quickly as it came. "Come over to me, John, but make sure you don't get between him and me. And you," she directed at Josh, "toss me the keys to the handcuffs."

He just stood there, perfectly still.

Kim cocked the hammer back. "Give me an excuse, you piece of shit- believe me, I don't need much of one. Now, *give me the key*!!"

"Do you want to know what happened to your father, John? If you do, call her off."

Goosebumps broke out all over her when he said that. She recalled the cryptic remarks he'd made about John's heredity, including the 'chip off the block' remark shortly after he abducted her. But, knowing his nature as well as she did, she quickly shook it off. "You really are sick." She glanced at John. "Baby, you know he's-"

"No, I'm not bluffing. I've got no reason to lie about this."

"Bullshit! You have the best reason of all- trying to save the miserable era of destruction you call your life, which I'm about to bring to an end!"

"I swear, John, I'm telling the truth! I know how he died, why he died and who killed him, but if she kills me, you'll never know what I know. Think about it: think how much peace it would bring you to know what happened. You could even prosecute the man responsible for killing him- the one who sanctioned his death! Yeah, he's still alive! Think of the closure you'd have by putting all of them behind bars, or on death row! I know everything. What do you say?

"And what about you, Kim? Would you deny him that? Would you deny him what he needs to know and what he can know? Is your need for vengeance against me stronger than John's peace of mind and finally being able to put his father to rest?

"You say he's the love of your life. Prove it."

"Honey? Do you believe him? What do you want me to do?" Kim glanced at him again as he stood still, deep in thought. "John?"


Josh was a master manipulator- no question about it. *He definitely could be lying through his teeth...*

310

John's desire to know what had happened to his father, which now was even stronger than before, grappled with his desire to see Kim's tormentor dead. There just was no way of knowing if Josh was trying to pull a fast one and turn the tables. Chances were this was the only card he could play that might save his life...

*...but he seemed pretty sure of himself when he made that remark about what happened to my father, like he knew the answer. He did it again just before Kim fired...*

*...of course, he could be full of shit on both counts...*

Another question was, how could they get the information out of him if he *was* being honest? Was the information worth allowing him to stay alive- maybe even releasing him?

It didn't take John long to answer that.

*No. Even if he did know something, I couldn't allow that. The world's better off without him in it.*

There was, however, one problem: he didn't want Kim to have to pull the trigger.

"That's pretty creative, Josh; way to pull a rabbit out of your hat. The thing is, I don't buy it. Why don't you do the human race a favor and jump? Grow a pair of balls for once in your life and make the jump your-"

"Drop the gun, Miss Francis."

Now, there was a different problem.


Kim gasped upon hearing the voice behind her, but she didn't move. "Are you the police?"

"Not hardly. I'm sure you'll remember me, though, since a couple 'a my partners and I were sent to jail and a couple more died because 'a the sting you just mentioned." He whistled at her. "Still are quite the looker, aren't ya? I got a great view from back here; I sure like your choice of clothing."

"Deano! It's good to see you."

With those words from Josh, Kim's resolve was hardened even as she felt herself blushing from Dean Rollins' comments. "No. I won't put this gun down. Even if you kill me, it won't be before I kill this bastard who kidnapped me twice, made me have to watch over my shoulder for the past eleven years and almost took the love of my life from me twice in addition to everything else he's done. It's not going to happen. Plus, Josh, I don't believe

311

you know a damned thing about what happened to John's father."
She aimed at his forehead.

"Listen to me; drop the-"

"*No!* I'm *not* going to let him get away with what he did!"

"He won't," Dean said calmly. "He's gonna pay for everything he's done: make no mistake about that. I did ten years of hard time while my partner over there lived like a king off my share and the rest of the crew's shares. If I were you, Strauss, I wouldn't be so happy to see me.

"But if you kill 'im, Miss Francis, I'll have to kill you- both of you. If he dies, I won't get my money and have a way out. I'm not goin' back to the Pen and this backstabber's my ticket to freedom. You might find this hard to believe, but I wouldn't like havin' to kill you. I got nothin' against you and Governor Stratton anymore. You both did what you had to do."

She still didn't budge.


Lisa shifted around for what must have been the hundredth time as she lay on the floor. Finding the slightest bit of comfort was becoming more and more difficult. She also was a bit chilly, since she wasn't wearing much in the way of clothing.

*I hope Joshua comes in here soon and lets me out of this- my legs will start to cramp up before long and this gag is unbearable- my jaw is killing me...*

*...damn that little bitch for doing this to me!! When I get my hands on her again, I-*

Suddenly the back door opened.

*Joshua?*

"Mmmmph!!!"

"Well, what have we here? Who is this cute package someone left for me?"

Lisa froze.

*That voice...*

She only was left in suspense for a few seconds before she was rolled over and the hand touched her face and turned it up, making her wince as a fresh rush of pain shot through it.

*Oh, my God...*

*...no, not you...*

"Hi there, Lisa! How sweet of you to remember me. I didn't count on there being a fourth passenger, but I'm glad you'll be coming with us. We have some catching up to do, don't we?" Vanessa slapped her behind hard to give her a taste of what was to come, making her jerk in response.

Lisa yanked at the cuffs and cursed into the gag for a moment while her nemesis, having given Lisa the exact same treatment that she in turn had given Kim a very short time ago, made certain she would stay as she was.

"Somebody sure did a good job on you. It looks like you're ready for- ah, some luggage, eh?" Vanessa spied the bags.

"Let's have a quick look and see what you brought…"


"You're doing fine, Honey. Keep the gun on him." John turned to face Rollins. "How can we believe what you're saying? That you wouldn't kill us anyway? Kim was in on the sting that netted you and I was the one who prosecuted and convicted you. Plus, you've killed again: that guard during your escape, not to mention Mark Peters. How do we know you're not here to bail out your partner?"

Dean nodded. "I can see how you'd think all that. For the record, many a time I thought about takin' revenge on both of you when I got out. For a long time I saw you as the ones who fucked things up for me, but then I started to see things differently.

"Eventually, I figured out who it really was that screwed me over: none other than Mister Strauss here. He played you two just like he played me, from what I found out about the shit that went down between the three of you in '89. You almost became one of our partners, and Miss Francis here was Strauss's guest.

"As for Peters, he was dirty in more ways than one. He played a part in the big picture by launderin' a lot 'a money for our friend over there, and you'd better believe he got rich himself. I'll be honest with you; I had no problem icin' that fat little cocksucker. He an' Strauss invested our fuckin' money an' got filthy rich while I stewed away with my buddies- both of which were murdered while we were in stir. I got a feelin' you were in on that, too, ya fuck," he gave Josh a very cold glare. "That's one of the things I plan on gettin' out of you, one way or another.

"As for Sam Raymond at the Pen, I didn't wanna kill 'im. I know you probably won't believe this, but that's what *he* wanted. I liked the guy; a lot of us in stir did. He was a good man who had bad luck. He was dyin', ya see- cancer was eatin' his guts away.

He told me he'd lay awake at night, tryin' to keep quiet but wantin' to scream 'cause the pain got so bad. It hurt me just to listen to him say that...

"...anyway, there was a problem with his medical coverage. He said those worthless pukes in his healthcare program told him they wouldn't cover the costs of any treatments he had to get 'cause he had that condition before he signed on at the Pen. He had a lapse in coverage when he was between jobs and neither of the programs he had would pick up the costs, so he was fucked. He couldn't even come close to payin' the bills.

"So he was lookin' for a way out, but he wanted his wife and kids taken care of. He didn't have enough time in his job to draw a pension, and social security's too far off for his wife. I shouldn't be tellin' you this, Mister Governor, but I got no choice 'cause I gotta get outta here, an' quick. I promised Sam I'd take care of his family with part of my share, which is what I'm gonna do as soon as I can.

"Now, Kim- if I may call you by your first name- I need you to drop the gun."


"Mike One, this is Two-Niner. I'm two minutes from Suicide Ridge. Be advised, there are four access roads with multiple turn-offs leading up to numerous points of the ridge, which is a pretty long one. I don't know how familiar you are with the area, but I wanted to give you that info just in case, over."

"Damn...roger, Two-Niner, it's been a long time since I was up here last, and I wasn't all that familiar with it to begin with. Thanks for the tip. I do have some good news, though; I contacted your HQ and they're giving us a chopper. From what you told me about those multiple roads, we'll be able to put it to good use. The pilot's call sign is Air One and he should be on our frequency momentarily. His ETA is approximately 30 minutes."

"Roger that, Mike One; that *is* good news. Why thirty minutes, though? As quick as those choppers are it shouldn't take more than ten."

"I agree; ten would have been nice, but it needed refueling. All right, I'm two miles away from the ridge."

"Roger. I just turned onto the first road, which is just past mile marker twenty-eight. I'll take a look here. The second one's about a mile and a half past this one."

"Copy, Two-Niner, I'll take that one. Contact me when you find something or when you clear your section. Mike One out."


John had heard about the autopsy report. Rollins was telling the truth in that Sam Raymond had terminal cancer throughout his digestive system. John had no way of knowing if he was being honest about wanting to take care of the man's family, or if that was just a ploy, although it did seem like he was being straight about that.

One thing John couldn't deny was the animosity Rollins felt for Josh, who was beginning to look nervous...

He made his decision, which really was the only one he could make in spite of his reservations. He also had his other reason for it.

"Do what he says, Kim."

"But...but what if he's lying? What if all of what he said is a smokescreen? We can't let this scum get away with-"

"I don't think he will get away with what he's done. I have a feeling Dean here will follow through and make him pay. Plus, I think I have a good idea as to how he knew we'd end up here, which also is how he knew about what happened between Josh, you and me.

"Back to the matter at hand, I don't want to die and I know you don't, either. There's another thing to consider besides that. I know your instincts are telling you to kill him; I want him dead, too, but I don't want you to be the one who kills him. As much as you want to end his life, think about what it would do to you if you did. It would haunt you. No matter how much he deserves death, you never would stop seeing his face.

"You know all I've told you about what killing Clyde Davis did to me and you've seen some of the effects for yourself. Although I did what was necessary in that case and I don't regret it one bit, I never want you to go through that. Given your nature, the effect on you would weigh much heavier. I'm not saying you're not capable of handling it; I think you know that. I just don't want you to *have* to handle it, Ok?

"Go ahead, Kitten. Lower the gun."

\* \* \*

315

She knew he was right, despite how she felt about Josh. Killing him *would* haunt her, probably for the rest of her life.

Although she hated to, she did what John said...


Josh saw a small opportunity and acted, but he didn't cover two feet before he saw the flash and felt the very sharp and hot pain in his right thigh.

He fell to the ground after his abortive attempt to move to Kim in order to put her in between Rollins and himself. He was going to grab her gun and use her as a shield to take any bullets from Rollins' gun while he put a couple into Dean.

Instead, he rolled back and forth, yelling and cursing as he held his leg where the blood was seeping out.


The slight wind on the ridge had died off, allowing Kim to see the smoke wafting up from the barrel of her gun. In the matter of a second, she'd raised the revolver, aimed at his leg and fired, hitting him right where she wanted to.

"Would you care to underestimate me one more time, Josh?" she said to him as he looked up at her with hate-filled eyes. "I'd be happy to make you a neuter."


"All right, *now* drop the gun. I think you got your point across." To Dean's relief, she obeyed.

"What happened, Babe? Was somebody hit?"

He turned to the latecomer. "Yeah, you missed asshole over there gettin' part of what's comin' to him. And, *Christ*, is your friend ever a crack shot!"

He turned his attention back to the others. "Now, put your hands up, Kim; turn around and walk back to me. You come over here, too, Mister Governor."


Kim couldn't believe her ears. She'd been so focused on Josh that John's hint also had gotten by her.

"*Vanessa*?!" She turned, hands in the air as she'd been ordered, and gaped at her.

"Hi, Kimmy. I'm so glad you're all right; it's great to see you again, although this isn't exactly what I had in mind for our reunion." She smiled and, like Dean had, whistled at Kim as she took her in. "Look at you; you still look *fabulous*! Seeing you in that outfit sure brings back some memories. Oh- careful in those heels," she said as Kim faltered a bit while making her way toward the van.

"It's good to see you again, too, John. I was sure you'd pick up on the fact that I told Dean about our conversation. In truth, that's one of the main reasons I came to see you. I was worried about Kimmy, but Dean and I also needed to find out if you had any info that would help us in our search. I apologize for that, although I'm glad we all ended up here together like this without any of the wrong people getting hurt...

"Anyway, you're going to get your wish- both of you. You'll be together and you'll never have to worry about *him* again," she spat as she gestured toward Josh.

On his way over to Strauss, Dean picked up and pocketed the revolver Kim had used so effectively. When he got to his former partner, he grabbed him by the collar and dragged him away from the edge. He responded to the man's protests by telling him in no uncertain terms to 'shut the fuck up!'

John and Kim watched as Josh was manhandled and deposited back onto the ground not far from the van. Rollins didn't look like one to be trifled with, so neither entertained any thoughts of doing that. Neither was in a position to, anyway, with Kim in her high heels and John's hands still cuffed behind him, let alone the fact that Rollins had the gun.

Dean rejoined Vanessa and handed the revolver to her. "Anything of interest in there?" He gestured to the van.

"Oh, yeah- a duffel bag full of money! At first blush it looks like somewhere between three and four million, maybe more. Your share and then some, Baby." She kissed him.

"Hot damn!! All right, Sexy, we need to get outta here. First, let's make sure these two won't be able to try and follow us. Is there anything in their van to tie her up with?"

"Well, there's a single glove that was cut up, which I think she must have gotten out of; too bad we don't have time to hear how she managed that! There's another gym bag in there with a bunch of handcuffs, though, among other things. I'll grab a pair."

317

"Bring a few of 'em. We'll need some for our other travelin' companion here. It'll be good to have more company, ya know?"

"I agree completely! Our other passenger's all ready to go, too. We just have to toss her into our van." With that she went to fetch the cuffs.

While she was in there, Kim turned to Dean. "You don't have to cuff me. We won't follow you, and John's already-"

"Well, that's just it. It wouldn't be right to have him handcuffed and you free, now, would it? Besides, we'll leave you a key where one or both of you can get to it. All that'll be is a delay so we can get a good bit down the road."

"But...please, you don't understand. I've been tied up for the past three weeks, and-"

"And now you'll be handcuffed. Hey, at least I'm givin' you a change of pace, right?"

A frown quickly wrinkled her brows and she opened her mouth to retort, but thought better of it. However, her frown stayed.

He turned as Vanessa reappeared with several sets of handcuffs. "Good. You can put 'em on Annie Oakley here."

He couldn't help but smile while she scowled at him, and he had to stifle his laughter while Vanessa cuffed her wrists behind her back. "You know, Babe, Miss Kimberly's even a little hotter-looking when she's pissed. Better go easy on the temper-you're about to pop out there," he jibed, glancing at her breasts.

"*Oh*!!" Kim exclaimed, gritting her teeth as her ire went way up over him making light of her plight. At that point, Kim had had enough of being toyed with. She had no doubt her cheeks were as red as she was angry.

He couldn't resist that one, but before he got her to the point of breaking the link holding the cuffs together and strangling him, he let her know what else was on his mind. His levity disappeared accordingly.

"Hey, I'm sorry. I was just messin' with ya. And for the record, I'm glad I didn't end up kidnapping you that night you came to my place an' brought the cops on that sting you helped set up." He nodded when Kim's eyes widened at what he'd revealed to her. "Yeah, you heard me right. You were gonna be our bargaining chip to make sure Strauss here didn't end up keepin' all our money for himself, which he probably would've done even if the rest of us didn't get busted. I would've turned you over to him. Back then it wouldn't have mattered to me to do that, but now... well, I think you know what I'm getting at.

"You did good with the gun. That was a hell of a shot you made- two of 'em! Make no mistake: Strauss would've killed your man. You saved his life. You did right by him."

"You sure did," John added as he kissed her cheek.

That calmed her. She smiled and lowered her head.

"To put it in an even better light, you saved the life of the man who just might end up savin' America- who knows?" He gave her a wink. "You're all right in my book.

"OK, into the van with you two. We gotta finish up here..."


"Mike One, this is Two-Niner. First access road's clear- no vehicles at all. I'm heading back to the highway. I'll take the fourth one and leave the third for you, if it's all the same to you, over."

"Copy, Two-Niner, works for me. We're just about finished with the second one. Air One, what's your status, over?"

"This is Air One. I'm topped off and airborne. I have two sharpshooters on board along with my copilot and myself. ETA to your location is ten minutes or less, over."

"Roger, Air One- outstanding. Head to the southernmost point of the ridge and sweep from there north when you arrive. Victor Three-Three, what's your ETA, over?"

"I'm about five minutes from One-Six's location, over."

"Roger. Hang tight when you get there. Mike One out."


"How did you end up with him, Vanessa?" Her friend turned her attention to further securing Kim by putting the collar on her and tethering her by chain to the cot. She'd already done the same thing to John and gagged him as well. "I mean, you could have..."

"What, done better? Between the guys I had and all the others who wanted me, maybe you'd have thought that, but you know what? With one exception, all they ever did was lie, and the richer they were, the worse they were. Most of 'em were married, anyway. You remember their routine- laying the bullshit on you about how they'd take care of you and set you up in a place and all that crap. Let's face it: we had a lot of undesirables all across the spectrum coming into the club, anyway. When it came time to deliver on what they offered…well, you can do the math. Hardly any of them ever measured up in bed, either; again, the performance level dropped as their net worth went up.

"The only other man I came across with whom I would love to have ended up…well, you know like I do that he just wasn't an option. He knew it, too…" She took notice that John frowned a bit when she said that and cursed herself for drifting. Hoping he didn't catch on, she continued. "As for those other guys, believe me- you didn't miss a thing when you turned all of 'em down. In spite of that they sure missed you!"

She threaded the chain through the D-ring on the front of Kim's collar and locked it. "There was something about Dean, though. He never had a lot to say, but when I asked him something, he'd give me a straight answer every time. I like being with him…no, it's a lot more than that.

"We just fit; I can't explain it. He's so good to me. I never would have thought we'd end up together, either- especially when he went to jail-, but here we are. I know it's weird, but hey- I never was mainstream material, anyway, right? Neither were you, as I recall. Most of all, I guess I just got sick of the same old routine. Yeah, I know things could get dangerous, but I have to tell you, this has been pretty exciting so far. I'm happy. I made my choice and I'll live with it, even if things go south on us.

"Well, that about does it. You'll be able to reach the gun and the cell phone easily enough once you free yourselves, but I doubt you'll get out of the tethers. I'm sure you'll be all right, though. Now, for the key." As a final touch, Vanessa took the handcuff key and buried it in the cleft between Kim's ample breasts. She grinned as her friend's eyes narrowed.

"Oh, come on, Kimmy- have a *little* sense of humor, anyway. Let me see a smile before we go, OK?" she asked as hers disappeared. "I'll probably never see you again. You always were my dearest friend. No matter how you might feel about me now, you still are and you always will be." She leaned toward Kim to kiss her.

Kim mewled a little as she closed on her lips, but she didn't turn away. At the last second, Vanessa took a detour and kissed her cheek. "The lips wouldn't be appropriate now, since you're far from single...but then again, you never really were single, were you? Ah, there's that smile!"

She reached for the ball gag. "You two take good care of each other and be happy."

"We will. 'Bye, Vanessa. I-..."

As they always had, Kim's eyes conveyed much more than her words could. Even in situations like this when she couldn't express her feelings verbally, her message came through clearly. "I know. 'Bye, Sweetie. Oh- by the way, John, you don't know it yet, but soon you'll find out that I left you a present. You'll find out what it is, too, Kimmy. You might be a little angry about it at first, but I think you'll enjoy it, too," she said while she gagged Kim. She couldn't resist another little joke at Kim's expense when she finished buckling the strap. "You know, it's funny, but I seem to recall doing this to you a couple times before..."

Kim blushed in response, then looked up at her with that playful 'you just wait!' expression Vanessa had seen on many occasions. Kim usually evened the score.

At that moment it sank in fully. Both women realized that Kim wouldn't get her chance this time.

"Ya ready, Babe?"

"I just finished, Dean; I'm coming." Vanessa brushed away Kim's tear and then her own before she moved to the front of the van. She turned the engine off and took the keys out of the ignition. "Oh, don't forget your suitcase, Kimmy."

Just before she left, she turned and looked at Kim and John once more. Not wanting to leave her friend on a sad note, she said, "God, what a threesome we would have made!"


Dean climbed into the big black Ford van he'd had Vanessa purchase for them with some of the hundred thousand dollars he'd confiscated from Peters. "Looks like my buddy here traveled light, which is fine with me." He glanced down at Josh. "I don't think he'll be gettin' outta that."

"I believe you," Vanessa said as she looked down at Strauss, who almost was in the same predicament as Lisa; they lay side by side on their stomachs. Vanessa looked her in the eyes. "While I'm driving, I'll have to think of some things to do with you. It's been awhile since I've had a woman to play with,

321

especially one who's so fond of me, like you are," she smiled and moved to the front seat. She took great delight in the hatred she saw on Lisa's face, which looked so severe that Vanessa was certain she'd burst a blood vessel.

"Hope I'm around for whatever you have in mind for her."

"Of course you'll be around; I would *hope* you'd want to join in!" She started the van, turned it around and headed back the way they came as Dean laughed heartily.

He took his seat behind Vanessa and looked back at the hog-tied couple. "Guess I should fill you in on how you ended up in this predicament, eh? Well, we got lucky tonight. We'd been waitin' at another section of the bluff when we saw your headlights further down from where we were. It took awhile to find your ass. Fortunately, you fucked up an' left your van runnin', or else you might've heard us as we came up. Glad we turned the lights out, too- my Girl's idea."

"Thank you!" Vanessa chirped.

Dean chuckled and gestured toward her. "Gotta love 'er, huh? I sure do." He leaned around and gave her a peck on her cheek. "Anyway, with every overlook point we checked, I had Vanessa park the van and wait while I walked up to take a look. We ended up parkin' maybe a hundred feet away from where you had the van idlin' Once I knew it was you, I guided her to a spot that was even closer, but still shielded from your view.

"Then I made my move, and here we are. I got my share plus interest, so I'm happy. We'll see if you have anything else to offer me before I grease your ass. No biggie if you don't though; I mainly wanna see you suffer some. I wanna give you a little taste of what I went through for ten years.

"I'll tell you this one time only: make things hard for me any step of the way an' I'll take great pleasure in breakin' all your bones, one at a time, startin' with the smallest ones. They hurt more. You'll be beggin' me to put you outta your misery, which I might or might not do. When I'm done I might just dump your ass out on the side of the road somewhere an' cut ya so you'll bleed to death slowly. You get no warnin'- understand?"

For the first time since Dean had known him, Joshua Strauss looked afraid.

*I'm likin' this...*

"We're coming up on the highway," Vanessa said. "You wanted me to go right, didn't you?"

322

"You got it. Right turn, then keep goin' straight for about twenty minutes or so. Tell me when you see the sign for I-81."

"OK."


As soon as the other van pulled away, John and Kim focused on getting free. Kim tried to slide her cuffed hands over and past her rump with the intention of working them down behind her legs and under her feet to bring them up in front of her.

Two things prevented her from doing that: Vanessa used the cuffs on her that had only a sort of swiveling hinge connecting them, which held her hands together too closely, and this was one instance where her womanly hips and athletic 'bubble' butt worked against her. With a frustrated groan she gave up, knowing her only immediate hope of being let out of her cuffs rested with John.

She turned to face him and found that he was attempting the same thing she just had.

However, he stopped at the sound of a faint buzzing that steadily was growing louder. They looked out the windshield to the extent they could- they knew the buzzing sound was that of an approaching helicopter.

John and Kim looked at each other, wide-eyed.

Sensing how close they could be to the end of this second nightmare in the span of just a few months, Kim encouraged John as best she could as he went back to trying to work his hands to his front.


"Mike One, this is Air One. I have Suicide Ridge in sight. I'm moving to the southern end to commence my sweep north, over."

"Roger, Air One, I have a visual on you. That's me coming up on the third access road."

"That's a-...Mike One, be advised- there's a black vehicle approaching the entrance you're about to turn into. Looks like a full-sized van, over."

"A *black* one, you say? Wait, I see it. We'll check it out, Air One; go ahead and start your sweep." Tom looked closely as they reached the junction at the same time as the van.

"Roger. Air One out." The chopper headed away.

"Damn, what a honey! Great rack, too- even though she's wearing a loose shirt I can tell. Shame it isn't warmer yet or we might have gotten a better view," Rogers commented as he saw the driver.

Tom shook his head and grinned as he also got a look at the beautiful, long-haired brunette, who turned to them as she checked for traffic, smiled and waved flirtatiously. She couldn't have looked any less nervous than she did and she definitely wasn't Lisa Meyers- this woman had a more exotic look. As he and Rogers waved back, Tom couldn't see any reason to stop her other than Rogers asking her to join him at the nearest motel. They turned onto the road she just came off; she turned right and went south.

"I see your eyesight's just as good as ever, Bill. That was quite a smile she had, too- reminds me of somebody I met a while back. Had she not been wearing the sunglasses..."

He trailed off as it hit him.

The more Tom pictured her face the more he realized how much she resembled Vanessa Chamberlain, whose smile was unforgettable, just like everything else about her.

*Was* that her driving the van?

And if that was the case, what was she doing on Suicide Ridge in western Virginia at six in the morning?

She'd been in his office talking with John right after Kim had been abducted and John said he'd shared things with her...

*...could he have told her about the night he and Josh came* here?

"Tom? What's going on? Who did that girl remind-"

"Mike One, this is Air One. I have a white full-sized van in sight and my snipers have confirmed the license tag as Pennsylvania, Kilo-Foxtrot-Juliet-Sierra One-Two-One. I say again, I have a visual on the suspect vehicle, over."

# Chapter 13

"Victor Five, this is Mike One. Suspect vehicle has been spotted in the vicinity of Luray on Suicide Ridge overlooking the Shenandoah River. I need all available units to proceed to that location as soon as possible, over."

"Roger, Mike One. An hour ago I pushed Two-Two and Three-Four out west on 66. They're patrolling near Manassas and they'll be the first ones to you. I'll let you know ASAP who else I can round up, over."

"Copy, Five. Sounds good. Air One, is there any activity there? Anyone moving around outside or inside the vehicle, over?"

"Negative, Mike One. Zero activity outside and we can't see any further than the driver's compartment inside. You're the closest ground unit to the vehicle; make that first left off the access road and follow it all the way to the ridge, over."

Rogers hated to bring this up, but he had to. "Uh, Tom, you'd better have him check below the ridge, too- just in case…"

Tom looked away, then nodded. "Take a look below. Are there any bodies you can see on the rocks down there, over?"

"Wait one…" The ensuing silence on the radio seemed interminable for Tom…

Finally, Air One came back with, "that's a negative. Water level's low from the drought, so they'd have stuck out, over."

Tom breathed a sigh of relief. "Roger. Move out of there, Air One. We're dealing with a guy who won't hesitate to pull the trigger, so the ground units will have to take 'em down. Victor Two-Niner, get over here right now. Same goes for you, Three-Three."

"Roger, Mike One. I'm already on my way."

"This is Three-Three, I'm inbound, too."

"Copy, Two-Niner and Three-Three. You heard the directions from Air One. Remember: no sirens or flashers. Move in slowly, park a safe distance away, turn your radios down so only you can hear 'em and proceed on foot toward the vehicle. Once you have it in sight, take up the best covered and concealed positions you can find and stand by. Two-Niner, you take charge there and find a good avenue of approach to the vehicle for a possible assault. Let me know when you're in position." Both units acknowledged their orders. "Air One, go ahead and keep moving north for the time being. I'll get back to you shortly. Mike One out." Tom put the radio down.

He was stuck right in the middle of two choices at a critical juncture. There was a chance- maybe a good one- of catching Strauss asleep in the van. He had to sleep sometime...

...but as smart as he was, wouldn't he have picked a better hiding place to sleep in? The air unit had seen him almost immediately. Something didn't feel right.

On the other hand, he was nearly certain that Vanessa Chamberlain was driving the van they'd just seen, coming from where the suspect vehicle was parked. It had to be more than coincidence. Even if it ended up not being her, at least he would know...

...and if it *was* her...

"Mike One, this is One-Six. Where do you want me?"

Tom watched as Two-Niner hauled ass up the highway and turned onto his road. "Turn us around, Bill. Follow that black van." He grabbed the radio. "One-Six, I want you to move south on the highway from your rally point. I'll be in front of you and heading in the same direction. You'll be shadowing me, but don't follow too closely. I'm in pursuit of a black late-model full-sized Ford van that possibly has the suspects and hostages inside."

"Roger, Mike One. We're moving now, over."

"Roger. Air One, I also want you moving south along the highway. That same black van you pointed out to me a few minutes ago? That's the one we're looking for, and south is the direction the driver took. They couldn't have gone far. Try to be as inconspicuous as you can- we can't take any chances, over."

"Understood, Mike One. I'm on the way, over."

"Roger. Out."


For him, it was working.

John got his hands down past his butt, then bent his legs at the knees and drew them in as much as he could. It took a little work, but gradually the chain of the cuffs slid up over his feet. The hard part was done. As soon as he got his hands in front of him, he reached up and removed his gag.

"Mmmph!"

"Hang on, Kitten; I'll have us out of these cuffs in a sec."

Kim smiled as he reached up and undid her gag, then pulled it out. "Thank you, Honey. I can't believe I'll *finally* be able to spend more than an hour at a stretch with my hands free!"

Right at the end of that thought came another that she still puzzled over. "Do you have any idea what Vanessa meant when she said she left you a present?"

"Maybe this," he said as he slipped his hand in between her breasts to retrieve the key. He took his time, smiling all the while.

Kim blushed and lowered her head. "You could be right." She settled back and sighed as she shifted around. "Mmmm... don't have *too* much fun in there, you! Not just yet, anyway."

"Hey, I have a lot of territory to cover in this search. Have to be thorough, don't I?" She giggled as he leaned over and kissed her, then extracted the key.


"So where are we going? Any place in particular?"

"Nah, not yet, Babe," Dean replied. "I just figure it's a good idea to head away from all the activity. We'll take I-81 south all the way outta Virginia- that's the first order 'a business. Once we're in Tennessee, we'll see which way we feel like takin' from there. We'll need to stop for gas by then, prob'ly, an' we'll think 'a where we wanna spend the night. Doesn't look like money'll be a problem," he said as he fingered the cash Strauss had brought.

"A lot 'a coin here. You took a big chance carryin' so much around. Wonder what you had in mind for all this? Hey, I bet you were gonna head outta the country, weren't ya? That's what Peters was gonna do before I took care 'a him. Figured the pilot flyin' you out would keep 'is mouth shut if ya handed 'im enough loot. Looks like this woulda done the trick, too, but see-you got careless. If you hadn't tried to rub the Governor's nose in it an' wasted all that time, you prob'ly woulda gotten away before we got there. All ya had to do was take 'im out 'an put one in 'is head- that woulda been the end of it. You'd've had Kim Francis, too- you'd've had everything. Matter of fact, why'd ya come here at all? Seems to me you had 'em dead to rights wherever it was that you had 'em before ya came here...

"Whatever the case, you wouldn't've ended up in some 'a your own handcuffs, lookin' like quite the dumbass an' lyin' next to one 'a your girls." Dean laughed at him.

327

"You wanna talk about some poetic justice? It just doesn't get any better than this!"


"Mike One, this is Air One. I have the black van in sight. It's still heading south on the highway. Will advise of any change in direction, over."

"Roger, good job. You're the only one with eyes-on, so stay with 'em. Mike One, out." Tom's radio wasn't silent for long.

"Mike One, this is Victor Two-Niner. We're in position and standing by for orders, so is Three-Three. We're ready to approach to the vehicle, over." His voice was low since he was in tactical mode.

"Copy, Two-Niner; that was quick. Still no activity you can make out?"

"From what I can tell, zero activity, over."

"Roger. You have the green light, Two-Niner. Conduct your assault and use whatever force you deem necessary, including deadly force, over."

"Copy, Mike One."

"Keep in mind that's my-...well, I'm sure you know. Do it, Two-Niner. Do what you have to. Mike One, out."

*I should be there.*

That thought haunted Tom as he lowered the radio.

*Christ, what if something goes wrong and John, or Kim, or both of them are killed?*

"Don't, Tom." Rogers could tell the state of worry he was in even though he could only cast fleeting glances at him while they rolled down the highway going in excess of a hundred miles per hour. "You went with your gut and made the decision. Suppose we'd stayed there with all the units and nobody ended up being in that van? We'd be holding our dicks in our hands and the bad guys would be getting away. For what it's worth, based on what you told me, I think you made the right call.

"They'll be all right and we'll get the shitbags that did this."

Even though it wasn't to a great extent, what Rogers said did help. Tom knew his best detective and trusted friend was right and that he wasn't just saying that to make him feel better. That was something the man would not do under any circumstances.

"Thanks, Bill. If I haven't said so, I'm glad you're here."

"As a matter of fact, no, you haven't said a damned thing like that." Both men laughed, which helped Tom a bit more.

In spite of all that, however, Tom still felt the heavy weight of worry on his shoulders. It would stay there until he knew John and Kim were safe.

Corporal Jim Brewer, Victor Two-Niner, gave the signal. He and his partner, Trooper First Class Dan Russ, converged as stealthily- but also as quickly- as they could on the van from the rear. From where they started, it was no more than fifty feet away across the slightly uneven ground. It helped that there were no windows on the back doors.

The Victor Three-Three unit provided support for them- they took up position closeby, one facing each side of the vehicle.

The unit in motion had covered more than half the distance to the van when the two men halted.

Corporal Brewer shared a worried glance with his partner- both had heard the voices inside.

They had to assume it was the perpetrator and his suspected accomplice since it was believed that Governor Stratton and Miss Francis were subdued.

*We still could take 'em by surprise, but we'll have to move fast.*

Brewer could feel the adrenaline kicking up. He took a deep breath and looked at his partner, then went to give the nod.

John quickly undid his cuffs and Kim turned onto her stomach so he would have easy access to hers.

They covered the rest of the distance to the van without incident and took their positions on either side of the back door.

When Trooper Russ reached for the handle, the occupants started talking again. He slowly depressed the button and Corporal Brewer leveled his .45 automatic in preparation.

"Oh, shit."

Kim looked over her shoulder at him. "What's wrong?"

329

"The key doesn't fit. I can't unlock yours."

"You're kidding me..."

"I wish I was. It won't go; the hole's too small."

"*Dammit*!! John, I want *out* of these things!"

Both officers froze.

Trooper Russ looked at Corporal Brewer, who held up his hand.

*She said 'John'...*

After her outburst she tugged at the cuffs.

"Take it easy, Honey; don't do that. You'll hurt your wrists. Just calm down now."

As he caressed her, hoping that would help, it dawned on him. "I think I just realized what Vanessa's present was."

"What's that? Giving us the wrong-" suddenly she stopped fighting and looked up at him. "Oh, my God, I think you're right. This absolutely is something she would do."

Even as frustrated as Kim was, she couldn't help but laugh along with him.

"FREEZE!!!"

John had reached over to grab his cell phone when the back door flew open and he found himself looking down the barrel of one gun, then a second almost right away when the other door was yanked open.

"Governor Stratton? Miss Francis?"

"Yes...yes, Officer. It's, um-...it's us."

"I apologize for that, Sir, Ma'am." The visibly relieved policeman lowered his weapon and his partner did the same.

"You were doing your job and you did it well. No apology necessary." It took a moment for John and Kim to collect their wits.

"You can move now, Kim- it's all right."

Right after that he asked, "Would either of you happen to have a key that might fit Kim's handcuffs?"

\* \* \*

Tom picked up his cell phone. He had to swallow to push his heart back into his chest when he saw the number of the incoming call. He jabbed the button. "John?! Is that you?!"

"Yeah, it's me, Brother. Kim and I are all right. We-"

"Where are you?! Are you inside the van on Suicide Ridge?!"

"How in the hell did you know-"

"Hold on." He picked up the two-way immediately. "Victor Two-Niner, Mike One. Stand down- I say again, *stand down*!! Those are our friendlies inside the van- give them whatever assistance they need, over."

"Roger, Mike One. We're already here with 'em, over."

"Thank God. Mike One, out."

He put down the radio as a great surge of relief rushed through him and he shook Bill's extended hand. "John, it's great to hear your voice. You're sure you and Kim are all right?"

"We're fine, but we can't seem to get Kim out of these handcuffs. Nobody has a key that fits; I was hoping you might. Are you on your way?"

"Not just yet. I'm down the road from you and involved in a pursuit, but I'll be seeing you soon enough. Corporal Brewer and the other three troopers will stay there with you two and coordinate transportation back home for you. Just sit tight and relax for a bit."

"Sounds good, we'll do that. Kim was something else. You should have seen how she handled a pistol! I'm thinking about incorporating her into my team of bodyguards!"

Tom chuckled. "I want to hear all about it when this is over. For now, I have to concentrate on stopping this van that I think has Strauss in it."

"Hey, you need to know that Dean Rollins and Vanessa Chamberlain were here, too."

"Vanessa's the one driving the van. Rollins is with her?"

"Yeah, he put cuffs on Josh. Seems ol' Dean wants revenge; he thinks Josh is responsible for the deaths of his accomplices while they were in prison, among other things."

"So they're all inside that van...all right. Thanks for the heads-up, John. I'll talk with you soon." He hung up with John and grabbed the radio. "Air One, this is Mike One. Did you copy my last traffic with Victor Two-Niner, over?"

"This is Air One. Roger, our friendlies are safe, over?"

"Roger that! Get a tag number on that van right away and get it out to the whole team."

"Wilco, Mike One. Moving in now-...stand by, vehicle has reached an intersection and it- they're heading west. Suspect vehicle is now westbound on Route 6 and heading toward the I-81 interchange, over."

"How far away is that?"

"Approximately fifteen miles, over."

"Copy. Get us that tag number, Air One. Victor One-Six, light 'em up, go loud and haul ass- no need to be covert anymore. I want to intercept them before they get to the interstate. We have fifteen miles of leeway, so that shouldn't be a problem.

"Victor Five, I'll need you to alert the State Police barracks closest to here. Get any and all available units up and mobile. We could be in need of reinforcements, over."

After receiving acknowledgements from both, Tom put his siren up on the dash and turned it on.

"Step on it, Bill. The gloves are off now- let's get 'em."


The officers didn't have any luck getting John or Kim out of the tethers, and had just as little success in getting Kim out of the heavy handcuffs that still were locked securely around her wrists.

"Sorry about that, Mister Governor. We have somebody coming with a pair of bolt cutters. We, um, might have to call a locksmith to get you out of those cuffs, though, Miss Francis. I don't think we'll be able to get the cutters in between 'em."

"I can't believe this!" she exclaimed in annoyance as John pulled her against him.

"Is there anything we can do for you in the meantime, Ma'am?"

"You guys have done all you can for now. If you don't mind, would you give Kim and me some time alone before everyone else gets here?"

"Absolutely, Sir." Corporal Brewer closed the doors behind him and walked over to the patrol car with Trooper Russ.

When they were a safe distance away from the van, Russ couldn't hold it back anymore. "Jesus, Jim, what a *knockout* she is! Have you ever seen a hotter-"

332

"No, I haven't, and yes- he's one lucky guy. Now, shitcan any more talk like that about Miss Francis. Remember: she could become the First Lady one of these days."


"Can you see it, Babe?"

"No, it must be behind us. You think it's following us?"

"I have a feelin' it is. I been hearin' it for a while now, an' it just got louder."

Dean stepped over the shackled couple and looked out the back window.

There it was.

As he feared, it was a police chopper and it was bird-dogging them.

*He's awful fuckin' close, too...*

Dean looked at his AK-47 assault rifle, then back out the window at the chopper. When he'd bought the rifle from his connection, he figured it couldn't hurt to have it. Now, it was starting to look like the smartest purchase he'd ever made.

There could be only one reason the helicopter was tailing.

They knew. He couldn't afford to assume otherwise.

He'd come too far for it to end here, like this.

He picked up the AK-47.

*I got no choice...*


"Is it really over?"

"It is for us, Kitten. We're safe now; it's all right." He pulled her closer and cuddled her as she began to weep.

It finally settled in when the officers closed the doors and left them alone. Josh and Lisa were out of the picture and probably meeting their fates. His influence over her was broken completely.

She and John had survived once more.

Kim lay against him and let it out.


"...Roger, Air One, good copy on the license tag. I think-"

"Oh, *shit*!! We're taking fire, we're-"

There was no mistaking what had happened; the pilot cursed and his transmission cut off at that point.

"Air One, what's your status, over?"

333

Not a minute earlier, Tom had gotten his first visual on the chopper. Now, he saw it yawing and starting to spin.

"My hydraulics are gone; he must have hit the line. I'm losing power fast. Stand by, One- we're going down…"


Corporal Brewer monitored the radio. Immediately upon hearing the chopper had been hit he turned to the other troopers.

"Listen up: the two reinforcing units should be at this location soon. It sounds like those guys in pursuit are in a lot of trouble. Dan and I are gonna help 'em out, so you two will protect the Governor and Miss Francis and wait for the others. Got it?"

"Got it, Jim. Go kick some ass."

Brewer nodded; he and Trooper Russ were quickly underway.


Tom held his breath and watched the helicopter go down. The only good thing was, it wasn't very high up when it was hit.

With the rate of speed Rogers had the car up to, they were able to see the end of the descent. It looked like the pilot had some semblance of control, although it still turned out to be a rather hard landing in an uneven field off the road.

"I just went by you, Air One; good job on the landing. Do you have wounded, over?"

"Roger, Mike One. I'm hit and so is one of my snipers."

"How bad?"

"Hurts like hell, but not life-threatening- seems to be the case for both of us. Otherwise, we're just a little shaken up. We'll manage until medical assistance arrives, over."

"Copy, Air One. Give Victor Five your location and he'll get an ambulance out to you.

"Victor Five, you're in command now. I'm coming up on the suspect vehicle as we speak and Victor One-Six isn't far behind me. We have to stop 'em before they get to the Interstate, or this could turn into a bloodbath. Mike One, out."


"Dean, what did you do?!"

He'd broken out the rear window of the van with the barrel of the AK. Almost in the same motion, he took aim at the

334

chopper and emptied a full magazine, leading the chopper a little as he fired. Obviously, the bird was within effective range.

He was in a haze momentarily as he watched it go down, but Vanessa's voice snapped him out of it.

"Gun it, Babe- we gotta get onto 81 an' quick!"

"What did you-"

"Vanessa, if you don't drive as fast as you can, we're *dead*! We gotta get onto that interstate an' get the fuck outta here!"

*We're prob'ly dead, anyway…*

"There they are; it looks like they just sped up. How are we gonna handle this, Tom?"

Tom looked in the mirror on his side. Victor One-Six was close behind them.

I-81 was only three miles away. The reinforcements wouldn't make it in time and no other units were close enough to stop them. It was all on Victor One-Six, Rogers and him.

"One-Six, this is Mike One. Stay with me, but keep a comfortable distance back. We're gonna get as close as we can to him so I can shoot his tire out and hopefully get the shooter, too. He has an assault rifle, so watch for his fire and wish me luck. Mike One, out."

He took out his .45 automatic and clicked off the safety. "Pedal to the metal, Bill, and crouch down as low as you can because he'll be firing at us. There's no other way. Go."

Rogers did what he said and jammed the accelerator down as far as he could while Tom leaned out the window and took aim.

Both knew what they were up against and what easily could happen.

They were up well over a hundred and closing quickly.

*So far, so good; we're almost in range. Just a little closer.*

The van crested a small hill and briefly disappeared.

*Once we hit the other side, your ass is mine…*

For a second, the car went airborne.

Tom quickly reacquired the van…

…and saw the muzzle flash.

Vanessa called out, "One mile 'til 81. We're almost there."

Dean didn't even hear her. He was focused on the road, particularly the police car that was gaining at a frightening rate.

*It looks like the crazy son of a bitch wants ta ram us...*

Since there was no need to worry about his captives, he paid them no mind.

He poked the rifle barrel out the window again when they went over a hill and took aim right when the car would reappear. As soon as it did, he pulled the trigger.


John kissed her forehead as he felt her shifting around. "You must be sore. Here, let me rub you down a little."

Kim relaxed against him and sighed as he massaged her shoulders. Just as it always did, his touch turned her to mush. Her tears had abated, but the emotions that brought them on lingered.

As she reflected on all that had happened, she realized that something truly had changed within her. There was no danger whatsoever. She was completely safe and, just like when she was in the cage, instead of putting a damper on her re-emerging passion, the element of safety was air fanning the rising blaze.

Her hands twisted in the cuffs as the fire began to shoot through her so quickly and so suddenly that it almost was frightening. She kissed along his neck and rubbed her breasts against him.

"John..." She moved around to his front and climbed on top of him. Her trail of kisses started anew at his earlobe and moved across his cheek.

It was déjà vu. This was the state she'd been in back at the house, only she wasn't restrained so severely this time.

There was no mistaking what she wanted.

"Here?...*Now*? Honey, those guys are rmm- mmmm..."

"Get my suit off me, Baby. Don't worry about the nylons-they're crotchless. I, um, think you'd better gag me, too...

"...and *please* hurry..."


The car landed amid a flurry of bullets. Steam began to pour out of the engine. The windshield was hit multiple times almost immediately and was on the verge of shattering.

At the same time, Tom returned fire. His first round struck the right door below the window and close to the seam between the doors. The second and third hit the base of the right rear window, from which Rollins was firing.

Tom heard a bullet whiz by his head, then felt a nasty sting just below his left ear that almost made him drop his .45 just as he squeezed off his fourth round.

He saw the reaction of the shooter, knowing that round had found its mark. The rifle fire stopped, and Tom didn't hesitate.

He aimed at the same point and fired two more rounds.


Dean screamed and clutched at his shoulder, but on adrenaline raised the rifle back up and emptied the remainder of his magazine toward the car as two bullets struck him square in his chest.

He was dead as he fell across Lisa.

He never saw that his last several bullets went over the first car and struck the police cruiser that had just crested the hill.


Tom fired two times at the right rear tire, but his third shot went somewhere off to the right as the car careened wildly. He was yanked back inside as they went off the road.

He lost consciousness sometime during their first or second roll.


Vanessa already was slowing down when she heard and felt the tire blow. She had to apply the brakes anyway because she was approaching the curve in the road just before the I-81 overpass, which at most was only a couple hundred yards away.

She hit them hard when the tire went. The van went off the road and into a drainage ditch, but stayed upright and came to a stop.

Dean was dead- of that she was certain.

It was over.

She didn't even think to turn the engine off. She just sat there in a daze and waited for the police, whom she suspected wouldn't be long.

* * *

There didn't seem to be much of a cool down period afterwards- not for Kim. After John removed her gag, which had served its purpose well, she began to kiss and nibble on his shoulder and work her way up toward his neck once more.

John sighed deeply as he ran his hands down along her sides. He took hold of her sheer nylon-covered rump and squeezed, which made her tighten up. "Damn, Kitten, from the way things are going here, *I* might have to tie you up sometime."

"Oooo!!" She faced him with a very seductive grin, then kissed him again.

"This really does get you going, doesn't it?" he inquired as he reached up and caressed her cheek.

"Being tied up?" Her long lashes drifted together slowly and she smiled as she responded to his touch. "You know, a simple 'yes' would have been an honest answer up until recently, but...it's a little more complex now. In a good way, though...oh, I'll just start from the beginning. I want you to understand where I'm coming from."

She rested against him. "One day shortly after I turned thirteen, I was out for a walk and came across a group of boys along with a few girls from the neighborhood. I didn't pay them any mind because they didn't think much of me. For some reason they had this impression that I was stuck up and thought I was better than they were, even though I never felt or acted that way toward anyone. In spite of that they came over and started talking with me. They were nice, too, which really threw me for a loop.

"They told me they were playing cops and robbers, but there was a problem. One of the girls had to leave and they needed me to take her place. Even though I was a little leery, I also was glad to be included for once in something they were doing. At the time I was naïve as to why they wanted me to play...then again, I think deep down I knew why.

"That just happened to coincide with the tail end of my puberty, which I'm sure was a factor. My waist always was really small, and my butt and my legs developed and took their present shape early on. That was a result of the combination of genetics and the sports I'd been involved in- mainly competitive figure skating. Then came the big transition in '81.

"It started early that year when I noticed my 34B-cup bra was too tight, and I was having a little trouble getting my jeans past my hips. By the middle of summer when the growth spurt pretty much stopped, I was about ready for a 34DD-cup and my hips had become those of the childbearing variety. When those ingredients were added to the mix, the direction of my life changed completely. Sometimes even now it's a lot to handle, but at thirteen...

"It was bad enough for swimming because my boobs slowed me down when I was getting pretty good, but it was worse for skating- they really threw my timing and balance off. Until I was in my late teens I wasn't able to compensate and regain the ability to do my jumps. Even when I did I never got back to the level I reached during the winter before puberty, so the damage was done. I was good, too, Baby; I was *very* good, and I wasn't the only one who thought so. I won the 1981 state championship, went on to win the silver medal in the regionals and competed in the nationals- and that was the first year I competed seriously.

"I was so caught up in the whole thing, especially since I accomplished all I did not long after the Olympics were held. My coach was certain that's where I was headed and so was I, but then...with the changes to my body and those few pounds I gained in certain places, that was the end of my aspirations. I had to drop out of competition, which really hurt."

"I never knew that, Kitten. I know you always loved skating in all its forms, but...why didn't you tell me you were a champion? Even though you didn't go all the way, you did so well as it was; you should be proud of that. You still have your medal, right?"

"Oh, definitely- that and my trophy from the state competition. I was very proud, and still am, but at the time I also was really upset about it- even while you and I were together in '83. I'm sure you can understand why. I was on track for my shot at skating greatness and then- bang! Just like that my ability on the rink, which took me years to regain- and then, only to an extent- was gone."

After a brief pause, she reflected further on that. "Looking back, I probably should have been able to overcome it, but...well, maybe those hormones played a part, too. The sudden loss of confidence was the killer. I guess it just wasn't meant to be. So, that's where I was on the day of August 18th, 1981. A big part of my life was over; I went from possible Olympic figure skater to Miss T & A of Hamilton.

"That's not to say I didn't get over it eventually and start to adjust to my new status. Better yet, on that day of the 'cops and robbers' game I was wearing a pair of shorts and this little top, both of which fit fine the year before but suddenly were *very* tight and covered significantly less. So, here I am in hot pants, my top is straining, I'm bare from midriff to waist; I was young Daisy Duke that day! Not that I had much of a choice there; my clothes would have to have fallen off me before the wonderful Steven Francis would fork out any of his precious money to buy new ones for me.

"I can't put all of it on him, though. Even then I already was becoming another kind of exhibitionist, sashaying around in that little bit of clothing, showing off my new curves and my suntan. I enjoyed all the attention I got- even the catcalls-, which was a welcome change from the neglect at home. It also was a way for me to rebel against his puritanical code, but as great as it felt to do that...well, sometimes when you rebel against people or circumstances, you get so caught up in it that you forget to concentrate on finding out who and what you are. I don't doubt for a minute that all that negative energy hindered me in some ways for a number of years.

"Even so, I held so much in, too; you know how much worse it is to do that. When I think about it, it was such a small measure of retaliation that I took against him and I did it when he wasn't around. So, I guess in the respect of getting back at him, it was totally inconsequential. He never said a word about it anyway, although I'm sure at least one of our neighbors mentioned to him how I was dressed, so he probably just kept true to his pattern of not giving a damn about anything I did.

"However, that display I put on and all the focus on me sure played a part in other decisions I made in the years to come...

"Anyway, I found out I would be the girl who was taken and held hostage. It was so weird...I'm sure I said 'yes', but I don't remember saying it. I didn't know why I wanted to play that role; I just knew that I did. Suddenly, everyone wanted to be with the criminals. They looked ready to *fight* over it! I've never seen so many cops wanting to turn bad!"

John laughed as she continued. "I found out why very quickly. With no warning at all, a couple of the bad guys grabbed hold of me and led me between a couple houses into this grass alley. I was caught off guard completely and slow to react. I tried to resist but wasn't very effective in that; even though I was in far better shape than any of them, I had no chance against the whole group. They stopped me and held my arms while another one produced a length of rope. When it set in what he was about to do, I stopped resisting. Another emotion started to seep in as he tied my hands behind me, and then gagged me with a couple scarves he also had. They all stood back and just stared at me. They were in a trance- at least, it sure looked like they were.

"Either it was cold feet or wanting to add to my role and to the game, but suddenly I got an urge to run, so I took off. Considering the way things progressed from there, I'd have to say it was more the latter- my adventurousness taking over, that is. I was a decent runner at best- and only in short distances. Then, with my hands tied as they were and the wedge sandals with the three-inch heels I was wearing, I was slowed even more. The sexy look sure didn't help in that regard; I didn't get far at all before they got over their shock.

"My adrenaline kicked up initially when they hauled me back there and tied me up, and it flowed even more when I ran, but when they caught me…God, what a rush that was! It scared me and thrilled me at the same time, but since I was so young- and suddenly daring as well-, it was more of a thrill at that point. I'd never felt *anything* like that! So, the guy who'd bound my hands took another piece of rope and tied my ankles. He said something like 'try to run away now!' after he finished. What neither he nor any of them knew was, all of a sudden I didn't *want* to get away. I was glad my little escape attempt had failed.

"Then, one of them blindfolded me and took hold of my upper body; he used my boobs as carrying handles and squeezed them at will. Another grabbed my legs and they carried me off. I had no idea where they were taking me. I fought with them and tried to work my hands loose, but that was an exercise in futility. They were all over me, groping my legs and my butt and making all sorts of comments as they kept walking.

"I'm sure this will sound terrible, but…well, the more they felt me up, the more I started to respond to what they were doing rather than struggle against them, but I don't think they caught on. I-…I climaxed at least once while they manhandled me like they did, but since I'd never done that, I didn't realize that was what happened until later in the day. What I *did* realize was how much I was starting to get into the whole scenario.

"They stopped walking and suddenly I was being pulled up; I knew it was this guy Timmy's tree fort. I was pushed onto the bed and my blindfold was removed. Then, I was afraid. They must have thought I was acting the whole time, but at that moment I really was frightened. I mean, gosh- I'd daydreamed on occasion about what it would feel like to be one of those heroines in books or on television who was abducted, but that was the closest I'd ever come to what they were doing to me. Talk about making a sudden leap...

"I was isolated inside there and completely helpless, and these were the same people who didn't like me much, anyway. They gagged me so effectively that I couldn't make them understand that they were scaring me. I spent a lot of time straining and writhing on that bed while they watched me again- they were even more transfixed than before. I really had cast a spell over them.

"Then, it happened. The longer I struggled trying to get out of those ropes, the more I realized that I was becoming every bit as spellbound as they were. I was tied up good and tight, too; the one who did that to me was an Eagle Scout who sure knew his knots. At first I was trying to get loose and hopefully escape, but gradually it started to dawn on me, how much I was coming to enjoy being the distressed damsel and how much that was turning me on. As soon as I realized that I couldn't free myself- that there was nothing I could do- it was like somebody plugged me in. Plus, I still was afraid because I didn't know what they would do with me, although I have to confess: that also excited me.

"I wanted someone to touch me again, even though that notion scared me, too; all these emotions were just stirring me up and pushing me higher and higher. The thought of any of them hurting me faded into the background. My life was so tedious and painful otherwise; even skating and swimming weren't good refuges anymore, so at a pivotal moment, along came this new thing. I just let go and the sensation took hold of me. I could feel myself losing control completely and I *loved* it! I loved the effect I had on all those guys, I loved how the whole thing affected me and I loved that I had absolutely no control over *anything* I was helpless in every way, yet I wielded such power over all of them at the same time. Nothing had ever gotten to me so much.

"I think I made them nervous, unless they were having second thoughts about what they'd done. Or, maybe they knew I wanted someone to touch me, which could explain why none of them did, although they sure felt differently when I was blindfolded! Maybe they just wanted to see me suffer- who knows? I doubt any of them had ever seen a girl in the state I was in. They must have thought I was possessed! Then again, I guess I was, in a way. At any rate, they left me alone.

"I was so hot and bothered that I could not stay still. It got even worse as time passed by and worse yet when I began to fantasize that what was happening was real- that I *had* been kidnapped and I *was* being held captive by dangerous people. I was in dire need of a release and there was nothing I could do about that either, which turned me on even more. I literally was burning up! Then, I saw something I could use.

"I, um…I saw a baseball bat lying on the floor, so I got up and hopped over to it, bent down and picked it up, and then carried it back to where I was. I knelt down onto the bed and gradually maneuvered the bat into the right position. Of course, there was some trial and error involved, considering the state I was in. The 'error' parts frustrated me and served to fire me up even more, as if I wasn't stoked enough! I mean, I was desperate at this point!

"Finally I got it right. I lay on my stomach and rubbed myself against the bat. It wasn't long at all before I had a *monstrous* orgasm. I realized that was what had happened earlier, too, when those guys carried me and copped their feels while I fought them. Even though I was tied so securely, I'd never felt so free. I wanted more, so I did it again and again; I kept rubbing against that bat. Eventually I got enough- for the time being, anyway. It's a good thing I was gagged so well! It was better that no one came up to check on me until after I was finished, but they didn't miss my display by much. I have to admit, though, I think the fear of being caught in the act made me hit it even harder. Every factor contributed, and the result was just overwhelming! That was my first sexual experience, John."

"Wow…" That was all he could say.

"They kept me in there all day long. Without realizing they'd use it against me, I made the mistake of telling them my parents were away until late the following night. Soon I noticed that it didn't sound like they were even playing the game anymore. I heard the digging again; I figured they were helping Mister Weldon. I was sure they'd let me go, but they took turns watching me. I'd try to ask them to free me and the jerks would say 'what? I can't understand you'. Then they'd laugh and leave me alone again. I tried to find something to cut the ropes when I had a couple chances, but I didn't have any luck.

"By dinnertime, I still was in the same predicament. Two of them brought some stuff up for me. One took off my gag, then fed me and gave me water. I wasn't even allowed to do those things for myself! I asked if they would *please* let me go, but she said the game was still on and I still was their hostage. After my little break, she gagged me again.

"The one who'd tied me came over with more rope and pushed me down. He took one length of it around my waist, pulled it tight and fed the remainder between my thighs while I fought him, not that that did me any good. He turned me onto my stomach, yanked the rest up behind me and tied the ends off around the rope holding my wrists. That anchored my hands, so any chance I had at getting free was gone. He also tied my thighs, and then my elbows, too- the little shit! I sure seem to bring out the sadistic side of some people...anyway, for the finishing touch he put a tether around my neck and tied it off to the frame. When all that was done, he informed me that I would remain their prisoner overnight.

"I was stunned! Here I was, a few blocks away from my house, tied up so tightly that I barely could move, being held captive in a treehouse! The girls had these evil looks in their eyes; I figured they had a lot to do with the decision to keep me in there all night. That especially rang true when the one who fed me gleefully told me the group was going to a party and she hoped I would enjoy myself. She said she might even come back later with a surprise for me. With that, she blindfolded me, turned the fan up- probably so I wouldn't hear anyone coming and no one would hear me-, and I barely could tell that she turned this little lamp on, too. Then she slapped my butt really hard and left me there. I was sure I heard a 'click', so I figured she'd locked me in.

"I was even more helpless than before. The only way out was through the door, which no longer seemed an option. I'd have had to climb down the ladder, anyway, which would have been impossible given the way I was tied. I couldn't break or untie the tether and I couldn't even cry out for help, so I was stuck there until they came back for me.

"I couldn't believe it, but I was *so* turned on- even more so than before- that I felt a little strange, sort of lightheaded. Talk

344

about intensity…I sure put that rope between my legs to good use! I don't know if that was why he tied me that way, but since I needed the outlet again I was glad he did. I wore myself out before too long and fell asleep."

"Jesus, Kim…didn't you feel like you could be in danger? I mean, *real* danger?"

"At the time I didn't think about it…well, in a way I felt like I was, but not so much from the boys. For the most part, they were stoners, alcoholics or both. They were a lot more interested in partying than they were in sex, although in later years when I thought back on it, especially now…they literally could have done anything they wanted to me- *anything*- and there was no way I could have stopped them. I don't even want to think about what they might have done if they'd caught me making creative use of the bat, or the rope.

"You know, not long before I fell asleep, I got the weirdest feeling that someone *was* watching me. I-…I'd just climaxed again and I could swear I heard something while I was coming back down; it felt like someone was there with me, so I lay still and listened for a moment, but nothing happened. My heart was pounding and not just because I was scared to death that I wasn't alone. I also was really tired, though- actually, I think I passed out.

"More than anything, I worried about the girls and what they might do. They loved having me in the position I was in. I couldn't take attention away from them while I was bound, gagged and locked away. If they had their choice that's how they might have kept me permanently. Even two who'd been my friends were in on that. They just *hated* me. Jill Weldon, who was my best friend during elementary school, was the one who taunted me the most, slapped my ass so hard that she probably left an imprint of her hand on it, and then shut me in. I bet she was the driving force behind the whole thing."

"Jill Weldon? The Attorney-General's daughter?"

"Mm-hmm, that's her. For her family's sake- especially her children- I hope she's not the cold-hearted, conniving bitch she was back then. Her father was at the other end of the spectrum, though; he always was so nice to me."

"He's a good man- one of the best friends my family and I have ever had. Jill was cool enough around us, but in a way I can see how she wouldn't be like that with you. Jealousy makes some people do ugly things, although keeping you tied up and locked inside a tree house is an extreme measure to take, to say the least...

"So, you were like that for the whole night?"

"No, I'm happy to say. A couple of the younger boys in the neighborhood, for whom I happened to baby-sit regularly, knew the older ones were elsewhere and they knew what the group had done with me, so they decided to try to rescue me. They were only seven years old. I really was surprised to see them; I was so out of it I never heard them breaking in. They took my blindfold off and had to shake me several times before I finally woke up.

"I was so uncomfortable; by then I really wanted out of there. I begged them to untie me, but of course they couldn't understand me. Frustration took over then; I started to cry and thrash around. That made them try to help me, but the knots were too tight for them to undo. I 'mmphed' until they took the gag out of my mouth. I asked one of them to get something sharp to cut me loose, which he did. He just opened a drawer and found a pocketknife almost right away, which ticked me off in a way because I'd missed it earlier when I looked. It still took some work because the knife was pretty dull, but finally he was able to cut the ropes holding my elbows and my wrists.

"I still was so caught up in the whole thing; when I was freed I felt so exhilarated- for a moment, that is, until I tried to stand up and realized how light-headed I still was. I gave each of them a big hug and a kiss after thanking them. They were so cute- both were really happy to have helped me, especially when I called them 'my heroes'. I asked how they got in since I never heard them- I figured they'd found a key or something, but they said the door wasn't locked, which puzzled me to no end. I was certain Jill had locked me in...

"Anyway, Mister Weldon happened to be in his yard next door; he had to help me down. Then he carried me over to his porch, set me down and gave me some water. I was groggy and really weak. I could tell he'd been working in his garden again. The grounds around his place were immaculate; it seemed like he always was doing something in there. Actually, that day he had someone there with him working in the yard; I remember watching this good-looking guy digging earlier that day who turned out to be Mister Weldon's nephew. He was there for a while, but I guess he'd gone by then."

346

"Nephew? I wasn't aware he had any nephews...sorry. Go on, Kim."

"Mister Jack offered to let me stay the night at his house when he saw how out of sorts I was, but I was worried about little Davie and Darren. I didn't want the older kids to be angry with them for freeing me. I told them I'd walk them home; they'd already insisted on walking with me since I wasn't feeling well. Once my circulation was normal again, which took a few minutes since I'd been tied up for eight hours straight, we left. They held my hands the whole way.

"But when they found out I'd be alone, they made me go inside with them and told their parents, who insisted I spend the night at their place. I was glad; I didn't want to be by myself after all that had happened that day. Mrs. Griffin noticed the rope marks and demanded that I tell them what happened to me. I didn't spill everything, of course, or they might have called the police. They gave me the evil eye because of what I was wearing, but I told them I'd gone swimming and tanning earlier, which I had done. It's good they didn't see the bikini I wore underneath; they would have hit the roof!

"Fortunately they didn't keep me up too long. Of course, they wouldn't have been able to, anyway, since I was so exhausted. Boy, did I ever sleep that night! Afterwards, I always let my little buddies stay up late the rest of the times I watched them. We've been close friends ever since; they turned out to be wonderful men.

"I figured the reason why the group wanted me to play in the first place was to have the neighborhood sex symbol under their control since none of them thought I'd go out with them. If that was the case, they were right- especially after the game. Of course, the girls had their reasons, too. I think the whole group was afraid I'd tell on them because hardly any ever spoke to me again, which I had no problem with. They just went back to their pattern of avoiding me in general, and even more so than before.

"On the other hand, Mister Weldon was nicer to me from then on, and even- I don't know- a little more concerned and protective of me. He always knew how little my so-called guardian cared about me and I think he wanted to fill in the void as well as he could. He really was upset when he saw what the group had done to me, but I didn't tell him that Jill was involved. In spite of how angry I was with her I didn't want to cause problems between them. With such a great father I don't know how Jill turned out like she did.

"If something bad had happened that night, there's no question I would have looked very negatively- to say the least- upon being tied up, especially during sex. I mean, I have no way of knowing what they might have done to me if Davie and Darren hadn't rescued me. What if that bunch came back all messed up? They could have had every intention of raping me and...maybe worse- who knows? As it turned out, the only bad thing I walked away with was a little rope burn on my wrists and ankles. Since I was freed while the experience still felt so intoxicating, that was the imprint it left on me.

"Unfortunately, Josh ended up using that against me very effectively when I was involved with him. He had that way of prying things out of me; in fact, it was like he knew about that event- or at least my tendency- before I even told him, which was pretty weird. I was so vulnerable then; he picked up on that, too. I really fell for him, but then, after you and I made love at the Memorial Day party..."

"Vanessa hinted at what he did to you afterwards."

"He almost broke me. If I hadn't escaped when I did, he probably would have, but he didn't- not then and not now." She smiled at him. "I'm all right, John. It took time and effort, but I got past it. I almost can't believe how drastically my perspective has changed over the past couple weeks- and tonight especially, when I was in that cage and facing everything that haunted me from when I was a little girl up until now. In a way, Josh did me a huge favor by putting me in that position, which I'm sure he knew was exactly what he was doing. I bet he also was convinced that the combined assault of all those ghosts from my past would end up defeating me, but he was wrong. The last thing he expected to happen *did* happen; I defeated them, and him as well. I'd rather have had this come about sooner, but better late than never."

"No doubt about that, Kitten. Even when the odds must have seemed overwhelming to you, you didn't give up. Then, your string of successes, including freeing Jenny, led to your ultimate victory- and not just over Josh. I think your escape from that thing he had your arms tied with was the final phase of you overcoming those inner demons, or weaknesses."

"I believe you're right, Baby. Now, as for being tied up and dominated, it never was something I *needed* in order to be turned on. I think you know that, too. It's just...well, as a counselor- and also as a dancer- I always was the one in control. I got used to that in my work and in my life. I guess part of what drew me in was my desire to have one part of my life where I'd give control, if only temporarily, to someone else. Sex was where that fell.

"And let's not forget about that little episode when I was thirteen and the role it played in making me lean in that direction. It's such a turn-on for me to feel so helpless and at the mercy of my lover- and not only for the sexual part. Just knowing that I don't have to make any decisions or be responsible or...normal, conventional. I mean, the last thing that should be routine is sex- at least *I* think so. The added elements of intrigue and fantasy, the sexy lingerie and the total surrender of myself...that combination really does get me going!

"Josh thought one reason I was so into it was because of how cold my parents were. He does have a point; in a way, their near-rejection of me and their frigid relationship with each other also pushed me toward the other extreme of falling into the hands of someone who was obsessed with me. I came so close to losing myself; I was right on the edge with him. Part of me wanted to give in, but the other part wouldn't let me. It was a very hard fight, though...

"I don't feel that way in the hands of just anyone- not any more. Being taken by someone dangerous never to be seen or heard from again and becoming his toy is not what I want at all. After having been through that with two different men, I don't want it to happen to me ever again. If I did, I'd agree that there's a problem. I've learned that I need to feel safe, too. I need to have complete trust in the one I give myself to, which is where you come in, John.

"With you, I *can* lose myself. I want that part of me kept inside our bedroom when we make love- as long as you're up for it. I have a sneaking suspicion you might be, especially after the way you reacted to seeing me in the cage, dressed as I was and all chained up- sort of like I am now. I saw and felt how turned on you were, too. Then, knowing that you never would harm me in any way if you had me in that position...well, you saw what it did to me. I felt like I was melting down! And let's not forget the night we had at the pool party where you showed a dominant streak yourself...

349

"I don't mind being put in my place sometimes. To be blunt, I like that. I don't want someone telling me it's wrong for me to feel so turned on when I'm being subdued and tied up- like I'm some sort of deviant or something. I don't want to be like everyone else, or conform to more acceptable behavior or whatever some psychiatrist will tell me. I know what I like, I know what I want and I'm comfortable with that. Plus," she kissed him, "I know *who* I want. I'm not damaged- a little shaken, maybe, but I'm OK. I think you see that, too. I don't want to be kidnapped again- unless *you'd* like to abduct me," she said, smiling wickedly.

"Maybe. We'll see about that," he grinned back at her, but his expression quickly turned serious. "So Josh didn't..."

"Not this time. Daniels was on the verge, but he didn't, either. Had things not gone down as they did today...well, we both know what would have happened. I'd have had no way of stopping him from doing that or anything he wanted to me. Then, there was Lisa; she might have ended up treating me even worse than Josh, given the way she was talking just before I knocked her out.

"I hope they're getting theirs. The things they did to me... they were so cruel. They were arranging their transportation out of the country when you found me. The time I spent with them was bad enough as it was, and knowing how much worse it would have been if you hadn't come..." She shivered at the thought. "Would you hold me, Baby?"

"Absolutely." He smiled tenderly and pulled her closer.

She took a moment to simply appreciate the feeling of being in his arms as he held her and caressed her. "We certainly were lucky. It frightens me so much to think how close we came to-...well, to not being able to do this again- twice in a few months, yet."

"I know. Even though it was more than luck that got us through, it seems like someone's watching out for us, doesn't it?"

"It sure does. I'll never take another day- another *minute*- for granted. Not after all that's happened this year..."


"Jesus Christ..."

After getting no response from either Mike One or Victor One-Six, Corporal Brewer had pushed the car up to a speed that was almost dangerous as he retraced the route they'd taken. He'd rushed past where the chopper crew sat waiting for the ambulance.

When he saw what lay past the crest of the small hill in the road just before the interstate, it felt like his heart had stopped.

To his right, lying upside-down in the culvert just off the road was a dark blue sedan with Maryland tags. The roof was partially collapsed, all the windows were broken out and the right side was dented badly. The engine was running and steam was pouring out from under the hood.

Further down the road and close to the overpass was the black van the units had been pursuing. It had slid off the road as well; the vehicle was canted so only its blown right rear wheel was in the culvert. Its right rear window was gone.

What worried him most was Victor One-Six's patrol car. It had hit the abutment of the interstate overpass head-on.

"Victor Five, this Two-Niner. I need immediate assistance on Route 6 just east of the I-81 overpass..."


Kim ended the few minutes of silence. "While they had me locked inside that room and after it became clear that there was no escape for me, I thought about you- a lot. I began to picture you busting down that door and just ravishing me. Rescue just didn't seem realistic and it only upset me when I would think about it and hope for it, so I kept going back to that fantasy.

"The longer my captivity went on, the harder it became for me to fight that image off, but with the ways they tied me up I had no means of release at all. If my hands weren't bound behind me, I was spread-eagled. There was nothing I could do- it was *awful*! It got to where I felt like I was going crazy! It was his way of torturing me and trying to divert me from finding a way out of that mess, keeping me restrained like he did. He didn't even have to keep me tied; he just did that because he liked it.

"But still, you played a big part in my ability to stop them from defeating me, or even damaging me emotionally, especially when Josh was about to-...well, you know. I would close my eyes and just drift away. They would disappear and you would be there with me..."

She was kissing his neck and her voice was taking on a dreamy inflection.

For John it was becoming almost surreal. He could see vividly what she was describing and he could feel every bit of her arousal as his also intensified by the second.

351

"I imagined you teasing me the way you do, running your hands all over me and kissing all over me while you had me under your control...in time it became so real, though- Baby, I could *feel* you. Wherever I imagined you were touching me would feel so warm and when you kissed me it almost felt like you were branding me..."

Her kisses and nibbles were becoming much less gentle as she moved up to his earlobe. A short while ago he and she had turned her fantasies into reality, if not bettered them.

On top of that she couldn't stop reflecting on what probably would have been if John hadn't found her, and she was more than ready to show her appreciation once more.

She was unable to finish what she wanted to say, and didn't care a bit that her train of thought was lost...

...neither did John.


"How do you feel, Sir? That bullet came awful close to-"

"Yeah." Tom lay on the slightly sloping ground above where the remainder of his car was. A slight variance in a couple different directions of the bullet that clipped his neck could have caused an awful lot of damage, or killed him outright. Tom considered himself very lucky, but he wasn't quite ready to talk about it yet.

He looked at the trooper who'd crouched down next to him and read his name badge. "I've been better, Corporal Brewer," he replied, wincing as he applied the ice pack to his throbbing head. "Thanks for helping pull us out of there. What about my partner and One-Six? And the chopper unit?"

Brewer looked away. "Thad Blanton's dead. He was driving the patrol car. He got a bullet right in the middle of his forehead- probably never knew what hit him. Virgil Pryor's gonna be medevac'd out along with Detective Rogers. The medics said they're not critical, but they're both in serious condition. The chopper guys weren't too bad off; the shake-up from the impact of going down so hard seemed to be worse than the damage the bullets that hit 'em caused. The ambulances'll take those guys to the hospital along with you."

Tom looked away and slowly shook his head.

"I heard your last transmission, Sir. You stuck your head right into the lion's mouth."

"I guess you could say that." He could see the muzzle flash of the assault rifle every bit as clearly as he did when they went over the hill.

"I'll be honest with you; I don't know if I'd have been able to do it. You were outgunned and behind him, yet. He had every advantage."

"We didn't have a choice. It was that or let them get onto the Interstate. There were no units that could have cut 'em off and we'd lost the chopper with the snipers on board, so it was all on us. If you'd been in the same situation, I bet you'd have handled it the same way, especially if you knew innocent lives would have been at risk. That's what we do: protect the innocent. That's why we take the oath."

"Pretty costly sometimes..."

"It sure is."

"Well, at least you were able to take the shooter out. You hit Dean Rollins three times- twice right in the chest."

"And the others? There were four in the van, right?"

"No, Sir."

"*What*?! How many were inside?"

"One other- Lisa Meyers, who also was killed, but we're not sure by whom. She still was cuffed hand and foot, and was shot in the head. She and Rollins were the only ones inside. The passenger door of the van was open, too. From the looks of it, whoever else was inside got away. As close as the Interstate is to where the vehicle ended up, it would have been easy for the remaining occupants to walk down the embankment and flag somebody down. They could have had as much as fifteen minutes between the end of the shooting and the time my partner and I got here. We were the first to arrive."

Tom closed his eyes and leaned back. "*Dammit...*"

*They won't like this...*


It took a couple tugs and a little assistance from Kim for John to get the Tigress suit up over her hips. They knew it wouldn't be long before their transportation arrived.

"You know, Baby, if we ever see Vanessa again, we should *thank* her for using these handcuffs on me!"

"No argument here," John agreed amid a very satisfied smile. Once he got the suit past her hips, the hard part was done.

He pulled it up as far as it would go. "I can't believe I have to ask you of all people to do this, but go ahead and suck it in."

She giggled. "Well, this is quite a bit easier than lacing me into one of my corsets, which you'll get plenty of practice doing."

"There's another thing I'll enjoy getting used to; this just keeps getting better." She took in a very deep breath and John worked the zipper up, then adjusted her suit.

"I thought you said playtime was over," Kim mirthfully chided as he took some time in making sure her breasts were contained as well as they could be.

He grinned as he finished with the adjustment. Although she continued to smile as well, her eyes took on a serious aspect. "What is it, Kitten?"

"Even though you knew he would kill you, you still came for me. I'll never forget that, John, and I won't let you forget it. You were so brave; your damsel is very grateful."

He clearly saw the depth of her gratitude and love, and then felt both as she laid another breath-stealing kiss on him and pressed herself against him. That kiss temporarily chased away the anger that came up when he thought of his inability to rescue Kim and the fact that Josh, in reality, had out-thought him. If not for Kim's resourcefulness and daring, they'd have been done for.

With that in mind, he returned her kiss with just as much fervor, pulling away only when he heard activity outside.

Kim's focus stayed on him nonetheless; she wasn't ready to stop just yet. "You know what else?" she whispered as she nuzzled his neck again, knowing how much he loved that. "She's just coming into her sexual prime."

A low, throaty growl escaped him. It was so easy for her to charge him up... "Cool yourself down there, Honey. If you go much further, I'll have that suit off you again before you even see me reaching for the zipper."

"Is that a promise?" She laughed and tried to get away as he tickled her, but it wasn't long before he pulled her against him again, drawing another sigh from her. "Of course, you realize you'll just have to make all that lost time up to me- not only from what Josh did, but also when we couldn't make love. You'll be a *very* busy man."

"I'd say so!"

They were interrupted by a knock on the van's door. "Sir? Ma'am? Is it all right to open the door?"

"Didn't make it by much, did we?" John said to Kim in a low voice. "Sure, Officer. Go ahead."

"I just wanted to let you both know that your transportation's turning onto the access road now. A couple escorting units are with 'em- they have some tools that'll get you out of the tethers. Hopefully we'll get you out of those cuffs, too, Miss Francis.

"I also have to let you know, Sir, your brother's being taken to the hospital. There was a shootout during the pursuit and he was wounded. The medics on the scene listed his condition as good."

"He was shot?!"

"Take it easy, Sir. A bullet grazed his neck and he suffered a concussion and a few bruises, but they think he's all right otherwise. Sounds like they'll want to keep him overnight for observation. We'll be taking you to the hospital so you can be with him."

"OK, thanks. Was anyone else hurt?"

"Yes, Sir. Four other officers were wounded, including Detective Rogers, who was with your brother. I don't know their conditions. We lost one of ours, too."

"Oh, no….I'm sorry to hear that. What was his name?"

"Thaddeus Blanton."

John nodded. "Did they get Strauss?"

"I don't have any other details, Sir. They mainly wanted me to pass on to you the condition of your brother. I guess we'll have to find out the rest later." He turned at the sound of approaching vehicles. "Ah, here they are." He signaled to the lead car. "Hey! Tell 'em to get the locksmith over here!"

"I can't believe we need a locksmith for my handcuffs. I guess he'll love this job, won't he?" Kim whispered to John.


Ricky Mason lay on his back, perfectly still, staring up at the morning sky. It was quite a day; very few clouds disrupted the sea of blue. Soon the sun would clear the treeline and bear down on him full force, but Ricky didn't have to worry about getting burned.

In fact, Ricky didn't have to worry about anything- all his problems were gone. He'd given a lift to a couple who were in dire need of one, especially the guy, who walked with a limp. After

355

tossing their luggage into the trunk, they climbed in. The woman, who was very beautiful but a little strange, sat in the front seat and didn't say a word the whole time. The man was profuse with his gratitude and seemed cool enough. Better yet, he handed Ricky ten hundred-dollar bills and promised him more.

It was Ricky's lucky day. Normally it took him two weeks to clear that much!

The man pointed out an exit after they'd only been driving for about fifteen minutes and said that was where they needed to go, so he took it. Next, he said he needed to take a leak and asked Ricky to pull off onto a side road they came up on.

When Ricky stopped the car after they passed a bend in the road that would give the guy some privacy, out of the blue the man presented him with an offer he couldn't refuse.

Fifty thousand bucks for his car! In cash, no questions asked.

'Why are you doing this?' Ricky asked him.

'Because you strike me as a man who could use a turn of fortune, and I'm in position to make that happen for you' he said as he handed Ricky the stack of bills.

Ecstatic, Ricky got out of the car and went around to the other side to get in the back after the man promised to take him where he needed to go.

As it turned out, he wouldn't need to go any further than where he was.

Ricky lay on his back, perfectly still, staring up at the afternoon sky.

His stare met that of the blinding sun, but Ricky didn't blink.

His journey was over.


When she felt the cuff open, Kim was exultant.

She'd sat patiently for about twenty minutes while the locksmith worked. She became worried when he said he'd 'never had to work on a pair of handcuffs like this before' Just after he said that, however, he successfully picked the lock. John rubbed her shoulders again as she brought her hands around to the front. The other cuff opened fairly quickly since by then the skilled technician knew how to tackle the problem.

"Thank you so much." She kissed the man on his cheek.

The surprised and red-faced locksmith seemed to have more trouble saying 'you're welcome' to Kim than he had with freeing her from the handcuffs. With shaky hands he accepted the tip she insisted on giving him and began to gather his tools.

"Do you need a jacket?" John asked as he stood.

She shook her head. "I'll be fine like this, especially considering how warm it is already. Let's get out of here." She followed John as he got out of the van. She lay her hands onto his shoulders as his hands encircled her waist and he helped her down.

She couldn't suppress her desire to lay another one on him as the feeling of total freedom finally sank in to her- that which she'd been deprived of for so long. Even though her exit from the van into the outside world was almost purely symbolic, it still felt marvelous. She wasn't even mindful of the cameras that were filming them and all the accompanying camera flashes until she pulled back after the lengthy and very steamy kiss.

When the small group of reporters starting throwing questions at them, suddenly she was fully aware of their presence.

As the effects of her kiss wore off, John asked, "You're sure you don't want a jacket?"

She looked up at him and smiled. "I'm sure. I dealt with lots of drunken and sometimes-vulgar men while I wore this uniform, so I can handle a few reporters. They've already seen me, anyway. Besides, I think I still wear it pretty well. Don't you?"

He chuckled. "To say the very least, hell, yes!"

It wasn't long, though, before he saw the change in her. Her frivolous disposition was gone. "What's wrong?"

"Do you think…well, that it might look bad for you somehow? If you want me to-"

"I don't care how it 'looks'. All that matters to me is that you feel comfortable, which apparently you do. Don't change a thing. I don't want a version of you that's altered to be palatable for the public or any faction of it. I want you to be you. Period."

She gave him another little smooch. "I love you."

"I love you, too, Kitten. Come on; let's go to the hospital. I'll buy you breakfast."

Kim laughed and turned to walk with him, but he stopped her and swept her up into his arms.

"Hey, don't look so surprised. I actually have a reason for doing this other than the fact that I love to hold and carry you.

There's a chance you could fall and hurt yourself, walking on this ground in those shoes. Sorry I couldn't do this earlier."

She lay her head onto his shoulder. "Thank you, John- I love when you carry me, too. I always have." She fondly recalled their first date, when he noticed that her first experience with high heels wasn't going so smoothly, then picked her up and carried her to his car. She could tell he had the same thought.

"Mister Governor, can you tell us what-"

"We won't take any questions now- it's not the time. One Virginia State Police Officer lost his life a short while ago and several others are in the hospital, which is where we're going so we can be with my brother, who is among the wounded. We'll give a statement later. Thank you."

John put Kim into the limo as the driver held the door open for them and climbed in behind her.

"Oh, I almost forgot. Excuse me, Officer," he came over when she signaled to him. "I nearly left here without my suitcase; would you mind grabbing it for me?"

"No problem, Miss Francis. Be right back."

"Ah, Vanessa reminded you about that. What's in it, anyway?" John asked.

"A lot of my lingerie and my shoes, too. That's probably why she winked at me; she knows how much I love all of it. I might as well keep it. I've already broken in the corsets and the pumps, which can be a pain on both counts. It's very high quality stuff, too. Also, a girl never can have too many sexy bras, thongs and pairs of silk stockings, which I'm sure he packed enough of to last me several months, if not longer, since they were about to take me out of the country. Hopefully he packed some sort of jacket or long shirt in there, too. I should be somewhat covered up while we're in the hospital." She looked up as the trooper came back with the suitcase. "I'll take it in here, Officer. Thank you."

The policeman smiled and tipped his cap to her before walking back to his cruiser.

"I *hope* he did that, anyway, or else-" She stopped cold when, upon opening the piece of luggage, she saw a laptop computer sitting on top of her lingerie. She looked over at John, who also had a perplexed look on his face.

He took the computer out and opened it up as the driver pulled the limo forward and they left Suicide Ridge. There were several sticky notes on the periphery of the screen.

When he and Kim read what was written on those notes, they turned to each other in utter disbelief.

"...I promise I'll be back by tomorrow...I love you, too, and I'll see you then...I will. Tell the kids I love 'em and I'll see 'em tomorrow. 'Bye, Honey."

Just after he hung up, Tom looked toward the doorway and saw John and Kim. "Am I ever glad to see you two. Come here, both of you." He hugged them, then gestured to the seats.

"They told us about what you did. Jesus Christ, you could've been killed!"

"I know. Donna wasn't too happy with me, either. It had to be done, though; the alternative was unacceptable. I guess my number didn't come up today, even though it sure could have...

"So you're both all right?"

"We're fine, thanks to this beautiful and multi-dimensional woman I'm so crazy about. Josh was ready to pull the trigger on me and Kim shot the gun right out of his hand."

"No kidding! I heard you put that marksmanship training to good use, Kim. Nice outfit, by the way," he said with a grin. Beneath her flashy tiger-striped cape, he saw the uniform that went with it.

"Thank you on both counts," she replied as she blushed. "So you got them? You got Josh and all of them?"

Tom's smile was gone immediately. "Rollins and Lisa Meyers are dead, but Strauss and Vanessa are missing. They've disappeared." Kim's eyes widened at that. "I'm sorry, Kim, I know it must be very upsetting news for you. Losing the chopper was a huge blow to our pursuit. Otherwise, we probably would have had 'em all. There's a possibility that Strauss killed Lisa before he took off. The crime scene people will determine that."

"Oh, Tom, don't apologize. Like John said, you could have been killed doing what you did to stop them and I have no doubt you did your best. I just hope somebody ends up getting him."

John put his arm around her. "I'll take every measure I can to make sure you're safe, Kitten. He won't take you again."

"It wouldn't be smart for him to come after me now. Then again, I never thought he would after '89, either. I guess there's no telling what he might do, but...you know, I don't care what he does. Never again will I live my life in fear of him; those days are over. I just hope Vanessa's all right."

She leaned against him, noting the pained expression on Tom's face before he turned away briefly after the last thing she said. "All the same, I wouldn't mind a few safety precautions. They certainly couldn't hurt, especially given what we have."

"What do you mean?" Tom didn't like his brother's curious mien as he stared back; he could see the wheels turning. *Shit, he probably knows...* "John, what's wrong?"

"Nothing. I just spaced out for a minute," he replied, averting his eyes he produced the laptop. "You'll like what's on this, Brother. I bet you'll agree with what I plan to do about it, too..."


"Tell me what's on your mind, John," Tom asked after Kim excused herself to make a phone call and walked out of the room. He worried more and more that John had figured out what had happened between Vanessa and him. *It's bad enough that I know,* he thought as John turned away...

...however, he also noticed on a couple occasions- particularly when Josh was mentioned- how John's face would cloud up. He was harboring something and didn't want Kim to know what it was. *That could be it.* "You can tell me, Brother."

Still looking out the window, John finally said, "I failed. Badly. He had me, Tom- I walked right into it without thinking it out and almost got myself killed. I couldn't-"

After a moment of silence, Tom put it together, mainly by way of John's attitude. "Listen to me; you can't always win. As you just found out, you're not infallible. You won't always be the hero, you won't always be right and right doesn't always prevail. Sometimes the shitbirds live to fight another day, unfortunately. Don't worry, though- he'll get his."

"Yeah, I suppose," John replied. He managed a smile as well. "Thanks, Tom. I needed a pep talk."

"I figured as much. That's not all you need, either; you and Kim should go home, get settled in and spend a good, quiet night together."

"You seem to be the doctor today, even though you're laid up."

"Yeah, yeah," Tom smirked as Kim returned. "I hope you didn't walk by the cardiac unit, Kim; they have enough work on their hands as it is!"

"Listen to you with the wisecracks! And here I was, all worried about you! Seems like you'll be back to normal in no time, if you're not there already."

His smile turned into a yawn. "On that note, get out of here, you two. I need a nap about now, anyway. I'm glad you came by."

"So are we. We'll see you back at the ranch."

# Chapter 14

"That was a very good idea you came up with for what to do with Josh's money," Kim told John as they turned onto I-66 and headed east toward D.C. Before they left, they'd visited with and thanked the other police officers who ended up in the hospital as a result of the gunfight that marked the end of the pursuit.

"Well, it's the least he could do for having uprooted all those women and all the damage he's caused them. I just hope eventually they'll be able to lead normal lives."

"So do I. It'll be more difficult for those he kept longer, but at least with two million dollars each, they'll have the freedom to do whatever they want- go to college, buy a home, travel..."

In spite of that her face hardened the more she thought about the whole situation. "*Damn* him!! It makes me *furious* that he got away! And worse, he has Vanessa- I'm sure he knows she's the one who put his computer in my suitcase. When I think about what he's doing to her...I know she made the choice, but..."

"Don't, Honey- you know that'll only make you feel worse. Josh is slippery, but he's demonstrated that he's not infallible. You foiled him in more than one way and I've gathered from Vanessa that she's a pretty crafty and clever lady herself. It wouldn't surprise me if she found a way out, just like you did."

"You're right, this isn't helping. It's just...she's my friend and I hate to think of her in such a predicament. Not that I'd wish being with that piece of shit on anyone, but...all right, I'll try not to think about that. It's too bad he didn't make a traceable transaction from his bank account to whoever he met up with to fly him out of the country. It would have been nice to possibly nail him that way."

"It sure would have, although once he realized his computer was gone, he would have known his way out was compromised..." John was distracted by a pending transaction he happened across.

*I'll be damned...*

*'...the dumb bastard almost killed you, which he will pay for.'* Josh's words, and the way he said them, came back.

*It looks like I just have to click the 'execute' order, or...*

*...no, I don't have to do anything. It's already set to go...*

Kim looked up at him as he trailed off. "Honey? What's wrong? Have you found something else?" She leaned closer to look at the screen.

"Hmm? Oh, no- nothing of consequence. Not this one." He closed the file before she could get a look and quickly went to another folder. "This is the one I wanted to see."

Kim regarded him curiously for a moment, but when she looked back at the screen, she shook her head in disgust. "This would be one of his stupid jokes, no doubt..."

"Yeah, I'd say-...wait a second..." The folder he'd opened was labeled 'other assets'. There was a file with the address of his house- the one he'd sold to Josh- as its title. John opened the file to find that Josh had scanned the deed to the house and the property into the computer.

Both deeds were dated June 28$^{th}$, 2000 and were notarized.

Both listed the owner's name as Kimberly Elizabeth Francis.

"Believe it or not, these look like official documents. You just might own the house, Kim. A quick phone call will confirm or deny."

Not even five minutes later, John got his answer.

"So it's true..." She'd listened in on the conversation and heard the clerk.

"Looks that way. The question is, what do you want to do about it?"

She looked out the window, her brow furrowed in thought.

"I just want you to know that if selling it is what you want, I understand completely and I wouldn't even think about holding it against you. To say the least, you had some horrible experiences there The last thing I want is for you to have to relive them. Your happiness and well being are much more important to me than any house." He waited, but she didn't respond. "Kitten?"

She smiled. "Have I ever told you I love when you call me that?"

He kissed her and said, "Come to think of it, you might have."

She snuggled against him. "With my mindset regarding the house before last night, I would have been on the phone right now contacting a real estate agent, but...I want to keep it. I want for that to be our home."

"Really? What changed your perspective?"

"As I alluded to earlier, shortly before you came for me I managed to exorcise one of my worst inner demons while I was being kept in the study- one I thought never would stop tormenting me. As a result, I'll never shrink away from a thunderstorm again.

"And, let's not forget what you did with me while I was locked up in that cage. Talk about chalking one up in the 'good memories' column!"

John laughed. "Here, here! But, about the storms- I know how much they used to frighten you and that was a bad one yesterday. You told me that you were afraid of them for almost as long as you could remember. How were you able to get past that?"

"Believe it or not, it happened in an instant. I just realized that I'm tired of being afraid, and not only of storms. I made a vow to myself never to let anyone or anything get to me like that again."

"You sure proved that point on the ridge."

At that moment he became aware of the object touching him, appropriately enough, right over his heart. It was like he'd gotten a nudge from some unseen entity.

John knew it was time.

He backed away a little and touched her chin, making her look up at him. "The only reason why we're here is what you did on that ridge; that's something I won't ever let *you* forget. You came through, Kim- for both of us. No adjective could possibly nail down how truly amazing you are, not to mention how beautiful you are and how much I love you. For the rest of our lives, I will do my utmost to make you the happiest woman in the world, starting right now."

Kim's eyes already were glistening, but when he moved around and knelt in front of her, then reached inside his suit coat and produced a tiny black box, her hands flew to her face. She was so overcome by joy that she couldn't move a muscle.

"Will you marry me, Kitten?"


"Hi, Phil. I guess you know I've run into a slight problem. You wouldn't happen to know of a place where I could hole up in until we take off, would you?"

"Are you by yourself? I heard Lisa died- sorry about that."

"Yeah, she was a big help. I'm not alone, though." He looked at the back seat of the car where Vanessa lay. "You'll see my travel companion shortly. I'll have to decide whether or not she'll make the flight. In the meantime, you can enjoy her company, if you like. Once you get a look at her, I'm sure you *will* like."

"Sounds good to me. Where are you now?"

"A couple miles from the airport at a rest stop."

"OK. Let me give you the directions…"


Kim gazed at it. "This is the most beautiful ring I've ever seen. Baby…"

Just when he thought her very welcome barrage of kisses had stopped, she reloaded and came at him with more. When she pulled back, he kissed away the last of her tears. "I'm glad you like it so much. It's certified flawless; I wouldn't have given you anything less. As far as I'm concerned, you're the only woman who could wear it."

Her appreciation was abundantly clear as he took her into his arms again.

"I've kept it with me constantly, ever since the day you were kidnapped. I didn't know when or how I'd be able to give it to you. Things weren't looking too good there for a while, but I'm glad they turned out the way they did."

"So am I." She gave him another peck. "Now we get to plan our wedding. Oh, John, this will be so much fun! But…I hope it won't be too hard on Leslie. It's still so close to-…I'm sorry."

"I know; it's all right." John thought back to when he visited Doug on that fateful day. "The last thing I said to him was that…that I wanted him and Tom to be my Best Men. It's partly his doing that led me back to you- the way he got on me about pushing you away. I know he'd have been happy to see us now. Christ, I miss him…

"Maybe it'll help Leslie, though- she likes being involved, especially in events like this. She has a lot on her plate, but she'll want to pitch in. We'll find a happy medium."

"Right, and we can involve the kids, too…"

Saying that made her think of something she hadn't in quite some time.

"Speaking of 'kids', do you remember when you dropped me off after our first date, when we weren't much more than kids ourselves? Gosh, I thought it would take me forever to fall asleep that night! When I finally did, I had the most wonderful dream-I've never had a better one. You proposed to me, John, almost exactly like you just did...

"I, um...I never felt comfortable enough to tell you this. Even now it's giving me butterflies!"

"What's that?"

"For a long time, what I've wanted most is to be your wife and the mother of your children. I can't tell you how many times I would look up at the stars at night and pray that my wish would come true; the more time passed, the more I began to wonder if it would. The things we want most can make us so insecure- we're afraid we might never have them, or that we'll screw them up if we're granted them. Our fondest dreams can be our greatest fears, too, and boy, was that ever a case in point. Look what I did as a result; I'm sure that was a big part of why I ran away to the beach in the first place...

"You know what, though? I don't feel the least bit afraid now. In fact, I feel like I just woke up after that dream of you on bended knee...or maybe I'm still dreaming."

"You're not, although as terrific as this feels I can see why you might think it's a dream."

It didn't take any deliberation for him to make his next proposal to her. "You know, we can do that. If you want- and when the time comes- I'm in the position where you can stay home full-time and raise our children. I can't imagine them being in a better situation. Keep in mind also that it's not permanent for you- once I'm elected President I can't serve any more than eight years. I have no doubt I'll be ready to stay home full time after that, so you'll have the chance get yourself out there again and take on any career you want."

"That sounds wonderful! I feel more ready now to be a mother than I ever have. That's the most important undertaking there is, and with all the negative examples of parenting I've seen, I know how to avoid becoming one- not that I'd follow their examples, anyway. They just made me see more clearly how important it is to be a good parent. Our situation will be better in part because I'll be able to stay home, so on that subject you're right, Honey: our children *will* be in the best environment we can possibly make for them.

"One of the reasons I want so badly for you to win is because I'd love to see it become more common that a family can afford to have one parent at home full time, which I'm sure most of them want. Granted, there are a lot of bad parents out there, but there also are a lot who would be better if they didn't have to spend every waking minute working."

"That's one reason why I want to redistribute the wealth and improve the pay scale in the important positions. It'll help single parents, too- on the financial end, anyway. That's a hard life, and I have nothing but respect for single parents who raise good kids."

"I couldn't agree more. Back to your original subject, on the personal front, with all I've experienced I won't feel like I'm missing out on anything for a while by staying at home with our children. After more than a decade of having the constant fear of being hunted, I could stand to be in a situation that was- shall we say- less exciting? I have a decent nest egg myself from my dancing days and the bikini circuit. We can put together what we have; it sounds like we should be pretty comfortable. We know we won't have to worry about buying a house, and like you said- once we end up in the White House that won't be an issue, anyway. A lot's up in the air at this point, but I have no doubt things will work out for us in one way or another."

With a sigh, she added, "At any rate, as of today I'll be unemployed."

He took her hand into his. "So you do want to see the principal first?"

She nodded. "I called him when you and Tom were alone that last couple minutes. There's no sense in dragging this out. As kind and helpful as Doctor Harris has been to me for all these years, I'm not going to put him in the position of having to fire me, which is what he would have to do. I'm not going to resign over the phone, either."

"Even with all the good you've done he'd have to fire you?"

"I deliberately held something back from the board that would have prevented me from being hired in the first place. I know what you're thinking and I agree, but the fact remains- with my omission, I misled them. Doctor Harris's was the deciding vote."

"Look, I usually don't agree when people say the means justify the end, but I also know no one is perfect. Anyone who doesn't believe you covered that up because you felt so strongly

367

about being a counselor and that you wanted to do good, plus the very logical assumption that the board wouldn't allow a former exotic dancer to counsel students- they just don't know or understand who you are and what you're about. That's something employers and decision-makers miss when they look at a resume and cast judgment based solely on that before they even meet you. It's not like you killed somebody.

"Who hasn't held something back sometime during his or her life, anyway? Can you show me one person who has never lied? You were in a no-win situation, Kim. Had you told them, you never would have gotten the job and you never would have been such an influence on so many lives. Would anyone else have been any better than you've been with all the students you've come into contact with? And do you really think all those kids have lost their respect for you? Maybe some have, but those who really understood the message you conveyed and made themselves better because they understood and were willing to do something about it? I bet they don't feel any different about you."

She didn't reply and her expression remained unchanged.

"I can see you've made your decision and I understand where you're coming from. I think I have an idea how much it's hurting you, too, so I won't try to talk you out of it any more. I want you to remember this, though- there are a lot of young adults out there now who benefited plenty from what you did for them. Look how Jenny and Kelly turned out. My niece Jessica is yet another; soon, she'll be your niece as well. Those are three I can name right off the top of my head. I can't begin to imagine how many more there are.

"You did your best, which you've shown is very impressive. You have an awful lot to be proud of. Now, some people will vilify you for not making the disclosure, but others will look at what you did with the opportunity you were given and applaud you. Whatever the case, you can't control what other people think about you, so I hope you won't worry too much about that. You also can't keep beating yourself up over one mistake you made, which I bet you've been doing for a very long time. In fact, I recall someone very close to me telling me something to that effect a few months ago."

Kim giggled and embraced him and her feelings of remorse and guilt abated a little. "I had a feeling you'd bring that up."

"Well, you were right and you should advice. Never be ashamed of who you are accomplished."

She pressed herself against him. "You alway the right thing to me when I need you to- you're star me! I know this is what I have to do, though. With n out in full view for everyone, I doubt I'd be a very counselor anymore. My bit of celebrity most likely would with and taint any advice I was to dole out from this poin the parents probably will want me to resign once they what I did, and I wouldn't blame them.

"There's one more consideration as well. I'm glad y still running; I know how much you want that and I know yo right for the job. As much as I would have hated for some low- like Josh to ruin your plans and deprive the country of such wonderful leader, I'd hate more than anything else if I ended being an anchor for you, which could still happen."

"Don't even think that, Kim. It's only because of you that I'll get my chance at all." He stroked her thigh as he went on. "I hope you won't get tired of me thanking you, which I'm sure you realize won't stop anytime soon.

"But, since I believe in 'show, don't tell', I will be hard at work to come up with ways of expressing my gratitude that will tickle your fancy among other things, especially when I take you away before things heat up with the race."

"Take me away? Where? Will we have enough time for that? It's pretty late into the race now, isn't it? The other candidates have-"

"Honey, we'll make time. I'm not the least bit worried about what the other candidates are doing. My focus right now and for the next month or so is and will be entirely on you- on *us*-, which is right where it should be. I want to find some secluded, beautiful place where we can just enjoy each other. If I'm elected, we won't have the chance to be together without interruption, which is a chance I'm not willing to take."

She smiled. "As always, you make a very convincing argument- not that you had to try very hard. I'm looking forward to that very much. I guess all that remains is for us to decide where we'll go…unless you've already come up with a place."

"I have a couple of possibilities- nothing final yet."

"Well, it sounds like that will make another great story I'll [shar]e with my classmates at the Princeton reunion this fall." Amid [a ya]wn she added, "Wow, I just realized how tired I am! I don't [kno]w about you, but I sure could use a nap."

He also yawned. "I'm with you there. We're still well over [an] hour away from your place, so let's take advantage." He lay [ac]ross the seat and waited for her to join him.

Kim undid the clasp holding her cape closed and removed [i]t.

John shook his head slowly and grinned in appreciation of his view. "Damn, I hope you'll wear this outfit for Halloween. Of course, if you do, there's a good chance we won't get out of the bedroom."

"In that case, why should I wait until Halloween?"

His grin broadened. "I love the way you think."

She lay across him and used her cape to cover them up.

Not a minute later they were fast asleep.


Josh had been to Phil's place before; it was fairly isolated and had very little traffic.

It was perfect for a temporary hideout, especially since he was paying the man a large sum of money and offering him quite a fringe benefit as well. He pulled into the garage and the door closed behind him. He shut the car off, then looked behind him.

"I'm glad you had a good laugh at my expense when you and Dean had me in a similar position; that'll just make me enjoy taking revenge on you all the more. Not only have you cost me well over a hundred million dollars- I bet you're also the one who poisoned Kim against me from the beginning. However, I'll get to pay you back some by doing the same thing to you as you did to Kim in the little scenario you concocted while you two were at the Silver Palace. How fitting, that you'll get the same exact treatment you inspired me to give to her, and all the others.

"Let me also give you this to consider: neither you nor my deceased partner thought to get the handcuff keys out of my pocket. By that oversight- nah, let's call it what it is. By that *fuck-up* you helped me out of the cuffs, Vanessa. How does that make you feel?"

* * *

370

"Hey, Tom, it's me…oh, Kim's fine. She's having a bath right now. After that we'll be going to the conference.

"Look, I wanted to ask you about the autopsy on Lisa Meyers- has that been done?…It hasn't? Good. I just thought about something and I wanted to run it by you. Maybe I'm reaching, but then again, with what we saw in Josh's file, maybe I'm not…"

Kim ran her hands along her freshly shaved legs as she slowly raised them, one at a time, out of the sudsy water. *You do a better job of it than I do!* She smiled as she thought back to a short time ago when, after bathing her, John again performed that otherwise tedious task, which of late had become an eagerly anticipated and very pleasurable experience for her. The memory of it also had helped so much in her psychological war with Strauss, particularly when he had her in the tub.

It was obvious that John loved shaving her legs as much as she enjoyed letting him, which made the experience all the better.

This time she even let him go a step beyond her legs.

Just before he left her alone to soak for a while longer, John alluded to a surprise that he was going to put together for her while they were on their getaway. That was all he'd said in spite of her pleas for more information. His refusal to budge prompted her to splash him repeatedly until he ran out, laughing all the while.

*That's all right, Mister Stratton. I have my ways of making you talk,* she mused, smiling wickedly.

*Just* wait *until I get you alone later…*

*…in fact, I think I'll employ one of those weapons on you tonight…*

"For now, I suppose I should get ready."

"Now, where's that sexy babe of mine?"

"Here I come," she purred as she walked into the front room to greet him, dressed in her version of the 'power suit'.

With the exception of her pumps with the skyscraper heels, everything she wore was silk- suit and lingerie alike,

371

although in the case of the latter, she'd left a little something out. Except for her white blouse, everything was black as well.

He was speechless as she moved toward him slowly, hands clasped behind her, breasts thrust out proudly, eyes fixed on his. Every bit as titillating as the visual feast was for his eyes, so was the enchanting symphony for his ears. The tapping of Kim's shoes on the floor had started it off. Soon followed the seductive whisper of silk from the rather short and tight skirt hugging her undulating hips, and from her stockings as her legs brushed together while she closed in on him. The pounding of his heart as she approached added the background rhythm.

She stopped a few feet away from him and slowly pirouetted, very pleased that she had the desired effect on him, and then moved into his arms. The look in his eyes more than made up for his lack of words.

His olfactory senses weren't left out, by any means; she was wearing the perfume she knew he loved, as subtle as it was powerful...

"Baby..." That was all he could manage to say before they tried to devour each other with a torrid kiss. She had so many charms, all of which held him enrapt. As elegant- even regal- as she looked when she modeled for him, she also looked indescribably alluring. Kim had an unmatched talent for maximizing her boundless sex appeal no matter what she wore. Although she certainly didn't need to expend any effort to that end, when she pulled out all the stops, most- if not all- who saw her took notice, to say the very least.

None, however, took more notice than John. He knew many an envious look was cast at him along with the awestruck stares at Kim when they were together. He knew she loved the attention, but because she made it so clear that she loved him more, he didn't feel insecure. On the contrary, that attention so often bestowed upon her made him feel even more proud to be with her.

"Let's try to save some of this for *after* the speech," John managed to slip in between their necking.

"Now, Honey, you of all people should know that I have more than enough saved up. Maybe we'd better put you on an all-oyster diet, or call your pharmacist for some you-know-what, because I'm going to keep you *so* busy while we're away that you'll need the whole *next* month to recover...that is, if I let you.

"And make no mistake- I *will* get that little secret out of you."

"We'll see about that, although I do look forward to your efforts." He gave her one more kiss. "Are you ready?"

She nodded and looked away. She'd managed to distract herself temporarily from focusing on what she had to do, but now it was time to face up to it.

"I'm ready. Let's go."


Del pulled over because it looked too suspicious.

The recent rain had softened the ground considerably- enough so to allow him to see that a vehicle had pulled off to the side of the road very recently.

A squadron of buzzards circled overhead. When he got out of his truck, he heard the growling of a wild dog. All the commotion was happening just opposite where the vehicle had pulled off, on the other side of the tree line there.

He took the semi-automatic twelve-gauge shotgun out of the rack behind the seat of his pick-up and began to walk toward the area. He chambered a round as he stepped off the road. When he hit the tree line, a couple wild dogs ran off in the opposite direction and the buzzards took to the air.

Immediately upon clearing the trees, he saw what had brought the animals there.


"Thank you all for coming. Given what's happened over the past several weeks, and especially over the past twenty-four hours, I'm going to keep this conference brief.

"By now you're probably aware of all she did and the risk she took in bringing about the freedom of most of Strauss's captives, but as of yet, you don't know the entirety of the critical role my fiancée played in foiling his plan to leave the country. You'll know it soon enough, though, and yes- I did say fiancée.

"Kim and I are engaged. For those of you who are well acquainted with one or both of us, I'm sure you're saying 'it's about time'. We'll be spending at least the next month together and away from everyone and everything. We need time to ourselves in a peaceful setting where all we'll need to worry about is what to have for breakfast or what to see that day. Shortly after we get back, I'm sure things will get pretty hectic pretty quickly.

"This morning I handed in my formal resignation as Governor of Maryland. I'm still in the presidential race and it looks like I'll finally be able to lay out my platform, which I will do upon my return. We'll take a few questions, but that's all."

"First of all, congratulations to both of you on your engagement and I'm glad you're both all right. Have you set a date for your wedding?"

"Thank you, Jane. I just proposed a few hours ago; we don't have a date yet."

The same reporter followed up. "When do you plan to return from your trip?"

"We'll be back in mid- to late-August, after Kim's birthday and in time for the trial of my former chief of staff."

"Speaking of that upcoming trial, it could prove to be quite a distraction for you and for Miss Francis as well. Will that interfere with your campaigning?"

"I can't imagine it'll be too much of a distraction. That's a cut and dried case; Walter Daniels will get what's coming to him."

Another piped up. "Don't you think that's cutting your campaigning time awfully short? Or is your intention merely that of playing spoiler?"

"What, so I can't be considered a legitimate candidate unless I spend hundreds of millions of dollars from fat cats, corporations, unions and special interest groups on negative campaign ads? And also on the junkets around the country via corporate jets while making the empty promises- or deceptive ones- that these poor excuses for party candidates make? Promises that amount to nothing more than business as usual? It won't take me over a year, or even six months, to lay out what I plan to do when I'm elected President. In fact, I think two months is more than enough time. The real question is, will the democratic and republican candidates agree to debate me? The answer: probably not. I doubt they have the guts between 'em."

"Whoa, that's a very bold statement there, Mister Governor."

"Well, think about it. They have everything to lose and nothing to gain by including me. They offer the same tired solutions, which solve nothing and serve only to perpetuate the cycle of futility we're in. I offer a genuine alternative that will call for considerable sacrifice but, when all is said and done, will make this nation strong again- possibly stronger than it ever has been. There will be bumps in the road and growing pains along the way; it will not be easy, which brings me to my last point.

"According to most who analyze elections and determine how a candidate won, what I'm doing by calling for sacrifice and accountability for one's actions- and also by telling you the solution I'm offering will be a difficult one- is sabotaging my own chance to be elected. In essence, what they're telling us with that statement is that Americans don't want to hear such things; we only want to hear that the outlook is bright and that we have nothing to worry about. I don't buy that, because sacrifice and hard work are what built this nation.

"What I'm telling you is, that's what it will take to save it. I'm talking about a change in philosophy and the way we live and how much individual wealth we can keep, and a radical overhaul of our system of elections and government, which is failing us. Once we achieve those goals we can focus our energies on following up on an earlier success. We can end our stagnation and move full steam ahead in a new and exciting direction."

He looked over at Kim. "Ready to go?" She nodded, then stood and joined him. John turned back to the reporters. "If you'll excuse us, we need to-"

"Miss Francis, is it true you were just fired from your job as a guidance counselor because of your past as an exotic dancer?"

Kim was so focused on what John said that she momentarily was taken aback by the sudden and accusatory question. "Well...no, I wasn't fired. I resigned."

"Did you resign because you would have been fired? And did your wardrobe at the high school consist of short skirts, high heels, garter belts and back-seamed stockings, like now?"

The temporary effect was gone and she found herself trying to hold back her anger, knowing this man was trying to provoke her. "You must be looking awfully closely to know I'm wearing a garter belt. Do you usually do that with women you interview?"

"Only those who dress like pole dancers when they're supposed to be mentoring children. Do you even regret having been a stripper?"

"What did you say?! Where are you getting this crap from?!"

"I talked with a couple of your associates at the school who were only too happy that you no longer would be in the position. They said you never were or would have been promoted because of the inappropriate style of dress you have- to put it lightly. They did give you credit in that you at least had the good sense to resign."

"Who? Who did you talk to?" *Wait a minute, I think I've seen you before...*

"I protect my sources. That's how I get my information."

"Oh, your 'information'- is that what you call it? That's another way of saying either you're inflicting your own opinion on anyone who cares to listen and citing undisclosed references that you don't even have, or you only are interested in getting dirt on me. But you know what? I'll answer your charge.

"No, I did not wear garter belts and stockings while I was at the school- neither as a student nor as a counselor. Did I wear short skirts and high heels? Yes, I did. Why? Because that's how I dress. I love being a woman and I appreciate the fact that I have the freedom to dress as I choose. Did I do that to entice any students or faculty members? No, I absolutely did not and I never led any of them on. Anyone who says otherwise is a *liar!*

"For what it's worth, I regret very much keeping hidden the fact that I was a dancer. I ended up betraying people who have been so good to me over the years, like my fiancé, my adoptive mother who took me in and mentored me. Same with Doctor Harris, who recommended me to the school board back in '92 and has been a wonderful influence on my life and so many others. I shouldn't have held that back from them and I'll never do such a thing again. I can only hope my students won't think too badly of me, either...

"But you also ask if I regret being an exotic dancer. My answer is 'no', from my own standpoint. No one held a gun to my head and forced me to dance; I made that choice on my own because it was something I wanted to do. I won't make any excuses."

Kim hesitated. At that point, some other memories started to seep in. She'd constantly tried to see only the positive in that phase of her life and block out the negatives, but it wasn't working anymore.

That especially rang true when her instincts as a counselor kicked in and she realized how much of a slanted picture she would present to a young girl considering dancing for whatever reason. In reality, it became a very ugly life for lots of women, and Kim knew she'd be committing a terrible injustice if that was all she revealed about the industry.

*Even though what I've said is true- that for me personally it* was *positive, that's only part of my experience. God knows there was plenty of the other extreme...*

"On the other hand, I can't deny that terrible things happened during that time besides my encounters with Joshua Strauss. Some of my friends and acquaintances succumbed to drugs and either ended up strung out or dying very young. I was able to preemptively steer a few friends away from them altogether, but of those who were on them already I only was able to help one break the cycle. As much as I tried to help the others, it didn't do any good. When it came time for me to leave I saw still more of them spiraling down. It was hard...

"Worst of all was what happened to my friend Roxanne. She came across a similar version of Mister Strauss, who ended up murdering her. I just pray that doesn't happen to my friend Vanessa as well. It's bad enough how the same thing can befall any young woman in any vocation- or in school, or anywhere- who happens to cross paths with some psychopathic stalker. Of course, you do increase the chances of such a thing happening when you choose the path I took. For those reasons and others, dancing can be very dangerous; I don't recommend it as a way of life. It's easy to lose yourself in it- in the bad way as well as the good. From that perspective, I was one of the lucky ones..."

"I just hope, if any school board in the future comes across a woman with a similar background as mine who wants to change her life and to help students, the members at least will hear her out and give her a chance. Being a dancer doesn't automatically make you a bad person."

"Don't you even care about the adverse effect you're sure to have on Governor Stratton's already-slim chances at being elected President? Do you really think people would react well to the prospect of having a stripper as their First Lady? We'll be the laughingstock of the world- not that you care, obviously. I could see you on Inauguration Day wearing your Tigress uniform from that sleazy club where you worked."

*A-ha!!* That's *where I saw you!* "Actually, I believe John will win. As for my Tigress suit, I'd *never* wear it outside in late

January! Gosh, I'd freeze! On the other hand, there's always the reception afterwards, which I'm sure is held indoors...hmmm..."

She winked and grinned as much of the rest of the group chuckled. "Why, Mr. Dalton, I do believe you're about to burst."

"How do you re-, know my name?"

She smiled at his slip. "Well, it's easy to *remember*- as you meant to say- lousy tippers like you that get loud and obnoxious. People are supposed to mature with age, but apparently, you haven't changed much at all. I also remember arrogant, *married* jerks that pinch my rear end, make me drop my tray and then laugh about it. To top it all off, you just couldn't understand why I didn't want to get a room with you that night in '88, when you offered to '*make it all up to me*'." She rubbed it in by doing a rather good caricature of his voice and laugh. "I hope you didn't bounce *too* hard when Paul and Joey threw you out the door...then again, yes, I do."

His face turned beet-red as everyone there, after a stunned silence, erupted into full-fledged laughter. "I...I have no idea what you're talking about. Look, perhaps you think it's funny to make a mockery of this, but I doubt any *decent* American thinks that way. Did you ever stop to think that you might have brought all the danger you were just in on yourself with the shameless way you act along with your dancing and dressing like-"

"*That's ENOUGH*!!"

"What's the matter, Mister Governor? Don't you think we have the right to-"

"What, the right to smear Kim?! The right to drag her through the mud by passing judgement on her past life?! From the sound of it, you have no moral high ground from which to cast your stones- in fact, I doubt you have any morals at all. You propositioned a young cocktail waitress while your wife was at home. You had children at that point, too, right? You're the very definition of a hypocrite.

"On top of that you presume to lecture *me* about rights?! I'll tell you this- you spout off to my fiancée again and I'll give you a right you'll wish you never got!"

"Sir...*Sir*! We've got this." Two of John's bodyguards took positions with their charge. A couple more materialized on either side of the loudmouth and seized him. The man was about to protest, but the bodyguards presented him with a scenario that dissuaded him from that course and he accepted their invitation to leave under their escort.

Kim saw that John was about to blow and tried to calm him, like she did at the last press conference she'd accompanied him to.

*I'm surprised you held off as long as you did.* "Honey, it's all right. I can handle-"

"No, Kim, it's *not* all right. I know you can handle him; you did that very well. The thing is, you shouldn't *have* to handle him. Nobody has the right to talk to you that way, especially some sanctimonious, hypocritical, piss-poor excuse for a reporter who's too stupid or ignorant to understand what you said. In fact, he seems to have paid a lot more attention to your legs than your words." John held her with a tenderness that stood in stark contrast to the anger he felt toward the reporter.

He turned to the group. "I expect that will be the last time such an ugly display will come from any of you. Kim has addressed her past as a dancer to the extent it needed to be addressed- probably more than she needed to. I think most of you will agree with that assessment, so unless Kim brings it up again, the subject is closed.

"That said, I'm going to tell you some things you *don't* know about this woman." He revealed to the group Rollins' intent to abduct Kim and use her as collateral against Strauss after luring her to his place to dance, and how she turned the tables on him in the form of the sting she helped set up. "Had that gone the other way, I can guarantee all of you that Kim never would have been heard from again. For the rest of my life I'll thank God that didn't happen, just as I know Kim and everyone else who knows and loves her will. But she still lived in fear over the next decade because she had a bad feeling that the whole gang had not been caught. As we know now, she was right.

"In spite of the fact that she had to look over her shoulder constantly, she graduated with high honors from Princeton University and also with high honors from her Master's program at the University of Maryland. All she did from the fall of 1992 until this past spring was help hundreds of young students find their way through high school, and find themselves in the process. I don't need to elaborate on her record as a counselor- it speaks for itself. No one can take away or minimize all the good she's done.

"Lastly, I want to tell you what hardly anyone knows about this final chapter of the mess Joshua Strauss caused. Jenny Jacobson told you about the vital role Kim played in her liberation and that of all the other women Strauss held captive. If not for Kim's bravery, she and the other eleven might never have been rescued.

"But, had it not been for Kim's bravery early this morning, I wouldn't be- period. Strauss was going to kill me before leaving the country. He had me at point-blank range, but Kim managed to free herself and she saved my life by getting the drop on him.

"When you choose to focus only on a couple aspects or phases of Kim's life, you miss entirely who and what she really is and you end up putting a label on her that she does not deserve. I've never come across a woman who has more love, warmth and goodness inside- that is her legacy in every walk of life she's taken. She turned her back on certain stardom because she wanted to help children- especially those who came from dysfunctional families, like she did. I can't put into words how fortunate I feel to be the man she loves- there's not a luckier man here or anywhere. To think I almost lost her on more occasions than I even realized..." He turned back to her and said, "I love you, too, Honey, and I'm damned proud to say that.

"Come on, let's get out of here."


"His name's Richard Mason," the detective said to his partner as he looked at the driver's license he pulled from the dead man's wallet.

"Let's find out what his story is and why he ended up here..."


For some time, all Kim could do was smile at him as they rode toward the house.

"Right now I'm looking at another wonder of the world- and this one blows all the others away," John said as he touched her cheek.

That finally loosened her tongue. "You know what they say about flattery."

"Absolutely." He gave her a little peck.

"I always enjoyed listening to you speak. You made me feel even better about myself- just then and also earlier, during our ride back. You defended me again, too."

"I'm sure you knew I would. Seeing you upset brings that out of me, but I did refrain- barely- from going after him. I loved the way you made Dalton eat his words, especially with your comeback about the Tigress uniform- not that I would mind in the least if you wore it on Inauguration Day."

She giggled and shook her head, but he saw her uncertainty came back as she shifted, then turned away. "What's wrong?"

As much as she hated to, she had to get it out. "John, I'm worried about something. Since it's happened twice now, I think I have cause. Both times reporters have made rude comments to me you almost tore their heads off, and-"

"Of course I almost tore their heads off. You heard what-"

"Please listen to me; I'm not finished. I love how protective you are of me, but those who don't want you to win have seen those interviews and I'm afraid they might have a weapon to use against you. I'm willing to bet that the closer we get to the election, the more incidents like that we'll see. They'll try to knock you off balance and keep you that way by these cheap attacks on me and anything else they can think of along those lines that will make your blood boil.

"You can't let them get to you so much- you have to work on curbing your temper in situations like that. Senator Gray discussed this, too; no one wants a hothead as President." She reached up and touched his face to stop him from turning away. "Baby, I didn't mean it that way. You know I'm not attacking you. I'm just concerned and I feel like I'd be doing you a disservice if I didn't let you in on it."

"It's all right, Kitten. I see what you're saying and you're right. I'll work on that."

"There are times when you're fully justified in letting loose with your anger, but today wasn't one of them. At the risk of stating the obvious, I know things will get worse before they get better- and I'm not just talking about the flak we'll take over my past and anything else. I guess I'm trying to prepare myself for what's coming, too."

"You're afraid…"

"Yes, and that's another reason why I'm convinced your cause is the right one. There are very powerful people out there who don't agree with what you want to do and they'll use any means to prevent you from doing it. Those who stand to lose the most will fight to keep it, and their attacks might not only be verbal ones. The closer you get to victory, the more dangerous they'll become. In spite of how rough it gets, though, I know you'll fight back and I know you'll win, but you won't be alone. I'll be right there with you, for better or for worse. I won't let anything else come between us: that's a promise."

Although he had no doubt that was how she felt, it warmed his heart even more to hear her express those feelings. That was her nature; Kim always had been an open book. Keeping the dark chapter of her past hidden from him was an aberration he knew would never happen again.

The same went for him; although she hadn't asked about his fateful jump off Suicide Ridge, or about his role in the planning of the big heist, he would tell her about both later on...

Then, once more, she looked up at him but quickly looked away. This time she preempted his inquiry. "I, um...I just started thinking about your mother. I can't help but wonder, with everything I've done and with what I did at the conference...do you think she would-..."

Her discomfort was obvious and he had a good idea about what was causing it. "I think I see where you're going. She still would have approved of you, Kim- I think even more so now than ever, if that was possible. I'm so proud of you with the way you handled yourself and there's no question in my mind that Mom would have felt the same way. She would have applauded you for standing up to that guy and giving as good as you got, if not better. I'm sure my father would have loved it, too. Now, lighten up, huh?"

Kim laughed and gave him a kiss. Once more, he'd dispelled so easily the dark clouds that hovered around her.

She looked up at him after he fell silent. "Hmmm...that's a very interesting smile on your face. Care to share with your fiancée what it is you're thinking about?"

"Just the fact that the woman I'm going to marry has yet another exciting dimension. From the way Vanessa talked about you, you really must be one hell of a dancer. I sure would love to have seen you perform."

She blushed deeply and looked down. "What else did she tell you?"

"A lot," he replied as he kissed her forehead.

"I bet she did! So, you, um…you know?"

He nodded. "Like I told her, I can totally understand that happening- not just because both of you have cornered the market on beauty, but also from the depth of your friendship and the circumstances of that night."

"I figured she spilled that, especially with the 'threesome' comment she made before she left! It *was* a strange night, and I admit: it was one for the books, although I never felt such an urge again. Anyway, thanks to Josh, you can see me perform."

"How-…video? Did he tape you?"

"Mm-hmm. There were a few DVDs in that suitcase. He got some of my best work, especially this one routine I did that became my signature. In a way, you were there when I made it up, because I thought of you as I did it. I imagined there was no one else watching me but the only man I really wanted to dance for.

"Along those lines, if you ask me nicely, you can see the real thing, too. I'm sure I'm not very rusty. In fact, I was thinking of a little surprise I want to give you. And don't even think about asking me to elaborate! You'll just have to wait and see."

It took all of a split-second for his imagination to go with that and about as little time for the visions conjured up by her last statement to commandeer his train of thought. There just didn't seem to be anything she wouldn't do to please him, and again, it was time to show her that she deserved- and would get- the same from him.

He reaffirmed his eternal gratitude for the act of God or simple twist of fate that brought them together that day in front of his locker. Their bond seemed invincible; it had been tested and strengthened by all that had happened to them. There was no doubt in his mind that they would go through any more such trials in the future if they had to, and that they'd come through them together as well.

He pulled her into his lap and kissed her as his hands experienced their greatest pleasure with the attention they bestowed upon Kim's body. He purposely was slow and gentle as he stoked her- he spread kisses along her jaw, down to her neck and toward her earlobe as he stroked her thighs, which she parted for him as his hand moved between them and began that most pleasurable journey.

He pulled back a bit and looked into her eyes. She squirmed as his hand coursed higher ever so slowly and cried out softly as his fingers reached the top of her stocking and touched the bare, highly sensitive skin of her inner thigh.

But in spite of her escalating passion, she couldn't suppress her smile. When John regarded her curiously, she lowered her head as she felt a progressively hot rush of blood into her cheeks and neck.

He was even more curious now- the higher his hand moved on her thigh, the deeper she blushed, so he continued his deliberate journey along the very curvy, scenic, well-constructed and maintained highway- there was only a little further to go…

…when he reached his destination, he quickly discovered why she was blushing, and his touch made her gasp and quiver.

Kim looked up at him to see his reaction, then giggled and looked away again.

"*Kitten!*" To say the least, he was pleasantly surprised to find that she'd left out one very small item when she dressed that morning. "With all those people there…no wonder you sat the way you did!"

"I know. I'm so bad…"

Recovering from his surprise he traced along her cheek, thinking how funny it was to hear her say that while the color of her face was approaching that of an apple. "No, you're not. You *are* naughty, but you're definitely not bad."

After a moment she looked back up at him. "Naughty, huh?" That word reminded her once more of that little treat she had in store for him and suddenly, triggered by that word and what just transpired between them, a little scenario that was a take on an old fairy tale began to form.

*Oooo- I* know *he'll love that…I can't believe it's all stemming from the little striptease I wanted to put on for him!*

I *can't wait for this, either…* Her excitement over what she knew would be a very steamy evening sent tremors through her.

Just before his 'discovery', not to mention on several other occasions, he'd seen that secretive and wicked little smile on Kim's face. "Oh, yeah- *very* naughty, especially with that smile. And there you go blushing again! Just what is it that's brewing in that devious mind of yours?"

"As I said, you'll find out later. You won't be disappointed- that I promise you."

"I don't doubt it. Every time I think I've experienced your best, you seem to top it the next time and you don't even have to try. I've never been so excited to be alive; falling in love with you is by far the best thing that ever happened to me, and it always will be."

Her appreciation of what he said came through clearly in her kiss. "Mister, you'd better prepare yourself for a very special night," she purred, then slowly pulled away.

Then, that little smile returned. She reached down and undid his suspenders and his pants.

"But as for right now," she hiked up her skirt as she mounted him in preparation for the exclamation point, "I'll show you naughty..."


At 6:00 PM exactly, a wire transfer of one million dollars was made into the bank account of Stanley Jeffries.

# Chapter 15

John's sense of anticipation had him on the edge of the bed as he waited for her.

When she stepped through the door, his heart leaped right out of his chest.

She stood across the room, wearing a full-length red satin cape that she held closed. She also wore a matching bonnet, which she'd fastened under her chin. Desire already smoldered in her eyes...

"There you are, Mister-" she stopped short. "My goodness, look at this place! Such clutter- I'm surprised at you!"

She pranced around the room and surveyed it very superficially, turning up her nose as she did. There still was a bit of the mess left over from when the police units checked through the house to make sure it was clear of explosives; she and he would deal with it, but obviously not tonight. Although she hadn't planned on incorporating that into her role-play, she was enjoying it nonetheless.

John already was practically mesmerized, but he became even more transfixed when she gradually changed her pace. Her moves became even more graceful and beautiful...

...and so sensuous. She just flowed naturally from one captivating rhythm to the next, taking his libido higher as she teased him with her performance and the all-too-brief glimpses of her body that she allowed him. *I see why you had such a following. My God...*

She glanced over toward him again and smiled; clearly he was enjoying her show. *I guess I do still have some moves left,* she thought as she basked in his attention. *Of course, what I felt for you is a big part of what brought it all out of me, so it's no surprise...*

But then, as she began to hum a little tune, she spied the items on the nightstand. Raising her brows, she got back into character. "And just what do you mean by having those silk scarves and sashes on display?! Shame on you, Mister Wolf! Why, a girl might be led to think you were lying in wait for her, to bind her and gag her and have your way with her, which is exactly what that scoundrel who resembles you would do. Oh! How *vile* he is!

It's lucky for you that I know you better than that," Kim scolded in her haughtiest voice and demeanor.

She finished her circuit of the room and turned to him again. "Also fortunately for you, I'm not here to discuss your utterly hopeless mess of a dwelling and appalling lack of manners and decency, which I promise you I will *not* soon forget.

"I am very glad you're home, though, Mister Wolf. I had to sneak away from Grandma's house. I was afraid you might not be here and I would be all alone and defenseless if that bad, bad wolf was lurking about. Whatever would become of me if I fell into his clutches?" she drawled winsomely as she strolled slowly toward him.

Her eyes never left his and she saw him glancing down as her bare, tanned, silky-smooth legs alternately emerged from under the cape and were swallowed back up by it. She was capable of taking only very short steps given the height of the heels of her shoes.

When she stopped and carefully reached up to untie her bonnet, she smiled inwardly. That little gesture had marked the beginning of a new era for her one fateful Halloween night- the night she threw her inhibitions to the wind, which she was doing now in her relationship with John.

The difference this time was that she only meant to seduce the man she loved. She'd bewitched the patrons of the clubs she worked under the guise of fantasy- look and imagine, but don't touch.

Now, her audience of one would touch her on yet another level.

She removed her bonnet and with a little shake of her head, her shining mane fell free, tumbling down in a golden cascade.

"You see, Mister Wolf, Grandma doesn't approve of me spending time with you. She doesn't understand how nice, ordinary and completely harmless you are, and I'm glad she doesn't know how slovenly, lazy and inhospitable you are."

John couldn't help but snicker. *You just wait...*

"She was so mean before she sent me to my room! She told me I've been a *very* naughty girl lately..." she undid her cape and let it slide down slowly from her shoulders, along her body and onto the floor "...and I just don't know why she would say such a thing!"

She pouted expressively, hands on her hips, completely immersed in her role and loving her effect on her fiancé. "You don't think I'm naughty, do you, Mister Wolf?"

He was struck dumb. Kim never would cease to amaze him by how much she made him want her and his desire was reaching yet another peak. Every bit of her femininity came to bear. Her expression was a perfect- and devastating- blend of innocence and seductiveness, with some indignation thrown in for good measure.

And her body...all she had on was a tiny, ruffled red g-string and a red pair of her trademark pumps. As with the black pair she wore while she lay corseted and fettered in the cage, the heels on these were almost perilously high; they looked high enough to induce vertigo. John was amazed that she could even stand in those shoes, let alone put on such a captivating performance for him as she had just a little while ago...

...*and do you ever know how to walk in them,* he thought as she so effortlessly sauntered toward him like a lioness sizing up her prey. She reached the bed and climbed onto it, then began to crawl toward him ever so slowly.

As she closed in on him, she went on. "I don't mean to be. Sometimes I wish *you* weren't so nice. I can't help picturing you as being just a little more like...well, like that other one. I get so warmed up whenever I imagine you that way. I think about us being together and the things I want you to do to me that you simply *never* would do and I get so-...oh, maybe I *am* naughty!"

She was face-to-face with him now and she leaned closer. Her lips brushed his ear as she whispered, "Maybe you should punish me." She lay down and looked up at him invitingly.

After a moment she propped herself back up. "But you're not like that, are you, Mister Wolf? Even though you have such a notorious reputation, you're always so nice and such a gentleman. I wonder why people confuse you with the Big, Bad Wolf. I don't think you're bad at all. You *look* like a foul, intemperate and ill-mannered beast, but I guess appearances can be deceiving, can't they? In fact, I'm starting to wonder if you're a sheep in wolf's clothing..."

She giggled, then moved in closer to him again as she continued her taunting and teasing. "I bet that's just what you are! You *never* would punish me! You probably wouldn't even chastise me, no matter how naughty I- *hey!*"

She never saw it coming as he pulled her into his lap and rolled her over, face down. He quickly grabbed her arms and bent them up behind her in a hammerlock, then clamped both her wrists together in one hand and held them like that.

Belatedly, she tried to fight him, attempting to maneuver herself out of the vulnerable position he had her in.

Despite her efforts, so far she couldn't escape his grip. She had no leverage, and his hand imprisoned her wrists like a band of steel. She played possum for a moment, and when she felt him relax his grip a little she twisted and pulled as hard as she could and almost broke free. That made her redouble her efforts.

"I bet you saw me as a pushover, didn't you? Sorry to dispel your- *ah!*" She cried out when he delivered a slap to her rear, then tried still harder to wrench herself away from him. "How *dare* you?! Let me go this- unh! *Ah!!* OW!!!" He'd followed with three more, after which she lay still and fell silent.

"You were saying?" She shot him a look and turned away in a huff, making him chuckle. "No, you're certainly not a pushover, although apparently you assumed that *I* was one, didn't you? I doubt you're ready to behave just yet, Little Red; actually, I hope you'll resist me even more. I look forward to the challenge very much…"

She felt quite shamed, but she also was extremely horny. *You took it right to heart when I told you how I like being put in my place, didn't you?* Since she'd sprung her little fantasy on him without giving him any hints about it, she had no idea how John would react- especially since it also was a thinly veiled challenge for him to put his money where his mouth was. Apparently, he'd picked up on that.

*I wonder what else you have in store for me…*

Already, her breathing was quickening; she loved the direction he was taking and was very eager for his next move. She was amazed by how erotic the spanking was- even more so since he restrained her while he did that. It was similar to what Vanessa had done to her that night on stage, and like what Jill had done to her while she was held captive in the treehouse, although she hated to admit even to herself how much that had stimulated her as well.

This time, however, it was so much better.

*I never thought you'd spank me!*

*Of course, if it makes me feel like this, I hope it's not the last time you do it,* she thought as she smiled to herself again.

"A bit more agreeable after all, are you? At least for now. In that case, would you care to tell me about those things you want me to do to you?"

She jerked as she felt his hand on her bottom again, but this time his touch was gentle as he caressed her where he'd just spanked her.

"Or maybe you'd like me to guess..."

The quick transition from mild pain to major pleasure fueled her more. She knew he also saw that as she wriggled and cooed while he massaged and squeezed her firm 'caboose', as he called it.

He loved how her hands clenched and released as she responded to his touch. It was just like Vanessa had described.

"...maybe you want me to do..."

She felt his free hand slide down between her thighs while his other hand continued to imprison her wrists. Her slight wiggling quickly turned into urgent writhing.

"something like..."

Her body begged him and her sensuous cries further emphasized her need as she anticipated what was coming.

"...this."

His finger slowly traced along the edge of her g-string, then slipped inside it...


"Got somethin' for ya." He handed the prisoner the cup.

The man took a whiff. "Is this what I think it is?"

"Yep- Irish coffee, just like I've been telling you about. Made it myself- thought you might like some since you probably won't be getting much other than standard prison-issue coffee soon enough." Daniels had made the means of bringing about his own end surprisingly easy with his repetitive requests for the drink.

"Don't count me out too early, Stan," he said to the guard as he raised his mug in salute and took a long sip of the coffee with the special ingredient. "I haven't been condemned yet."

*I beg to differ,* the guard thought as he stifled his smile.

"Mmm- not bad! It's a little stronger than I'm used to."

"Probably because you haven't had any for so long, or you got it from people who don't know shit about making it."

He laughed. "Could be. Well, I guess it'll help me sleep even better than usual."

The guard smiled. "I'm sure it will. Enjoy."


He took the rest of the coffee down quickly after he took a seat on his cot.

Just as he finished, he dropped the cup.

A huge, invisible hand took hold of his body and squeezed.

Falling back, he gasped for air.

He knew what had happened.

Death came for him as quickly as it had for his former tenant Andy Edison, who'd died the same way by Wally's doing.


As he let go of her wrists and reached over toward the nightstand, she slid off his lap, got up and half-walked, half-ran somewhat unsteadily for the door. He immediately came after her.

Kim's heart was pounding as she heard him behind her. It was the same way she'd felt as he closed in on her during that Marco-Polo game so long ago...

Even if she wasn't wearing a pair of her sexiest and most precarious stilettos, she knew it was highly unlikely that she would get away from him, especially since she also was just coming down from a couple very potent orgasms.

Better yet, in those shoes a full-out run was not an option. She had no chance at all of escape, which quickly became another reason why she loved wearing such high heels- especially now...

...not that she *wanted* to elude him, of course.

Kim squealed in delight as he grabbed her and easily hoisted her over his shoulder while she struggled with him. He carried her back to the bed and dumped her onto it.

She propped herself up and faced him defiantly. "You *are* that villainous lecher! You let me go at once!"

"You're not going anywhere! Better yet, I'm going to teach you a lesson that'll make you think twice about walking through the woods with hardly a stitch of clothing on!"

"I can if I want and there's *nothing* you can do to stop me!"

"Oh, really?! Well, this'll take care of that urge and keep you right where I want you!" He produced one of the long sashes from the nightstand. When he saw her eyes light up- and especially after what she said next-, he continued on course.

"You *fiend*!! First you spank me and now you want to tie me up?! You're no gentleman at all! If you think I'm just going to lie still and let you do this to me, you're sadly mistaken!"

He was on top of her before she could evade him again. He took hold of her wrists, pinned them over her head and once more imprisoned them with one of his hands. Her eyes widened and she gasped, unable to contain her thrilled response to his aggressiveness. She resisted him again, which added yet more excitement to their play. She wanted him to totally subdue her…

…which he went about doing right away. He even taunted her a bit. "Come on, now- surely you can do better!"

When her eyes narrowed, he saw what was coming, and after their moments in the van he was prepared for it. He well remembered how difficult she'd been to control then, even with her hands cuffed behind her. He'd experienced something similar with her one night in '89; when her furnace reached full blast, she was quite a handful, which she became again- and quickly.

He held on for the ride while she employed every bit of strength she could muster and every move she could think of to try to turn the tables on him in one final, sustained burst…


…when it dissipated, she still was where she wanted to be: pinned to the bed. This felt a lot like that amazing night at the pool party; the look in John's eyes told her he was thinking that, too…

At that point, Kim willingly surrendered control of her fantasy- and herself as well- to him and began to writhe under him, fully aroused once more as she eagerly awaited his next move. She licked her lips as he tied her wrists together and then to the middle of the headboard. She still was panting, now more from excitement than from her exertions, and she softly cried out as he finished the knot.

"Not going anywhere, are you?" She tried to turn away when the blush he loved to see crept up her cheeks, but he turned her face back to his. She seemed unable to stay still, which reminded him of what she'd revealed to him on Suicide Ridge. "Yes, Little Red- I am him, and now you're my captive."

John had to pause for a moment to catch his breath. No doubt about it: subduing Kim was far from an easy task. However, that 'task' was every bit as stimulating as it was difficult. It really was an enhancer- no question- and it was about to be one again. He saw and felt the powerful current shooting through her, which started when she tried to break his grip, intensified when she realized she couldn't, and now was on the verge of taking her over completely on when the full effect of his last statement set in.

"Fooled you, didn't I? I've waited a very long time for this moment- to have you as my own. So many times I've thought about the things I would do with you. Now that I know you've had such thoughts of me, I'll show you the many, um, '*punishments*' I have in store for such a naughty and wayward young lady as you. A sheep in wolf's clothing, eh? After I'm through with you, I bet you'll see things quite differently."

The look in his eyes further fueled her already raging fire. She saw his craving for her and a touch of mischief, but most clearly of all, she saw his love for her.

Kim couldn't believe the heights he was carrying her to. John seized upon her submissive impulses and was stoking them to the point where any lingering fears and doubts she had about her darker side were being incinerated by the all-consuming blaze he was helping to generate in her yet again. He was masterfully and lovingly dominating that part of her like only he could; he was giving her what she'd yearned for in this part of her life.

She simply needed to let the right man experience her alter ego- the one who loved and accepted her completely and unconditionally, and the one she knew wouldn't abuse or betray her trust. She knew she was as safe with him as she possibly could be and that she could reveal herself to him completely.

That made all the difference.

She also detected a bit of hesitation on his part- no doubt because of all she'd been put through while in the hands of her two abductors. Even so, the last thing she wanted was for him to stop, so she helped keep his wheels turning.

"So you think! Well, I will have none of this!"

Kim twisted her hands and tugged at the binding…

…to no avail. The futility of her efforts further enflamed her, more so now than at any point before.

*You sure know how to tie a girl up, too, don't you, John? I can't slip out of this…*

"Oh, yes you will, my Little Red. You'll have *all* of it…"

Her little grunts and cries as she struggled also were invitations for him to silence her, which he did with a very hot kiss. She found it increasingly difficult to stay in her role as raw lust began to take over, further heightened as he cupped and fondled her breast. With his thumb he teased its pink peak, which made her arch her back. "Oooo…my, what big paws you have…mmmm…" she moaned as he nibbled on her earlobe.

Amazingly, it seemed to get better and better. She felt absolutely wicked, a little lewd, and more seductive than ever before, including her stage time. She *was* performing for- and better yet, with- the man she loved, who also was totally in to the little scenario they were improvising. At this juncture, John seemed even more excited to be with her and she felt the same way about him…

…and it was only the beginning. They would spend many more nights like this…

Clearly ready for the next step, he practically ripped the g-string off her. She helped him by raising her hips in an effort to save her racy piece of lingerie.

*Time for a finishing touch,* she thought as he got on top of her. "Now that you have me at your mercy,…" She slowly wrapped her legs around him,

"…whatever will you do with me,…" and raised herself up enough to kiss his chin,

"…Mister Big…" then the tip of his nose,

"…Bad…" and lastly his lips.

"…Wolf?"


The guard opened the cell door and walked over to the corpse he'd spoken with only minutes earlier. He picked up the coffee cup, walked out and closed the door behind him. It was the easiest money he'd ever made.

Better yet, the piece of shit deserved it for what he'd done. *Too bad I couldn't have beaten you to death…*


"Mmmph…"

Kim looked every bit as exhausted as he was, if not more so. He'd felt- and 'Little Red' herself had agreed- that she needed to be further restrained as a way to help with her punishment. So, he'd spread her legs and tied her ankles to the footposts and gagged her as well- both her suggestions- and took full advantage. By doing that, both figured they were less likely to be overheard. However, Kim fully covered the spectrum from squirming so submissively and mewing so softly in the beginning to yanking and twisting with total abandon and crying out while lost in the throes of passion. Her staying power and the frequency and magnitude of her orgasms were nothing less than stupefying. John wondered if the bed frame would survive and was a little surprised that the bodyguards didn't burst through the door en masse at some point during one of the many opportunities...

...needless to say, neither of those considerations slowed him down in the least...

"I'll never look at that fairy tale the same way again; I sure do love our version," he said as he unwound the silken gag and removed the balled-up part of it from her mouth.

Kim licked her lips as she drifted back down to earth and emitted a deep, contented sigh as she lay limply. John quickly untied her legs, then moved up to free her hands while she kicked off her shoes. "Mmmm...I must say, Mister Wolf, if this is your idea of punishment, I plan to be naughty a whole lot more."

"I look forward to that! One thing *I* have to say, though, is you were just as much of a wild animal as I was- if not more so! Restraining you was more a necessity than an option. You wore me out..."

She giggled and cuddled close to him once he finished untying her and lay next to her. "Believe it or not, I wore myself out, too! Seems to me we both could use some recuperation. After all, we have to be ready for the next episode of the Erotic Adventures of Little Red Riding Hood, don't we?"

"You know it!" He kissed her hand. "As for now, what do you say we get some sleep?"

"I say, good night, Honey."

He chuckled. "'Night, Kitten."

Kim dozed off rather quickly, but John looked over at the phone on the nightstand, wondering if it would ring anytime soon with the news he expected.

He didn't have to wait very long.

* * *

395

No longer would Kim have to worry about reliving in the courtroom the nightmare of her captivity in the hands of Walter Daniels.

She came back to the present when John embraced her from behind and kissed her neck after having draped the comforter over her. "You chilly, Kitten? I saw you shiver."

She leaned back and returned the kiss. "I don't think it's possible that I could be chilly right now," she replied as she settled back against him and looked out into the night. "Apparently, someone was watching out for us again. It's weird how Daniels just dropped dead, but I'm sure it goes without saying that I'm not the least bit sorry he's gone."

John nodded. "Neither am I."

"So, for the next month, all we need to focus on is each other." She guided his hands down to her hips. "Baby, I have to admit, I really underestimated you before. I never thought you'd be so-…well, so adventurous, not to mention assertive! I wondered if what we did at the pool party was a one-night-only sort of thing, but I think it's safe to say we picked right up where we left off, and then some! You had me to where it felt like all you'd have to do to send me over the edge was look at me…"

"How can you ever know what you like unless you're willing to experiment a little? Of course, a big part of why I was right up there with you was because it was obvious how much into it you were. Still, these fantasies are just one ingredient for us.

"You know, it's totally clear now, even more so than a few months back when we really came together. When a couple has what we have, everything else is just another log on the fire."

"You're right." She looked out over their backyard, their small pier and the water, enjoying the feeling of serenity that, until just a couple nights ago, she was certain would not come for her in this house. It seemed so long ago when she'd seen that horrible vision- the one she felt confident she never would see again.

*If for whatever reason you do come back, I'm even more confident that I'll be ready for you- we'll be ready for you…*

It wasn't long at all, however, before her advanced state of fatigue reasserted itself. She yawned and looked up at John. "Now I'm *really* tired. Since you and I enjoy so much when you do it, how about a lift?"

"But of course." He picked her up and carried her over to bed, lay her down and joined her. After they kissed good night, he reached over and unplugged the phone.

Kim slept like a baby for the rest of the night.

So did John.


They pulled right up to the plane, which was fully fueled and ready to go.

Other than a minimal amount of ground personnel who were elsewhere, the airfield was deserted. Since midnight was less than an hour away, that was no surprise.

Best of all, there would be no co-pilot on this flight.

After a quick scan of the area to confirm they weren't under observation, Phil gave Josh a hand with their beautiful and scantily clad cargo, who was securely bound, gagged and hooded as well. She knew where they were and what was happening and fought them hard every step of the way. She cried out repeatedly, desperately.

No one heard or even saw her. The men got the very athletic and feisty- although quite helpless- Vanessa into the plane quickly and dropped her onto a seat in the passenger compartment of the Learjet.

Given his leg wound, which had hindered him a lot, Josh was glad the hard work was over. He strapped her down so she'd be ready for takeoff. He'd considered killing her, but decided to wait and see what happened. She'd already demonstrated that having her could compensate in one way for all he'd lost, in large part because of her, although she wasn't his first choice...

...or his second. As he envisioned the one he wished he had with him besides Kim, bound the same way Vanessa was, he wondered if she would have struggled at all...

On the bright side, Phil wouldn't spill the beans, especially given the airfare he would receive and the extra incentive he'd enjoyed that he wouldn't have had.

He took the seat next to Vanessa and turned on the TV while Phil got their bags. *Might as well get a last look at the news before we take off,* he thought as he tuned to his usual channel on the satellite system. The international segment was just ending.

No sooner did the anchor start on the national part than Josh saw a clip of John helping Kim out of the van that morning.

397

Now, it hurt to see her in that Tigress uniform. He longed even more to somehow relive the happiest period in his life, when he saw her in it, smiling as she walked over to him on New Years' '89. *As much as I'd love to have that again, I guess he's right. I might have to cut my losses and accept that that probably won't happen with Kim.* He'd failed with his last and most promising attempt.

It pained him even more now to see her kissing John the way she was…again.

Then, he heard those reviled words.

"…at the same conference, Governor Stratton also announced that he and Miss Francis are engaged, although they haven't set their wedding date as of yet."

He tuned out at that point. A saber had run him through; he felt the cold, hard steel, just as though it really was buried to its hilt in his chest.

He was about to turn the TV off when his ears pricked up at the follow-up the anchor gave to that story.

"…that Walter Daniels, who was to be tried in early September on multiple felony charges stemming from his alleged acts against Governor and the future Mrs. Stratton, died earlier tonight in his holding cell in Baltimore. The cause is unknown and is the subject of investigation by local authorities.

"In other news-"

Josh turned the set off.

"I'll be damned…"

*It went through- the transaction went through!*

*Daniels was healthy; there's no way he just drops dead.*

Josh was certain that the death warrant on Daniels that he'd initiated, which was to be executed by Stan Jeffries- the guard at the lockup- had been served.

But Josh had been without his computer since early morning. If the police had gotten it right away, surely they would have frozen the accounts and the deal would never have gone through. Apparently, that was not the case.

Did John still have the computer? Did he see the transaction? Did he know?

*If he did…*

There was no way for Josh to tell right now, but who had better motive than John to want Daniels dead? That transaction would have given him the means and opportunity to make that happen and he wouldn't have had to lift a finger.

A big smile broke out on his face.

*He knew about it- there's no doubt in my mind...*

*...you have to love the irony...*

"We're all set, partner; strap yourself in. We're short a lifejacket, but our guest here has quite a nice pair of natural flotation devices of her own, so we're covered, anyway."

Josh chuckled, especially when he saw Vanessa bristle. "Just a sec, Phil," he said as a notion came to him. He reached over to her and removed the leather hood. She tried to wrench herself away, but he grabbed a handful of her long, thick black hair and forced her to face him.

A multitude of straps bit deeply into her tanned skin and bound her to the point of reducing her mobility to that of a caterpillar. A wider, thicker strap sealed her mouth and held the large ball inside it that forced her jaws open nearly as wide as they would go.

Every bit of hostility she could muster shot out from her dark, tempestuous eyes.

"I want you to know that this probably is the last time you'll ever see America. I thought you might want to take a final look." He let go of her and she turned away.

"OK, Phil, we're ready. Let's get out of here."

He buckled his seatbelt and lay back.

As the plane lifted off, he looked over and saw a tear in Vanessa's eye as she gazed out the window, now subdued in another way. She lay motionless in the chair, her fight apparently gone- at least for the time being.

Josh smiled and settled in for a nap.


"That was quite a breakfast. You know, I don't think I ever saw you eat so much."

"I have a feeling you know very well why I was so hungry! Anyway, I'm glad you liked it, and that you finally were able to take me up on the rain check you got a few months ago."

Kim moved the tray further down on the bed and was careful not to upset it as she turned onto her side and lay against him. "I think we did it even better this way. In our bed, with this view we'll wake up to every morning…"

"It sure is a sight to behold," he said as he took her in.

She looked up at him and smiled, then got on top of him. "With a lead-in like that I hope you're ready for the second course. I wouldn't mind building up my appetite again."

"Oh, I'm ready, but you might want to think about giving me another rain check."

"Now, just why would I want to do that?"

He ran his hands down along her sides and rested them on her hips. "Well, first of all, we're only talking a matter of hours before I take you up on this one. Secondly, I'll have plenty of opportunity to make up to you for all the lost time- not just over the past couple months, but also over the past seventeen years. In addition to being happier than I've ever been because of the prospect of us being alone, I'm also feeling *extremely* invigorated from that. I think *you're* the one who'd better be prepared!"

"Oooo!! I'll just have to prove to you that I'm totally up for that challenge- and you'd better back it up, or else!"

He laughed heartily. "The gauntlets have been thrown down! And keep in mind that just in case you become too much to handle, I know how to, um, reign you in, shall we say."

"You certainly do, Mister Wolf! So, you'll *finally* tell me where we're going?"

"How does Hawaii grab you?"

Kim gasped. "Oh, John, I've always wanted to go there! This is awesome! For the whole month?!" When he nodded, she hugged him and planted another big kiss on him. "I can't wait! I'll call Mom first and ask her if she'll keep my kittens for a while longer. She loves them, anyway; I'm sure she won't mind."

"Tell her we'll stop by on our way to the airport. I want to see all the family before we go. I figured you would, too."

"Yes, definitely! I guess we'd better get packing, then. There's so much I'll need to bring…"


Josh had to stop looking at the picture. Her youth and purity were getting to him and making him feel it again. Now wasn't the time for that, so finally he had to look away.

He'd done it- he'd left the country without incident. At least this part of his plan had gone smoothly; they almost were safe. He winced as he got another reminder of the part of the plan that had not gone smoothly, to say the least. He touched the bandaged wound on his thigh, glad that at least the bullet from the revolver Kim had used on him had gone clean through; it didn't hit bone, either. He'd disinfected the wound at the points of entry and exit while at Phil's place, so chances were it would heal without complication.

In one way he'd been able to channel his fury away from what the injury represented. That had helped considerably in passing the time of the flight, but it hadn't tamed Vanessa at all; she had plenty of fight left. She was facing away from him and nude- almost. He'd re-tied her legs after she landed a kick too close to his groin, then he kept going with the straps. When he finished, she was tied into a ball and couldn't budge.

His anger came back yet again when he stood up to go to the bathroom and the pain shot through his leg, as it did whenever he moved. The last thing he needed was another memento of Kim's victory, which that bullet wound would be for some time.

Even more infuriating was the fact that he'd titled the house he'd bought from John- in cash- in Kim's name, largely as a joke. At the time, what were the chances that she ever would own anything again? It was a nice way to rub it in- so he thought.

His joke didn't merely backfire: it blew up in his face like an ink bomb planted in a briefcase of ransom money. Like that ink, the effects of the reversal would take an awfully long time and lots of effort to wash away. He'd never felt so stupid in his life.

*Have a nice honeymoon, John and Kimberly Stratton. Enjoy it while it lasts and enjoy the fucking half a million dollar wedding present I ended up giving you. I can't believe I might have to let you get away with that and everything else, although it is the smart play. I have been lucky, even when I nearly was caught. I still managed to get away.*

*Maybe I should just fade into the background...*

*...all things considered, though, it sure would be nice to see you again,* he thought, gazing at the picture once more.


"There you go with that smile again! You're driving me *crazy*! Why are you being so mysterious?! I know you have something up your sleeve and you'd *better* tell me what it is!"

"If you'll exercise the slightest iota of patience, I'll *show* you what it is. We're making a stopover very soon. In fact, we might be there now." He checked with the pilot, who confirmed it. "Indeed we are. Get ready to land, Honey."

"Where are we?"

John pointed out the window as the plane banked into a turn for its approach.

Kim looked down over the desert and saw the city that had sprouted out of it. She'd seen the familiar features over a decade ago when she'd come out here to perform. There was no mistaking the casinos and hotels of Las Vegas, where that big billboard image of her as she posed with the tiger had ended up.

As she wondered if that billboard still was displayed so prominently over the famous strip, realization of why they were stopping here took hold. "Oh my God- we're eloping?!" John smiled in response and she practically jumped into his lap. "Baby, this is so romantic! It's exactly what my grandparents did-...you remembered that, didn't you?" Still smiling, he nodded, prompting her to show her appreciation with a kiss that made his head spin, until she thought of what they'd discussed the day before.

"What's wrong, Kitten?"

"Well...I thought we were going to-"

He knew what she was thinking about and headed her off, wanting to dispel even the slightest worry she had. "We're going to do both. I don't want to wait another minute longer than I already have for us to be married, and what better place than Vegas to make that happen? While you were packing, I found your birth certificate and tucked it away with mine to bring along. This won't be the only time we say 'I do', though; I want to keep this one secret- just for us- and then we'll have the full-blown ceremony later, sometime after we get back. What do you think?"

Her smile was just as radiant as it was when he proposed to her. "It's perfect; I couldn't have planned it better. Actually, if you haven't picked out a chapel here, I know of this quaint and adorable place that will do just fine. I'm pretty sure it's still around. It's a little off the beaten path, too, so we should have plenty of privacy."

"Good, I was hoping you might know of a place that would work for us. I like the sound of that one; we'll check it out."

She embraced him as the plane touched down. "If the chapel *is* still around, its element of privacy will help with my next surprise for you, which just came to me..."

"Would you spare a little hint?"

Kim gave him a mysterious smile of her own. "Let's just say, it's a way to cut out the middleman and it has to do with what I'll wear. You'll see what it is just before we say 'I do'. I think you'll find it fitting, given where we are and who you're marrying."

Eight hours later, in a quaint little chapel off the beaten path, John was treated to Kim's version of a wedding ensemble, which was her surprise for him.

*And what a surprise it is. No wonder they called you Aphrodite...*

At that point he also understood why, according to their bodyguards, she'd insisted upon waiting until she got to the chapel to change into that ensemble, and why she made extra sure that their ceremony would be a private one.

He understood as well why she needed help with her outfit.

Now, he couldn't wait to help her out of it...

Vanessa was right again when she said Kim was the sexiest, most beautiful bride there could ever be- not that he wouldn't have known that anyway. What she was wearing, which was almost exactly what Vanessa described, added further emphasis to that statement.

Better still, she would be *his* bride in a matter of minutes.

All John could do was smile as she made her way toward him- those killer heels she wore ensured her slowed but steady pace- and it seemed that all she could do was blush.

With Kim's help, his plan had turned out even better than he'd hoped it would. For both of them, it really was perfect.

*Who says traditional is the way to go?*

## September 1

"…We now turn our focus to the bizarre and frightening story of the alleged criminal activities of Joshua Strauss, which from all indications will remain an ongoing story- at least for now. State Police in Virginia surmise that after surviving the shootout and freeing himself, he took Vanessa Chamberlain with him, flagged down Roanoke resident Richard Mason, then later killed the young man and took his car. The car was found abandoned six days later. There are no clues whatsoever as to where Strauss could be now and it is quite possible that he's fled the country, according to the FBI. Miss Chamberlain, who, according to Baltimore Homicide Lieutenant Thomas Stratton, was driving the van, remains unaccounted for.

"As many of you viewers probably know by now, Lieutenant Stratton risked his own life to stop the van from reaching Interstate 81 during the deadly high-speed pursuit that could have cost even more lives. As many of you also know, had it not been for the courageous exploits of Miss Kimberly Francis, Strauss might never have been uprooted from his Pennsylvania dwelling where he held a dozen women captive for a decade. Actually, I have to make a correction; Miss Francis has changed her surname to that of her birth father, who was killed in the Vietnam War. Now she goes by Kimberly Russell, but in the near future she will change her surname yet again; after all, she's engaged to be married to Lieutenant Stratton's younger brother John, who is one of the subjects of our next story.

"On the political front, we're hot and heavy into the primary elections. The presidential frontrunners are campaigning in their key states. So far, both have been dismissive of Governor Stratton's very provocative comment that both major party candidates 'didn't have the guts between them' to debate him on the challenges facing our nation and what needs to be done to handle them. They seem to be equally as dismissive of the Governor as a serious candidate, but interestingly enough, both candidates danced around the question as to whether or not they would agree to debate the man. Governor Stratton has scheduled a press conference for later this afternoon, during which he will lay out the fundamentals of his plan to attack the many problems we face. This morning he had a routine checkup with his doctor, who gave him a clean bill of health.

"The Governor and his lovely fiancée have been back from their getaway for a little over a week. We still have no comment from either of them as to the nature of their mysterious one-day stopover in Las Vegas other than their repetitive claim that it was for a slight mechanical problem and refueling. Some speculation persists that they might be married already, although no witnesses to that effect have come forth and no pictures have emerged. If they *were* married, they pulled a fast one on all of us!

"But apparently, they weren't able to escape the paparazzi entirely. Lately, Miss Russell seems to be their most wanted. Many scandal sheets and adult magazines are offering substantial sums of money for topless or nude photographs of her. Apparently they have yet to find any, which given her background as a dancer seems to have befuddled the industry. The closest they've come so far were a score of recent photos of the very well-built, bikini-clad Miss Russell taken while she and the Governor frolicked in the ocean during their time away.

"Also, let's not forget the footage of her in that Tigress costume, which is what she was wearing in the most famous shot of her we know of- that being the billboard-size blowup of her lying right in front of a full-grown male tiger. That was used to promote the Kitty Cat Club in Atlantic City, where she worked. After the club closed in '92, the billboard ended up in Las Vegas to help promote a show. It's been there ever since and has become something of a landmark.

"Numerous shots of her have surfaced from her cheerleading days and also from the many bikini contests she won, including the one in Ocean City only weeks ago from which she was abducted, and also when she became Miss Celestial in 1990. There's rumored to be another highly sought-after photo from Halloween of '86 of Miss Russell wearing only lingerie and dancing on a bar at the original Hammerjack's, a Baltimore landmark that closed in 1995. That one has not been produced as of yet. Back to you, Hal."

"Thanks for that piece, Connie. I have to say that I find it funny how some reporters have blasted the woman for what she did in the past, which, from all accounts of those who saw her dance, is rather tame when compared to what we see today in the music scene. You don't hear such uproar from them about some of these so-called pop stars that wear almost nothing and gyrate around onstage.

"There's no question what they're selling, although they'll tell you it's music- that is, if you can call the crap they spew out 'music'. Sure, we believe that's all you're selling! I've said it before and I'll say it again: good music will sell itself, just like any product of high quality will. If you need to be naked on stage to help it sell, then you need to get into another occupation- and don't tell us you're selling music. Not all of us were born yesterday.

"At least Miss Fr- Miss Russell, I mean- took responsibility for what she did. She acknowledged that it was a decision she made of her own volition and she doesn't try to pass it off for anything other than what it was. You might not agree with what she did- personally, *I* don't condone it- but you have to respect her candor. Furthermore, as the father of two young daughters, I appreciate her statements that went toward dissuading other young women from dancing.

"When we return, we'll take a look at other stories around the nation, including the determination that Walter Daniels' death did not come about as a result of foul play..."

"What took you so long in there, Kim? You feeling OK?"

She sat with John on the couch after returning from the bathroom. "I'm fine- just a little girl stuff." Although it wasn't a lie, she didn't tell him everything, namely her disappointment at the negative result of the test she'd given herself.

*Those tests aren't always right, though, and it's only been a month-and-a-half. I need to give it more time...*

"Are you ready for your speech?" she asked as she glanced at his notes.

"Just about. All I need to do is finalize my cue cards."

"Need any help?"

"Nah- I'm fine. How are you ladies coming along with the feast? It smells terrific! I expect to see people coming from miles away wondering what you all are cooking."

John and Kim had been spending a lot of time with their families since their return from Hawaii. Today they were at Leslie's place where a big dinner was in the works in celebration of John's kickoff speech as well as his and Kim's engagement. It also served as a late birthday party for Kim, and her grandparents had flown in from New York for the event.

"We're doing very well with it. Everything should be ready by the time you finish with your conference."

"Excellent- I can't wait to dig in. So, are you getting used to your new last name?"

"Definitely. The less I'm reminded of-...you know, he doesn't even deserve to be called my stepfather, so I won't bother. In fact, I don't want to risk spoiling my great mood by thinking about him to any degree. I like my true last name much better, especially since I really am a Russell. Oh, speaking of which, another Russell is waiting for me in the kitchen. Grandmom wanted to show me something- one of her recipes, I think, so I'm going to get back in there, OK?"

She went to get up, but quickly found herself in John's lap.

He'd furtively glanced around and saw that the coast was clear, then pulled her down and kissed her. "I wanted to take advantage of this rare moment we seem to have to ourselves," he whispered before he went to the well again.

"Uh-huh, I should have known. I was wondering where you'd sneaked off to, Kim," Tom said rather loudly as he walked in on them. Kim sprang to her feet and some of John's cards went flying. "Damn, I don't think I've seen stop signs as red as your faces!"

John picked up one of the family dog's toys and threw it at him as all three laughed.

"I'm glad I found both of you together, anyway. I got some good news a few minutes ago. I've already told everyone else."

"I wondered what that commotion outside was about. What did you-...you were promoted, weren't you?"

Tom grinned at him and nodded. "Effective October 1$^{st}$. I'll be a Captain in the State Police."

"The *State* police? No kidding- how did that come about?"

"I think it's a case of timing more than anything. The right opportunity came up, and I made more contacts with the State guys when a couple department heads and I put together the multi-state task force to try to find Jenny, the other women, and you, Kim. Seems they liked the way I was able to coordinate and run things. The end result of my Wild West shootout with Rollins also impressed them. Based on those factors and my track record, I'm taking charge of their Missing Persons Division in a few months."

John went over and embraced him. "That's great news, Brother. You deserve it."

Kim hugged him as well and kissed his cheek. "Congratulations, Tom; I'm so happy for you. Now we have another reason to celebrate."

"Thanks, you two. It feels pretty damned good to get that second silver bar. I also wanted to double-check what time you're taking off for your conference, John."

He looked at his watch. "Wow- speaking of time, it sure has flown. I'll need to leave in half an hour."

"Do you need to be alone, Honey?"

"That might help. I should concentrate and collect my thoughts." He gave Kim another little peck. "I'll be out when it's time to go, OK?"

She nodded. "We'll see you in a bit."

"Catch you outside, John. Come on, Kim, let's rejoin the others."

They walked out and left him to his preparations.


Tom took hold of Kim's hand and gestured toward the basement door.

She looked up at him questioningly and he quickly turned away and headed down the steps. Kim didn't like what she saw in his eyes; it was a look she'd seen in them once before.

She pulled the door closed and followed him.

Once they were in the room Tom checked all around it to make sure they were alone. This was not a conversation he wanted anyone to overhear. Satisfied no one else was down there, he went back over to Kim.

"You're thinking about Vanessa."

She was right on it. *Christ, you're perceptive,* Tom thought, taken aback momentarily. He nodded and looked away. "Just my glimpses of her brought it all back."

His turmoil was painfully clear to her. She moved over to him and embraced him.

"It's been hell. Thinking about what that fucking cancer among humanity's probably been putting her through...killing her isn't his style, is it? You know that better than anyone."

"Unfortunately I do." She pulled back and looked him in the eyes. "Does John know about that night?"

"He knows I went up to Philly and saw you dance, and also that we went back to your place and that I ended up putting you to bed. I couldn't tell him or Donna about-...Vanessa and me."

Kim nodded.

"He suspects something, though. You know what the worst part about this has been? Keeping all of it inside and not being able to tell a soul, until now. You were there- you saw us, but even then you didn't judge either of us. You listened and you understood what had happened; you understood that it was the heat of the moment."

"Tom, don't do that." He tried to turn away but she wouldn't let him. "I can see how much you need to talk about this and I'll help you deal with it any way I can, but do not lie to me. You know it was more to both of you than just a moment. Vanessa knew that, too. It was something that couldn't happen, but did happen. You and she saw something in each other and you couldn't stop yourselves from acting on it, although you both were strong enough to not allow it to happen again. You can't always put the brakes on, though, especially when the spark is there.

"And, yes, I do know how much bearing a secret like that for so long can hurt you."

The way Kim laid it out was the way it had happened-almost.

However, something else he'd seen that night was what put him in the mood that made him vulnerable to such a thing happening. That was something Kim never would know.

"You're right. I'm sorry, Kim- you know I didn't mean to insult your intelligence. I-"

"You don't need to explain. I don't think any less of you and you shouldn't think any less of yourself. You're a good man. You always were; it's natural for you. I love how you are with Donna and your children. You're right where you should be- that much is perfectly clear to me. Vanessa also knew that you belong with your family, which is why she never tried to contact you. You've never done anything like that since, have you?"

"No. I never was with another woman and I've never wanted to be with another woman afterwards. Things are great between Donna and me, and our children."

Kim stepped back. "I think you should keep your situation as it is. I want you to think about this, too: telling Donna would be a selfish thing to do. While that might alleviate your guilt and make you feel better, both would come at her expense. Think about how she and your children would suffer because of that knowledge. We're not talking about an ongoing affair, anyway. It was one time."

"It would hurt her. A lot..."

"This is your decision, of course. Keep in mind that in the eleven years since that happened, you've done all the right things, and I don't believe you only did them because you felt guilty. I can say that on good authority, because I was in something of a similar situation when I had to resign from being a counselor. What you do with the opportunity you're given really does matter, as John tried to explain to me. I'm finally starting to take that into account, although it still hurts when I think about how things turned out..."

"As for you, I don't want you to do something that might end your marriage. You're with your family because you want to be with them."

"Absolutely." He hesitated, then asked, "I'm curious: why did you resign?"

She looked away for a moment. "It was a fight that would have caused more harm than any good that could have come from it. I also think it simply was time for me to move on to the next phase in my life. I want to be a mother; I've wanted that for a very long time and I know I'm ready for it now. Don't get me wrong, it still was very difficult to walk away from what I loved to do. It's just time for me to do it on a smaller and more personal scale."

He nodded. "I can't wait to be an uncle again. You'll be a great mother, Kim."

"I'll do my best; that is a promise."

Immediately after saying that, her thoughts drifted back to the pregnancy test she'd given herself earlier and her concern about the negative result. She contemplated sharing that concern with Tom, but the nature of the subject made her a bit skittish.

*Maybe I'm just being silly with this...*

"Kim? What is it?" Tom noted her prolonged silence after her smile faded. Obviously, there was something on her mind.

She contemplated a bit longer. *I need to tell someone and Tom's a good choice. He's a father, and he's my brother-in-law now.*

*He always was a good listener, too...*

Gradually, she relented. "Well, we've..." she knew she was blushing as she went on. She even glanced around a couple times and lowered her voice despite her knowledge that they were alone.

"John and I have been going at it like rabbits for over a month- two or three times each day is our average- and we never use any birth control. Plus, we were together several times back in April during what I know was the right time in my cycle. I'd have thought I'd-...I'd be pregnant by now."

"Well, I'm not sure about what might have happened in April, but as for your recent activity, I wouldn't sweat that just yet. In fact, you might have been using a natural form of birth control without even knowing it."

"Really? How?"

"It took Donna and me several months before she became pregnant with Jess. We didn't know why; we were twenty-four and having a lot of sex, like you two are now, in part because we were trying for a baby. We figured the more we did it, the better our chances. As it turned out, we were doing it too much. My sperm count got pretty low and I wasn't allowing it to replenish itself, which might be the situation with John.

"For now, enjoy yourselves and don't worry about it. When you slow down a bit, I'm sure it'll happen for you. It's good to hear my brother's making the best use of the time you two have together, anyway." He winked at her and laughed as she blushed again.

"In all seriousness, I know I've said this before, but I'll say it again: I'm glad you two are together. Sometimes when you look at a couple and see how they are with each other...sometimes you just know. I couldn't picture you or John with anyone else. I have a feeling he's really going to need you over the next couple months. This run will be a lot tougher on him than he thinks, and I hope he really is all right. I can't believe he's doing this without a campaign manager."

"I know. That's the other reason why I resigned. He believes so strongly in what he's about to do, though, which is why I'm not *too* worried. I don't think Doctor Reynolds would

411

fudge on John's examination, so I'm glad he had it done but I'll still be watching him very closely. I want to help him manage his campaign somehow, too."

"I bet he'll be happy about that. I have no doubt you'll be more of an asset to him during this campaign than anyone realizes."

"That's my hope. So, do you think you'll tell her?"

Tom's eyes went out of focus as he thought. "I don't know. I'll say this: you've made a very good case for me not to. I never looked at it like that."

"There's a lot to consider; it's a tough situation. For what it's worth, I have a feeling you've done plenty of penance already."

"It sure feels that way. I'd say you've done your share of that, too." He took her into his arms. "Thanks, Little Sister. You've helped more than you know."

"I'm glad I could, and...it feels great to finally have a brother. However, you'd better watch it with the 'little' remarks! I get enough of those as things are, since everyone I know is taller than I am!"

"Fair enough," Tom replied as he laughed. "I guess we needed to lighten things up a bit, didn't we? Hey, we'd better get upstairs. It's probably about that time..."


"What do you think it means?"

Kim looked at the very cryptic note he showed her as they rode along in the limo toward the location for John's speech. "'Like father, like son?' Who could be behind this?"

"Well, some anonymous caller contacted the receptionist at the Mansion and gave her that message for me. Unless this is a prank, I only know of one person who could be behind it, especially given the turn our conversation took on the Ridge."

"Josh..."

"Yeah. He knows how stuff like that can get to me, so it's entirely within character for him to try and get under my skin this way. He also made some really weird remarks about his parents, but that could have been because he was frazzled...well, whatever the case, I won't let him get to me. They're trying to trace the call, but they don't have anything yet.

412

"Ok, enough about that. Did you hear about Jenny? She won the bikini contest in Ocean City last weekend and she'll be competing in their big end-of-summer pageant. Speaking of which, have they finally stopped calling you and asking if you'd be competing, too?"

Kim smiled. "Yes, I think they got the message, although it sure took them a while! This much is for certain; I won't be Maryland's representative in Miss Celestial 2000. That part of my life is over, which, as you know, is how I want it. I walked away from my last hurrah with a really sexy bikini, though, which I put to good use in Hawaii."

"That you did, although I must take issue with one thing you just said."

"Oh, really? And just what is it that you must take issue with, pray tell?"

"Your bikini's only sexy when you're wearing it." He eagerly accepted the kiss that remark earned him. "I bet those other girls competing in the pageant are glad they won't have to go against you; Jenny said so, too. That'll be great if she goes all the way. Talk about coming out of your shell…"

"You can say that again! I talked with her earlier today and she told me all about it. She apologized for not being able to make the party- apparently that contest is taking place this afternoon, so she has to prepare herself for it. I'm glad her friends are with her…

"You know, it's a little scary, in a way. That first night when Josh had us both, he put me into the van and then brought her outside, and-…John, I couldn't believe how much she looked like a 5'6" version of me ten years ago- and not just physically. Now that she's doing the bikini circuit and cheering for the same football team…it just feels weird- like I'm in a time machine or something. I'm glad she's doing well, though. This might be good for her, as long as she doesn't let it carry her in the wrong direction. It's very easy for that to happen."

"You've seen your share of examples, haven't you?"

"More of them than I'd hoped to; even one would have been too many. Really, when you think about it, I could have ended up as a statistic very easily if I'd fallen in with the wrong sort from the beginning- aside from Josh. I want Jenny to keep me in the know about what goes on in her life. She's stepping into a very unfamiliar realm that will chew her up and spit her out if she's not careful."

"I have a feeling she'll be careful, especially considering the fact that she already got a taste of what could happen if she gets mixed up with one of the undesirables. Speaking of him, I do want to ask you one more thing. Has Jenny talked with you at all about what he did to her, if anything? I know she told the other counselors that nothing happened and the physician confirmed she wasn't raped, but…it's hard for me to imagine that he had her for three weeks, yet he left her alone for the most part. It just doesn't jibe."

"I agree. It seems there's something she's not telling me, but if there is, I can't get it out of her. Or maybe I'm seeing something that's not there…I don't know. I also find it hard to believe that he didn't do anything more to her than abduct her and hold her against her will, but maybe he didn't. For the most part, she seems unscathed. He did seem to go comparatively easy on her. I suppose it helped that he was more focused on me, not to mention a lot more cruel, but it's better he was that way with me rather than with Jenny…"

"Sounds like you looked out for her in more ways than one; I know she appreciates that." He looked out the window when the limo stopped. "Well, here we are, Kitten. Are you ready?"

She took a deep breath. "I think so. The question is, are you?"

His initial response was to pull her against him and kiss her. "I am," he then answered verbally as Herb opened the door for them.

"Let's go see if America is ready for me."

# Epilogue

*November 9, 2000*

"We're back with John K. Stratton, former Governor of Maryland, who came up short in this election. He took the ten electoral votes of his home state, where he won overwhelmingly. Although he made strong showings in a number of states, Maryland was his only victory. Sir, it's been said by many that one reason why you lost was that you were overly combative toward the other candidates. What is your response?"

"Well, if they'd done the brave thing and debated me, maybe I wouldn't have been so blunt, shall we say? I'm sure they knew their stale agendas couldn't measure up. I stand by what I said, Daryn- all of it. My problem is more with what they represent than with them, but if they choose to continue to defend an unfair, corrupt and dysfunctional system, I must- and will- attack them for that.

"Neither of the other candidates has a clear vision for the present of our nation, let alone the future of it. The same can be said about the parties themselves- they have as little real direction and purpose as their candidates. All they're about is raising money and throwing it every which way in order to deceive or lie outright to enough voters in order to win the election. I'm here to tell you their days are numbered. I think the people realize deep down that the democrats and the republicans will accomplish nothing. You'll see four more years of the same old crap, same old rhetoric, same old bickering between the parties, resulting in nothing substantial being accomplished. Things are bad and they're going to get worse."

"That doesn't sound like a concession speech."

"Oh, it isn't, and it's not meant to be. I have nothing *to* concede. On the contrary, this was a great victory; we're on the map now. We've more than doubled the best showing ever by an Independent candidate and I have no doubt that we'll do even better next time. Add to that the fact that whoever those parties put their money behind in the next election will have no choice but to debate me- they won't be able to hide behind the rules and scurry away.

"Something significant happened with this vote; a lot of Americans realized that they have a viable alternative to politics as usual. I'm very excited about our prospects for future elections- not just for the presidency, either. Mark my words, when the time comes for the next election, you will see the largest turnout of eligible voters that we've had in decades- possibly the largest ever! I strongly encourage interested citizens who share my views and who would like to run for office to get out there and do it! Your fellow Americans need you; your children and their children need you. Let's get these perpetuators of the status quo out of office and let's do what needs to be done for our country."

"I take it that means you'll be back in 2004?"

"You'd better believe it!"

"Already we're hearing from quite a few democrats, who say you cost their candidate the presidency. How do you feel about that?"

John's first response was to laugh. He then added, "I'm sure they'll be crying for months. Look, all their candidate had to do was win his home state. If he'd managed that he'd have become the next President. Many would say- and I would agree- that if you can't even win your own home state, you don't deserve to be President. Walter Mondale lost big when he ran in '84, but he won his own state. Hell, I won mine and I'm an Independent!

"I have to say that I'm pretty ticked off at some of the democrats who, as far as I'm concerned, have betrayed the spirit of their party's name Many democratic members of Congress, much of the party hierarchy and a number of their wealthy contributors and most vocal supporters expressed their desire in lots of ways for me to drop out of the race because they were afraid I might cost them victory. What does that say about them? For one thing, they couldn't have had much confidence in their guy from the start. Also, if they truly believe in democracy, that's the very last thing they should have wanted- to try to persuade someone not to run for office. I find such people very un-democratic, to put it lightly.

"All that aside, what really cost the democrats victory was an outmoded and unnecessary system called the electoral college. Simply put, we don't need it anymore. It's one thing that perpetuates the two-party system, which we also need to do away

416

with. The popular vote is sufficient; if it alone determined the victor, the democrat would have beaten the republican 40% to 38%. Or, they could have had a run-off election between the top two vote-getters, which I can't imagine anyone would have had a problem with. Think about it: the President-elect only took *38%* of the vote!"

"Interesting point! Well, thank you for your time, Mister Governor, and best of luck to you. That'll do it-"

John clicked the TV off, then leaned back, relaxed and enjoyed.

"Have you ever seen anything so beautiful?"

Kim put her question, rhetorical for the most part, to him as they sat together in front of the large window that overlooked the water. They watched as the very early snow fell over the Bay; this bit of weather had caught everyone by surprise.

Better yet, it was laying- it wouldn't take too much more of it to cover the ground completely.

It really was amazing what time- and another reversal of fortune- could do. The feeling of peace John had told her about that had convinced him initially to buy this house was making its soothing presence known to her. It was the first time since she was fourteen and living with Diane that she felt this way.

She truly was home.

"Actually, I have," he replied as he nuzzled her.

Smiling, she turned a little so they could kiss. She hadn't asked him yet, wanting to give him the remainder of the previous day and the bulk of this one to let it all sink in. Now, however, she couldn't hold the question back any longer. "How are you?"

After a long moment, his answer was a simple one. "Relieved."

She kissed him again and she could see- and feel- his state of tranquility, although she hoped he wasn't trying to hide something else. "So am I. I think it's good in some ways that things turned out like they did. I know you must be disappointed, but even though you came up short in the election, you gave it your best and you made quite a showing. You have so much to be proud of in that."

"I know, Kitten, and I am."

"I mean, 2004 isn't so far off, and-"

He silenced her with another kiss. "If you're still feeling guilty in any way because of this notion that you hurt my chances at winning, don't. Above all, it's certainly not your fault that the pirated video footage of Josh's live feed of you tied to his bed is all over the place. We'll find the scumbags responsible for that, and they'll be damned sorry when we do. I'm sure you know as well as I do who's behind it ultimately, but I also have a feeling he has help."

Kim felt him tense up as soon as he mentioned that name, which didn't surprise her. *If Josh is what's making you so angry from time to time, I certainly can understand that.* "Just when I thought that part of the past would start to fade into the background...I can't believe how so many people seem to have a copy of that! Everyone knows that was made against my will, to say the least. The tabloids and paparazzi haven't helped with their rewards for pictures of me, and I wish everyone else would stop harping on it so much and let it go. It won't go away if so many keep talking about it.

"It burns me up that someone could be so unconscionable and vicious, and then profit from it. Even worse, by all accounts, we're talking about a *lot* of money, which will keep going into that vermin's pockets the longer it's in the news and these damned perverts keep buying it. They're just as bad as the maker and sellers.

"The only good thing is, I wasn't nude...well, no, I can't say that's the only good thing. So many people have been so sympathetic and kind, including the other candidates and their wives. They really helped in taking some of the edge off."

"That's true, and most also have the sense not to bring it up at all while in your company, since they know if the shoe was on the other foot, they wouldn't want it brought up to them. Of course, there have been exceptions, like the stupid reporter yesterday who asked how you felt about being named the sexiest woman on the internet..."

"I know. I couldn't believe it myself, especially since it was a female reporter! You'd think she'd have some sensitivity, or that she'd know better than to ask that! With some stations, it makes you wonder if they send their least intelligent people out to do interviews."

"That wouldn't surprise me," John said amid his laughter, which helped lighten Kim up as well. He touched her chin and turned her face up to his. "I want you to understand something, Honey. In every aspect, you've helped me more than I can put into words- and I'm not just talking about with the election. Also remember that nobody with any sense sees you as a villainess or a hindrance- least of all, me. Don't worry about that- just put it out of your mind. In fact, now we can concentrate completely on each other, just like we did a few months ago, and also give some thought to what we're going to do in between elections."

"Our main focus should be keeping you and your platform fresh in everyone's mind. Talk shows, editorials, appearances and the like- we'll need to keep you in circulation."

"You mean, 'us'. Don't forget that you're part of this, too."

"Right. The Governor and Miss Damsel in Distress 2000."

He glanced down and noticed she was smiling. "Don't you mean *Mrs.* Damsel in Distress?" She giggled and tried to push him away when he tickled her momentarily. "That day isn't too far off and the rest of the world remains blissfully ignorant of what we did out there in Vegas. Most bought off on our 'mechanical difficulties' story. Then again, given the looks we get from our families when that comes up, chances are they probably know. It'll be a great ceremony, though, and I bet everyone there will have a blast."

"No doubt about that; I can't wait! I still love that we both came up with the first day of spring as our date. As nice as it would have been to be married in the White House, I have to admit- I like how this unfolded for us as far as our wedding goes."

"In that respect, so do I. There's far less scrutiny this way, although we do have every fashion designer in the world wanting to make your gown. You really have 'em working! How many will you be trying on this week?"

"Four so far, although that's probably subject to change."

"Well, they sure won't top the one you came up with when we eloped."

Her little grin materialized. "I knew you'd love that ensemble, but that was one moment when it would have been nice if we'd had a woman on our security detail to help me with it. Speaking of which, I guess we'll be losing them soon, won't we?"

"Most of 'em, yes. I'm sorry. I wish-"

"I know, John. I wish we'd always have them, too, but apparently we won't. I admit, the prospect of being without them scares me, which brings me to my only real concern about the videotape and what it could bring. In that case, publicity is not a good thing at all, and the fallout is something we'll have to deal with. In that vein I really could hurt you in your presidential run because I know you worry about my safety. Things really could get dicey, couldn't they?"

He nodded. "It's four years before the next run. A lot could happen before then. For that reason I've hired Herb to stay on, and Mel, too- he's the guy Herb handpicked out of the rest of the team, and he happened to be looking, anyway. They've recommended two others, including a female martial arts expert. Mainly, I have them to protect you, Kitten. All things considered, I think it's for the best."

"I won't argue, especially since I have even more notoriety than I thought I would. I'm glad they'll be with us. Getting back to Herb, you should have seen his expression when he realized that I needed him to help lace me into my corset. I don't know whose face was redder- his or mine! I kept apologizing while I talked him through how to do it, which isn't exactly in his job description."

"Oh, I'm sure apologies were in order as that had to be a *most* unpleasant task for him," John said in a voice dripping with sarcasm. That earned him an elbow jab to the ribs.

"Smart-ass! I'll have you know Herb is quite the gentleman, which is more than I can say for you sometimes! Anyway, I doubt our families would react too well to seeing me walk down the aisle wearing a corset."

"This is true, and just think about how valuable that picture would be for those bottom-dwellers that call themselves paparazzi...

"On that subject, I'm glad you're able to make some light of that video of you. After we've rooted out the parasite or parasites in question, it'll be forgotten before long, anyway; you know how fickle those people are."

"I know, Baby. It's still pretty fresh right now, but I'll do my best not to let it get to me too much, and we're not going to let it get in your way- I mean, *our* way, either. We're going to build on what you made happen yesterday; we're sure not going to lie dormant for three years for any reason, especially not that."

"You've got that right- in more ways than one," he said as he began to caress her thighs. "And no matter what the doctors say, the stork *will* pay us a visit sometime in the near future. My domestic policy will reflect the adage 'if at first you don't succeed...'"

Kim smiled briefly, then turned away.

He kissed her temple and pulled her closer to him. "It'll be all right, Kitten. I know it will. Don't ask me how I know; I just do."

Even though she was getting better in dealing with it, John knew to tread lightly when it came to this subject. On numerous nights after they'd gotten the doctor's assessment- or lack thereof- from the tests, he'd had to soothe Kim after awakening to find her weeping. No one knew why she couldn't conceive and it was starting to get to her.

The mere thought of her crying induced him to cuddle her and kiss her. Gradually he felt her ease up, which made him feel better. When he looked out the window again, what he saw made him feel better still. "You know, this is the first time I've ever seen snow fall over the water."

"Really? It's my first time, too."

"Good. I'm glad we're seeing it together. I can't think of anywhere else I'd rather be watching it. I also can't imagine anyone else I would rather be watching it with." Still looking into her eyes, he added, "This was a hell of a year for us, wasn't it?"

"It sure was. I'm glad it's almost over."

"I second that. Hopefully, 2001 will be less- shall we say- eventful. In regards to this one, I don't want you to dwell too much on anything- especially the outcome of the election. For the record, I don't believe that crock of shit about winning being the only thing. Frankly, I think that attitude is something we need to steer ourselves away from because, along with greed, I find it to be a corrosive state of mind. You cannot win every time; life doesn't work that way.

"You know what *is* everything? The battle. Or the struggle, the challenge- whatever you choose to call it. It's about finding what you're good at, getting out there and giving your best effort. You do what you believe in- do what you believe is right. It's about legitimately taking your shot and not half-assing, cheating or selling out. So what if you fall short sometimes? Winning and losing are relative, and only temporary. You'll have your moments if you keep at it, try hard enough and believe in yourself. It's all about the way there. The game is always on- it starts when you come into the world and it doesn't end until you leave. I believe that every bit as much now as I did when I first heard it- maybe even more so now..."

Noting her silence, he glanced at her. "What's that smile for?"

"Your father gave you some good advice that day when you, he and Tom were fishing, didn't he?" That statement made her think more about something she'd pondered ever since John had revealed to her all he knew about her father-in-law- in particular, the final words Tom, Sr. said to John before he left their home for the last time...

That made John smile, too. "He sure did...wow- I sounded just like him, didn't I? Maybe he rubbed off on me after all..." He also drifted for a moment as that statement evoked another reaction.

She looked up at him and noticed he was somewhere else. *I really should tell him, even though I'm probably way off base with this...* "John, I, um...speaking of your father, there's something I want to run by you. It might sound totally out there, but-..."

"What is it?"

"Well, for some reason, from time to time I keep coming back to the last words he said to you the night he disappeared. I wonder... do you think he might have been trying to tell you something else? Maybe trying to give you some sort of message when he told you to go back to the fishing spot?"

"As much as he loved being out there, he probably figured it would be a good way for us to bond, and maybe even a way for me to feel closer to him somehow, especially considering the fact that he never came back. Considering all the tension there was between us at that point, I'm sure that's what he meant." He turned to her. "Why do you ask? Do you think he might have been getting at something else?"

"Oh, I don't know. If he was, I can't imagine what it could have been, especially since I wasn't there and I didn't know him. I'm sorry to bring that up, Baby; I just think about it on occasion."

He kissed her and said, "You don't owe me an apology; I can see how it might come across to you as somewhat cryptic...I'm glad you brought it up to me, anyway.

"Back to where I was going with that line of thought, from the get-go in this campaign I agreed with the pundits in one way. A victory for me now was extremely unlikely at best. The changes

422

I want to make are pretty radical and people are leery of making such strides overnight. But, like you said- there is 2004, and the seeds have been planted.

"That's going to be the one, Kitten. People are going to see that the system as is simply will not work; they'll come to realize it needs fixing, and badly. We're going to do some serious traveling- I want to hit as many cities and towns as we can and get the message out in person. There are the '02-'03 congressional and gubernatorial elections to think about, too; maybe we can lay some groundwork by helping to get some like-minded candidates elected to those posts.

"I want everyone to know that this is not a fad or an impulse; I know what needs to be done and I'm going to do it no matter how long it takes. Given the twenty-one percent we took this time, I bet there were plenty more voters out there who were on the fence and leaning in our direction, but weren't quite ready to come over. Four years from now they will be, along with a lot of eligible voters who've been staying home on Election Day for a long time. I'm every bit as sure of that as I am that I love you."

Kim's eyes glistened and they kissed again, then turned back to the view that looked like an oil painting. The darkening sky provided quite a contrast to the pure white of the as-yet undisturbed snow that lay all around their nest, which soon- they hoped- would provide shelter for at least one more. She snuggled against him and sighed as she felt his protective and loving embrace tighten just enough around her. He rested his hand on her abdomen.

"Maybe you'll have the magic touch," she mused as she lay her hand on top of his.

"Maybe," he said with a smile. "Let's see if later tonight I can do something that'll make your tummy grow in a few months."

She giggled and gave him a kiss, then settled back against him once more. For the time being, she decided to forget about her feeling about Tom, Sr.'s last words to John.

*It's probably nothing, anyway. Chances are I'm just being silly, or reading more into that than I should be...*

She glanced over and saw that her rambunctious kittens were curled up together and sound asleep in their basket. She nudged John and pointed them out, and both smiled at the two little black furballs. Apparently they still were exhausted from their earlier play.

After that momentary diversion, John and Kimberly Stratton gazed out into the evening as darkness began to fall with the snow. Enough of the latter had fallen to blanket the area, which the former also would do before long.

They didn't say another word for some time.

They didn't need to.


*You have to love the irony...*

*...who'd have thought you would end up benefiting me so much after all since you cost me so much?*

He was totally engrossed in his now-famous footage of Kim, struggling to no avail for over an hour. It had become a gold mine. At this point in the film clip, Josh watched the image of himself, poised to cut her tiny thong away as the sex goddess squirmed beneath him. He didn't even have to see her expression on the screen to remember it- the expression that clearly showed how humiliated, horrified and enraged she was from what he was about to do to her and her inability to stop him...

...even though she still flowed through his bloodstream, he didn't feel such a strong need for vengeance anymore- not against her, anyway, for what she'd done...

...at least, he didn't feel the need to retaliate against her directly. Soon it would be time to focus on a new target, who along with a couple others and their families- Kim included- would suffer when all came to light...

*My income from the video is some good payback for what she did. It's also good that she never found out anything substantial, but she came damned close- again- because she got to me so much and made me lose control. I really was lucky...*

Suddenly, however, something strange began to happen as he looked at the screen. It was the quite engrossing part of the film after the point where he ran out and conducted the fruitless search for Jennifer. Curiously, he found that the longer he watched Kim straining and writhing in desperation to free herself, the more he saw a face that was hers, yet wasn't...

*Hmmm...*

That line of thought stopped when her demeanor suddenly and drastically changed after she stopped fighting. Kim's face definitely was the one he saw now.

This was the part he hated.

He fast-forwarded past it to the next one. Watching while she manipulated her magnificent, securely restrained body as best she could to maneuver the knife up to her hand also was most entertaining and stimulating, as was her resurgent fear when he came back. However, this part also made him kick himself.

Only after all was said and done did he see that she'd managed to get the knife he'd forgotten about; obviously, she'd put it to good use, too. It was another small detail- this one lost in the moment of panic when Jennifer escaped- that had cost him so much. If not for that lapse, Kim would be his and John would be dead. Now, all he had was this footage.

*Well, it was a little stroke of luck when I forgot to put this in my suitcase with everything else. Otherwise I'd really have been left with nothing,* he thought as he watched her.

*What a woman...*

*...and you keep trying to be respectable. Sure pulled the wool over a lot of peoples' eyes, didn't you?*

*But not mine. I was on to you that first day. This'll remind you again of what you've probably always been and what you always will be, no matter how hard you try to convince all of us otherwise. It'll help keep you in your place, right where you belong...*

All that aside, she truly was a sight to behold...

...and so animated...

*...it's no wonder this footage is selling so much. I won't be surprised if it sets a record. Maybe in that way you'll come to appreciate the rebirth of your celebrity as much as I do.*

It took some effort for him to turn off the tape, which he was sure he'd come back to later. It was the only one of her that he had now, since the suitcase had fallen into John's and Kim's hands. He had to have something to help compensate for his losses in that realm. Vanessa no longer was much of an option- not that she ever really was in the first place. She'd broken quickly.

The tape of Kim gave him little satisfaction in that regard, however. They paled in comparison to the real thing- that which he had and that which was denied him.

He tried not to dwell on those unpleasantries. There were plenty more videos and digital discs to burn from the master copy- lots of customers to satisfy...

*...including me. As close as you, John and your bunch came to getting me, it didn't happen.*

*On the other hand, I can't believe how close I came to spilling everything...*

That thought made him angry with himself for nearly undoing all that had been accomplished over all those years. The timing was far from right- the situation too precarious, although he'd failed to see that. He'd been shaken to his core by that experience- by that loss of control, which had led to a lot more being lost. It was the first time that had ever happened to him- and it would be the last.

*Financially, I'll be back on my feet soon enough. I won't be where I was, of course, but I guess it'll be enough, in terms of money.*

*As for you two and those around you, when I'm set up and ready to get the wheels turning, everything will come crashing down on your heads when what I know comes to light...*

*...and it'll only take one phone call to get that juggernaut rolling.*

It wouldn't be an international call he'd have to make, either.

Unable to stand it any longer than a few months in the Bahamas, where he'd never reached any level of comfort, he'd decided to take the chance and come back. He'd been in country for a couple weeks now, hiding out at Phil's house. From there he was able to make the not too lengthy drive to the place and area he wanted to move back into when the time was right, which, by all indications, might come sooner than he'd thought.

As good as it was to be back in the USA, it would be better still once he was in his old stomping grounds and able to blend in once more, which he was very good at...

"Hi, this is Governor Stratton for Doctor Hughes."

Doctor Henrietta Hughes and her assistant at the FBI lab had conducted the autopsy of Lisa Meyers. Through Tom, John had contacted her when he found out she would be doing it. Even though the cause of her death was obvious, that wasn't what John was interested in. If not for his inquiry, and Tom's as well, nothing more than a cursory examination would have taken place.

Acting on the likelihood that Lisa and Josh had had sex sometime during the last couple days before she was killed, John and Tom figured it also was possible that a sample of semen could be extracted from her. They'd figured right. The inconsistencies John had pointed out in the background information that were based on what he knew about Josh had made both of them very curious, not to mention suspicious. Those inconsistencies were subtle and could have been explained away by logic, which John had tried to do by playing Devil's Advocate, but even when he did that his doubts remained. Furthermore, that only served to strengthen them.

As if he didn't have enough reasons to be concerned about Josh being on the loose, now he had yet another. He was determined to do whatever he could to help track down his archenemy, which led to him calling Doctor Hughes. There was no way he would sit still and wait for Josh to come back and try to harm Kim or anyone else again.

"Hello, Mister Governor, your timing is perfect. I just got the results. It looks like you and your brother hit the nail on the head. According to the bio, including the birth certificate, Joshua Strauss has type AB-positive blood. The type from this sample is B-negative."

"Can't say I'm surprised to hear that."

"Well, I'd say we've opened the proverbial can of worms."

"Yeah, I suppose so. Now we have to sort through 'em...

"...if he's not Joshua Strauss, who in hell is he?"

*March 21, 2001*

The day they'd anticipated for so long had come, and given the time of year, they couldn't have asked for a better one. The sun was shining in a cloudless sky, the mercury was reading nearly seventy degrees and there was a very gentle breeze, which lifted a couple loose tendrils of Kim's hair and caressed her face as she looked out over the courtyard.

Everything they'd planned had unfolded perfectly- all their guests were able to come and the reception was all set to go off at the grounds of their home. Even the weather, which was at no one's beck and call, had contributed the gift of an ideal day for a wedding...

*...which is yet another good sign,* she thought as she allowed the feeling to settle in. *I just hope this all carries over into the next phase of our life- if it happens...*

*...no- I won't think about that now. I'm going to concentrate on today and enjoy it. I have so much to be thankful for...*

"Are you ready, Sweetheart?"

She looked over at her Grandfather and nodded as a big smile blossomed.

"Looking forward to your second trip to the altar?"

"Oh, yes! Vegas was wonderful, but-..."

Bill laughed as her eyes widened and her hands flew to her mouth. "Don't worry, Kimberly. I doubt your Grandmom and I are the only ones who figured out what you two did out there in Vegas. Remember, we did it, too!"

Kim smiled warmly and embraced him. "I know. I told John when I got back home after that first weekend I spent with you. He remembered- in fact, it was his idea to elope first and then have another ceremony for everyone else. I love him so much..."

"I can tell; I see the same thing written all over him when he looks at you. By the way, speaking of your Grandmom and I, young lady, it's time for you to admit that we and your Mom are right about another matter, too. You know you'll cry well before the vows are exchanged; already you're getting teary-eyed!" He grinned and winked at her.

"Oh! As if you two aren't bad enough, now Mom's in on that?!" Kim retorted playfully as she laughed. "Well, I'll have all three of you know I will *not* cry- you'll see!" She walked over to him and took his arm, and both headed for the aisle.

It only was a matter of seconds after the most beautiful music she ever heard began to play when she proved them right- and mostly everyone else in attendance as well.


They'd concluded the event all the men were waiting for- the one where they got a look at the blushing bride's famous legs while her husband removed her garter ever so slowly, then tossed it into the crowd of bachelors. As that marked the end of the activities, the reception was winding down. John and Kim kissed her mother good night, then she and the friends she came with headed for the hotel. Among those who remained were Kim's grandparents.

"I'm glad you both were able to come," John said to Bill as the caterers started to clean up. "It meant a lot to Kim and me to have you walk her down the aisle."

"It was an honor. I couldn't be more pleased, seeing my Granddaughter well on her way to living a good life- especially after all she went through from childhood up through college. I can see how much making her happy makes you happy; I feel the same way with my wife. It seems to take awhile in some cases, but the good people of the world are rewarded in one way or another."

"They are indeed, Bill. Hi there, John- looks like we're finally able to talk for a moment! How are you?"

John turned, and smiled as he greeted Jack Weldon. "I couldn't be better, Mister Jack. Did you have a good time?"

"Most definitely- this was quite a bash the two of you put together." Jack turned to the hostess and took her hands into his. "And look at this young lady- still as radiant as ever. I haven't seen you in far too long, Kimberly. I've missed your company."

Kim smiled, hugged the Attorney-General and kissed his cheek. "Hi, Mister Jack- it's so good to see you again! I've missed you, too. Gosh, I can't believe it's been seven years!"

"I know. Time really does fly. By the way, I think we're at the point where you can call me 'Jack'. You're certainly not a little girl anymore, although you always were precocious. I don't think any of us ever saw anything quite like you."

429

Kim blushed. "Well, you'll always be *Mister* Jack to me."

"Fair enough," he said, and winked at her. "You need to come visit with me sometime; I'm still in the same place."

"I thought you would be. That's terrific; you always did have such a nice home. I remember how proud you always were of it and that you always kept it so clean."

"I still do. The old garden's there, the fence, the lattice work- I love that place as much as I always did. I never even considered moving- way too much history there. There's a lot of me in that old house, too. It really is home, and that couldn't be replaced."

"I think I know what you mean. Oh- speaking of your garden," she said as she giggled, "I remember way back one winter- I think I was only six at the time- when you really got an early start on it! I do remember it was January- shortly after New Year's- and there you were, out in your yard digging! Talk about dedication! I don't think I'll ever forget seeing you out there that day."

His face went blank for a moment, but then he grinned. "Ah, I think I know which one you mean. We had a warm winter that year and I jumped at the chance to get the soil ready and all. I ended up growing my best tomatoes that year, as I recall."

"You certainly did grow some great ones! Anyway, I'd love to visit you- in fact, I'll do it soon, now that we have some more time on our hands. How is Jill and her family?"

"Well, she and her husband are divorcing. It's a bad situation already and I'm afraid it will get worse. He cheated on her- for years, as it turned out. She and her children are staying with me for now, which I don't mind. They're the only family I have left since my brother passed away a few years back. It's no surprise he never married or had any kids; he was a good man, mind you- he just didn't have much in the way of paternal instincts or a desire to settle down.

"As for Jill, she was in a bad way for a while, as you can imagine. Come to think of it, I bet she'd like to see you again."

Kim was taken aback for a moment, dropping her inkling that there was a disconnect with what he'd said about his brother. *I never would have thought Jill would want anything to do with me...* "Oh...well, I-..."

"I know you didn't get along when you were younger, but my Jill has changed a lot over the years. Being a mother gave her a

430

new perspective- you'll be surprised by how she is now. In fact, she was very worried about you when you went through that ordeal last year."

"She was?"

"Yes, I can vouch for that. Remember, you two were close friends once. Who knows, perhaps you can be again. I know it would be good for Jill if that were to happen- might be good for you, too. Give it some thought, anyway."

"Ok, I will. Wow, we sure are stirring up some memories here, aren't we? Talk about not having been somewhere in a long time...I haven't seen the old neighborhood since I stopped babysitting for Davie and Darren Griffin. As you know, my memories there weren't all good ones."

"I remember. I saw the sadness in you in spite of your efforts to hide it with all those activities: the figure skating, ballet, swimming and cheerleading. You had an awful lot working against you. Along those lines, how are you coping with all this rigamarole over the videotape? Someone has sunken really low to profit from your captivity. I'll tell you this much- once we find who's responsible, if they live in this state, you'd better believe I'll go for the maximum punishment. To put a sweet girl like you through that...disgusting!"

"Oh, it's not so bad now- I actually haven't heard as much about it recently, so maybe people are starting to forget about it. You've done an awful lot over these months to try and track the guilty parties down, though- I think you've been my most vocal public advocate. This situation is just another reminder that we have our share of sewer rats in our society..."

Jack noted that she trailed off and saw a look of uncertainty and discomfort coming over her. "Is something wrong?"

"Um, sort of. I mean...I, um...I know why you're being so dogged in your pursuit, but...if you don't mind...I mean, I appreciate so much that you're looking out for me, but..."

"What is it?"

"Well...I was thinking maybe if we-...toned down the exposure and attention they're getting, in all ways...please don't misunderstand me; I do appreciate-"

"I know you do, and I think I know where you're going. You feel that any publicity this scum gets could prolong peoples' curiosity and therefore keep the video sales going and keep you in the spotlight in such a negative way." She lowered her head. "It's all right, Kimberly. I do understand and you make a very good point. I'll tone down the rhetoric."

She looked back up at him and smiled. "Thank you, Mister Jack. You always did look out for me; that's one reason why you're so dear to me. I have the utmost confidence that your team will find and deal with them, which is why I don't let it bother me so much anymore. Besides, I have plenty of pleasant diversions these days."

"I would bet one of them is standing beside you?"

"I was about to clear my throat or something!" John smirked as he glanced at Bill, "see how easy it is for me to become invisible?" That made all of them laugh.

"It's also easy for you to land yourself in the doghouse, Mister, so you'd better be careful how you use that wit of yours!" Kim responded light-heartedly, hands on her hips.

"See what I have to contend with?"

"Are you kidding? Where do you think that all came from?"

"I heard that, William Russell!" Salma took position next to Kim, and assumed the same posture.

"Oh, boy- now we've done it! Unless you're as good at appeasing your wife as I am mine, you could be in for a chilly honeymoon!"

"Actually, that happens to be one of John's many talents- we call it 'sucking up'," Kim said, smiling flirtatiously at her husband and causing even more laughter among everyone else.

When the merriment subsided, Jack's smile remained, but for a different reason. As he looked at the newlywed couple, he couldn't help but make his observation known. "You might find this a bit strange, but already I see similarities between how you two are with each other and how your mother and father were, John."

"Really?" Kim beamed at the comparison and moved into John's arms. He also smiled.

"Indeed. I would call that a good sign- in spite of a couple distractions they had to deal with, they had a very strong marriage, as I have a feeling you two will."

"How sweet of you to say that! I'm so glad you came."

"I wouldn't have missed your wedding for anything. I still think it's funny, in a way, how two young people I knew separately for so many years came together like you did. And, I'm glad both of you will be able to take it easy for a while, in a way." He looked at John as he changed the subject. "I suppose you'll be doing a bunch of travelling soon enough?"

"Oh, yeah. We'll be on our honeymoon for a couple weeks- maybe longer-, and then it'll be time to start working on how we'll get our message out. We won't wait too long before we get on the road. Kim's starting to make contacts in different cities and we're putting a plan together as to how we're going to reach out to as many people as possible. She's looking into getting me scheduled to speak in town halls, school auditoriums, theatres- wherever she can. There's a huge pool of disenchanted eligible voters who don't vote- and a lot more who aren't even registered-, along with a lot of disenchanted eligible voters who do. I'm going to make sure that every one of them gets my message and understands that I'm sticking around for the next election. I think a lot of those pundits in D.C. will be blown away, along with my competition, when the results of that one come in!"

"Or, maybe you're right when you say the time for real change has come, and it won't be such a surprise."

Kim affirmed that point. "I don't think it will be a surprise at all. I have a feeling that in a little less than four years' time, John and I will be throwing a party for an altogether different reason." She turned to him. "You're not the only one who believes the 2004 election will be the one, Baby."

After giving him a smooch, she shifted her focus. "All right, enough talk about that for now. You and I have other matters to attend to."

Salma piped up. "On that note, I think it's time for the rest of us to get to our hotel." Since the hour was pretty late, a number of the guests had left already. Those who remained took the hint and gathered their things.


It nearly was the end of one chapter of their life; this period marked the transition into the next.

Kim slowly- even somewhat timidly- made her way back into the bedroom after changing, which really amounted to shedding a layer. She was clad only in her sexy and scanty lingerie, along with her silk stockings and high heels- a combination that heated him up every time, although she certainly didn't need any help to get his heart thumping.

He lifted her into his arms and carried her to their bed, seeing and feeling her longing during their brief journey. Her hunger showed no sign whatsoever of subsiding; in that respect it seemed like this was their first night together. He gently laid her down and joined her.

"I'm yours now, John." There wasn't any of the playfulness and banter that got them started many times when they made love. Kim's heart and soul had spoken.

In regards to what was coming, his sole focus was to make that period last as long as he could. He wasted no time getting started...


...but later, as Kim slept soundly after they consummated their second marriage- with a few exclamation points for good measure-, he came back to something else that recently had been repeated, which was as far from pleasurable as it possibly could be. Even the exhilaration and bliss that Kim brought to his life coupled with his high confidence that he would win in the next election were not enough to wash away the stain on him that this episode with Josh had left, which wasn't the only one he had.

For the second time in his life, someone had humiliated him deeply. Worse, at this juncture, it seemed like the perpetrator would get away with it- just like the first one did. That instance was something he'd been able to bury, although it had taken a lot of time and effort. Nonetheless, all seemed to be going well at the start of last summer; it seemed like he really had glossed over that first black mark completely...

...until this very recent one was left.

In spite of his best efforts he couldn't look past it, or ignore it this time. Worse, in part because of this recent episode, the humiliation from his past was resurrected and thrown back in his face, adding to his focused enmity that as yet he had no way to unload. The main problem was, he had no idea where to start looking. Josh had disappeared- again.

Only days ago Doctor Hughes had finished checking that DNA sample against the national database: no match.

However, that did not and would not deter him. No matter how long it took or what he had to do, John would find him and have his vengeance.

*The following is an excerpt from the third episode in*

*the series, which is entitled:*

## <u>The Time of Reckoning:</u>

## <u>The Lion Strikes</u>

# Prologue

*March 12, 2003*

"Gee, Harry, I don't know if I've ever seen you so focused. I'd think you were watching one of those pornos you tell your buddies about."

That shook Detective Lawson out of his concentration and he glanced at his spunky partner, who was twenty years his junior and very sharp. Although she wasn't beautiful, she was quite sexy. Most guys on the force considered her aloof, unattainable and possibly not interested in men. She dressed very conservatively as part of her effort to keep her colleagues focused on her abilities as a cop, which, as Harry would attest, were very impressive.

She was Daddy's girl through and through, and had followed his path; her father served with distinction on the Force for thirty-five years. Inexplicably, in late '97, he committed suicide. No one brought that up in Danni's presence out of respect for both of them. "Uh-huh, I figured you were listening in on some of those conversations. If you're so interested, you could watch one with me- might loosen you up a little. How long has it been since your last date, anyway? You should try doing something other than working and working out."

Detective Danielle Searles held up her hand. "No, thanks- I'll pass. Maybe you should try *doing* either or both of those things for a change: might make you a better detective."

Harry laughed. "You need to speak your mind, Danni; you hold way too much back!"

She smiled. "I will say this, though: I'm glad you and Spence are so familiar with the area. God only knows how long it would have taken us to find this spot if you two weren't with us, although Spence seems a bit sharper!"

"Yeah, yeah! I used to know this watershed area- and this stretch of it in particular- probably better than anybody did. Guess I got a bit rusty, huh? I'll tell you this much; I wish we had a better reason to be here at this hour. Fuckin' guy and his 'anonymous tip'-how do we know he's not some worthless, brain-dead crackhead havin' a bad trip? Callin' the station at four-thirty in the morning…you know, this has all the makings of some damned wild goose chase. I was up way too late last night to deal with such bullshit since 7 AM."

The crew had been digging for an hour and so far, no body. Harry had suggested they pack it up a while ago, which was reasonable, no doubt, but Danni wanted to be sure. After all, they'd done this much already. "Well, they're about five feet down. If there is a body here, whoever buried it wanted to make sure it wasn't found easily. He or they might have gone the full six, or more…"

"Maybe, but I doubt it. I still think this is all a hoax. 'It's been there for some time'- what could he have meant? A few years? Decades? And why in the hell did he have to tell us this today, in a fucking cold rainstorm? Too bad his 'crisis of conscience' couldn't have come when it was a little nicer out. I'm tellin' you all, we need to pack this shit up."

"Has anyone ever told you that you bitch a lot, Harry?"

One of the guys in the hole piped up. "Yeah, especially when *you* ain't even doin' any diggin'!"

They all laughed and Harry retorted, "Hey, I'm only trying to look out for you guys."

"Yeah, right! Next you'll try ta sell me some-"

"Whoa- I think I've got something here."

Harry froze for a moment, then jumped down into the hole and looked at what one of the others pointed out. The digger had hit a wooden plank with his pickaxe.

"Gimme that shovel, Spence." Harry grabbed it and cleared away more earth.

It was what they suspected, and after several more minutes of digging, they were in position to pry the lid off.

"Stand back, you guys. Depending on how long this has been here, there's a chance what's inside might help reacquaint you with your breakfasts…"


"What do you mean, it's gone?! How could that have happened?! This had better not be some kind of joke."

"It isn't, John. The sample's gone." The semen sample from Josh Strauss, which was the only physical evidence of him on record, had been 'misplaced' at the FBI, according to the most senior official Tom had been able to reach. Tom decided that he should be the one to tell John. "I don't know what happened to it-your guess is as good as mine. No one can track it down; that's their story."

"Those people could fuck up a free lunch, then turn around and somehow make you pay for it. As much as we've been in contact with them about that sample, as many tests and checks that have been made and some incompetent idiot loses it…"

"I know. I'm not happy about it, either, nor is Doctor Hughes. Now we have nothing on him, and still, we have no idea where to look."

*"Dammit…"*

"We've been at a dead end since the beginning, anyway, and now this…we probably can expect that the investigation at the least will be curtailed further. It hasn't been a big priority for months. They might even drop it altogether; you can only bang your head against the wall for so long."

*"They* might drop it, but you can be sure that I won't."

"With nothing to go on, what can you do? I know how badly you want to-"

"No, you don't, Tom. You don't know how badly I want to get him," John said as his blood began to boil again. "I'm not gonna miss anything this time- count on that…

"…somehow, no matter how long it takes or what I have to do, I *will* get him."


"Well, hello there! How are you?"

Kim had walked into the convenience store, her mind set on an ice cream after the impromptu display she'd put on at the local ice skating rink. Even as cold as it was, which prompted her to add her mittens, scarf and wool hat to the ski jacket she wore over her leotard and tights, she had the urge nonetheless.

To her surprise she'd been able to land a double jump, which she was very happy with since she hadn't even attempted one in some time. She also pulled off a few tough spins along with two airborne splits. Some people had gathered around to watch her, their curiosity piqued when they saw the cameraman filming her. They were further intrigued when they realized who she was and they applauded her when she finished. After Kim curtsied to them, she and John greeted them and mingled while their bodyguards monitored everyone carefully.

439

Before long, they took off.

They were to go right to their bed and breakfast, but Kim's hankering for her favorite treat, which she allowed herself on occasion, delayed them in getting back there. The three customers in front of her delayed her a bit more, but that delay brought her face-to-face with the child, who stared at her.

"Oh, you're shy, aren't you?" Kim squatted down, now eye-level with her, and smiled. "My name is Kim. What's yours?"

Still no response. Kim looked up at the man with her, who held her hand with what looked to be a very firm grip, and faced forward. "What's her name?"

He didn't answer, and moved up to the counter when his turn came. He pushed his money toward the cashier before she even said anything and didn't acknowledge her greeting.

Kim frowned, and focused again on the little girl, who continued to look at her with the same expression. She began to worry about something she noticed in the child's eyes...

...then she sensed it and stood up. "Excuse-"

That was all Kim was able to say before the man turned and took a swing at her, but he was slow and clumsy, which the alcohol she smelled on his breath probably contributed to, and she was ready. She ducked and counterattacked, landing a shot to his solar plexus that staggered him just enough.

In the next instant, the man was on the floor and pinned, with Herb holding his wrist, having bent his arm up behind him in what surely was a painful position. Mel instructed the cashier to call the police, which she did quickly. Just like that, it was over.

When the little girl ran toward her, Kim knelt back down and took her into her arms. "It's all right, Honey- you're safe now," she soothed as she held the sobbing child.

"You were *great!*" The cashier gushed as she came around and stood next to Kim. "That was the most awesome thing I've ever seen! Where did you learn to fight like that?"

John rushed in with the other two bodyguards. "What happened?! Are you all right?"

"We're fine, Baby. That man over there had- oh, I still don't know your name, Sweetie." Kim brushed away her tears.

"My name is Rachel."

"I'm glad to meet you, Rachel. Do you have a Mommy and Daddy?"

440

"That's my Daddy," she said, pointing at the man subdued on the floor.

"Oh…well, we're going to get in touch with your Mommy and get you back to her, Ok? While we're doing that, Mister John, our nice friends and I will take care of you."

The police arrived quickly and took the man into custody after getting statements from everyone in the store. All present found out that the man indeed was wanted for suspicion of abducting Rachel- suspicions that obviously were well founded. Once they were finished, Kim took the girl's hand into hers and they walked to the car, flanked closely by the bodyguards.

It wasn't long before they reached Rachel's mother, who'd been watching the news when the story of the rescue came on. Her gratitude came through loud and clear over the phone and already she was on her way to be reunited with her daughter.

Rachel lay in Kim's lap as they rode to the place where she and John were staying. While she stroked the child's hair, Kim couldn't help but reflect once more on her inability to conceive that as yet no one understood. Her feelings of desolation were hitting her hard.

It didn't help when she looked up at John, who stared straight ahead, deep in thought, distracted and moody. That was becoming a common sight.

She was beginning to worry about him; more and more, she was convinced that he was slipping back into an old habit. *What are you keeping from me, John?*

*And, after all we've been through, why? Why would you do that?*

Also upsetting her was that she needed him and he wasn't available…

Kim wasn't aware that she'd drifted. He brought her back when he kissed away a tear as it fell, then traced along her cheek, smiling tenderly at her while he did. He looked at Rachel, who had fallen asleep, then back at her.

"You're thinking about it again…"

Compounding her deteriorating spirits was the guilt that rushed in over her touch of anger toward him a moment ago. The high she'd been on was all but gone, and so suddenly.

Knowing it would fail, she gave up her effort to stop herself from crying and let John pull her close to him. "I'm sorry."

"Shhhh. It's all right. I know where you are; I saw it as soon as Rachel ran to you."

"We're never going to have-"

"Don't say it, Kim- don't think that way. It's not your fault. We're doing everything right and we have to keep it up. I hate what this is doing to you- how much it's tearing you up. We have to keep believing that our day will come, though. I know how much you want a baby; I do, too. I also know it's hard to try to stay positive, but can you do that, Honey?"

She sniffed, but managed a smile. "I'll try. I promise."

After they kissed, she sighed and relaxed against him. She glanced at Rachel, who hadn't even budged, then turned back to John. "Thank you, John; I needed that."

Kim fondly recalled his similar reaction just a couple weeks ago when a reporter asked her if or when she planned to have children. The reporter wasn't being malicious, but it hurt nonetheless. John's protectiveness toward her kicked right in; he ended the interview, got her out of there and back to the privacy of their room. Contrary to her knee-jerk reaction minutes earlier, virtually every time when she needed him to be, he was there for her...

...which made her want to do the same thing for him, if he would let her. "May I ask you something?"

"Sure."

"Lately I've noticed that-...well, there are times when you're preoccupied, and you get really quiet. I've seen you that way before; I know it's something other than the campaign that's troubling you. Would you tell me what it is?" She was disappointed when she saw the shroud fall over him again, and knew what his answer would be before he even said it.

"It's...a little complicated. I don't have much information on it right now, so there's not much to tell, anyway."

"But what is it? Maybe I can help somehow."

John looked into her upturned face and gave her a smooch. "You already are, just by being with me. You shouldn't worry- it's not a big deal. I can handle it."

Not wanting to pester him, she relented for the time being. However, she wasn't able to do what he said and not worry. It had been a long time since he'd held anything back from her, which was something she'd hoped he'd never do again.

442

All she could do now was hope he'd either tell her soon, resolve the problem, or both, because in spite of what he claimed, this preoccupation was starting to take away from his concentration on the campaign, and also their marriage- at least, certain aspects of it. Valentine's Day had been a very welcome exception, but the overall trend was downward. It wasn't a case of him ignoring her, but it was clear to her that he was focused on something other than the race.

Worse, she was pretty sure she knew the identity of a major contributor to his increasing tension and occasional anger: Joshua Strauss. Every time his name came up in the news, conversation or anywhere, John's fist would clench, or his eyes would narrow.

*I guess I should have expected this...*

"...and the latest stop on their lengthy campaign trail is Boston, Massachusetts, where the couple was received warmly. The turnouts at his forums seem to be increasing as time goes on, and markedly so since this past November 4$^{th}$.

"I would say Mrs. Stratton has done her part to keep the trend of those turnouts on the upswing. This afternoon she took to the rink and showed that she's some kind of a dancer on the ice; there's no denying her talent in that realm. I wasn't surprised to learn that when she was only twelve she was a rising star in the world of figure skating. She sure came alive when the music started to play; those who were at the rink today stood back and watched her go. She fell on her first attempt at a double jump, but did that stop her? Unh-uh! She got right up, brushed herself off and proceeded to nail that same jump on her second attempt, which makes me wonder if we'll see a parallel drawn between that and her husband's run for the White House. He came up short in his first run, but he picked himself up as well and is going for it again.

"However, there's at least one man out there who underestimated the woman who could become our First Lady- perhaps *because* of her looks and femininity. That brings me to the main reason why she made the headlines today. Mrs. Stratton played a vital role in the rescue of little Rachel Williamson from her non-custodial father, who had beaten his ex-wife- the girl's mother-, abducted the child and fled. The Amber Alert had just gone out when the rescue took place. With that heroic act by Mrs.

Stratton, we see yet another dimension of this fascinating woman. The cashier at the convenience store where this episode took place had nothing but praises for her. Needless to say, a very grateful young girl and her mother echo those praises. Indeed, Kimberly Stratton is quite a woman, but not everyone sees her in a positive light, as evidenced by this rant from religious leader Pat Elwell:"

"...we Christians must unite and stop the march of this Godless, socialistic menace to our great nation and his Jezebel, who dresses and acts like the harlot she is. That billboard of this most sinful temptress hanging up for all to see over the most sinful city in our nation is all the proof we need! You don't fool us, Kimberly Stratton, making us think you're cleaning up your act! We see right through you! We will not allow you to represent our country and glorify the negative example you set for our young women!"

"Mister Elwell's reference, of course, is to that famous promotional billboard, which was moved to the Las Vegas strip, depicting Mrs. Stratton in a very sexy and revealing outfit as she posed in front of a huge male tiger. His hellfire-and-brimstone tirade went on for several more minutes, but don't worry- I won't subject you to it. I will show you Governor Stratton's retort, though:"

"That guy personifies narrow-mindedness. He's fixated on Kim's past, which is just that- the past. She posed for that shot when she was nineteen, for crying out loud! Any normal person who sees how she dresses now wouldn't come to such conclusions. My wife dresses a bit on the flashy side because she's very confident in herself and proud of the result of her efforts to keep herself in shape. I'm every bit as proud to be with her and I appreciate her efforts, too.

"Back to Mr. Elwell, he seems to get worse as the years go on. Isn't forgiveness one of the cornerstones of religion? Obviously, tolerance isn't in his mantra, which gives him a common point with the fanatical Islam fundamentalists. I think his congregation had better be careful with their loyalty to him."

The anchorman came back on. "No argument here. Mister Elwell is getting pretty extreme, and now, in light of Mrs. Stratton's action today, it looks like he will be dining on some crow for his remarks directed at her. Wonder if he prefers light meat or dark...but then again, it might be hard for him to eat anything with his foot so deeply embedded in his mouth! I know- I'm a baaaad boy...

"Anyway, Governor Stratton caused another- and a bigger- stir in the same conference that quip came from. It started when one reporter brought up an issue he had with a point of criticism the Governor leveled against the major party candidates during the 2000 election; he brought that up right after this succinct and poignant part of the Governor's speech:"

"...we need to simplify things in our country- our tax code, our election system, our health care system, our educational system, our legal system, our trade and immigration policies- everything. The way it is now, things are so complicated that you need to be Einstein to figure it all out! It's ridiculous and, contrary to what all these lawyers would have you believe, it doesn't have to be like that. Under my administration, it *won't* be like that. Speaking of the lawyers, they wield far too much power. I think it's time we took some of it away from them. We need far less lawyers and plenty more teachers and doctors."

"Mister Governor, you said just before the last election that you wouldn't even need six months to get your message out. Several congressmen who are presidential hopefuls- and President Black himself- brought up the point that you've been on the trail for the '04 election, on and off, since June of last year. What made you do what you railed against?"

"Necessity. The democrats and republicans get virtually all the media coverage; their message is the one that reaches so far because it's what's heard. Since the other parties like mine are left with the scraps, I had to take this action. The only real way I have to reach as many people as possible all over the country is to do what I'm doing. It's better having a forum, anyway, because I can answer directly the questions the people have. Best of all, based on some very good points some of the participants brought up, I've improved upon a couple solutions for the many problems we face. Their voices are being heard- and heeded as well."

"Mister Governor, I'm very curious about the remark you made a moment ago about reigning in the lawyers. How do you propose we do that?"

"Capping their salaries and fees, for starters. If lawyers don't have the financial incentive to defend high-profile criminals or to push these lawsuits in which they make ridiculous demands in terms of money, the frivolous lawsuits will drop off and it will become more difficult for high-profile defendants to abuse the system like they do and get away with all they do. The lawyers' motivation to help them buy their way out of the crimes they commit will be reduced, which I see as a good thing. It's a step toward equal justice for everyone- a step toward taking away the different set of rules that applies to the wealthy and also eliminating the excess of senseless lawsuits.

"Many lawyers complain about the outrageous tuition for law school- that's one thing they *won't* have to deal with anymore. We need to dissuade lawyers from the practice of twisting laws to justify even the most reprehensible behavior simply so they can win cases. In my system, lawyers who genuinely care about the underdog and also the pursuit and administration of true justice will be encouraged to pursue their quest while the greedy, unconscionable egomaniacs won't have so much motivation.

"Also in regard to civil cases, we need to place a cap on the maximum amount in damages a plaintiff can sue for. I suggest $5 million across the board for any individual civil case, including malpractice. I think that's reasonable. Plus, if we do that, insurance companies would lower their premiums in turn, so it would be better for everyone."

"Don't you think you're giving the insurance companies too much credit there?"

"Put it this way- they'd be given the opportunity to do the right thing and lower their premiums. If they didn't, we'd sick the consumer watchdog groups on them and they'd face stiff penalties along with plenty of governmental interference. Plus, there would be all the resulting negative press- not good for business! Finally, if those measures fail, we'll simply make them drop their rates by way of legislation."

"But what about the massive medical bills a plaintiff could have incurred?"

"That won't be applicable in my system- not with the new health service. Also, doctors will be held to the highest possible standards. They can't be perfect- that shouldn't be expected of them or anyone-, but incompetence would be very costly for them and not just monetarily. However, the ridiculous and excessive damages sought in these lawsuits have to be stopped. That practice is counterproductive on many levels."

"Sir, how do you respond to the latest criticism the other parties have directed toward you that you're an anti-capitalist, that you advocate overthrowing the government and that your reforms will spell the end of our way of life and possibly lead to anarchy?"

John laughed derisively. "That's how I respond! My reforms will end *their* way of life, which is what's scaring them. Make no mistake: they *are* scared and they have reason to be. With our victories in the last election and the multitude of promising prospects we have for those in this year and next, they know that they and their system are in deep trouble. They'll throw every distortion, concoction and outright lie they can at me to see if something sticks.

"That's what I expect from them, though, because the other parties don't believe in candor- they don't believe in being up front with you. That worries me. When leaders can't come clean and tell you things as they are, including when they make mistakes, they're not leaders at all and definitely are not examples for anyone to follow. Yes, that includes Mister Black. Despite how he wants you to believe that he sees things in black and white, he's typical of the state of politics today and also the state our nation is coming to. Many people are afraid- or for a host of reasons, unwilling- to say what they feel, whether it's right or wrong.

"Then, they figure their leaders lie or mislead, so why shouldn't they? The truth isn't fashionable; you're told to blunt your message so you won't offend anybody Is that how you want your country to be? The most powerful nation in the world, but one in which people can't or won't tell the truth for fear of repercussions? I tell you without hesitation that's not how I want America to be and I will not back away from what I say under any circumstances.

"As for the message of my competition, it's all smoke and mirrors- their platform is weak at best and broken at worst. In many of the recent elections you've seen people not so much voting *for* one candidate as they were voting *against* another- the lesser of two evils scenario. The problem with that is you still have an evil- in this case, stagnation. We get these people in office that do nothing but churn out watered-down legislation that benefits no one other than special interest groups and lawyers. No one takes a stand for anything; all anyone wants to do is compromise. Then, if you disagree with the major parties and their candidates, they want to throw every bad name they can at you because you've caught on to them and they don't like it. It's your duty to speak up if you disagree, yet they discourage that!

"The two parties see us Progressives with real solutions that will deliver a new and drastically improved country in

447

virtually every way. They can't handle that; they know they're not fooling anyone with their crap anymore, yet they still want you to vote for them and keep their corporate fat-cat friends in power. Their charges don't warrant a response other than for me to call them what they are: groundless, ridiculous and acts of desperation.

"To answer the other part of your question, I'll say this: capitalism as we know it is failing us, and badly. It's become a license for corporate robber barons to rip off stockholders and their country at large, and rewrite the rules to suit themselves.

"In light of that, certain aspects of socialism- a couple of which are part of my platform- don't seem so bad, do they? My platform can be called egalitarianism insofar as I want all Americans to be on the same starting line and have an equal chance to succeed in life regardless of socioeconomic background and race. That has not been the case at any point in our history, but it *can* be the case very soon. And, my platform is utilitarian, in that I want to do the greatest good for the greatest number of us.

"I do advocate the overthrow of *this* government because it doesn't represent its constituents or what's best for them; it routinely deceives and misleads. However, I call for a non-violent removal of them from office by way of the democratic process of voting. As for what my competition has to say, I'll just watch them wear themselves out while they throw their babble at anyone who will listen. The thing is, less people *are* listening to them. We're not buying this recycled garbage they're trying to sell us again."

"Sir, there's a constitutional question about you curtailing spending on campaigns, even when the candidate spends his or her own money. Isn't that a violation of free speech?"

"Maybe so, if you look at it from a purely legalistic standpoint, which is typical of the powers-that-be who want to use the letter of the law in order to keep us all in the doldrums of stagnation. Unfortunately, the double-talk and bait-and-switch tactics they use aren't considered violations of free speech, although they do violate the principles of common sense.

"In response to my critics and their charge, the war chest of a candidate with way too much personal wealth constitutes an unfair advantage over one who lacks that luxury. What they see as free speech, I see as a way for the wealthy to beat the people back and keep their stranglehold on power. Messages are lost in the money that affluent candidates spread around to buy votes and with all the advertising they can do that the other can't.

"In sum, many more people hear what the wealthy have to say in comparison to the ones with considerably less means. We need to put a stop to that. The same applies to the big cash-raising machines we call major political parties, which are a big part of the problem. I've never seen such hypocrisy as I see in them."

"How so, Sir?"

"During the primaries the democratic and republican candidates just beat up on each other endlessly. They smear and rip each other to shreds- tell us all the reasons why we absolutely should not vote for the other candidates. When the primaries end, they fall all over themselves praising each other, which makes you wonder why they even ran against each other in the first place!

"It's all a show. They just kiss and make up and put on their happy faces for everyone. They pander and they compromise their beliefs and ideals just so their party can win. That plays a big part in why nothing gets done; they're only energized in the race. I'm sick of it- sick of this endless cycle.

"Then come the favors for their friends and allies- big business and special interest groups. With as many times as the democrats and republicans have been bought and sold, they should be listed as commodities on the stock exchange! Even when those big businesses do us real damage, like Exxon with the Valdez disaster in '89, our government lets them get away with not paying the $5 billion in damages. They do little for the rest of our citizens other than throw us an occasional bone. That's the way things have been for a long time and that's another big part of why we're in the predicament we're in. It's a national version of the Tammany Hall days in New York City. The media hinders us as well by giving entirely too much airtime to two parties.

"So, in the final analysis, which is the real evil? Would you allow the current establishment to wield the Constitution as their sword to silence the voice of the people that cries out for reform? Would you keep their broken system in place and continue to drive this country into the ground, or would you opt for real, substantial change that would benefit virtually all Americans?"

"But surely the Supreme Court would step in and strike any such measure down; already they've indicated that they would. What you're laying out is a direct violation of-"

"I would hope the Supreme Court would do what's right and side with the 99% of us who would benefit from that change, which would allow those with broader interests to run for office. I'd also hope they'd support making life in general much better for the vast majority of our citizens via the cap on individual wealth.

"One measure I plan to take is to call for a constitutional convention during my first term as President in order to put into law my system- make it so no regressive-minded lawyers and/or judges can argue it away. In one fell swoop I would move to make Amendments out of my proposed changes that would benefit all of us except the wealthy elite. In truth, those changes would benefit them as well by making their country stronger, for those who choose to see the big picture over being selfish."

"What if the Supreme Court ruled against your programs and you couldn't garner enough support for a convention?"

"Well, I could to put those laws into practice bilaterally, via myself and the Congress, or unilaterally, if I have to."

"So you would defy the Court?! That is drastically overstepping your authority!"

"Perhaps it is, but if my options were to do that or allow the system as is to go on, as long as the people are with me I *would* defy the Court- no question about it. What is right outweighs what is legal. What we Progressives are laying out to you is the right course of action for all, whether or not the courts choose to see it that way. In the end, it's what the people decide is best for them that counts- not someone else's interpretation of it.

"Consider this: how do you think our founding fathers would feel if they could see how things are today? If they could see how big business runs America and determines the direction of our country, or the lack thereof? Things are bad today, everyone.

"Contrary to what some think, I hate having to stand before you and tell you this, but no one else will. They say we're in good shape when in reality we're foundering on the reef. We're living in a modern version of a feudalistic society; we have executives and other corporate officers and/or crooks robbing us blind, destroying our environment and keeping our country in a state of stagnation. All the power is in their greedy hands.

"As far as I'm concerned, those in our federal government are accomplices because they're letting it happen while getting and giving favors in the process. And here I thought prostitution was *against* the law! It's illegal for women to sell sexual favors, yet elected officials can sell political favors and nothing happens to them! We need to clean out that den of vipers, which we

450

Progressives already have begun to do with our victories last year and will continue to do over the next two.

"It all starts at the top. If we can't bring about the changes we need from within the system, then maybe we *do* need to go outside it. Maybe we need to create a new system, like our founders, who also experienced taxation without representation.

"That said, I vow to do my utmost to bring those changes about by way of the Constitution once I become President. If that doesn't work, then, with the blessing of the citizens of this nation, I will find another way, use it and make our country better."

The camera went back to the anchorman. *"Wow*!! I've never heard such language in all my years of covering campaigns! That is one powerful call to arms; he does seem to be trying to incite a revolution! Already there are strong reactions to it coming in from all over the country. No one can accuse this man of not telling it like he sees it! We really could have a battle royale in the works if he's elected.

"The Governor is spending a good bit of his own money on this tour. From the outset he's adamantly refused to accept any special interest, corporate or union money and he's been as good as his word. He's not advertising on television and he doesn't have a huge staff around him. Just as he said he would, he's keeping it simple. He is insistent that any contributors to his campaign adhere to his hundred dollar limit per individual, which is what he vows to make law- along with the other campaign reforms he's outlined- once he's elected.

"The political world continues to reel from the impact of this fledgling party that Governor Stratton officially formed early last year. The name 'Progressive' suits them well, since his programs certainly are that. He was smart enough to realize he needed help- and a lot of it- to advance his platform, so he embarked upon his campaign to recruit like-minded Americans to run for office. Scores of them stepped up to the plate and a number of them won their races.

"Although the Massachusetts contingent came up short in the interim election, all have said they will run again. Governor Stratton's prediction that we would experience bigger turnouts at the polls sure came true, too! His home state of Maryland, of course, is where the Progressives had their biggest victories. In addition to Mister Stratton's successor, Laura Collins, winning her race, Progressives from The Old Line State captured a Senate seat

451

from a long-entrenched democrat and sent six Representatives down I-95 to Washington, D.C. to boot! Along with their compatriots from other states, those new members of Congress are making their presence known in this legislative session.

"Although Maryland has the strongest voter base for the new party that poses the biggest threat to the established order that any third party ever has, that base is spreading rapidly across the country. Six Senators, one each from Arkansas, Delaware, Louisiana, Minnesota, Missouri and Oregon along with sixteen Representatives- four from California, three each from Illinois and Ohio, two each from Michigan and Louisiana and one each from Indiana and Iowa- form the rest of the Progressive contingent.

"With the gubernatorial races this year in Louisiana, Kentucky and Mississippi, we could see that contingent grow. Governor Stratton is stumping for Progressive candidates in all three states, which seem to be good prospects for the party to capture more Governors' mansions. Mister Stratton's rising influence will be pitted against that of President Black in what could be a preview of the presidential election next year. As for 2004, the Progressive leader says there will be plenty more victories to follow, which is a sentiment echoed by everyone in that young- but growing, determined and vocal- political movement."


"*Movement* my ass- this is a fucking *earthquake*!!" Philip Raines, majority owner and CEO of Tizer Pharmaceuticals, bellowed at the TV. After that he turned to his man- the one he knew only as 'Ray'. Raines often wondered about his background, which no one seemed to have much knowledge of. "So, do you still think I'm 'dreaming'? You still think 'those guys are a fluke'? That 'Stratton's a flash in the pan who will have faded into the woodwork by next election'? That 'any Progressive will become irrelevant almost immediately'?"

'Ray' shrugged. "Maybe I was wrong."

"*Maybe*?! To say the fucking least, you were wrong! You didn't only miss the bull's-eye, you missed the whole dartboard, not to mention the wall behind it! This fucking guy's banging the drums of a form of socialism and a lot of people are starting to dance to his rhythm! Do you have any idea what'll happen if he's elected?! Our way of life *will* disappear- that's what'll happen!

452

"We'll lose everything! All our hard-earned money will go toward educating a bunch of ignorant, lazy bastards from every fucked up race we have in this wonderful melting pot of ours- probably none of whom will do anything that'll make any kind of difference- not to mention this universal health care farce of his! That alone will destroy my industry!

"Who in the *fuck* does this asshole think he is, Robin Hood?! Trying to take away my right to keep what's rightfully mine...without me, twenty-four thousand people wouldn't have jobs! Every businessman I've talked to feels the same way! We deserve all we have- in fact, we deserve more than what we have because *we* make it happen! Our toils keep this country growing and moving forward, and he wants to penalize us for it!!"

After letting a lot of his steam out, he relaxed. "I'm sorry about that rant. I hoped you'd have ended up being right about this son of a bitch and his movement, but he's strong- even stronger than I thought he'd be. He's also dangerous- *too* dangerous to ignore. I doubt we can rely on the majority of the population voting the way we want 'em to and keeping our people in office. We might have to consider doing something about him...

"...we certainly know what his primary vulnerability is."

"You mean his wife." When Raines smiled, Ray went on. "Bad idea. She should not be harmed, even by accident, especially considering what she just did in saving that little girl. The public perception of her is sure to be even more favorable now. After today, most people might even forget that she ever was a stripper."

"Nobody who saw her dance will forget. I know I won't."

"Let's not digress here, all right? In the big picture, if she was to die, he'd fall apart or, more likely, become even more powerful and determined than he is. With the outpour of public sympathy for him, he'd be a shoo-in. You don't want that."

"I didn't mean we should kill her."

"What, then...kidnap her?"

"It could be a very effective way of controlling him; there's no doubt that would derail him, at the very least. We saw what it did to him the last time she was abducted..."

Ray stood and walked over to the large window that overlooked the harbor. "She was grabbed twice in 2000, though- before she had security around her, which she has now."

"Which means they might not think it could happen again."

453

"I don't know about that. It would be risky. Not necessarily impossible, but definitely risky, and potentially costly, too. I'm sure you're thinking about what happened today- the way that guy she helped bust for taking his own kid was close enough to take a swing at her. My answer is yes, we might be able to create a situation that would give us the opportunity we needed. I'm just telling you, in my opinion it would be a lot harder than you think."

After a moment of deliberation, Raines turned away. "I see your point. Let's keep that in mind as a last resort, maybe. We really need to deal with him directly- find some way to make him look bad or discredit him somehow. There must be a weakness he has other than his wife, although we have yet to find one. We sure as hell won't be able to tempt him with another woman- not even with Ginger, my secretary.

"The bottom line is we have to stop him from becoming President. We'll have to see how things go in the Governor's races this year- see if Black's boys can dust his ass. If they do, I think we're all right. If any of Stratton's people win and it looks like things'll get worse, we'll have to finish the job his former Chief of Staff started. John Stratton sure can't hurt us when he's dead and I bet if we kill him, we kill the movement. That's how it usually goes. Time is on our side, too; we have over twenty months until Election Day…"

He turned and looked purposefully at Ray before finishing his statement. "…a lot can happen in twenty months."